THE HIDDEN

Jo Chumas

THOMAS & MERCER

Published by Thomas&Mercer
P.O. Box 400818 Las Vegas, NV 89140

ISBN-13: 9781477848197
ISBN-10: 1477848193

Library of Congress Control Number: 2013909235

I dedicate *The Hidden* to the memory of Huda Shaarawi, early twentieth-century Egyptian Nationalist and feminist, and to the memory of my father, Henry John Chumas.

PROLOGUE

East of Lake Timsah, Egypt, July 1940

The strikingly handsome young man smiled to himself as he considered his good fortune. The rendezvous at the small desert village to the east of Lake Timsah, bordering the north of the Sinai, where he now found himself, on an icily still, crystal-clear night, was the culmination of a finely tuned plan. He had waited for this moment for months. Nothing and no one had stood in his way. His heart pounded as he searched the darkness. The sharp tang of wood smoke filled his nostrils, mouth, and lungs. In the distance, he saw a group of men lounging by the dying embers of a fire. They were smoking a nargila pipe, laughing drunkenly.

He made his way towards the peasant woman's mud-brick house on the far side of the village. He edged silently around the side of the building, then slipped through a narrow arch. He knew what he had to do—hand over the documents, maps, and key information. He fumbled with the canvas satchel he was carrying, and drew out a thick black cloak, which he hoisted around his shoulders. Everything was happening as his men had predicted. He saw the leaf mat at the back of the house and the red silk ribbon tied to a pole, the narrow entry, the back door to the woman's house. He heard the murmuring of voices and shrank back behind a date palm.

The men around the campfire were laying out mats, laughing, swigging back the last dregs from a whisky bottle. He stood silently, holding his breath, waiting, watching.

Suddenly a powerful blow struck him from behind. Arms were clamped around his shoulders, and his head was wrenched back by the roots of his hair. A searing sound slit the air; the glint of a dagger poised at his throat, the pain shot through him, tight and hot and numb. The smell and taste of blood curdled in his mouth, and his screams echoed across the emptiness.

CHAPTER ONE

Cairo, Egypt, August 1940

The man who telephoned Aimee identified himself as Professor Langham. He introduced himself not only as Azi's superior, but also his colleague, advisor, and friend. He asked Aimee to come to the university to pick up Azi's belongings. A parcel, he said, had been retrieved from his locker. She hadn't said much to him on the phone, simply agreeing to meet him for tea on the specified date. That Wednesday, Aimee went to see him.

"It's a real pleasure to meet you at last, Madame Ibrahim," the professor said, smiling warmly. Taking Aimee's tiny hand in his, he guided her through the thick oak door leading to his office.

She looked hopefully into his blue eyes and murmured a quiet thank-you. He escorted her to a low armchair, then sat down opposite her under the whirring ceiling fan.

"You're very brave to have come so soon," he said soothingly. "This must be a great ordeal for you. I had thought of paying you a visit and bringing you the parcel myself, but I didn't want to intrude and appear improper or forward."

Aimee straightened her back and jutted her chin out, looking him squarely in the eye. "That's kind of you," she said, holding herself tightly inside her grief. "I am rather grateful to you actually for the chance to come. I needed to get out of my house."

Her voice trembled slightly as she spoke. She bit her lip and casually gazed around the room, studying the heavy wooden bookshelves, the trophies and ornaments on display. The professor did not respond right away, respectfully allowing the silence to settle over them for a moment or two.

"The university was devastated by the news," he said at last. "Young Ibrahim was one of our most respected professors. He had such a bright future ahead of him. Of course, I was delighted when I heard of his sudden engagement and marriage, but then this."

He broke off with a melancholy sigh and leaned towards her pleadingly. "I want you to know, Madame Ibrahim, that I am at your service, if there is anything you need, anything at all."

Smoothing her skirt with her hands, Aimee flashed him a half smile, wriggled her toes nervously inside her shoes, and moved her neck discreetly to ease the tension in it. This was so hard for her. She felt uncomfortable sitting with him, alone, like this, in his office. It did not seem quite right.

"Azi spoke very highly of you, Professor," she said with a forced smile. "He loved his job, his students, the university."

Langham sat back in his chair, studying her closely. What a startlingly good-looking girl she was, but she was just a girl surely? Her alluring eyes glittered like cut crystal in the sunlight, translucent green, all observing. She wore her hair clasped at the back of her head, its inky darkness a stark contrast to the pallor of her skin. She spoke English flawlessly despite a heavy French accent.

"Have the police arrested anyone yet, Madame? Do you have any more information?"

"No, I don't."

"I'm so sorry, Madame Ibrahim," he said. "The wait must be agonising."

"Please call me Aimee, Professor. I wasn't married for very long. I'd hardly gotten used to being called Madame Ibrahim."

He smiled nervously at her and nodded. Aimee felt herself go hot at the obvious break in the conversation. She was struggling to hold back the jabbing pain taking hold of her, the feeling that made sitting here in the professor's office so excruciating. She thought of Azi, sitting in this same chair, talking to Langham and how he was dead now. She flashed Langham a grateful smile. He only wanted to help her, after all, but he couldn't bring her husband back.

"Professor, perhaps there is a way you could help me. I really would like to teach or translate perhaps, something to occupy my mind. It would make waiting for the police to find the killer easier to bear. I am fluent in English and French, and I speak a little Turkish and Arabic too."

Langham frowned thoughtfully and stroked his chin. "You're a talented young lady. If only it were possible for us to use you here. I regret that this is such a conservative institution. I have my aspirations for this place—we need to adapt to the modern world and educate our young men to accept women in the workplace; although some do, I am bound, you see, by our founder, and by outside money. A woman working here would be"—and here he paused—"difficult. For the time being, I could not allow it."

Aimee felt her cheeks redden. She shouldn't have asked him.

He decided to change the subject. He could see he had embarrassed her. "You have family here, Madame?" he asked with a smile.

"I'm an orphan. I have an aunt, but I never knew my parents."

She returned his smile, then studied her hands. It was humiliating to put herself at the mercy of a man she didn't know. And he was looking at her so inquisitively, as though he wanted to know more about her. But some things were private and sacred—looking back on recent events, even a little unreal. First the telegram from her aunt Saiza had come, summoning her back to Cairo after fourteen years in France because of the war. Then had followed the train journey with Sophie, her school friend, their voyage together across the Mediterranean on *Le Congo* from Marseille to Alexandria, their arrival in Cairo—a city she did not remember, even though she had been born there. Released from the confines of their convent education, Sophie and Aimee loved the freedom from school, the excitement, the invitations to soirees and nightclubs and dances, all organised by Sophie's uncle and guardian, Tony Sedgewick, who was based in the Egyptian capital. Cairo was a breath of fresh air after life with the nuns in Paris. Aimee hadn't even been in Cairo for more than a month when she met Azi. Her aunt Saiza had introduced them, and he had courted her with such passionate abandon that she had been almost shocked. She knew nothing about men— did not know the first thing about how to act around them—but she knew she was falling in love with him. He had promised her the world, if only she would agree to be his. Azi's world had fascinated her, and she'd been dazzled by his intellect, his plans for a dynamic new Egypt. He had a large group of male friends, academics and businessmen. Though she longed to live in his world, she knew that her shyness and her French convent-school upbringing had not prepared her for the cacophony of activity she witnessed every day in Cairo. Though she felt strangely connected to her birthplace, she was still a stranger here, walking blind. Like an invisible spirit, she could observe but felt barred from taking part. And her youth and her sex were barriers to this world. She was a young woman expected to act in a certain way. She knew so little of life, but sometimes her desire to know everything hidden to her shocked her.

"I'm sorry, I didn't know," Langham said. "But Ibrahim's family surely will look after you now. They will take care of everything?"

Aimee caught his eye. How could she explain to this nice man that the family she had married into was not interested in her?

"They're emigrating to America as soon as possible before things get too difficult with the war. I haven't been invited to join them, not that I would want to, you see—"

He looked on with interest.

"It's my aunt, Professor. She's been like a mother to me. I couldn't leave her behind. She's all I've got now."

"You travelled from France, I believe?"

Aimee nodded, searching his face. "I spent my childhood there, in the town of Neuilly near Paris, at a convent boarding school. My aunt thought it best, for my education. I taught there for a while after finishing school. Then the war started and my aunt sent for me. I've been in Cairo now for nine months."

"So you hadn't been here long when you met Ibrahim?"

She smiled and shook her head. "No. My aunt is a very social person. She's very active with the women's movement here. It was thanks to her that I met my husband. As you may know, he gave talks at the Society for the Status of Women on women's role in society and the future of families in Egypt."

"Yes," Langham said. "I was behind the research grant that sparked the talks."

She went on. "My aunt was very pleased with the way things progressed between us. She strongly approved of our engagement and our marriage. She thought it was proper that I marry, and to have me finally returned to Cairo to be with her was a blessing." Aimee stopped herself before she said too much and turned to look out the window at the dazzling cloudless sky.

"Of course," said the professor, though she wasn't really paying attention. Then out of the corner of her eye, she noticed him get up and go to his desk, unlock the drawer, and pull something out.

"Before I forget, I do need to give you that parcel. I'll order some tea for us, shall I?"

He passed a large parcel to her and picked up the telephone. Aimee shivered and stared at it. Wrapped in thick brown paper and tied with string, it looked innocent enough.

After speaking with someone in the university kitchen, Langham put down the telephone and looked at her hopefully. "Tea won't be long. Have you any idea what it is?"

Aimee shook her head and fingered the string curiously. "No. I'm afraid I don't."

"Do you want to open it here?"

She looked up at him reluctantly. "I think I will take it home. If it contains letters or documents that might help the police with their enquiries, then naturally I'll let them have it."

"Of course, you must do what you think is best."

"Is there anything you know, Professor? You must have known Azi better than most. You worked with him for a long time. Can you tell me anything? Anything at all?"

Langham paused for a moment. He seemed to be searching the room for inspiration.

"Your husband had many friends," he said. "But that's because he was well liked. Naturally he was opinionated, but it was important for him to be that way. He was a professor after all. But he also respected others who were prepared to voice their views. His students would say—"

As he fell silent, Aimee noticed his expression change. He was biting his lip, thinking.

"Can you think of anything unusual that occurred recently, anything he did that was out of character or that made you wonder?" she asked.

Langham looked at her and put his thumb to his mouth for a moment, stroking his nose, his eyes narrowing, as he cast his mind back. "He seemed rather more ill-tempered than usual. That is the only thing I can think of. I put that down to his having a lot of work. And perhaps he resented that it was keeping him from his new bride."

He smiled knowingly at Aimee. The tea arrived. Cups were poured and handed out. Aimee put the parcel to one side and sipped her tea gratefully. When he had finished, Langham put down his cup and glanced at Aimee, quickly taking in the soft curve of her shoulders, the long black eyelashes framing those haunting eyes of hers. He felt sorry for her. He had a daughter her age. She could be his daughter. He watched her stand up to leave. The meeting had obviously been difficult for her, and he didn't blame her for wanting to go.

"Promise me you'll telephone if you need any help at all, Madame Ibrahim," he said as a last gesture.

Aimee wondered what help he could be to her now.

"I need work, Professor. I need to support myself and my aunt. If you hear of anything."

He smiled and extended his hand to her. "Of course. I will make some enquiries. You must find time to enjoy yourself too, Madame, to take your mind off things. I've heard the great Noel Coward will be giving a series of war concerts. He's planning a tour of the Middle East, which should be good for the soldiers' morale and all of us really, something to look forward to."

He paused for a moment, studying her face. "As a matter of interest," he asked, "do you think you will attend the launch of *Monument*?"

She looked at him quizzically. "I—sorry?"

"The book of poems by some of the university's rising literary stars." Langham smiled.

"Oh—I don't know."

"Your husband was looking forward to going. I'm sure you were sent an invitation. It's been organised by Zaky Achmed, one of the professors here. I'm sure if you were to go, you would be welcomed with open arms. Many of the wives will undoubtedly be going."

Now that she thought about it, Aimee did remember the invitation. She'd seen it in Azi's study but had forgotten all about it. She smiled and said, "I'll give it some thought."

"It's up to you, of course, Madame, but sometimes it's better to be out among people, to know you're not alone."

She watched him as he talked, his idle chitchat meant to make her feel better, as though he were an ally. The rays of sunshine through the window highlighted the yellowing of his teeth, the lacklustre rings around his irises. He was an old man and he meant well. She understood why Azi had been so fond of him. But all the same, she sensed he was relieved the meeting was over.

"Don't be a stranger to us, Madame Ibrahim," he said warmly, his hand pressing hers once more. "You're always welcome here."

"Good-bye, Professor Langham," she said awkwardly, "and thank-you."

CHAPTER TWO

Haran Issawi was not in a good mood. His secretary had just informed him that his train from Luxor to Cairo had been delayed by another two hours. However agreeable the Winter Palace Hotel was, being stranded there was highly inconvenient. His temples pulsed angrily and he swore under his breath. He had engagements and reports to read over, and it was critical that the signing of the legal documents entitling him to an eighty-percent share in the trans-Mediterranean packing consortium went without a hitch. There was huge money at stake with this latest of his many business ventures. Although all of these endeavours yielded vast sums of money, this one would be particularly lucrative. It was typical of the inefficiency he encountered in every avenue of Egyptian public life that his chartered Luxor-Cairo train now had mechanical problems. And on top of that, he felt unwell. Beads of perspiration had formed on his forehead. His starched collar felt tighter than usual around his neck, and the buttons on his waistcoat strained. His eyes felt heavy and tired. Dinner the night before had gone on too long, and he had consumed too much whisky. Was it possible he was no longer young enough to enjoy the sensual pleasures of dancing girls, good food, and copious amounts of wine and spirits?

It was true that his body was not young anymore. His once-lithe frame was padded with rolls of fat. His moustache was no longer slick and dark, and his white hair fell out daily on his comb. His once-rich dark eyes had paled to a milky, nondescript colour.

Still, as chief advisor to the king, he commanded respect and fear. Yes, fear. The king and the government of Egypt were like putty in his hands.

He considered his brilliant powers of persuasion, his calculated finesse in convincing the chief councillor for the fellahin, Youssef Attwara, against allowing tax concessions for farmers. High taxes made the fellahin work harder, and the harder the farmers worked on their cotton plantations, the more money rolled into the coffers of the wealthy landowners—of which he, of course, was one. The fellahin must become more businesslike in their approach to farming, and concessions—tax or otherwise—would only make them lazy. At least Attwara had been intelligent enough to grasp the underlying message he wished to convey. Issawi would hear no more on the subject of rent concessions—or any concessions for that matter—and he had it in his power to ruin the business Attwara had painstakingly built up over many years. Attwara had stopped short of accusing Issawi of blackmailing him. Wise man, Issawi thought, to stop the discussion there and accept the inevitable. He did not like to be crossed. He had achieved all he wanted in his political life, and he wouldn't let some junior bureaucrat derail his plans. Now he could return to Cairo and report to the king that he had succeeded in stamping out any possible dissent among the fellahin and reassure him that aristocratic wealth would continue to flow in the right direction.

While he and his entourage waited for their private train to be repaired, he would discuss the continuing problem of the X. His top security men had just arrived. As they walked towards him, he examined their faces and saw concern there. Hilali and Gamal both saluted and stood to attention.

"What news do you have for me, Hilali?" he asked.

He listened as Hilali cleared his throat, and he saw dread etched on his face.

"We need to move fast, sir," he said. "We don't have much time."

"Yes, yes," Issawi snapped impatiently. "We must not lose any more men to them. What's your strategy? How much ground force do you need?"

"Gamal and I have nearly finished fine-tuning our strategy, sir. We're almost ready."

"Well, get on with it," Issawi said sharply. "You want to move? Then move!"

Issawi saw Hilali's eyes flinch, but his posture remained rigid, soldierly.

"Sir, you must prepare yourself," Gamal said. "Intelligence has uncovered another plot in which you are the target."

Issawi's eyes narrowed. "Go on."

"We believe it's only a matter of days before the Group of the X makes an attempt on your life."

Issawi's face was motionless. This news was nothing new to him. He was as hated as he was feared. His life had been targeted before. Now he travelled everywhere in armoured vehicles with a security entourage to protect him. But the way Gamal spoke alarmed him. He was usually practical and unemotional, but for the first time, Issawi saw fear in Gamal's eyes.

"Use your networks, Gamal," Issawi said. "Find out who the masterminds are and exactly what they are up to."

"Sir," Hilali said, "we already have dossiers on five possibles, but there are many branches of this organisation and it's likely the men at the top are just foils. The real enemy is the X's huge network of

spies on the ground, a massive web of agents, subagents, and coun-
teragents. We're deep in muddy waters with this one."

Issawi stood up and started pacing. The veins on his temple
throbbed. "Contact the head of Secret Police at HQ," he said.
"However big this group is, whoever the newcomers are, wherever
they hide out, we have the resources available to find them."

Gamal leaned forward, his voice lowered. "Sir, we can plan
raids, but we do not have the resources to raid the hundreds of
addresses this group uses. A lot of their men, we know for certain,
are also undercover agents gathering intelligence for the Germans.
As I said, we have identified five leaders so far, but this group is
clever. They move quickly. They change tack. They slip about invisibly. We have very few photographs of any of them. We think they
are using a tagging system, acting on directions, then passing the
information on. As soon as one of them passes intelligence down
the line, he disappears, changes his identity and his physical appearance. We believe they are running an identification-paper racket,
which serves them well, but their primary goal is to take over the
government and rule by terror. As you well know, the X is an old
network. They're artful and skilled. We don't know yet when they
are going to act, or how they plan to pull off the assassination. We
just know that you are in very grave danger."

Issawi ground his teeth and took a sip of water. Even with the
ceiling fans whirring overhead, it was still unbearably hot. Trust
nobody, he thought to himself. It was a mantra he had lived by his
whole life.

"Where are these dossiers?" he asked.

"With Operations and our key men."

"The men on the ground, who are they?" Issawi asked.

Gamal paused before he replied, studying Issawi's face. "Military
men, academics, businessmen, traders from all walks of life, as well

as thugs and criminals, who've all come together with the common purpose of a fundamentalist Nationalist takeover."

"How many belong to the X these days, did you say?"

Hilali studied a notebook in front of him. "We estimate that the Group is now at least five hundred men strong, but in reality, the network is without a doubt much larger than that."

Issawi wiped his mouth with the back on his hand. "Damn them all," he said.

Hilali went on. "We must use some of our men to go undercover and find out what they are planning. We don't know how much time we have. Although it could be months, we think it is a matter of days. The most important thing is to break up the networks from the ground up. It's the networks we need to target. We've been watching a few key people."

It was Gamal's turn to speak. He said, "Your engagements, sir? You should cancel your engagements for a while, until we can report back."

Issawi snorted. "Impossible. I will not change one thing. I have my security men. I have my armed vehicles, my private train. My family is well looked after. You must order Operations to move in on them immediately."

Hilali studied Issawi incredulously. It wasn't as simple as that. His boss was an arrogant, stupid man who had no right to hold the position he held. Hilali hated him, but he had to earn a living.

Issawi went on. "Don't just stand there gaping. How do you propose to organise yourselves?"

Gamal said, "We'll step up the undercover operation that we already have in place. We can scour the clubs, the brothels, the cafés, the streets, the addresses we have; tap phones; send in our men and women; but to really be effective, sir, we need more money from Operations."

Issawi smiled mockingly. This was one of Gamal's usual ruses to extract money from Operations, but he wouldn't allow it. "Impossible," he said. "That's exactly what the X wants. They're not important, Gamal. Thugs like the men in the X have been trying to take over Cairo for decades. Use your men to find out the nature of the plot and report back to me in forty-eight hours."

Gamal bowed his head respectfully, but he was seething inside. "Yes, sir."

Hilali bowed and saluted, then said, "Lunch has been ordered, sir. I'll just go and check to see if it's ready."

Issawi went to the window and stared out at the Nile below. The Group of the X did not scare him. He would not be intimidated by a pack of thugs. He would continue to wield his power unhindered.

CHAPTER THREE

Aimee clutched the package to her as she walked quickly through the archways of the university to the main streets of al-Azhar. She stopped for a moment to scan the streets for a tram or a car to take her home. The heat blazed down on her, and she felt stifled in her calf-length English wool skirt and her cream blouse with its innocent collar. Her low feminine shoes, which she'd bought on that trip to London, had been perfectly appropriate at one time for a French bride of Egyptian heritage, but they now felt over-the-top and excruciatingly uncomfortable.

Her charcoal black hair, which she generally wore long and loose or demurely plaited, felt tight and awkward, pinned as it was at the base of her neck. As she breathed in the heat, she was sure she was breathing white, chalky, poisonous dust into her lungs.

The loud Arabic voices, piercing the air with their guttural, impatient cries—a thing of joy to her in the early weeks of marriage—now made her body heavy with grief because the sound reminded her of Azi. He'd loved the Arabic language and had been encouraging her to read the new literature coming out of Egypt. With Azi, she had had the opportunity to embrace the language of her early childhood, which had stirred up memories of her time with her aunt Saiza in Alexandria, before Saiza had sent her to

France. Now those Arab voices mocked her. They spoke of a life alone in a city she didn't know.

As Aimee stood looking for a car to take her home, she observed the crowded streets. The sour odour of mud and under-earth and spice, vegetable peelings, and dank sewage lingered forever behind her nostrils. The vivid blue sky, the place she looked to for answers, never offered her any. She didn't know what to do now that Azi was dead. As she so often did, she wished she were older, more experienced. She felt as though the whole world was watching her—inquisitive men, desperate children, self-satisfied European women, soldiers, old Egyptian mothers with sagging, greying skin—and all she could do was stare back timidly at them all.

As she waited for a car to take her home, she stopped in the shadows of the al-Azhar mosque and the elegant stone houses built by the Europeans.

"A ride, Madame?"

A cab driver peered out of the car window at her. She nodded and climbed in, sliding the parcel onto her lap. Sinking low in her seat, she fanned herself against the heat. They drove along wide boulevards, tree-lined streets, and darker filthier harets crammed with people, goats, and donkeys, until at last they came to the Sharia Suleyman Pasha. When the driver stopped, Aimee thrust some coins in his hand and got out. Holding the parcel carefully against her, she walked towards the tiny haret, the alleyway that led to the courtyard at the side of her house. Samir, her neighbour's thirteen-year-old son, was standing against the door to the courtyard staring at her inquisitively with his huge black saucer eyes. Aimee was fond of him and touched his cheek as she went through the gate, then climbed the steep stone steps to her front door.

On the hall sideboard was a newspaper. The headlines blazed with ominous reports about the war, fatal predictions, and sensationalistic news. And there was a letter addressed to her. She recognised Saiza's handwriting. Good. It would be news of her aunt from Alexandria, where she was recuperating from an illness. She picked up the letter and pushed open the sitting-room doors. The balcony doors were open. Amina, her housekeeper, must be somewhere nearby. Aimee sat down in one of the rattan chairs on the balcony and stared at the street below. Men in long jalabas were smoking on street corners, European women were marching purposefully to their club or to some war meeting, and newly arrived uniformed soldiers were getting their bearings. She watched, momentarily entranced by the cacophony of noise and the sunlight. The parcel the professor had given her sat on her lap. She did not want to open it, not yet. Instead, she tore open her aunt's letter. When she had read it, she leaned back in her chair and closed her eyes for a moment. Then she put the parcel aside, got up, walked to the study, and retrieved the invitation to the literary launch that the professor had mentioned. She examined it. It seemed disrespectful to Azi to go out socially so soon, but he would want her to be happy. And the professor was probably right. No harm could come of going to Zaky Achmed's literary evening. She would take Sophie, her school friend, with her. She returned to the balcony to retrieve the parcel. The rough string encircling it was begging to be pulled and the brown paper wrapping removed. She burned with curiosity. If there was something sinister in it, perhaps the police ought to know? Any information could help. Anything at all. The dull brown wrapping paper felt soft and cool as she ran her fingers over it.

Then she started to loosen the string excitedly like a child on her birthday. Inside was a notebook with a battered leather cover, the type that could slide easily into a large pocket. Inside the front cover of the notebook was a white label, gone to a decaying shade of yellow with the passing years, with tiny neat words scrawled in

Arabic in an unfamiliar hand. She flicked through the pages, her heart in her throat. It was a journal, but whose?

She peered more closely at the flowing script. Then her heart began to beat wildly, and she held the journal to her chest. The words read *The journal of Hezba Iqbal Sultan Hanim al-Shezira, Cairo, 1919.*

Maman, she said to herself. Her diary. And Azi had had this in his possession. Why had it been tied up in a parcel, hidden away in his office?

Aimee flicked through the book. What secrets did Maman reveal in this little notebook? How strange to be holding the diary Hezba had written twenty-one years before. Aimee had known vaguely that the journal existed. Aunt Saiza had told her about it, but she had said it had disappeared. All Aimee had of her mother was a single photograph in an ornate frame in her living room.

She looked over at it. There she was, a defiant-looking Hezba wearing silky loose trousers and a little waistcoat. Aimee stepped closer and studied the photograph. What turmoil there was in those soulful black eyes. This burning connection between them was like gossamer on the wind, barely visible but always there, haunting her.

Aunt Saiza had told her little about her mother when Aimee had been a child, but what she knew had stayed with her, harnessing her to her past like the pulsing cord connecting babe to mother. Saiza said that Aimee's grandfather had called Hezba "Fire," an apt name since she had been so passionate and determined, as though a permanent fever burned through her. Their father had always favoured Hezba, and Saiza had been jealous of his love for her. Aimee examined the photograph carefully, though she was familiar with every intimate detail of it already. Aunt Saiza had told her that Hezba had had black eyelashes, soft caramel skin, and fleshy legs, and that she could often be seen running frantically to her papa with arms outstretched. He would dance her on his knee. Papa Sultan had been a formidable man, and Hezba had loved him the most out of all who lived at the sarai, the royal palace near the Nile. Hezba loved his long dark moustache hanging low over his fine jaw, his broad sweep of jet-black hair, his twinkling chocolate-coloured eyes, and his scent, which was a mix of starched cotton and pipes and perfumed kisses.

Hezba had loved pulling his moustache, making him wince and laugh. His other children would form a line to see him. One by one he would pat them, kiss them, and then send them away, but she was always allowed to linger. Saiza had told her all this with bittersweet regret, but Saiza had loved Hezba. Everyone had loved Hezba Sultan.

Aimee stared at the uneven walls of her home and the little sitting room with its European-style furniture. Aunt Saiza had spoken of the palace's gold couches, marble staircases, and ornate architecture, of the cool, shuttered quarters of the harem, where the eunuchs served coffee to the harem girls in Ethiopian silver coffeepots, and the girls exchanged secrets and laughter, their bare arms jangling with jewelled bracelets as they walked the corridors arm in arm.

She shifted uncomfortably as she recalled the stiff aprons of her convent years and thought about the chasm between her mother's life and her own. As she flipped through the journal again, a photograph and some folded pages with strange typewritten words slipped out. Her eyes narrowed as she studied them. The photograph drew her attention first. It was of a beautiful woman, an Egyptian, dressed in modern-day clothes, with a cocky half smile on her lips. It wasn't Hezba. The photograph was recent, new. Aimee didn't understand. She turned the photograph over, and her stomach lurched when she saw Azi's handwriting. She recognised his rich penmanship and the sepia-brown ink he loved to use. And there was a name: Fatima and an exclamation mark and a date, two months previous. Her heart sank. She steadied her breath and stared at the photograph, staring so hard she made herself dizzy, trying to understand, trying to remember. This woman. Who was she? Fatima? She and Azi had known no one called Fatima, and she certainly didn't recognise her. She turned her attention to the typewritten pages, hoping they would provide clarification, but they were filled with words in a language she didn't understand And then she started reading her mother's diary.

The journal of Hezba Iqbal Sultan Hanim al-Shezira,
Cairo, August 1, 1919

The beatings are getting worse, but Habrid's brutality serves no purpose. I won't be stopped. He can beat me raw, but he will never crush me. I am a seventeen-year-old woman, not a child, yet he treats me like one. He has no right. After his latest beating, I immediately defied him, marching straight into Papa's library, and stole a new journal for myself, the one I am writing in now. I am ecstatic that I have these beautiful new scented and blank pages to write on. I went there, unaccompanied, of course, because even Rachid would not be a party to my deception. I stole the blank journal openly, hoping to be caught. I want the whole palace to know that Habrid, the head eunuch, is an animal who deserves to be strung up like the lowest, commonest criminal, and that he has reduced me to stealing. He told me he had orders to keep an eye on me, that Maman wants me beaten, as a lesson. Papa would never order such a thing, but he is away, busy with government affairs, and chaos has once again descended on the palace. Habrid ripped the pages from my last journal, shredded them in front of me, and then ordered the shreds burned. After that, he took me to the solitary room and thrashed me twenty times with a wet rolled-up cotton sheet. I'm convinced Habrid is in league with my husband, al-Shezira. With great lacerations on my skin from the thrashing, I am no longer attractive. This is how they want me, scarred, unloveable, and beaten into submission. Al-Shezira and Maman think that if Habrid beats me, I'll grow tired of speaking my mind and I'll repent and become a good servile wife. Al-Shezira is a fool. They want me to be true as a woman. But I will always disappoint them. I know I am being watched. I feel their eyes on me. I hear the whispering among the eunuchs and servant girls. I can hear Maman's words, can see her face as she shames me, but she does not see what I see. Her world is jewels and low couches and delicious food and excursions. She thinks I am a shameful girl for looking at her with questioning eyes, for wanting to read the works of modern Egyptian writers, for the rumours she hears about me, rumours I cannot stop.

"What would a young girl want a notebook for?" Maman asked me yesterday. I can't believe she asked me that. She looked at me contemptuously as she spoke to me, her mouth frozen in a crooked half smile.

"Intelligence, curiosity, and distracting pastimes must be strictly controlled. Do not ask questions, Daughter. Don't question those whose place it is to guide and direct you. Don't question Allah's way, nor the look in my eyes when I tell you these things. Your father would not have chosen me for his bride if he sensed I was dreaming of books."

Maman doesn't know, nor will I ever tell her, that I want to start a school one day and educate girls so they can live useful lives, not be simply slaves at men's service. Girls are ignored and sold into slavery and subservience, or if they are from wealthy backgrounds, they are married off to the first good strategic match the parents can find.

Maman would not understand. She has served Papa since they were married, as his wife, as the bearer of his children.

Maman adjusted the silk covering her legs as she spoke. Then she snapped her fingers in the vague direction of her eunuch. I looked at her with pity and fear, secretly dreaming of a night at the theatre to alleviate my boredom. I wished Maman loved me. But she does not. It is so obvious that she has no interest in me or my education. She just wants me back with al-Shezira. It's Papa I really love truly, but I don't see him much anymore now that he is so often away on government business in Minya. Still, my mind is on fire and I confess I'm in love. It's a type of love I have never felt before. I think only of Alexandre. Thinking of him keeps me buoyant as I perform the mundane duties of the day. When I think of him, I can laugh and smile and be the happy girl I know I am. He's the most handsome man I have ever seen. He is Virginie's brother, an adventurer, a free spirit like me. Lucky for me, he is based in Cairo, though his travels have recently taken him to India and Persia. He has dark hair, a beautiful mouth, alluring eyes, and an aristocratic air. But it is difficult for me to see him. Our meetings are very few and far between, but we have arranged a secret message system. Virginie brings me letters. I read them, and then I destroy them because I hate to think what would happen if they were found. I would be sent away. I would be thrashed. Even more importantly, I would die inside.

Alexandre treats me as his equal. This was evident from the first moment we met, in a way that was totally haram, when he burst into the room where I was having tea with Virginie. Papa has allowed me to visit Virginie at her house, in another suburb of Cairo, providing I am escorted and chaperoned by two of my eunuchs. Papa trusts Virginie because of his connection with Virginie's husband. Virginie respects that which is haram or forbidden and had placed her servant at the door to bar entry by any other party. We were drinking tea and discussing little bits of gossip when the door was flung open. A man, tall and handsome, stood there. He stammered his apologies. I did not have time to cover my face with my veil. It was too late. Destiny had thrown us together, and from that day on, Alexandre has been a part of my life. He wants a better Egypt for our countrymen and women—and that includes a better future for me as well. He wants me to join him in this fight. I don't know how I can, but for the moment I live to see him. When I'm with him, I feel free. To my husband I am nothing but a source of money— the sultan's money—and an ornament. He has despised me since I was given to him at age eleven, but he has put up with me because of my papa. To my sisters in the harem, this is the way things are, but I can't accept things this way. Do they not see that our country is being destroyed by the political will of the British? Do we not have the right to forge our own destiny? Alexandre and I—in our rare meetings—talk about the political situation. It's getting dangerously out of control. Is it acceptable for the Sarai and its occupants to sit on gold cushions while our men and women are being tortured and killed in the desert? I wish I were a man so I could be a lawyer, a doctor, an academic. Why can't I be one? Is it my sex that is to blame for such inequality? I believe it is.

I want to live long enough to see fulfilled my dream of a new Egypt where women and men work together for the good of our country, and no one owns us, not the British, nor any other government. I love Egypt, but I hate what it has become. I am a fighter, like Alexandre. With such strong opinions, I have to be discreet and not let anyone know what is going on inside my head. And if that means guarding myself against idle chatter with the girls of the harem, then so be it. For the time being, thinking about my love is my private indulgence. It gives me courage to face the future. I know I am going to need it.

CHAPTER FOUR

At midnight on the outskirts of Cairo, near the northern suburb of Heliopolis, in an unremarkable, dimly lit, sparsely furnished house on the edge of a palm-fringed street, two middle-aged men stood with three younger men, Hamid, al-Dyn, and Hossein. One of the older men, Taha Farouk, was a tall, striking individual with a chiselled, clean-shaven face and thick, grey-streaked black hair. He stared ahead darkly as he listened intently to what the other older man, Littoni—of equal stature but more thick-set—was saying. Farouk's mouth twisted with bitter, inner torment.

"The girl must know something," Littoni said, pausing to light yet another cigarette, then blowing out great rings of smoke. "Mustafa from sector three believes that a report has been issued to all of Issawi's cronies detailing our movements, our code names, and sightings. It's only a matter of time before the Secret Police raid what they believe to be our venues. We have to get the girl on our side, find out what's going on. She might be our last chance."

"There's no time, Littoni," Farouk snapped angrily, shaking his head. "Issawi's due to return from Luxor tonight. Tomorrow, he'll go to his club. Al-Dyn has worked there every night for the last two weeks, and he's had his ear to the ground. In a week's time, Issawi will attend the celebrations for the king's birthday at the palace. I say we take him out this week, take everyone by surprise. Forget about the bomb. It's too dangerous for us. The Group's finished if we follow that plan. If they're onto us, they'll be expecting something big. We can only succeed if we take them by surprise."

Littoni shot Farouk a look. Anger coursed through his body. Farouk was determined to have his way. Hamid and Tashi had all the equipment necessary to make a bomb strong enough to blow Issawi's car sky-high, pulp the men inside, and destroy half the Abdin Palace. But Farouk had had his sights on Issawi for years and was convinced that pumping a bullet through his heart would be a pleasurable experience. He wasn't interested in impact or sending the king the message that the revolution was about to begin. It was almost as though he had lost sight of the bigger picture.

"Don't try and stir things up, Farouk," Littoni said icily. "You've been outvoted on this one. All the crucial X sectors agree that Hamid and Tashi's device will do the trick. That way, there's no chance of anything going wrong. And we'll be able to take out not only Issawi, but also the king and some of the politicians attending the celebrations. It will be headline news for weeks, a message all the die-hard supporters of the current government won't be able to ignore."

Farouk broke in. "You're lying. The committee of traders at Khan el-Khalili and the Muski are both against the idea. You have the halfhearted support of some of the Patriots, professors, and the university men at al-Ahzar, but you're dangerously out of your league with a bomb of this magnitude. It's not the right time. I say take Issawi out solo, without fanfare. Then we'll be perfectly positioned to stage a bloodless coup."

Littoni said, "Shut it, Farouk. You want Issawi to win? They'll have their own surprises in store for us, that much is certain. The girl's bound to be in on it for sure."

Farouk was growing increasingly agitated. He snarled, "For the last time, forget about the girl. Al-Dyn will be able to get us all the information we need. There's no time left. Issawi's not that smart. He loves his club. Thinks his security operation's the best there is. He's relaxed, off his guard. If there's anything we need to know, al-Dyn will report back to us. Besides, the girl's husband's taken his secrets with him to the grave. I heard they hadn't been married long. Hardly enough time to let his bride in on Issawi's networks."

Littoni shot Farouk a wrathful look and turned to Hamid.

"Regardless of what al-Dyn finds out, our boys need somewhere new to meet. Time's running out at the Café Malta; we've met there three times already."

Hamid said hopefully, "My uncle's house is perfect."

Littoni was about to answer, when Farouk began talking again, spluttering as a cough snaked its way from his lungs to his throat.

"You don't know what you are doing," Farouk said. Al-Dyn stepped forward and put his hand on Farouk's shoulder to steady him.

"I said don't make trouble, Farouk," Littoni warned.

"The entire network's agreed this is the right course of action. There's nothing you can do to change it now."

Farouk laughed bitterly, wiping his mouth. "You haven't thought this through properly. If Issawi's security operations are onto us, we must do it my way or wait, let a few more months pass."

Littoni snarled at Farouk, clicking his teeth, and turned to Hamid. "You're sure you'll have the bomb ready in time?"

"We can work through the night," Hamid said.

"And it'll be powerful enough?" Littoni asked.

"Depending on where it is put, it will rip through walls and demolish everything within at least a mile radius."

Farouk lunged forward, grabbed Littoni by the lapels, and shook him. "And you're proud of yourself, Littoni? Proud of yourself for plotting to murder innocents? This is not what the X is about. We agreed years ago that no civilians would ever suffer as a consequence of our actions. Our target is always—and only—the aggressor."

Littoni stabbed at his pocket, trying to pull something out. Farouk uncurled his fist and pushed Littoni back. A moment later, Littoni stood opposite Farouk with a gun raised at him.

Unfazed, Farouk turned to Hossein, al-Dyn, and Hamid. "You're all staring down the barrel of a gun if you do this. Death sentence for sure if we're caught. You're young, you three. I don't suppose Littoni here cares much how this turns out, but you should. What about your brothers? Your families? Your mothers? You joined the X to change things. You agreed when you joined to disassociate yourselves from your families, but when this is all over, what then? Surely you want to go back to your old lives? We want Issawi. One man. And now Littoni here is not content with that. You want countless politicians, their wives, even the king himself, assassinated, because you're too impatient to go about this intelligently? The king is incompetent, yes, that's true, but it's only a matter of time before we can demand the king abdicate, do this whole thing properly. We're strong enough. Your way, Littoni, is far too dangerous, for you, for everyone. You want the revolution to start now, but indiscriminate violence is no way to win. You think you're cleverer than Issawi's networks, but you're not."

"I said shut your mouth, Farouk," Littoni shouted.

"Put your pistol away, Littoni. We're supposed to be working together, not against each other."

Hamid approached Littoni and whispered something in his ear that seemed to appease him. Littoni lowered the pistol and put it back in his pocket.

"Those civilians won't matter in the long run, "Littoni said, "as long as it gets our message across. After all, we've been planning this for years. Do you think we're going to stop now just because you've developed a conscience all of a sudden? It's our present to the government. A nice little greeting card that will let that pack of incompetents know in no uncertain terms that the X means business. If there was ever any doubt in their minds about that, the assassination of Chief Advisor Issawi and the king will reinforce the message loud and clear."

"But this is supposed to be a people's revolution," Farouk said. "Get it into your head; Issawi is our target, not the king or anybody else. There must not be unnecessary bloodshed. We want the people of Egypt to join us. If we kill innocents, we will lose their support. The repercussions will be devastating." Littoni smiled importantly, walked over to Farouk, placed one hand on Farouk's arm to quieten him, and stabbed the air with his other.

"Do you think our men want things done your way, Farouk? Do you think they want Issawi kidnapped and cut up into little pieces and shipped to Assiyut in a perfumed wedding consignment? It might be enough for you, but it won't be for the rest of our men. We're ready; our men are ready. We've waited a long time for this, and we're going to strike now." He was so close, Farouk could smell whisky on his breath.

"The revolution will happen whether you bomb the palace or not," Farouk sneered, peeling back Littoni's hand in disgust. "Don't you think I want Issawi dead as much as you do? And I am just one among thousands who want to see it happen. But you put him out with a bomb, you'll have the government's entire security operation on our tails. We're so close. If we go about this properly, the revolution can start from the streets, just as it should. If we do it your way, we'll just end up going into combat with the king's security forces. Our men only follow you, Littoni, because you're a bully. I know you threaten them, their businesses, their cover if they don't comply with your wishes."

Littoni grabbed Farouk by the shirt collar again and snarled, "I won't tell you again, Farouk. Be careful what you say."

Hamid, Hossein, and al-Dyn looked on wide-eyed.

"You just can't bring yourself to admit that my plan will work much better," Farouk went on. "You blow up the government, and what then? Hitler will invade. You're courting chaos and the destruction of Egypt."

"You're so wrong. This is the real beginning for Egypt," Littoni spat. "With the X in power, Egypt will become powerful. Right now, Egypt is vulnerable. The government doesn't know what it's doing. This war has been our blessing. The government is preoccupied with a possible German invasion. All of its resources are taken with this. We must strike now while they've got other things on their mind."

"You're deluded, Littoni," Farouk said. "You're finished, but you're trying to hold on before younger men like Hossein, al-Dyn, and Hamid take over."

"You can talk, Farouk. Your revolutionary days are really over. You're losing your touch. You pass yourself off as a freedom fighter, but you have a private agenda with this Issawi. That's why you want everything your way. Some girl, some broken heart, some revenge bound up in a woman."

"The palace is too public," Farouk kept repeating, but his words fell on deaf ears. "I've been telling you this for weeks. Every security man in the entire force will be out checking identity papers. You won't get through. Issawi is expected to arrive at 8:00 P.M. He'll attend the dinner, then the dance, then be expected to join the king in his private suites. He'll probably leave not long after midnight.

His car will wait for him and then drive him back to his home. You expect to get a car close enough? You're crazy."

Littoni was smiling. Farouk didn't know that the palace security men had recently come over to his side. "He won't get home," he said with a laugh, "not if we have anything to do with it. This will be the last celebration at the palace for a while. They'll be clearing the mess up for weeks. Perfect timing for our men to hit the streets and start the revolution proper. Then we can really get started. Chaos and disorder, followed by a new beginning."

Suddenly, there was the sound of a car starting up. Littoni jerked his head towards the door, startled.

"Sssh," he said.

The five men were quiet for a moment. They had all heard it. After a minute or two, the car drove off. Littoni nodded and went on. "We have seven days, Farouk. Go to Achmed's party. Talk to the girl. Size her up. She knows something, I'm sure of it. Hamid and Tashi will get to work on the time bomb. Al-Dyn, are you sure your cover hasn't been blown?"

Al-Dyn shook his head. "No. I hear everything that's going on at the Oxford. There's nothing suspicious there."

Littoni said, "We'll meet again to decide where and how we'll plant the bomb. Hamid, you've engineered it so it will be small but very powerful, yes? So all we need now is an invitation to the celebration to enable us to get past security. Tashi knows what he has to do there. The old Greek, Papadopolous at the Bulac print-works, can arrange the invitation for us. All right, that's enough for now. It's time to get to work."

Farouk listened on in amazement. "I'm going," he said finally. "Think about what I said, Littoni. You're signing your own death warrant—you know that, don't you?"

Littoni stared at Farouk. Blowing more smoke rings into the air, he said, "None of us should meet again until I say so. I'll get a message to all of you, through the usual channels when it's time. We must cover our tracks."

Farouk shot Littoni and the others one last look before he turned and left. He slipped his hand under his shirt and rubbed his chest as he walked towards his car. He hadn't felt much pain today, and his convulsions hadn't troubled him a great deal. He had a rendezvous with Nemmat, the prostitute from the el-G, who had keys to the Abbassiya apartment. He would size her up, see if she could be easily bought. If he could trust her, he'd set his own little plan in motion.

The journal of Hezba Iqbal Sultan Hanim al-Shezira,
Cairo, August 15, 1919

I can't believe what's happened. My husband is charging me with nushaz. Claiming wifely disobedience, he has asked a qadi to charge me with Bait Al-Ta'a. This law means I will have to return to my husband's home, and there is nothing I can do to fight back. I hate these religious rulings that strip me of my freedom. I will die. I will run away.

My husband has told my papa that I have betrayed him, because I continue to live in the sarai of my birth, and I have not returned to live with him as his wife. He has told my papa that he will not forgive this betrayal. My husband and my papa consulted with the qadi, and it has been agreed. My husband told Papa my betrayal of him is the last act of disobedience he will tolerate of me. My marriage to al-Shezira was always a political alliance between him and the family of the sultan, and if I am not seen to be al-Shezira's wife by Egyptian society, then al-Shezira fears his name will be like mud. That's all they care about. How can I bear it? My only friend is my journal. My little notebook is easy to hide away. I carry it with me always, even to the hammam. I like to strap it to my body under my clothes. I like to feel its secrets close to me. No one will take it from me again. No one.

And Habrid's cruelty cannot stop me from dreaming. For the moment I have to be content with the brief moments Alexandre and I are able to share together. While I dream, I wait impatiently for Alexandre's return to Cairo. And while I wait, I try to celebrate moulids with my harem sisters with the appropriate enthusiasm, and bribe my servants to sneak me out to a zaar. I love the zaars, where we women can be rid of our tormenters and all our troubles exorcised by the drums and the lutes of the wandering peddlers and musicians. When the women become possessed by the spirits of the desert, their true natures are allowed free reign. But in reality, I have become jittery with nerves and depression and a desire to cause trouble. It is almost as if I am living two lives: the sedate, grateful harem life, and my true inner life, wild and free.

I know that tomorrow night there is a zaar in Shubra. One of the peddler women who came to the palace a few days ago told me about it. I pretended not to be interested, because we all know those peddler women are Cairo's secret messengers—if the face of the daughter of the sultan reveals even the smallest taint of emotion, the whole of Cairo will know. I don't trust these peddler women. They have an intimate network of friends whom they confide in. Thanks to them, every love affair, every betrayal, every sordid piece of information, is silently blowing in through the harem mashrabiyya and over the terraces of the mansions and palaces. Often they exaggerate and lie.

On the subject of gossip, I know of three notable women who are entertaining men in their salons while their husbands in the ministries are tying up the remaining threads of the war. I envy them their courage. One woman, an elderly European lady, employs little Egyptian boys to look after her. She is very wealthy and can afford to live in the greatest luxury. Her boys are kept in apartments of their own. They live *like we girls live in our harems. They must tally to her every wish, and rumour has it that she makes use of them on different nights of the week, taking her pick according to her mood and her desire. I have heard she is often seen around Cairo, goes to the theatre by herself, strolls along the Corniche, is seen with the British ladies at the women's clubs, and takes walks around Gezira Island all by herself. This woman has the armour of old age. I believe she is about sixty years old. She is Austrian, I think, and was married to an Egyptian who is now dead. She owns one of the newspapers in Cairo that is dedicated to Egyptian women, and she has a small staff of women somewhere who produce it.*

I envy her freedom so much. I don't envy her her boys, because that would be wrong, but I do envy her the freedom to be herself, to work, to make a difference to the lives of those around her. I want a life like that for myself. How can I make a difference to the world when I am caged in a harem and repeatedly told to be quiet and not to think? I cannot stop thinking. However, this Austrian lady must be proof that things are changing. Alexandre knows men who are challenging the age-old laws of Islam through scientific and academic enquiry. There is hope. There has to be hope.

How wonderful to be able to live like a man, to walk among them as a woman, unveiled, with simply a hat on and a pair of gloves and a lovely fashionable dress showing off feminine curves. How wonderful to be able to take tea at the Shepheard's Hotel and mix with all the influential and well-connected socialites that come to Cairo. For the time being, I content myself with my friend, Virginie. She is wonderful, a constant source of support and inspiration to me. I know she will take me to Shubra, to this zaar. She is allowed to accompany me on occasional excursions to the souks and salons, but only when Papa gives me permission.

I will watch tomorrow night, but I do not plan to dance. I will watch the exorcism of the poor young girls. I will watch them denounced as fit for nothing, possessed by the evil jinn, and watch them dance in a trancelike state in a dark room lit only by candles. I will watch the evil spirits that pollute their bodies vanish forever as they dance and twirl and throw themselves around the room. And I will not join them. To join them would be to admit that I am not pure. And I will admit no such thing. My thoughts are my own.

CHAPTER FIVE

Shrouded in trailing black robes, seventeen-year-old Nemmat Shanti stood on the corner near Ali's Café, waiting impatiently for Farouk to arrive. She held her chador over her mouth, her black, heavily kohled eyes scanning the crowds. Beneath her chador, she wore an exquisitely jewelled costume of Persian silk, a bodice over her pert little breasts, and voluminous trousers over her perfumed body. It was very late, hot, and sultry, and her chador was chafing her. She longed to remove it and lie with her master, Abbas, smoking cigarettes on the balcony of his Shubra apartment. But as it was, she had to wait for the newspaperman. She was glad Mehmed Abbas looked upon her so favourably. She was young and energetic and moved with a dancer's sensuality. Abbas was richer, she was sure, than the newspaperman, the man she called Monsieur Farouk, richer than any man she knew. Though she knew Abbas would take care of her, she still had a duty to her mother and herself to amass as much money as she could. She didn't trust her madame, the owner of the el-G, or the clients who frequented the place. The only sure thing in her life was Abbas. As long as she satisfied him, she knew his money would continue to flow in her direction.

Nemmat studied the faces of the soldiers as they lingered on the street corners talking, the men at Ali's clustered around tables, smoking, the other café owners standing outside and wondering whether to close up shop for the night. Still she waited. How she hated waiting, hated standing on this corner, hated being stared at by the people who passed. The looks they flashed at her made her squirm. Women were usually escorted by a male relative and rushed from place to place. A woman shrouded, standing alone, was not a common sight in these parts.

Her impatience at being kept waiting made her ball her free fist under her chador. This Monsieur Farouk would make her late for Abbas if he didn't turn up soon—which would make Abbas angry. Once the Monsieur had arrived, Nemmat would head straight to Abbas's apartment. If she wasn't late, Abbas would have a full two hours with her, before he went home to his wife—and Nemmat didn't like to disappoint him. If Monsieur Farouk did not appear soon, she would leave. She was also anxious because she did not want to risk anyone from the nightclub, the el-G, seeing her talking to Farouk. Word would get back to her madame in no time. And then her madame would question her, thinking she was soliciting more business for herself on the streets, and for that she would be in trouble.

She thought about Farouk. When at the el-G, he always lurked in the shadows of the bar, observing everything around him, and kept his distance from the other customers. When he had requested her services in one of the back rooms of the club, instead of expecting her to fulfil her usual fleshly duties, he had asked her to help him find an apartment, for temporary use, in one of Cairo's seedier suburbs. Nemmat had often wondered why he had asked her. Did he know something of her background? She hadn't said much at that one meeting in the back room of the club, but she had agreed to help him.

While she waited for him, Nemmat distracted herself with thoughts of magnificently furnished apartments, adoring servants, and grand trips abroad to London and America. She had Abbas in the palm of her hand. The newspaper monsieur, she wasn't so sure. He had treated her gently the night he had asked her for help, and spoke to her in a soft voice, but it was clear that he was a hard-edged character, not to be trusted. Like all the men who went to the el-G, he probably wore a mask. Their real selves were invisible. She didn't know him at all, but she knew his type. And then she saw him.

He had spotted her and was walking towards her. It was clear that he did not want to be seen talking to her and he knew he had to be quick.

"Jewel?"

Nemmat nodded at the sound of her code name. He took a wad of notes out of his pocket and slipped them into Nemmat's outstretched hand.

"Is it all arranged?"

"Yes," she said, sliding her hand from under her chador to reveal a bunch of keys. "Here are the keys. You can take the flat any time you like. No one will disturb you, but you only have possession for seven days. You must return the keys to me after that or pay double the fee."

Farouk took them from her and let his eyes wander over her veiled features. He was right; she was cunning. She had already asked for too much money. Farouk knew the price of those run-down apartments. He could have taken his chances with any of them, but the risk was too high. Jewel would keep her pretty mouth shut, and if the price was higher, so be it.

"You're a hard businesswoman," Farouk said bitterly.

"I know what my dead brother's flat is worth," Nemmat replied impatiently. "But don't forget, the price doubles if you take longer than seven days—"

Farouk put his hand up to silence her. "Seven days is all we need."

"You are very confident."

"We're ready," Farouk said firmly.

"Have you set a date?"

"Yes. You'll get all the details in twenty-four hours, timing, location, your new identity papers for entry to the club. This man Issawi loves beautiful women. You must simply play your part— seduce him, spike his drink, lure him away from the Oxford, and escort him in the car that's sent for you to this apartment. Once you've gotten him there, there will be nothing more for you to do. When you receive the exact instructions, you must memorise every- thing. Nothing can be written down. Do you understand?"

Nemmat nodded. "Yes, but I need the money you promised."

"You'll get your money when you deliver him to the apart- ment," Farouk said sternly.

"But you promised half up front."

Farouk examined her carefully.

"There's been a change of plan," he said. "One of my men has advised me against it. Complete the delivery to Abbassiya without a hitch and you get it all. We can't take any risks. This operation must not fail."

Nemmat eyed him coolly.

"Who else is involved in this operation?" she asked.

"I can't tell you that, but don't worry. You have nothing to fear. As long as you memorise your instructions and follow them exactly, you will receive your money and be promised a safe passage to Alexandria. Nothing more will be asked of you."

"What if I am followed?" Nemmat asked.

Farouk paused for a moment, staring at her suspiciously, and then said, "Mademoiselle, for the price you have asked, I am convinced you will move heaven and earth not to be followed."

She nodded slowly, searching his eyes.

"And you'll be ready when you are given the dates?"

Nemmat nodded again.

And in the blink of an eye, Farouk was gone.

The journal of Hezba Iqbal Sultan Hanim al-Shezira,
Cairo, August 23, 1919

It is early and deliciously quiet. I had to start writing by the light of a candle, but it is already growing lighter. There is pink in the sky, between the lattices of the mashrabiyya, far out on the horizon. The sun will be up soon. The muezzins will call us to prayer.

I write to release the burden of guilt in me. I feel guilty because I know I cause Papa such distress. He doesn't know what to do with me. I am not the person he would wish me to be, quiet and serene and unquestioning. I also hate myself because I am a hypocrite. I pray, but I do not say the words in my head, and the words that issue from my lips are uttered without sincerity. My nightclothes are sticking to me, and my head is heavy as I write. I can hardly see the pages of my journal because my eyes hurt. Rachid is dozing in the corner, curled up like a baby on his cushions. Last night Rachid gave me a little calming powder to dab on my tongue. I had become quite hysterical at the news that al-Shezira is travelling with his party to Cairo to get me. I don't know when he will be here. It might be days or it might be weeks. Nothing more has been said about my being charged with the crime of disobedience against my husband, but that doesn't mean this ruling won't be passed. I imagine it's only a matter of time.

Rachid tried to calm me down last night. He laid me on my cushions and held me close, gently muffling my sobs with the palm of his hand so that Habrid, walking the corridors, would not summon my maman's eunuch.

And then when I became calmer, he stared into my eyes and told me how afraid he too was of the future, of my going to Minya, of the possibility of him not being allowed to escort me.

He told me he loved me, and I told him I loved him. He is like my brother. I felt so bad that I cause him so much distress. And yet, despite that, despite my wilful ways, he is so loyal to me. If only things were different. If only I could take Rachid with me to live freely. He would not be my servant. He would be my friend, my confidant, as he is now. I would give him everything I could to repay him for his kindness to me. Though he is not that much older than I am, he has been with me since I was a very young girl. He was bought into slavery as a child and we became friends. I could never let anyone know this because it would be considered a shameful thing for a mistress to befriend her eunuch. I look at him every now and again as I write. He is sleeping so peacefully, but his cheeks are wet with tears. As he dreams, he is in torment. My rooms are now full of soft light, delicate and dreamy. When al-Shezira comes back, I suspect Rachid is right in predicting we will be prized apart. Rumour is going around the palace that my husband has the most terrible fate in store for me as punishment for my waywardness and my depression. His pride has been wounded and al-Shezira is a proud man. I see my sisters whispering when I walk past them in the corridors of the harem. I wish for some terrible accident, some disaster to befall him, a train wreck, the onset of some illness, food poisoning, anything.

Minya must no longer be amusing him, so he has turned his attention to me. Why, I wonder, when he has other wives to amuse him? It's because of Papa and their alliance, I am sure. I lived with him in his Cairo mansion only briefly when I was first married, but then I became ill, so Papa allowed me to return to the palace of my birth in our district of Cairo. After that, al-Shezira abandoned his Cairo mansion and returned to Minya with the rest of his wives. Al-Shezira's insistence that I return with him to Minya is political bargaining with Papa, and I am the currency.

Rachid moans in his sleep. I look up at him. His mouth is moist. He's such a pretty sight when he's asleep. "Rachid," I whisper.

My poor eunuch rouses and jumps up. Then he stumbles over me and lands on the floor, laughing. He is so funny. I am happy when I am with him.

For a moment I forget about al-Shezira and his wives. Rachid smiles at me, showing his beautiful white teeth. I love the little grey patches under his eyes and his cheekbones sculpted out of soft flesh, but his eyes are sad.

All too soon I have to face the reality of what lies ahead, a life as al-Shezira's fourth wife, an object of torment, of derision, and a future of indescribable boredom in the stuffy confines of the Minya harem, when inside all I want is to join Alexandre and be part of the change that's rocking my beloved country. I want to tear off my veil and shout that, as a woman, I will not be ignored. When I think of it, I feel this rage overwhelm me, that I have to suffer at the hands of al-Shezira and yet no one believes me when I tell them the truth about my husband. They make me feel I should consider myself fortunate to have a husband at all, that because of my wild, untamed nature, I am not attractive to most eligible men and that the only thing in my favour is that my father is the newly appointed sultan of Egypt.

There is no reason to believe that the marriage between my husband and me was anything other than a political manoeuvre on the part of my papa and al-Shezira. Still I remain faithful to my papa and unfaithful to al-Shezira.

Why do I live as a caged animal, constrained only because I am a woman when I want to do so much? Alexandre has told me all about his allegiance with the Nationalists and how he is part of the movement to overthrow the British and sever their stranglehold of our country once and for all. He is free. He can make a difference. One day this will be me, I pray to God, this will be me.

CHAPTER SIX

Aimee had no trouble getting Sophie to agree to go to the literary launch with her. Conversation over, she replaced the telephone in the cradle and went to get changed. Two days had passed since her meeting with Professor Langham. He hadn't telephoned with any news of work or any more information that could help the police. Perhaps Langham really couldn't remember anything of any interest about Azi's mood and activity in the weeks before his death.

She thought about her husband. Would he be angry with her if he could see her longingly finger the lovely red satin dress her aunt Saiza had bought for her when she had first arrived in Cairo? She shivered. Azi had loved her in that dress, thinking its fiery colour a complement to her pale skin and black hair. The fit was perfect too, beautifully tailored to accentuate the emerging curves of a young lady. Tonight she would wear her hair up, the way Azi had liked it. Tonight she would go out for him, make a big effort to sparkle. At school she had worn starched shirts and simple ankle-length wool skirts and black boots. The nuns had taught the girls how to make their own uniforms, for economy's sake as much for the grace of God. God, Aimee had been told, had no time for vanity. Simplicity was the first rule of presentation.

Yet Maman had given birth to her in a robe made of gold thread, her aunt had told her. That birthing robe was a symbol of her heritage, a symbol of the royal blood that coursed through her veins.

Stained with the blood of new royalty, the golden robe had been passed down through the generations. Aimee had been born straight into the arms of her aunt Saiza, and her tiny, misshapen slippery body had been washed with coconut oil. From gold thread to starched shirts and invisibility, the road didn't make sense. It was hardly a normal trajectory.

A little while later, Aimee was in the car with Sophie. Their driver, Sophie's dragoman—employed by the Continental Hotel where Sophie had a private suite, paid for by Tony Sedgewick— knew the whereabouts of Zaky Achmed's house. It was at the end of a wide lane, away from the main souk of al-Qadima, a fashionable residential area with lovely old houses.

Sophie tapped the window of the car, and the driver stopped. Aimee stepped out onto the pavement, and rang the doorbell while Sophie instructed the dragoman on the hour he should return.

A small pretty woman opened the door and introduced herself as Achmed's sister. She led the way up some stairs and along a maze of corridors to a large room at the rear of the house, atmospherically lit with fashionable lamps and tables of thick honey-coloured candles.

The room opened onto a large balcony filled with men and women deep in conversation. The room smelt of spice, leather brogues, and floral perfume laced with musk. The scent of Shalimar by Guerlain, liberally applied by the ladies, tickled Aimee's nose. She overheard a group of women speaking Turkish, others speaking French. Laughter. Shouting. Jazz. Snake-hipped boys with greasy faces carried trays of delicacies. Sophie whispered to Aimee that she had spotted the friend of a friend who disappeared. Achmed, fetched by his sister, emerged from a crowd of animated intellectuals.

"Madame Ibrahim, I'm so glad you came. Your aunt has told me so much about you."

Aimee smiled and extended her hand. Achmed was a short rotund man of about thirty with dark tightly curled hair receding past his ears. His brown eyes gazed kindly at her. His mouth was full and downturned. Dressed in an immaculate pale suit and tie, he clutched a small silver cigarette case.

"I knew your husband, Madame. I'm so terribly sorry for what happened."

Aimee examined him carefully before she said anything.

"I am not sure if my husband mentioned you," she said. "It is possible, but as you can imagine—"

He bowed amiably and put up his hand. "Please, it's quite all right. It's such a sad day that we meet in these circumstances. I have been away, teaching at a country school in the Delta. Perhaps that's why you may not have been aware of me. But I used to work with your husband at the university. He was a wonderful man, an honest friend, a good sport—"

Achmed produced a large handkerchief from his breast pocket and wiped his eyes. She touched him briefly on the arm, and he tried to pull himself together, smiling once more and turning to wave to a group of men talking in the corner.

"A few of Azi's friends are here," he said. "I'll introduce you, but first I'd like you to meet my wife." He wiped his nose and replaced his handkerchief in his jacket pocket.

"You have children, Monsieur?" Aimee enquired.

"Yes, four daughters. They're in the sitting room with some of my cousins. They must go to bed soon, but if you'll wait just a moment, I will have them fetched."

"Are you expecting many people here tonight?" Aimee asked Achmed, scanning the faces of the men and women already present.

"The more the better, Madame," he replied, and she saw his eyes glitter happily as four young girls approached from the other side of the room.

"These are your daughters, Monsieur?" Aimee smiled. "They're lovely." The girls appeared to be between five and ten years old. They curtsied politely and gave a little bow. They were dressed identically in tight dresses of pink lace with sleeveless bodices, gathered at the waist with red satin ribbon.

"Daughters, this is Madame Ibrahim, the wife of Professor Abdullah Ibrahim, Uncle Azi as you remember him." Achmed coughed, then added, "It seems that my wife is detained at the moment."

"Good evening, Madame," the little girls said with uniform sweetness.

"This is Naima, Huda, Attilya, and Luisa," Achmed said with pride.

"Luisa?" Aimee looked at Achmed quizzically. "Surely that's not an Egyptian name."

"A friend of my wife is Italian," Achmed explained, smiling. "We thought it a beautiful name. She is the youngest, and we felt we could be a little freer with our choice."

Aimee studied the girls carefully, their soft, cherubic faces, big black wandering eyes, their glistening black hair smoothed into two gleaming plaits. Out of the corner of her eye, she saw a man eyeing her. Tall and smartly dressed in a dark suit, he stepped forward and placed his hands indelicately on the shoulders of the tallest of Achmed's daughters. The girl did not flinch and simply stood there, looking up at the man as though she knew him. Achmed's eyes narrowed slightly. Aimee saw a tiny, almost imperceptible tilt of the head, a flash of knowledge, some secret message, relayed to whom, she did not know. Then Achmed smiled at the man who stood so protectively close to his daughters. She looked at Achmed, then back at the man. In his midforties, he had a dark Mediterranean-olive complexion. His night-black eyes stared at her unwaveringly from under arched eyebrows. He had no trace of a fashionable moustache or the much-loved Arab beard. Who was he?

"Achmed, I knew you'd be behind *Monument* and your writers," the man said with a laugh. His voice was low and seductive, and he obviously knew Achmed very well.

Achmed smiled at his daughters, then pushed them gently away. They retreated to the other side of the room.

"I had no idea you'd be coming tonight," Achmed said soberly.

Farouk grinned as he took a cigarette case slowly out of his pocket and nonchalantly lit a pale Turkish cigarette.

"You didn't think I'd miss the chance to profile your launch, did you? This kind of thing is perfect fodder for the paper. I love a good book launch. Any chance to write about the burgeoning talent of Cairo's literati."

Aimee shuffled uncomfortably.

"Well, Achmed, aren't you going to introduce me to your guest? I'm sure this young lady must think you've no manners."

Achmed turned to Aimee.

"Madame, let me introduce you to the editor of one of Cairo's newspapers, the *Liberation,* Taha Mohammod Farouk. Farouk," Achmed went on, "this is the wife of an acquaintance of yours. Madame Abdullah Ibrahim."

Farouk shook Aimee's hand, his eyes devouring hers, taking in her softness and warmth. He studied her features curiously. He had not seen eyes like hers since his time in northern Afghanistan. How beautiful she was, such an exquisite face, such a young girl.

"Madame."

Aimee shivered. She didn't like the way he was staring at her.

Farouk went on. "I'm so sorry about your husband. I met him briefly a few months ago, at—let me see, a function given at the university."

Aimee smiled with effort. She was sick of smiling at strangers, sick of making polite conversation. She suddenly regretted coming to the launch. It turned out she did not really feel like being out in company.

"I got the impression from our brief encounter that your husband was very ambitious," Farouk went on. "Such a brilliant theorist and speaker on all subjects. He would have made an excellent politician, but instead he wanted to put the world to right using the long and dreary intellectual strategies of academia. If only he had used his intellect more wisely, but then, I can see he had excellent taste in matters of beauty."

Aimee straightened her back and flushed scarlet. Swallowing hard, she scanned the room for Sophie, searching for some excuse to leave.

"I don't think he mentioned you, Monsieur. I think he would have told me if he had met the editor of a newspaper like the *Liberation*."

Farouk looked at her with surprise.

"I see," he said, frowning. "I'm sure—oh well, Azi Ibrahim had many friends. It's quite possible. Anyway, he was a young man with a great future ahead of him. I liked him very much on first meeting and was shocked and disturbed when I found out about his death."

Aimee's eyes narrowed. She didn't know what to make of this man. She was not sure if she liked him. There was something about his mouth, his eyes, something that she couldn't identify, but that she found disturbing. "You're kind, Monsieur. But my husband is gone, and my only concern now is that his murderer is found."

Unable to take his eyes off the girl, Farouk took a long draw on his cigarette. How cool she was, how calm. Azi's confident young wife was one of a new breed of Egyptian women. But she was so young. He knew women like her. Perhaps her confidence was an act. She looked so virginal, so pure; yet she had married Ibrahim and was no doubt properly a woman in every sense, perhaps cunning, perhaps secretive, perhaps in possession of the type of information Littoni would give his eyeteeth for. Maybe Littoni had been right about the girl.

"A gang of thugs, no doubt, Madame. I regret your husband's death, but I have no time for emotion or sentimentality. Your husband was spared the fate that will soon come to so many of our men. The Egyptian Army must prove itself. The Anglo-Egyptian Treaty has done nothing for the self-esteem of our soldiers. The British government is supposed to be supporting the Egyptian Armed Forces. Academics like our friend, your husband, Abdullah Ibrahim, will be prime fodder for eventual conscription. Before too long, your beloved academic husband would have had to don a soldier's uniform. He would have been out there in the desert, fighting the Germans. All of al-Qahire's young men are destined to succumb to some sort of North Africa campaign."

Farouk did not really care about the Egyptian Armed Forces or the Western Desert military lieutenants whose ultimate goal lay in strategic war manoeuvres. He knew his words would mean nothing to a young girl like Ibrahim's wife.

"It does not alter the fact that the police are taking their time finding Azi's killer," Aimee said bitterly.

Farouk nodded. "It is likely they're occupied with other things they consider more important. Even as we speak, officers of the Egyptian Army are preparing extensive plans on how to fortify the city against attack. Twenty-three strategic sites have been pinpointed against the Italians and Germans. Cairo is shrinking into itself. Who knows if we will get out alive? And all the while, we are being entertained by the up-and-coming cultural elite of the city. We are enjoying a drink and good company. Perhaps we should be ashamed of ourselves. Perhaps the Almighty has been kinder to your husband than you think."

Aimee recoiled in horror. She had no patience for the likes of this man. And she had no desire to be lectured. Though she trembled inside, she was determined to speak her mind. As she spoke, she regretted her youth and inexperience.

"My husband was passionate about education, Monsieur. You talk about my husband becoming a soldier and joining the war like all the other young men, but he was arming young Egyptian men with a better weapon to fight injustice—knowledge. You talk about him fighting this war, of perhaps dying a noble death, but he has not been given the chance to serve his country. His life was taken from him by criminals. He will never be able to serve Egypt again, either by educating its young men, or by defeating the Germans."

Seeing that he had offended her, Farouk bowed and smiled in a conciliatory manner.

"Please forgive me. I suppose I have become unnecessarily hard. Nothing shocks me anymore. My poor beloved Cairo has suffered so much over the years. And death comes to everyone eventually. If I seem brutal, I apologise. You are young after all. Your husband was a good man. He did not deserve what happened to him."

He bit his lip and their eyes met again. She wondered why he was studying her so closely. She stared into his mesmerising eyes, wondering what secret thoughts lay beneath. If he was the editor of the *Liberation*—a newspaper of some repute in Cairo—he must have contacts in the underworld; he must know someone who might be able to help her find Azi's killer.

Farouk dug in his pocket, pulled out his wallet, and extracted a card with his telephone number on it. "Here, if you ever need me," he said with a pleasant smile. "I might be able to be of some use to you, you never know."

A shudder slithered down Aimee's spine. She studied the card and slipped it in her handbag.

"Thank you, I'm not sure—"

"You're French," Farouk broke in, trying to lighten the mood. "How do you find our city? Does it live up to your expectations, or do you long to return to your homeland?"

"I'm as Egyptian as you," Aimee said defiantly.

Farouk shook his head in confusion and studied her features more closely. She didn't look Egyptian exactly. There was something about her that perplexed him, something he couldn't quite put his finger on.

"I see. And do you plan to help with the war effort? You will work for the war?"

His inquisitive thin smile put her on edge.

"I'll do whatever I can. I don't want to be idle. I owe it to the memory of my husband to do as much as I can. Women should not sit by and let the work be done by men alone. I have no children, and my husband's family is leaving for America soon. If the people of Cairo can work together to support the soldiers, we must do so. I'm good at languages. Translating, interpreting. I'll find something to do."

"Your husband would have been very proud of you. You sound very determined and resourceful—admirable qualities in a young lady."

A hot, irritated shudder prickled her skin again.

"I must go now, Monsieur. I've just spotted my friend Sophie on the other side of the room, and I want to introduce myself to Monsieur Achmed's wife."

"Don't forget to telephone me, Madame, if I can be of service."

Aimee nodded, offered him a vague smile, and turned to Zaky Achmed. "Would you take me to your wife? I would very much like to meet her."

Achmed edged away and went to find his wife. Aimee followed. But she could feel Farouk's eyes on her. Their meeting had intrigued her. He was a strange character, abrupt and hard, lacking in social graces despite offering to help her, but that aside, he was almost certainly someone who would be useful to know. All the noise, the celebratory clapping of hands, the deafening laughter, the readings by the poets, the music and the animated chatter—none of it could stop her from thinking about the man on the other side of the room. She decided to make an effort to enjoy the party. From time to time, she looked over in Farouk's direction and saw him deep in conversation with other men. Their brief exchange had disturbed her. He had spoken so coldly about her husband, as though his death had been as natural to him as the sun rising. It was almost as though death and murder were nothing to him. She shivered a little.

When she and Sophie eventually decided to leave, she looked around the large room one last time to see if she could spot him, but he had vanished.

The journal of Hezba Iqbal Sultan Hanim al-Shezira,
Cairo, August 18, 1919

I am at the Theatre Madeleine near the Tahrir Bridge. As a present for my birthday, Virginie gave me tickets to see La Jolie Madame. I am sitting in the sultan's private box with two of my half sisters. I am covered from head to foot. Over my face I am wearing my niqāb. We are accompanied by our aghas, Rachid and Tindoui. I had to ask Papa for permission to go, and, surprisingly, even though Maman is furious, he defied her and said I could.

Monsieur Alexandre is sitting in a private box next to ours with his sister. He cannot see my face, but I can feel his eyes on me. I saw him bow discreetly in my direction. He is dressed in government uniform, a dark fitted jacket and a tarboush. He has adopted the dress and the standards of our country, because, my tutor tells me, he has taken al-Qahire into his heart and considers himself one of us.

As he looks out over the stage, I stare at him, pulling my niqāb closer to my face, gripping it, my heart beating wildly. Little beads of perspiration have gathered at the base of my spine, and my belly feels as though it is hollowing out with nervous anticipation and desire. This is the first time I have seen him in weeks. I don't know what is going to happen to us after I go to Minya. I want to be his amour. Will we be able to continue? I try not to think about this for the moment though. He wrote me a letter last week, which was delivered in the usual way, through Virginie at our lessons. I read that he has become involved in an underground branch of the Egyptian Nationalists and that he wants me to help him. He has a job for me, and this knowledge fills me with joy. He asked me in his letter to tell no one, not even Virginie. He wants me to prove to him that I am sincere in my desire to help ordinary Egyptians and wants me to go with him to a meeting of his group, out in the desert. My heart was racing as I read his words. I had withdrawn to a corner of the room to read the letter in private, and it was hard to keep my features serene and unexpressive, but I succeeded. When I finished his letter, I ripped it into little pieces, then returned to my lessons.

Madame Virginie sits very erect in her startlingly turquoise silk dress, hiding behind a beautiful ivory-coloured fan. The play is long and tedious. I cannot concentrate.

Alexandre's attention is not on the play either. Every now and again he looks over at me, and I notice a faint smile.

The play ends. We stand. The audience applauds the actors, and then they applaud us. We bow at them and leave our private box, marched by Tindoui and Rachid to our horse-and-trap waiting for us outside. As my sisters and I prepare to step in, Virginie approaches. She pulls me aside and invites me to have supper with her at her house in Zamalek. My heart expands with excitement at the prospect.

I nod and press her hand. She says she will expect me at my convenience. I tell her that as soon as our driver has escorted the ladies back to the palace harem, our driver will continue on to Virginie's house. Rachid will accompany me. It is unusual that I should make such a trip on my own, but because Rachid is accompanying me and because the invitation has come from a dear friend of the sultan's family, it will not be viewed as shameful.

I climb into our carriage and sit with my sisters. As we are driven through the streets, I break my news. Even in the dark, I can see my sisters' eyes twinkling at my adventure. I say nothing to suggest that my visit to Virginie is anything more than an innocent supper party for her and her special lady guests.

"Rachid will escort me home," I say, waving them good-bye at the palace gates as Tindoui escorts my veiled sisters through the palace to the harem. On we go to Zamalek. I pull my veil down over my face as I step out of the carriage and, accompanied by Rachid, I mount the steps to the front door. Virginie opens the door herself. She smiles. She says she has been waiting for me. She is excited, she says. Did I enjoy the play? Would I care for refreshments in her sitting room?

I dismiss Rachid. Virginie tells him he can go to the kitchen. Her boy-servants are preparing a supper feast, and he is welcome to have whatever he likes.

I follow Virginie. We walk up the stairs together with arms linked. She unfurls my veil and looks into my eyes.

"He's here," she whispers. I nod, hardly able to speak.

"I know," I reply.

"I will leave you alone for a time. No one will disturb you. As you know, my husband is away in Malta. My servants are under my supervision. They will not go to the second-floor sitting room."

"Why are you doing this, Virginie?" I ask her, holding her hands in mine.

"I want you to be happy, Hezba," she says, hugging me.

I wish she were my mother, my sister. I cannot imagine a kinder or better person than she. She knows that al-Shezira is on his way from Minya to get me. She knows that I hate him. She knows too that I dream of being allowed to divorce him, but she knows this will never be allowed. Still, despite this knowledge, she does not judge me. She wants me to be happy. She leads me to the door of the sitting room, pushes it open, and nudges me in with a little laugh. Alexandre is standing by the divan. He is smiling. He says nothing. I stand with my back to the door and unravel my veil, then remove it entirely. For what seems like an eternity, we stand at opposite ends of the room, staring at each other. I step forward with my heart in my mouth and clear my throat.

"Monsieur Alexandre," I say.

He puts his finger to his mouth and comes to me, enfolding me in his arms.

"We don't have long, Hezba," he whispers.

I bury my face in his neck, wrap my arms around his neck, and inhale his scent. I feel warm and protected. Then I look up at him and say, "Is it all arranged?"

He nods and looks into my eyes. "We're meeting next week at Kerdassa. You must come. Do anything you can to come. I am going to discuss the whole operation with my men, the Rebel Corps. But we need the money you promised us. Can you bring it with you?"

I assure him that I will have it. I have been amassing my allowance for a long time, and it has turned into a small fortune, which I keep locked in a jewelled box in my rooms. Alexandre needs it more than I do. He asks me to sit with him on the divan. Then he gently folds me in his arms once more and reaches for my mouth with his own. I tremble inside. I stare into his dark eyes, and I see the love he feels for me shining there. He holds my chin as he kisses me. Then he pulls me closer. Lying back, I let him press his body onto mine. He is gentle and loving. He does not force himself on me like al-Shezira used to. I feel his hands on my flesh and I shudder inside. I desire only to be with him, to feel the pressure of him inside me, to extinguish the entire world so that no one exists except for us.

CHAPTER SEVEN

Littoni closed up the Café Malta early and pushed through the crowds towards Sharia Suleyman Pasha. No time like the present, he thought sinisterly. He would risk it. If he could force his way into the girl's house, he might find something. One of the sector members had flagged up the girl as a key player in Issawi's band of spies. Issawi's men were planning a massive counteroffensive; that much was obvious from the information the Khan el-Khalili sector members had gleaned. He'd tried to play things down with Farouk—who was a dead man anyway. Farouk was old, a shadow of his former self, and he wasn't thinking clearly anymore. Littoni just wanted him out of the way. Littoni had been told Abdullah Ibrahim, the murdered man, had had a coded document in his possession with key information, maps of underworld Cairo, terrorist lairs, and entry points to strategic sites. With this document decoded, Littoni would have the last piece of the puzzle. Though he already knew a good deal, he wanted this document. So it figured that it was now at the girl's house. Farouk was useless. The only thing to do now was to search her house for information himself.

With the girl out at Achmed's launch and Farouk on her tail, the chances were good that her housekeeper, if she had one, would have gone home—and if she hadn't, well, Littoni had never been afraid to use his fists. He wasn't afraid of a woman.

Though the sun had set, the heat was still stifling. He tugged at his shirt collar and pulled out another cigarette from a tin in his jacket pocket, lighting it as he walked. He lowered his hat to partially shield his eyes, thinking some more about Farouk. He had a reputation for stalling, buying himself time. Littoni had seen him do it before. The time to act was now.

If he were honest with himself, he wondered why he hadn't done away with Farouk long ago. He wouldn't be missed. What would become of Farouk after the revolution? Littoni had not really given it much thought until now. Perhaps it would be better to eliminate Farouk.

For the moment, however, Farouk was in al-Qadima at Achmed's house with the girl, and Littoni could proceed quietly with his plan. His heart pounded as he raced along the street, bumping into people as he passed. As he rushed towards the girl's house, he went through the manoeuvre in his mind. Too wired to take a tram or a car, he found that walking fast gave him time to plan. He'd give himself fifteen minutes to do the job, not one minute more, in case she came home. He slipped down a narrow haret, found the archway into the courtyard, pushed open the iron gate, and was on the stone steps in a second. No lights were on. That was good. No one was home. He peered around him, his eyes darting in the gloom, searching the shadows for a human presence. He was alone. He gave the door a swift kick, felt it give a little, and decided that the door had been badly fitted. He pushed against it with his entire body and felt the frame give some more. His hands methodically and mechanically felt every part of the door frame for the weak points. Another shove. Still not quite there. Littoni raised his leg and kicked the lock panel. The door gave way. He was in.

He found himself in a dark narrow hallway. He stood for a moment to let his eyes grow accustomed to the dimness. The hallway smelt faintly musty, as though the place had been shut up on a hot day. Once his eyes had adjusted to the slatted moonlight dappling the room, he saw the double doors leading to the living room. He entered and scanned the furniture. He walked over to the desk and gave the desktop a yank, dragging down the foldaway lip. Inside he saw partitions for correspondence, envelopes. He flicked on a light and began pulling drawers out, searching, searching. Nothing. He spotted a small clutch of letters tied up with string and scanned them. No good. Wrenching open more drawers, he discovered a flat parcel tied up with string. He grabbed it and opened it. A notebook fell out. He flipped through it, held it upside down, and shook it. Nothing.

"Damn," he muttered under his breath. He ventured into the bedroom and lifted up the mattress, pushing it off the bed frame onto the floor. He wanted to find something there, a box with secret papers, but there was nothing. He flung open the doors of an armoire, found a suitcase, jacked it open, extracted a man's suit, fumbled in the pockets, and pulled back a sheath of fabric hiding a revolver. Seeing that it was loaded, he slipped it in his pocket and stood up. His eyes darted around manically, his mouth was parched, and the sound of his heart was vibrating and crashing against his eardrum. He was running out of time. There must be a safe, a vault. He padded over the kilims, treading carefully in an effort to locate an uneven floorboard, something that would indicate a hiding place for secret papers. He went to the farthest corner of the house. Huge windows overlooked Sharia Suleyman Pasha. From the window, he saw a smart-looking car draw up and two women get out. A blond woman with ringlets looked up at the window and pointed. He drew back from the window, not wanting her to see him. The other, a dark-haired girl with pale skin, shook her head and kissed her friend four times on the cheek. Was she the girl? Already home from

Achmed's party? Littoni slipped invisibly through the darkness and hid in the shadows of the courtyard to wait for her.

The journal of Hezba Iqbal Sultan Hanim al-Shezira,
Cairo, August 19, 1919

Papa is here. He has summoned his Fire to his library. I can't wait to see him. He has been away too long. I am not sure how long he is in Cairo, but I must not waste another moment. I must go to him. Fire is the affectionate name he has for me. I used to sit on his knee, curl up in his lap, pull his moustache, and tickle his nose. Papa loved to stroke my face back then. As a young child, barely older than four, I remember him remarking how hot my forehead and cheeks were. Since then he has always called me Fire. Oh Papa.

I walk through the long corridors of the harem towards the salam-lik and my father's quarters. As I walk, I am transported back in time. I am the Fire of the Sarai, the five-year-old who is held down by her nurse and her eunuchs and her mother while she is circumcised and made pure, who screams in pain, who doesn't understand why she is being mutilated. I am the Fire of the Sarai, the six-year-old who plays hide-and-seek with the other children of the palace. I am the Fire of the Sarai, the seven-year-old who is separated from her dear brother, Omar, and sent to live in the harem because that is the way of our people. I am the Fire of the Sarai, the eight-year-old who sings the suras of the Qur'an while Maman scolds me. "You should not sing them, child. Recite them with heart, not in a flippant voice full of light and joy. Be serious for once. Have some respect for the Prophet."

I am the Fire of the Sarai with a voice that can be heard through the marble corridors, the great dining rooms, the bathhouse, the stables. I am the Fire who begs Papa for riding lessons and a horse, who promises to be a good girl forever. I am the Fire of the Sarai, the ten-year-old child who puts her arm around Papa's shoulders and kisses him on the cheek, who dances and runs from room to room, who hides little poems under her maman's pillow, wanting her love so badly, who writes verses about the sun and the moon and the silvery light that falls on the trees in the palace gardens at night.

I am the Fire of the Sarai, the young girl whose body is no longer hers, whose blood starts to flow, who is scrubbed of womanly impurities, who is stripped of all her body hair, who is perfumed and veiled. I am the Fire of the Sarai who is married as soon as she is old enough to be opened up, so she can bear children.

I shiver when I remember all these things, my girlhood taken from me. And now I have to face my destiny as a woman, a life segregated from the world when I want to be part of it. If you were a living thing, journal, flesh and blood, you would pray for me. My rendezvous with Monsieur Alexandre seems like a dream. He has asked me to go to the desert to be part of the Rebel Corps, but how can I if I am sent away? This is why Papa has called me to his study, to tell me the details and to prepare me for what is to come.

In front of me is the door to Papa's library. I knock and open the door. It is a warm, welcoming room. I know every locked bookshelf, every floor tile, every chaise and leather tome intimately. I spend a lot of time here when Papa is away, just whiling away the hours, happy to be among knowledge and books. Papa does not like me lingering here, but he encourages me to take whatever volumes I want for my studies. He is sitting in his armchair near the window. I must make sure my eyes don't wander as he speaks to me.

"Fire," he says.

"Yes, Papa?"

"You know the time has come, don't you, to be a wife again to your husband."

My eyes become wet with tears.

"Papa?"

"You have not lived as your husband's wife for nearly six years."

I purse my lips and swallow. This is so difficult for me. To look at the face of the man I love, my father, and know that in my heart I am betraying him. I remain silent.

"Why don't you answer me, Hezba daughter? You must know it's your destiny to be a good wife to your husband and to have a child. Why do you insist on being so difficult? Why do you not rush to prepare yourself for his coming?"

"Papa, I—I don't know how to answer you."

"If you cannot talk to me, talk to your mother."

"Maman won't listen to me. She thinks I am impulsive. She thinks I have ideas that are too grand. She is not interested in anything I have to say."

Papa cocks his head at me. "That is not true, Hezba daughter. Your mother wants what is best for you. She wants you to have a good life. She does not want the whole of Cairo to be talking about you. She does not want you to shame the name of the sultan. Nor do I. You know you are my favourite daughter, Hezba child, but I will not tolerate this behaviour for a moment longer."

I stand before him and feel nothing but shame burning through me. I want to burst into tears, but I do not dare. Papa hates shows like that. It would upset him further. I decide to try and remain composed and wait for the awful news, which I know deep in my heart he is going to tell me, that al-Shezira will be here soon, and I will be robbed of my chance to go to Alexandre's rendezvous in the desert.

CHAPTER EIGHT

Farouk didn't stay long at Achmed's literary launch. Ibrahim's wife did not want to talk to him; that much was obvious. As he'd listened to speeches and the readings, and flicked through the book of poetry *Monument,* he had studied the girl's demeanour, her facial expressions, the way she held herself in public, trying to get an idea of what type of person she was. No ordinary girl, he had concluded. Something of an aloof character, poised, holding herself well in her grief. There was nothing more he could do tonight. If he had tried too hard to befriend her, she might have gotten suspicious. Besides, he was only doing what Littoni had suggested to put him off guard.

He took a taxi to Jewel's dead brother's apartment in Abbassiya. Farouk found the building and let himself in through a dull brown door. Before closing the door, he swung round and shot a look at a cluster of children playing in the corridor. The door to their apartment was open, and a woman was moving between the apartment and the corridor, checking on the children. It was late. He could not imagine why they were up at this hour. Maybe the heat was keeping them up. He counted seven of them, and they were all eyeing him curiously. Seeing him, the woman gathered the children impatiently to her and ushered them back into her apartment.

He closed the door gently. The place was still furnished. Dust sheets had been thrown over the sofas, chairs, and tables. The air was musty and stale, and it was clear that no window had been opened in weeks. A family of dead cockroaches lay huddled by the doors to the balcony. He stood and listened, eyes darting in all directions. This building was occupied by hundreds of poor Egyptian families, who would take no notice of the comings and goings of his group. He knew that the *Liberation* offices in Bulac were being watched. The group had to keep moving fast to confuse onlookers. His houseboat was too public and his private mansion was out of bounds, a private place that few, if any, knew about. In the gloom, he fingered the dust sheets. A smile spread across his face, and his eyes twinkled darkly.

There was a knock at the front door, and it opened quietly. It was Mitwali, a tall, lean well-dressed youth of eighteen with thick black hair, a hooked nose, and wide-set eyes that pierced the gloom eagerly. Mitwali bowed at Farouk.

"You weren't followed?"

Mitwali shook his head.

"What do you think?"

Mitwali was smiling. "Perfect. Far enough away, anonymous enough."

"Exactly," Farouk said. "You understand what is required of you, Mitwali?"

Mitwali grinned nervously, his eyes searching Farouk's face as he wondered what exactly he was thinking. He dug in his jacket pocket for a cigarette.

"I'm at your service, Sayyid. For the money you are offering me, I'll do whatever you ask of me."

"And Ali Khaldun? Is he reliable? Can he be trusted?" Farouk asked.

Mitwali watched Farouk closely.

"He's my brother. He is loyal to me. He needs the money too. He will send the money back to his wife and children in his village, Mit Abul-Kum. He hasn't seen them for months, but when it's all over, he wants to return there and try to start a school for the little ones."

Farouk bit his lip. These young men were so easily bought; the girl too. He'd searched long and hard for them. They were simple country people, young boys. He'd secretly checked them out and knew everything was in order.

"You must be ready as soon as you hear from my group," Farouk said.

Mitwali nodded.

"You must not talk to anyone about what you are doing," Farouk went on. "And I have to warn you, I will know if you have spoken out—and the repercussions will be devastating for you and your family. But if you follow my instructions, you will be paid well and you will be safe."

"We'll be ready, Sayyid Farouk," Mitwali said.

"You will be given suitable gear and provided with an appropriate vehicle. You simply have to bring the man here to this address. Then you'll be required to help me transport some boxes out of Cairo into the desert. For this, obviously you will need another disguise and another vehicle. This will be organised for you."

Mitwali nodded eagerly.

Farouk stared at him for a moment. "You're the right sort for this job," he said.

Mitwali nodded, his eyes widening.

"It will be an honour," he said.

"You feel strongly about this man Issawi, don't you, Mitwali. It's not just about the money, is it?"

Mitwali shook his head.

"My father, an honest, hardworking fellahin, was wrongly arrested for stealing government money, some years ago. His taxes were so high, he could hardly afford to feed his family. He worked sixteen-hour days in his cotton fields in the Delta, and the rent on his land kept going up. He was harassed constantly by this Issawi, who owned the land. Eventually he was tried and convicted based on nothing but lies. Issawi had put himself in charge of the Council of Fellahins at the time. My father was innocent. Issawi ruined our family, our business. My mother never recovered, and Ali, my brother, still has trouble sleeping. My father's a shattered man. When I told my brother about this job, it was the first time I've seen him smile in a long time. We lost our livelihood, our business, our identity, our dignity; we—"

"Don't say another word, boy," Farouk said, patting Mitwali's arm. "You are no different from the thousands this man has destroyed."

The journal of Hezba Iqbal Sultan Hanim al-Shezira,
Cairo, August 19, 1919

I was right, painfully right. Papa will not be swayed. How depressed I am that I have lost my power over him.

His message was clear.

"We allowed you a period of grace," he said, "but you cannot still be in the depths of depression. After six years your husband wants you back. Don't you want to be a good wife, have children, live in happiness, without worries, without the label of being an abandoned wife?"

I decided to speak boldly. "You made a mistake when you and Maman chose al-Shezira for me."

It was hard to say these words, because I was defying my father when I uttered them. My voice trembled. I felt like some lowly servant about to be beaten by his master.

Papa thought for a few moments and then he said, "The union of the al-Shezira family and ours is a good one. Think of the wealth that will be passed down to your children."

I don't care for wealth or our family line, but I said nothing about that.

"My husband is a violent man, Papa."

Papa eyed me icily for a moment. His handsome face flashed with what must have been a myriad of feelings. I don't suppose he knew how to answer me.

"Are you sure you do not provoke him? He has waited a long time for you. First there was your depression. The doctors advised that we allow you to stay here in Cairo until you returned to better spirits and became happier. We were delighted when you took your husband back into your arms again for a brief time and he gave you a child."

"He did not want me after Ibrahim was born," I said.

"Your baby died, Hezba. You pushed your husband away."

I did not want to have this conversation with my father. I could not bear the way he talked to me now, as though I were nothing to him, as though our association was simply one of business or fortune.

"Al-Shezira is not content with having four wives, Papa. He has taken another."

"And you are jealous of the attention he pays them?"

"No," I said, "No."

But Papa went on. "It is true, the pasha al-Shezira and his new favourite, the beautiful Iqbal, make a handsome couple, and their children are fine examples of nobility, but that is no reason to think you are not held in equal regard, my child."

"I want a divorce, Papa. Don't you want me to be happy?"

I could see Papa's face harden. I knew I had insulted him. Immediately I regretted saying such a thing.

"I want all my children to be happy, Hezba," he said sternly. "I am certain that you don't know your own mind. You are a young woman, and your mother is right to say you are impetuous. You have a responsibility as my daughter to behave properly. Divorce is out of the question. I won't hear of this happening. I have heard many things about you, things that are reported to me—"

"Who tells you things?" I was getting angry now. I could feel a tingling of rage rippling up my spine, making me feel hot, then cold.

"Habrid."

"Habrid thinks it is proper to thrash me with a rolled-up sheet."

He looked aghast.

"I did not order him to do that."

"He follows Maman's orders."

"Well, that is all right then. He is just following orders."

"I will be happy if you let me divorce al-Shezira, Papa."

"It is not that simple, Hezba," Papa said irritably. "You want to take the easy way out of everything. I am your father. I cannot allow a divorce to take place on your whim."

"But, Papa—"

He put his hand up to silence me.

"I don't want to say another word on the subject. Al-Shezira and I have decided that you are to return to take up your position as his wife, as soon as possible. Now you may go."

I stood there, tears veiling my eyes. Papa looked away. He could not hold my gaze. He fumbled with some papers on his desk and turned a key in one of the drawers.

I left his library and returned to my apartment.

CHAPTER NINE

The poetry-book launch was over. Aimee had just been dropped off and walked purposefully along the dark haret to her home. Pulling her shawl closer, she pushed open the iron gate to the courtyard and started up the stone steps. All she could think about was that man Farouk, studying her intently, hardly taking his eyes off her for a moment. The evening has passed pleasantly enough, but she didn't like the way his eyes had searched her face and travelled suggestively over her body, examining her every curve in an almost-predatory way.

And he'd given her his card. Would she ever have the courage to telephone him?

The moon lit the way. At the top of the steps, Aimee noticed that the front door was ajar. What on earth? Her heart expanded in fright, and for a moment she thought she felt a cold clammy hand clutch at her throat. She swung around in a panic. Nobody. At the bottom of the steps she saw Samir's little black cat padding silently along the rough stones in the moonlight.

She stood back against the wall for a moment, unsure what to do. Then she kicked open the door with her foot and reached for a light switch in the hall, calling out, "Hello, anyone there?" There was no reply. She slipped into the hall and reached for a lone golf club—one of Azi's—that had been left propped up behind the front door for some reason. She picked it up and swung it back over her shoulder, then tiptoed farther into the house.

The sitting room, the bedroom, and the small dayroom were now splashed with shadows from the light in the hall. "Hello?" Aimee shouted again. Her heart thundered in her ears, and her body turned to ice. She was shocked at what she saw. Papers were strewn everywhere. The lamp in the corner had been knocked over. The desk gaped open, and her furniture had been pushed to one side. Shattered glass glittered on the floor, shards from the framed photo of her mother. She gathered up the photograph and picked her way across the glass. Then she went to her bedroom, sliding along the wall of the hallway, stiff with fear.

The bedroom was in disarray. The mattress lay on its side against the wall. The armoire doors had been flung open. Suitcases and clothes were splayed across the floor. Her hand flew to her mouth. Shivering, Aimee sank down to the floor and gathered up Azi's suit in her arms. She fumbled around in it, looking for his revolver. Gone. Stolen.

She jumped up and raced into the hall, still clutching the photograph of her mother tightly. Standing out on the landing at the top of the stone steps, her eyes darting wildly, she scrutinised the shadows. There was a man. She identified the silhouette of his squat, hatless body as he moved silently towards the iron gate. She shouted after him and flew down the stone steps, waving the golf club high above her head. Then she poked her head around the iron gate. She wasn't losing her mind. It was indeed a man, racing along the haret to Sharia Suleyman Pasha. Soon he was lost in the throngs of late-night revellers.

Aimee bolted the iron gate and flew up the stairs to phone the police. She paused for a moment at the threshold, listening to the sound of her own heavy breathing. Fear squeezed every muscle. She could not stay here alone. Sophie had gone on to another party at Shepheard's after her driver had dropped Aimee off at her place, so there would be no point in calling her at the Continental. She thought of Farouk and remembered the card he had given her. It seemed logical to try him, especially since he had insisted that he was at her service if she ever needed help of any kind. She reached for her handbag and picked out the card with Farouk's telephone number on it. It was very late. It was quite possible he would not be there. She dialled Farouk's number with a shaking hand.

"Yes?" a voice answered.

"Monsieur Farouk?"

"Who is this?" said the voice.

"Madame Ibrahim. We met at the book launch tonight."

"Madame?" said Farouk. Aimee heard the surprise in his voice and the softening of his tone.

"I need your help, Monsieur." Aimee had trouble steadying her nerve-rattled voice. She clutched the telephone receiver, trembling.

"Are you in trouble, Madame?" Farouk said.

"My house has been broken into. I'm all alone here."

She sensed Farouk stiffen on the other end of the line.

"I'll come right away. What is your address?"

She gave it to him.

"Thank you," she said.

Aimee replaced the receiver, took up the golf club, and tiptoed through her house again, straining for any sound. She tiptoed over the glass shards and knelt down to pick up stray bits of paper. Her mother's journal lay on the floor by the sofa. Aimee grabbed it and examined it. It didn't appear to be damaged. She slipped the photograph from the damaged frame into it and went to the dayroom near the balcony. She knelt down by the skirting board and pulled back a small section of carpet, lifting a tiny piece of floorboard that opened to a cavernous hole. Extracting the photograph of the mysterious woman and the typed document she'd found in her mother's journal, she put the journal down there in their place.

Then she replaced the small piece of floorboard, laid the carpet across it, tucked it back in place against the skirting board, and stood up. She put the photograph of the woman on the mantelpiece and hid the encoded letter behind it as a reminder to ask Farouk about them if the opportunity arose. She returned to the top of the stone steps by the front door to await Farouk.

The journal of Hezba Iqbal Sultan Hanim al-Shezira,
Cairo, August 21, 1919

Two days have passed since my meeting with Papa. Two days of utter misery, during which time I have felt so alone and so bitterly despised by my parents. But this nagging unhappiness starts to disappear when one of the lower eunuchs, a little boy called Karim, comes to tell me the wonderful news that my husband has been detained. I bend down and kiss him, and I swear he reddens with embarrassment, his little chubby cheeks aflame. How funny he is, how adorable, and now I am bursting with happiness because my God has allowed me two more days of freedom.

I ask to go and see Maman, and with a lowered head and suitably demure expression, I ask her why my husband has been detained. She is reclining on her cushions with a little tray of pastries by her side. One of her eunuchs is grooming her hair. She looks at me curiously, and I can tell from her face that she is pleased, that she thinks I'm changing and will honour the wishes of the sultan, my father. Her prayers have been answered after all.

She says, "The pasha and his family are attending to a sick relative, but they are anxious to get to the Sarai. Your husband has sent word that he is waiting impatiently for the day when he can see you."

Though I shudder in horror inwardly, I reply as respectfully and deceitfully as I can that I too am waiting for that day, and I wait with a light and happy disposition.

She smiles at me.

"So, child, you have changed your mind about the kind al-Shezira. He is a good man, is he not? You have lived here long enough. The Minya palace will welcome you with open arms. They want to forget the past and the pain you have caused them."

"I know, Maman," I say quietly, with downcast eyes. "It is for the best."

Maman looks at me again strangely. Her eyes are screwed up in confusion. As her eunuch placidly pulls a comb through her hair, I notice he looks up at me and then away when he catches my eye.

"I must go now, Maman. Madame Virginie will arrive soon, and I must prepare for my lessons with her." I kiss her and leave, looking forward to my lessons and news of my lover. Papa wants me to read the old Arab masters, but I am interested only in the new literature coming from France. I take guidance from my teacher, Virginie. I love her with all my heart. She is a kind and gentle soul who only wants the best for the palace girls. She wants us to learn, to be educated and informed. "Education is the foundation of life," she says, shaking her finger when we are inattentive, her eyes smiling mischievously.

I am grateful to Papa for ignoring my mother and engaging her as my tutor. Papa has been known to be on my side when it suits him. It breaks my heart to deceive him, but I can't stop now.

CHAPTER TEN

The minutes dripped by slowly. Aimee ran down the stone steps, unlocked the iron gate, and ran back up the steps so she'd have a good vantage point with her golf club at the ready in case the man decided to return. She stood shivering with fear by her front door in the moonlight, not wanting to go back inside. The mess scared her, the destruction, the madness of the attack. Whoever had broken in had obviously been searching for something, but apart from the pistol, nothing appeared to have been taken.

The paralysing realisation that the burglar could be involved with Azi's killer or *was* in fact Azi's killer sickened her. If only Farouk would arrive. Then she saw him push open the iron gate. He paused for a moment and looked up at her.

"Are you all right?" he asked.

Aimee nodded. "Come up and see for yourself."

As he started to walk up the steps, he glanced at her. How frail she looked, white as death. Her large glistening green eyes, flashing in the moonlight, made him shudder. She reminded him of young girls he used to meet on his travels to northern India, when he was a young man—girls with pale skin and green eyes who would smile provocatively at him. Aimee stepped aside, and Farouk pushed open the front door.

"In there," she said.

Farouk switched on the light. The damage was considerable. Knife slashes gouged great holes in the sofa. A vase of flowers had been knocked over, and the stems lay on the floor. Water trickled off a small table.

His heart beat strangely. He swallowed and turned to face her.

"Do you have any whisky?"

"Yes, over there." Aimee pointed to a decanter on a silver tray.

Farouk went over and poured her a drink. "Here, drink this," he said, handing her the glass.

Aimee sipped the whisky gratefully, enjoying the sensation of the warm liquid as it slid down her throat. She had begun to shake and could hardly hold the glass. Farouk slipped off his jacket and slid it around her shoulders. Taking the glass from her hand, he set it down, then pulled her over to one of the armchairs that had been left untouched.

"Sit down," he said, kneeling down in front of her. Cupping her hands in his, he rubbed them gently to warm her up.

"Now tell me what happened."

Aimee looked into his eyes, examined the curl of his mouth, the arch of his eyebrows, the jutting line of his jaw. She saw kindness and tenderness in his face, and for a moment she felt comforted and eternally grateful for having met him. But still, he was a stranger.

"Sophie's dragoman drove us back. I was dropped off on the Sharia Suleyman Pasha about half an hour ago. I came upstairs and found this, exactly as you see it."

"You saw nobody, heard nothing?"

"I saw someone downstairs lurking in the shadows, a man with a stocky build, but he disappeared before I could run after him."

Farouk looked back around the room.

"I must ring the police," Aimee said resolutely.

"No, not yet. Let me have a look around. Whoever did this might have left behind some sort of clue. Was anything taken?"

Aimee stood up. "My husband owned a revolver. He kept it hidden in a suitcase in the bedroom. That was stolen."

Farouk didn't say anything. He walked into the bedroom and surveyed the damage. As he heaved the mattress back onto the bed frame, something grabbed his attention—a cigarette butt. He picked it up and examined it, sniffing the tobacco. It was a Kyriazi Freres, Littoni's favourite cigarette. He put the butt in his pocket and returned to the sitting room. Aimee looked at him hopefully.

"Anything?" she asked.

"No, nothing."

He walked towards her, took the glass from her, and set it down on one of the little tables. She was feeling warmer now with his jacket around her shoulders.

"Did you look in the study?" she asked him, jerking her head in the direction of Azi's room.

"Anything to see?" he asked her.

"Someone was rifling through papers, looking for something, a document of some kind perhaps?" she said.

"Come with me," Farouk said, pulling her up by the hand. She walked with him into Azi's study. Farouk pushed open the door and stepped aside as she brushed past him.

"What a mess," he said.

Aimee began scanning the bookcases crammed with books, the wooden filing cabinet, and Azi's desk, which was covered with newspapers, past editions, photographs, pamphlets and great dusty volumes, all sprawled in disarray. This was a man's room, an academic's room.

A low dull pink couch was partially covered by boxes of papers. On a small table, she saw Azi's dusty Corona typewriter, the one he'd used to type his articles.

"I can't imagine what they wanted. There's nothing here except Azi's academic papers," she said.

Farouk furrowed his brow. "Are you sure you have no idea, Madame Ibrahim?"

Aimee didn't know what to say. How could she admit to this stranger that she hadn't really known her husband all that well, that theirs had been a very brief love affair, that she was not the keeper of his darkest secrets, his ally in his private affairs, or his equal in any way. It was especially hard for her to admit that her husband had had a life, in some outer social sphere, that she knew nothing about and that she would probably never have been admitted into his secret world. And then she considered the pieces of paper that had fallen out of her mother's journal. Azi must have hidden them there, knowing that it was highly unlikely they would ever be discovered locked away at the university.

"There is something," she stammered. "The university asked me to pick up something they found in his locker. Inside a notebook was a piece of paper with some strange letters on it. I have no idea what they mean. It's probably nothing, but—"

"Do you have them? May I take a look at them?" Farouk asked her, plucking his cigarette tin out of his pocket. He eyed her quizzically as he lit one.

"Yes, I'll get them." She disappeared, returning moments later with the document and the photograph of the woman. She handed Farouk the paper first. He studied it, his heart beating excitedly in his throat.

"Do you know what it is?" she asked him.

He shook his head, studying the shapes on the page, running in columns up and down the page. He checked for patterns, familiar lines, anything he recognised—to no avail.

"No, but it looks like code of some sort. Can I hold on to it for a little while? I might be able to decode it. It might help the police with their enquiries. I won't keep it long, just long enough to work out if it could be of any help to you."

Aimee nodded.

Farouk folded the paper and put it in his top pocket. Then she handed him the photograph, asking, "Do you know who this woman is?"

His eyes narrowed as he studied the photograph. Fatima. The flash of recognition chilled him. He turned the photograph over and saw the loops and swirls of Arabic writing.

"I'm not sure—I—"

"It was in my husband's possession. Why would my husband have a photograph of this woman?" Aimee heard herself say. She knew she was just thinking out loud. "Judging from his scrawl on the back of the photograph, it seems my husband knew her quite well."

Farouk looked at Aimee, moistened his lips, and studied the photograph again.

"She looks familiar. I think."

Aimee stared at him, hating the burning sensation in her throat, the dizziness welling up from her stomach to her mouth.

Farouk went on. "I'm not sure. I think she runs a club in Wassa. The face looks vaguely familiar, but then—"

"Is that all you know about her?"

He looked up at the ceiling, then at Aimee. If he inspired confidence in her, she might confide in him in turn. She looked innocent enough, but beneath the façade, what did she really know?

"I know of a woman at this club, the el-G, who works as a double agent for the Germans and the British. She sells secrets, information. This could very well be her."

Aimee shivered. Was he telling her that her husband had been in love with a spy? "Why would my husband have a photograph of this woman?" she asked him more directly this time.

Farouk didn't know how to break it to her gently. "I think he used to go there, Madame, to the club. Many of the university men go there. It's a popular club, well established, with a fairly well-to-do and diverse clientele."

He fell silent, discreetly running his eyes over Ibrahim's wife as she stood before him, trying to come to terms with the news he had delivered. He handed her back the photograph, and she studied it for the thousandth time, silently memorising the woman's face, her blood hardening in her veins, her mouth paling to silver. She shot him a dark angry look and shook her head.

"What do you know about my husband's death? You must know something. You have contacts, don't you? You write about the underworld, about breaking news. There must be something you can tell me."

Farouk knew he had to speak carefully. "I know your husband rubbed a few people the wrong way. He had certain loyalties."

Her eyes narrowed suspiciously. "You told me tonight that you had only met my husband once. Is that true? Were you really just acquaintances?"

"His circle of friends overlapped a little with mine. I used to hear people talking about him. People liked to talk about Azi Ibrahim."

"So what did you hear?"

"That Azi was thinking about moving into politics. That he'd been approached, was considered one of the few academics in Cairo who could be primed to run for government."

Her eyes darted around the room. "Are you saying he had enemies, Monsieur?"

He cleared his throat. "Tell me something, Madame. Your husband's university department is partially funded by royal money, is it not?"

She held his gaze, unsure where the conversation was leading. "Yes. The young men are from wealthy families and the fees are high, but a department like that always needs extra money. I believe Azi told me once that the king had a financial interest in it. His sons were students there."

Farouk blew smoke into the air. "Madame, there are many poor people in Cairo who are ignored—men who would hate the privilege and wealth of those who can attend Cairo's most prestigious university. Perhaps the men or man who murdered your husband saw him as a target for their personal vendettas. Perhaps they thought a man like Ibrahim would get too powerful and he was murdered to send a message to those who operate within Cairo's elite. Perhaps he was a scapegoat. I don't know."

"But the woman?" Aimee said. "Is it possible that my husband was having an affair with her? Why would he have a photograph of her locked away at the university?"

He took a deep draw of his cigarette. "I'm not sure. It's possible you're right. You didn't suspect?"

She shook her head miserably. She felt sick, and her body was trembling. Suddenly her vision blurred, and she stared blankly into space. She couldn't answer him.

"Madame Ibrahim? Are you all right?" Farouk went to her and held her elbow, steadying her.

"You asked me whether I suspected, Monsieur. No. I knew nothing. My husband worked very hard. We hadn't been married very long. I had no reason to suspect anything."

Farouk stood silently for a moment, watching her, thinking.

She looked so drained, so tired. At last she slumped down in one of the chairs, holding the photograph, not speaking, hardly moving.

She looked up at him. "Is there anything more you can tell me about this woman?"

Farouk walked over to the French doors and stared out through the glass. "I don't know much really. She runs a club, as I said, in Wassa, called the el-G, a gentleman's club, a dancing club."

"Did you ever go with him?"

Farouk shook his head. "No, I never went with him, but I have been there and I have seen him there."

Aimee closed her eyes and urged him to continue. Farouk watched her carefully. He saw her trembling slightly, every tiny muscle in her face contracting with some inner shock.

"Up until recently the el-G was owned by Horzog Esfahan, a Persian businessman, but I was told that this Fatima Said paid him a very handsome sum to take over the place," he said.

She listened blindly, her body growing numb. Suddenly, she stood up, her face set. She wanted air, wanted to get away, to get outside. "Take me to this club. I want to see this woman for myself."

He moved closer, close enough that his scent and the aroma of Turkish cigarettes—the same brand Azi had smoked—tickled her nose.

"Are you sure?" he asked quietly.

She shot him a dark look, then turned away and ran her hands over her face. "Yes," she murmured. "Yes, I am. Very sure."

They were quiet for a moment. Aimee turned to examine him, her eyes running over his taut, sculpted face, his furrowed brow, the little beads of perspiration that sparkled on the bridge of his nose.

Music was heard outside, a local moulid. Spirits were high, even at that late hour. Farouk touched her arm. "If you're sure, I'll take you."

"I can't stay here," she said, "They might come back."

"Can you stay with your friend?"

Aimee looked around for her purse. "Sophie? Yes, I'll stay with her."

Farouk watched as a mask slowly clamped into place over her features. Iron bars closing down on her soul. He nodded slowly, biting his lip.

"Come on then. We'll go now."

The journal of Hezba Iqbal Sultan Hanim al-Shezira, Cairo, August 22, 1919

Tonight, Virginie, my tutor, is attending a costume ball at Shepheard's, one of the great European hotels here in Cairo, a place that's a favourite destination of the wealthy. I have written about Shepheard's before. It is a very popular place, where the British elite come for their holidays.

She tells us all about it, as she has attended a ball there before. I'm entranced and jealous. How I would love to go. How I would love to dance like those European ladies with jewels in my hair, wearing a floor-sweeping gown, my arms and my décolletage bare. I love talking to her about things like this. For the time being, al-Shezira is on the outskirts of Cairo visiting relatives, and I decide to focus on happier things. Some government business will also hold his attention for a few days. The stars are shining on me at the moment.

When the lessons are over and the others have gone back to their apartments, she pulls me aside and hands me a red handkerchief.

I take hold of it, my heart pounding, and I feel suddenly breathless. It is from Alexandre. Our rendezvous is on. I start mentally preparing myself for my escape into the desert and walk around on air for the rest of the day as happy as can be, taking interest in every little detail of the palace, every silly domestic argument, every face that passes me. That evening, as I am imagining Virginie twirling around the ballroom at Shepheard's, I hear Nawal shouting, "Hezba, where are you?"

I rush out of my rooms to see what the noise is all about. There are Battna, Nawal, and Amina, my half sisters, in the small corridor outside the girls' apartments.

"A peddler woman has come to the palace. Come on, let's go and see her."

Nawal drags at my arm, her face lit up with excitement.

"Rachid has spoken to her and has gone to get Uluk's approval. Habrid will not find out. The peddler is selling little bottles of ink, perfumes, and paper. I thought you would want to see her. Come on, hurry up."

Rachid appears. I am glad he is here.

"Has Uluk agreed?" I say. "How can we be sure Habrid will not find out?" I try to sound like I am in charge, but Rachid pats me on the arm and turns to lead the way.

"Just a quick look, Mesdemoiselles," Rachid says, laughing. "It is late and I have strict orders to send you off for your beauty sleep as soon as possible."

Just then Anisah, my maid, appears. She is as excited as I am. We love to buy things together, and even though she is my maid, she is more like my sister. She often accompanies me when we are allowed to go on excursions to the local souks. I link arms with her and we walk together. Anisah is a pretty girl. The whites of her almond-shaped eyes contrast shockingly with their charcoal colour, and her cherubic face reminds me of that of a very small child. She is beautiful really, slender but shapely with small pert breasts that often get an admiring glance from Rachid. Sometimes I can actually admit I am a little jealous, but Rachid is not my amour, I keep reminding myself. He does not make my heart pound the way Alexandre does.

We find the peddler in the ladies' hall. The woman stands grim-faced between two palace guards. I examine her face, her features. Peddler women are reputed to be able to read minds—to tell the truth from deceit—and I've been told I have a deceitful face. Perhaps the old woman has heard rumours about the Sarai and the "unsettled one" who lives within its walls and has come to examine the specimen for herself. But I try to ignore my feelings because I am eager to inspect the nibs and inks she is selling, lovely treasures, as important to me as the oxygen I breathe. I want to write about everything that happens to me.

Uluk arrives and we are allowed to approach the woman. Uluk hates Habrid, so he is glad to help us out. The peddler woman is shrouded in heavy robes. She greets us with a bow, kneels down on the floor, and lays out a swathe of silks on which she places a selection of beautiful bottles, ivory-boned nibs, and marbled papers.

I gasp in amazement at the beautiful colours: sepia, honey, rose, and dusky grey. I can hear Maman's words in my head.

"People will talk about you even more than they do already, Hezba."

The old woman tells us she is a peasant from the country, but she was once blessed by the khedive himself and is admired for her wisdom and her ability to recite suras from the Qur'an.

She must have been beautiful once, this peddler woman. Perhaps she is, as she says, much admired. But she looks tired now, and I feel sorry for her. I ask Rachid to bring her some refreshment.

"In the name of God, the Merciful, the Compassionate," she says. "I simply ask for your help to feed my family. My wares are quality

and inexpensive. Nowhere else in all of al-Qahire will you find such beautiful things. No souk sells these goods, no other peddler. I beg you, Sayyidas, please buy whatever you want."

I cup the little bottles in my hands and close my fingers around them, feeling the warmth of the glass. I pick up some of the paper and stroke its silky surface. I handle the bone attached to the pen nibs. Then I open a flat parcel filled with pages of different hues, a hundred pages at least, held together in a little folder of their own.

"Here," I say, handing her more money than she needs with a little extra for baksheesh. "I will buy all of this," I add with a sweep of my hand.

I wish I could tell her I am like her, that although I live in a palace and wear beautiful clothes and have everything I want, I am unhappy. I wish I could tell her I would gladly change places with her. I don't suppose her husband beats her and tortures her. I don't suppose she has given birth to a dead baby. I don't suppose she hates and fears her husband. But I can say none of these things, for these things are not talked about. This peddler woman thinks I am a rich princess.

"With thanks, kind Sayidda," she says with a smile. I bow to her, leave the others to their purchases, and return to my rooms.

CHAPTER ELEVEN

Aimee and Farouk walked together to the Wagh-el-Birka district. She had returned his jacket to him and thrown a thin scarf of dull-coloured silk around her shoulders. Loose pieces of mud fell away under her shoes as she walked. This was how she had walked with Azi through the Khan el-Khalili bazaar. Together they had tiptoed among seated fruit and tobacco sellers, basket weavers and purveyors of elaborate kilims, buoyed up by their like-mindedness, by their love, breathing in the odour of spices and hookahs, secretly holding hands, always secretly holding hands.

Now she walked with Farouk, down similar streets, inhaling the same scents of the night. It should have been Azi with her, but Azi was dead. She had to tell herself this, had to keep herself from breaking down without him.

Farouk walked protectively beside her; he knew these harets and sharias of old, having walked along them many times. He knew the faces of the locals and the traders, the women and their children. The piece of paper with its encoded messages burned in his top pocket, and he longed to study it. He felt smug about the advantage he now held over Littoni, but for the time being, the girl who walked by his side demanded all his attention. She did not walk quickly but carried herself with determination, her head held high, her eyes alert, as though she expected to see someone—the ghost of her husband perhaps. Farouk did not hurry her. Up ahead, a group of soldiers lurched and fell forward towards them, swearing loudly. He steered Aimee gently past them, his hand firmly on her shoulder. Farouk's touch made Aimee's heart jolt strangely. A shallow breath caught in her throat and little tingles danced up and down her spine. Her reaction to his touch shocked her. He was a stranger, yet she felt drawn to him. As someone who could help her get justice for Azi, she told herself. To distract herself, she turned her gaze to the noisy cafés, still open and packed with men, playing chess, drinking coffee, smoking hookahs, and talking. She studied the occasional chador-wearing woman with a baby in her arms being ushered home by her stern-looking husband.

"You won't like what you see at this club," Farouk said after they had been walking for a while.

Aimee did not know how to answer him. She simply stared ahead, trying to quell the anxiety flooding through her. Her head throbbed with the thought that Azi had been having an affair. She felt so young, so inexperienced. Azi had wanted more than she had been able to give him.

"I need to see her in person," she said quietly. "Surely you understand that?"

She felt Farouk's hand reach for hers in the darkness, and she let him take it.

Aimee dared to look at him for a moment. His aged face softened when he met her gaze, becoming fuller, younger, as though he knew how she felt. Perhaps there had been a girl, long ago. Perhaps he understood how distraught she was, how much she had loved Azi.

"Do you have a cigarette?" she asked him. Farouk fumbled in his pocket, produced one, and lit it for her. He watched her mouth tremble as she took the cigarette between her lips.

"You don't mind my smoking here in the street?" she asked him. "Azi used to hate it."

He shook his head and grinned, pointing up the street to the maze of narrow alleys and forbidden passageways.

"The el-G is not far," he said. "You'd better finish that before we get there."

Aimee inhaled slowly and looked around her. Everything seemed unfamiliar now. She didn't know this neighbourhood. Azi would never have taken her to a place like this. It was rough and dirty. She puffed on her cigarette nervously.

"Is it unusual for a woman like me to go to a club like this, Monsieur Farouk?" she asked him.

"That depends. What type of woman are you, Madame?"

She threw her head back and searched the sky for inspiration. She was hardly out of her girlhood, a young woman, a wife, a widow, the daughter of a royal bloodline but without any claim to it. She was unremarkable in the crowded streets of Wassa. She tried to see herself as others might see her: an Egyptian girl, not veiled, perhaps not yet married, for here she was out on the street with a strange man, who could be her brother, or perhaps an uncle.

"I'm not sure, Monsieur, but I know I am certainly not familiar with places like these."

Farouk smiled and watched her closely. She was losing the prickly anxiety that had cloaked her when they had left her house. She had aged ten, maybe even fifteen years in the space of a few minutes, and she looked better for it, not so vulnerable. The nervous puffing of the cigarette indicated that she was still on edge, but the walk from her house to the club had obviously done her good.

"You don't have to worry too much. Although I've never seen a woman in the audience at the el-G before," he said, "I know that women have been and do go there. Mostly European women, tourists who are after a little adventure or who are invited there as guests."

She looked up at him, amused. He was trying to protect her dignity. She knew what type of place the el-G was. As elite as its reputation was, it was still, essentially, a brothel.

She threw her cigarette on the ground, stamped it out, and looked up at him. "How did you get that scar on your face?" she asked.

Farouk's hand flew to the silvery stripe that ran from his hairline to his jaw on the left side of his face.

"It happened a long time ago, in the Libyan desert. I was a young man then and very foolish. I was in love, you see, and full of insane passion. The girl had a violent brother who did not want me to touch his sister. She had been promised to another, and I was getting in the way. He took his anger out on me, and I have the souvenir to prove it."

The speech was a convenient lie easily recited. As with so many things, Farouk knew he was a skilled actor, and he could tell from the look on her face that she believed him.

"You must have loved her very much," Aimee said vaguely. He didn't say anything. There was no possible response. He gently steered her towards an archway, feeling her stiffen under his touch this time. He glanced at her face but could read nothing in its expression.

"Are you all right, Madame?"

"It's no good," she said bitterly, chewing her bottom lip, feeling suddenly vulnerable and very afraid. "I don't think I can do this."

"Just stay close to me and don't say anything. Just watch. Trust me."

They turned into Sharia Wagh-el-Birka, then down a few narrower streets, lit with duller lights. Farouk and Aimee shouldered past raucous Americans, laughing street girls on their way to work, and overfed businessmen carrying wads of notes in their greasy hands. Dirty glass shop-fronts displayed scantily clad Russian girls, who sat on stools and smoked while young men gaped.

"The el-G's a little farther up," Farouk said, "towards Derb-el-Wasa'a."

Up ahead, Aimee saw the flashing neon blue light of the el-G. She held back, hiding like a coward behind Farouk.

A fat Turk in a greasy fez, a black waistcoat, and stained white shirt stood guard. His huge face broke into a smile when he saw Farouk approaching. He shouted out to him in French.

"Welcome. Monsieur. The club is busy tonight."

Farouk's features were set hard, as he pushed past the doorman.

"Yes, enter please." The doorman bowed again, sweeping his arm to the left to usher him in. Farouk pulled Aimee from behind him, his arm outstretched around her.

"Ah Monsieur," the doorman said abruptly, putting a fat hand up to stop them.

"I'm sorry, this is a gentleman's club. No ladies are permitted inside."

Farouk stared slyly at the doorman.

"This lady," Farouk said slowly between gritted teeth, "is my wife. She's coming in with me."

The doorman looked confused for a moment, and then a slow grin fanned out across his mouth. His filthy eyes consumed her. Aimee felt the slick seediness of his gaze crawling all over her. She shivered and looked away.

"I can assure you, Monsieur, it is not customary, but if Monsieur wants to spice up his love life—perhaps his little lady would like to observe the pleasures of Madame Fatima—then who am I to come between the master and his wife."

The doorman grinned at them, showing off his decaying teeth. Aimee flushed a deep red, hating Farouk for possessing her, for calling her his wife, hating the grimy, sordid street they stood on, hating herself for pressuring him to bring her here.

"Well then, enter, Monsieur and Madame, and enjoy yourselves." He laughed hoarsely. Aimee swallowed hard. She stumbled behind Farouk down the slimy stairs to the basement below. She could hear laughter and music, and then the smell hit her. It was the smell of damp, the smell of tombs, of strange burning oils, of death spiked with wilting flowers starting to rot. Farouk led her through a door to a large, dimly lit room filled with hordes of men sitting at small dining tables. On each white-cloth-covered table was a tiny ruby-red lamp with a low burning bulb, surrounded by clusters of glasses and ashtrays. Aimee scanned the crowd, which— according to Farouk—comprised a mix of soldiers on leave, Turkish and Maltese businessmen, Egyptian men, and university types—all of whom had been lured here by the prospect of seeing Fatima. All of them appeared to be transfixed by the empty stage in front of them, their eyes trained on the multicoloured sequinned curtain shimmering before them. They were waiting for the next act, their hearts beating in a wild, alcohol-driven stupor. Farouk led her to an empty table at the back of the room.

"What do you think?" he whispered in her ear. "Rather grimy, isn't it?"

Aimee studied what she saw, wishing she were invisible, wishing she were a man, dressed in a suit and tie and sturdy brogues, smoking a cigarette, laughing at it all. She sank lower in her chair.

Dancing girls appeared, seemingly out of nowhere, and started to circle the tables, stroking the faces of the men, coaxing them as they reached out and grabbed at pieces of their flesh, shoving money into the intimate crevices of their jewelled costumes. She could hear many languages being spoken, words she did not understand.

A waiter took their order. He did not look at Aimee.

"Two whiskies," Farouk said. The waiter left, and Farouk reached for her hand to comfort her.

"Are you all right?"

"I shouldn't be here. What possessed me to ask you to bring me here? I shouldn't have come. I've made a terrible mistake."

"You came because of your husband," Farouk said reassuringly.

Suddenly he noticed a group of men in the far corner near the stage. His mouth thinned as he studied them. He was thinking, thinking how he could throw the girl off guard, try and find out what she knew about Azi's involvement with Issawi. He needed to play the game as skillfully as he could, not for Littoni, but for himself.

"Do you see that table over there on the left, near the stage?" he asked her. Aimee peered over at it discreetly and nodded.

"Can you see that man, the one with the greying moustache, the big head, high forehead, hooded eyes, balding? He has a red bow tie on and a waistcoat. He's laughing right now. With the dancer in front of him who is licking her fingers, rubbing her hands all over her breasts. There, now she's running her hands all over his face. Do you see him?"

Aimee nodded, her belly knotting uncomfortably. She shot Farouk a look and then looked back at the man.

"His name is Gad Mahmoud. He's a disgruntled ex-politician, a friend of someone I think your husband had a great deal of respect for, a man called Haran Issawi."

He stared at her to gauge her reaction.

"Issawi?" Aimee said, looking at Farouk.

"Do you know him, Madame?"

"I'm not sure, I don't think—"

Aimee turned to stare at Mahmoud again.

"Do many politicians come here?" she asked.

"A few. Mahmoud's known to be mixed up in all sorts of dubious affairs. He's a member of a fundamentalist Islamic group called el-Mudarris, a breakaway Wafd movement that now works against it. The Wafd was the first nationalist group that fought to restore Egypt to independence in the twenties, as you no doubt know. El-Mudarris and the Wafd have been fighting for years. Both want supremacy, both are fighting for the same thing, but each group hates the other. This man, Gad Mahmoud, is dangerous, an underground terrorist. He has many aliases, and he's been linked to Haran Issawi, the king's advisor. I once saw your husband talking to Mahmoud here at the club."

Aimee eyes widened. She took a mental photograph of the man, watching him closely as he thrust his face deep into the dancer's cleavage. Though his party included three other men, Gad Mahmoud was obviously the leader. The men at his table were watching him in awe.

"Are you saying Azi was involved with an underground terrorist organisation?" Aimee said, biting her lip. "That can't be right. He wasn't really interested in politics. He was an academic. I never heard him even mention this man Issawi."

She was lying. Farouk knew that. He could tell from the way her eyes flickered as she spoke. Yet she was so innocent, this girl, so obviously naïve. Farouk continued to study her face, wanting to believe her.

"Where does this woman come into all this?" she whispered.

Farouk put his hand on her arm.

"Stay calm, talk to me, and don't look over there. Those men are looking this way."

Gad Mahmoud and his table were twisting around in their seats, scanning the room with smiles on their faces and jokes on their lips, slapping the dancers on the thigh whenever they came within reach.

Just then, the music changed. Flutes and sitars and a loud drumming started up, and then, as the curtains drew back, a high-pitched trill was heard. The audience clapped and screamed in unison. Fatima had arrived. A small, buxom woman in a sequinned bodice and flowing floor-length skirt sashayed onto the stage from the wings, her arms outstretched to her beloved fans. A dwarf with a scarlet fez, waistcoat, and bare tattooed arms joined her on the stage and cried out, "Madame Fatima Said."

Aimee shrank back. Fatima appeared to be about thirty, with thick jet-black hair that flowed freely down to her hips. She had a sharp chin and high cheekbones, and arched eyebrows over startling shimmering eyes, which glittered in the low light of the club like smouldering coals. Those eyes took in the face of every man in the room, seducing them all simultaneously. As she started to dance, the men cheered and whooped, reaching out for her while the dwarf stood guard at the side of the stage. She thrust her stomach forward in time to the drumming, her arms raised, her eyes sending daggers of desire from under hooded lids, her breasts and belly moving at full-tilt to the music. When she moved off the stage into the crowds, pulling provocatively at her skirt, she devoured the face of each man she saw. Aimee pushed her chair back and pulled at Farouk's sleeve.

"I've seen enough," she said in a panic. "I want to go."

He tried to calm her down. If they left now, he told her, they would attract attention. Fatima would pick the man of her choice soon, and take him backstage and upstairs to one of the girls. They could leave then, but not now.

"Sssh," he said, his arm around Aimee's shoulders, whispering closely in her ear. "We'll go soon, I promise."

As the music got louder, Fatima curled herself up like a snake and reached into the air. Then, feigning a fainting fit, she threw herself into the lap of one of the men, collapsing over him as he roared with laughter. She repeated this routine with several men in the audience, throwing herself into their laps and then bouncing up again before they had time to grab her.

Gradually, her clothes started to disappear. First she pulled at the tie of her skirt and off it came, falling to the floor in a heap to reveal a pair of slim, shapely legs.

A young soldier scooped it off the ground and buried his face in the fabric, inhaling the scent. Slowly, she removed her jewel-studded bodice, sweeping her long hair over her shoulders so that her breasts were perfectly hidden by her thick black tresses. Then she started to remove the small white silk culottes she was wearing, fingering the edges seductively while the men yelped and screamed and clapped.

A man got up from one of the tables and lunged forward, ripping the silk culottes from her. Aimee saw Fatima flash a look of warning at the dwarf, but he nodded at her and the plastered smile returned to her face. She reached for the man, stroked his cheek, and allowed him to undress her further, helping him to pull the remaining fabric from between her thighs. Aimee could not see the man's face, but the crowds cheered him on and his friends jeered and called out his name.

"Go on, Hawky, give it to her," they shouted. "Give her one from us too."

The man turned around triumphantly with Fatima's culottes raised high in the air, like the flag victorious. His face was scarlet, his mouth loose, arrogant. He wrapped his arm around Fatima, a large hand over her right breast.

She was naked except for the tiara on her head and a pair of thin spiky heels. The young soldier pulled Fatima close to him, his hands travelling hungrily to places forbidden.

The journal of Hezba Iqbal Sultan Hanim al-Shezira,
Cairo, August 22, 1919

I am counting the days until I see Alexandre. Tonight we celebrate the Prophet's birthday, the moulid-al-Nabi. Nawal, Bathna, and I decide to partake of a dangerous herb, just for a little fun. Bathna bribes Tindoui to get it for us, and we harem girls like to take it for our amusement. I mix a tiny amount of the powder with water and lemon juice in the palm of my hand and lick it away with my tongue. Bathna and Nawal do the same. After a while the world disappears into a blur. We watch a dancer perform for us in our private parlour. Watching her thrills me. I look up and see Rachid looking at her longingly while he stands guard. Five women, including me, are lying on cushions, watching the girl—a beauty of no more than twelve—as she dances to music that reaches an exotic frenzy. When the dancer finishes, I ask Rachid to come to my room after the midnight raka to talk.

He waits until I finish my religious recitations. I am worried about him. He is wretchedly unhappy and sometimes he tells me that the only thing keeping him from taking his own life is his love of his harem sisters. I know how he feels. I have felt the same way.

I try and remind him that Papa treats him well, so he has less to complain about than he thinks. Nevertheless, I understand him and he understands me.

Tonight we talk well into the night. If our hours together are numbered, we must find happiness together. The warm, dreamy sensation from the powder, running through my body, stays with me until I fall sleep. When I awake, Rachid has gone and Habrid is standing over me with his arms crossed.

I sit up groggily and stare at him. "What do you want?" I ask him.

"Come with me, Sayyida," he says, yanking me up by the arm. My robes feel sticky against my skin. I am sure my blood is coming. I feel this strange sensation in my belly, a pulling pain, a sure sign that I am unclean. Habrid should not be in my rooms now. He must not touch me if I am about to get my womanly blood.

"Where are you taking me? What are you doing?" I demand to know.

"I know what you have been doing," he says, escorting me to the thrashing chamber, commonly known as the Red Room. "I have orders to see you are punished."

"For what?" I shout at him.

"For cutting short your prayer time and for engaging your servant in conversation while your thoughts should be on your religion. You neither submit to Islam, Hezba, nor do you honour your position as the sultan's daughter. Your mother heard what was going on from her own spies in the harem. Two sins that are punishable in whatever way your mother sees fit."

I gape at him and pull away, but he is strong and I am weak. His large hands bruise the flesh on my arms. He pushes me into the Red Room, then nods to one of the lower eunuchs on guard there. Together they rip my gowns from me. I am shivering, naked on the stone floors. There is a lump in my throat and tears of rage behind my eyes as I bend over, covering my head with my hands to wait for the first crack of the stick against my flesh.

CHAPTER TWELVE

In a secret, darkened room, at the back of the Sultan Hassan Mosque, lit by a single desk lamp, the HQ chiefs of Security Operations, Hilali and Gamal, sat hunched over a pile of telegrams. Their most skilled code-cracker, a young Oxford graduate, James Lambert, sat with them.

Gamal spoke first.

"There are three here that have been sent from a kilim shop in Bab al-Luq to the Café Malta in Garden City on three consecutive days," he said. "We're looking for a synchronicity, evidence of a plan, a link that spells out the X's next move."

Lambert held a magnifying glass up to his eyes and ran it back and forth over each telegram. While he examined them, Gamal said authoritatively, "Have the Café Malta telephone tapped straight away, Lambert."

Hilali pointed at the words on the telegram and said, "Can you see the symmetry between the dates?"

Lambert bit his lip. "Carpet order processed. Consignment due in four days. Esteemed thanks sent."

Gamal leaned over him and read. "Carpet order shipment problems. New order required. Delays expected. Esteemed thanks sent."

Hilali pointed at the third. "Carpet order problems rectified. On target. Esteemed thanks sent."

The three men stared at one another.

"The Carpet Seller," Lambert said, his hand outstretched. "The dossier, please, Gamal."

Gamal flicked through a pile of cream-coloured folders and dug one out. He opened it and pulled out the contents. It contained newspaper clippings, reports, and fake rubber-stamped identity cards but no photographs.

"Carpet Seller. Code name Thunderbolt, code name Centurion, code name Smith: a man of many disguises and hundreds of aliases. But we don't know what he looks like. No one has ever managed to take a photograph of him."

Lambert took off his horn-rimmed glasses, blew on the lenses, retrieved a handkerchief, and wiped them clean. "I'm sure Centurion is probably the code name of three different ringleaders," he said. "They use the same name to confuse us."

Hilali picked up the telephone and dialled a number. "I'll send a message to Ringwood at HQ," Hilali said. "We have something for him. Tell him to prepare the troops. I think we finally have something we can work on."

"The Café Malta is a popular hangout with soldiers, isn't it?" Gamal said.

"We've been watching that place for weeks and seen nothing at all," Lambert said. "It all makes sense. The X move around a lot. They are deliberately evasive. This is the first coding consistency— the use of three linked words—we have seen in a long time. When Lambert here cracks this code, we'll see we were right."

Gamal stood up and started pacing around the room. "We don't have long, Hilali," he said. "We should put Operation X into action right now."

"Relax," Hilali smiled. "We have to have a strategy. Lambert's report will tell us what we need to know and enable us to target our efforts more intelligently. Then we can draw our networks together. I want Operation X to start at eighteen hundred hours on the night of the celebrations at the palace. If we bide our time, we can round up most of them before there's any real chance of trouble."

"You're quite confident, aren't you," Lambert said.

Gamal checked his watch. "There's a weakness in the chain. Lambert has discovered it. They're slipping up, using their code too casually, and this proves they're not invincible. Their stomping ground is the Muski district. All Intelligence reports point to the Café Malta being one of the X's headquarters. It makes the most sense to start there. In the Muski they can recruit more sector members."

"We don't want to alarm any civilians," Gamal said. "That's why we must be careful, do our work invisibly. Tell headquarters to send in their plainclothes men to scour the Muski district. Lambert had resumed his work on the telegrams. "Ah," Lambert said excitedly. Hilali and Gamal abruptly stopped talking and looked over his shoulder.

"Yes. Yes. I was right all along."

"Well?" the two other men asked impatiently. "What is it?"

Lambert didn't answer. He kept referring back to his codebook, smiling. He did this for more than five minutes while the two others waited.

"There's a date here."

"Well?" Hilali shouted.

"If I'm right, we're . . ." Lambert took a deep breath and ran his hands through his hair. Each telegram had been placed side by side. His eyes darted euphorically from one telegram to the other.

"What, man?" Gamal was getting impatient.

"Well I'll be damned," he gasped. "This is sophisticated, this one. They've made these telegrams look so damn innocent, but wait a minute—" Lambert sucked in a breath and screwed up his eyes.

"We're not out of the woods yet. Every letter has been triple-coded. This will take longer than I thought, but I think we've broken through. I think—"

The journal of Hezba Iqbal Sultan Hanim al-Shezira,
Cairo, August 23, 1919

Picture the scene. I wait for the depths of the night to come. I sit here alone in my room on my favourite gold cushions, waiting for Tindoui to fetch me in secret and take me to the stables. I am concealed behind the mashrabiyya in a little alcove. Then I lie down on the floor, on my cushions, my face pressed into the silky fabric. I breathe hard, trying to steady myself. It is very dark, very hot. I am writing by the light of a little candle. The harem is asleep, and I am trembling with excitement. I can hardly hold my pens, and I am sure I will smudge the ink. I want to summon Anisah, to get me a drink of sherbet to calm me, but I am scared to move towards the bell rope. I feel there is someone watching me, someone lurking in the shadows.

I want to get out into the air while I wait for Tindoui to come and get me. Perhaps I should sit on the balcony for a while, but I mustn't do so for too long because it isn't proper to be seen out on the balcony in the depths of the night. I swear I will die from this heat. There is no air. I can see Uluk asleep in the old rattan chair in the garden. Little patches of perspiration on his forehead are glimmering in the moonlight. His tunic is stretched tight around his fat waist. He looks so uncomfortable. It has been said that he doesn't feel safe with Papa away. This is why he sleeps in the garden. He is nervous about the Nationalist rioting in the streets, and he wants to be able to call the servants to order quickly if needed.

My hair is wet. It feels sticky and tangled. Anisah prepared my hair when I went to bed, tying it in a thick roll with calico ribbons, but now it is coming loose and feels hot around my neck. Little streams of perspiration trickle down my back.

Perhaps I have Maman's infection. Perhaps this is further punishment. I am afraid. The evil jinn is here to claim me. The jinn reads your thoughts. The jinn knows of the shame and longing in my heart. At last, I can hear heavy footsteps outside my rooms and Tindoui quietly opens the door.

"Here you are," he says. He carries a thick, dark cloak and hidden within its folds, a rough soldier's uniform. In the other hand, he carries a tall yellow candle.

He puts the candle on one of the small tables and looks at me.

"I am afraid for you, Hezba," he says. "You are taking too many risks. I shall never forgive myself if something happens to you."

"I will be fine," I say.

"Don't fool yourself, Hezba. If you are found out, you will be sent away forever. You are close to being found out. I am just warning you."

"Look at the streets," I say. "They are full of foreigners, women, young girls my age, living their lives while we are caged like little golden birds. I must go to him."

"But Hezba," he says softly, "your husband is your master, not this man, Monsieur Alexandre."

"No man is my master," I say. "You least of all. You are my servant. You speak too freely."

Tindoui stares at me with his wide, black eyes. He is trying to distract me from what I am about to do.

"Take me to the stables immediately," I say.

He bows, but his eyes quiver with concern.

I change quickly, and we creep quietly through the harem and out to the stables. I breathe in the night air, trying hard not to think about what I am doing. The night guard is asleep and we creep slowly past him. My heart beats so loudly, I think I am going to faint. My narrow slippers do not give me good protection against the hard stones in the courtyard leading to the stables at the back of the palace.

"Mustafa, find me some boots, before we mount, will you," I order one of the palace's horsemen. He appears with a pair that looks suitable for the ride into the desert. I put on the boots and throw on the thick cloak to hide my gear. I suddenly feel ready for anything. My hair is plaited in a single braid down my back. I put on the peaked cap and pull it down over my eyes, straightening myself against the rough uniform chafing my skin. I feel every inch the Australian lieutenant, and with thick boots and a rough satchel attached to my horse, I am transformed—no longer an Egyptian. I am a man, free at last.

CHAPTER THIRTEEN

While Aimee was at the el-G, one of Littoni's head sector men, Mohommad al-Dyn, was staking out Issawi's club, the Oxford. He loved his job, loved acting the part of waiter. It had been his secret desire as a young boy to work on the stage, but his parents had disapproved. No matter, he thought sinisterly, he had become an actor of sorts anyway, working for the X, playing whatever part was assigned to him by the Group of the X. Tonight, Issawi was scheduled to make his first appearance at the Oxford since his widely reported return from meetings in Luxor.

Al-Dyn's job as a waiter at the club gave him access to a great deal of information. He was on good terms with the doorman, Hagar, who had told him excitedly the night before that Haran Issawi was back. His eyes had glittered hopefully as he delivered the news.

"We're in for some big baksheesh. The pasha loves to throw his money around. He can't have the faintest idea of what anything's worth. He just spends and spends and spends. I know the government gives him a blank cheque and he certainly uses his position to maximum advantage. If I were that rich and powerful—well, it's good for us, is it not?"

Al-Dyn had smiled passively at this. The doormen at the Oxford ingratiated themselves with their clients, as they relied on big tips to support their families. His job as waiter, however, was as far down the scale as one could go, right next to the kitchen hands. He stood to gain little from Issawi's generosity as a big tipper, but he didn't care—it wasn't Issawi's money he was interested in. The X looked after him in that respect. Their coffers—it was rumoured— were kept full by wealthy sponsors and supporters.

Tonight al-Dyn was in a good mood. With Issawi due any moment, he felt in control, on top of things, and useful to the X's cause. It felt wildly exciting to be at the forefront of the mission, and he enjoyed working at the gentleman's club. Located on Gezira Island, the Oxford was a far less stuffy and sultry environment than the cloistered confines of the old city.

A deliciously cool Nile breeze fanned the faces of the men as they stepped out of their cars. Inside the club, al-Dyn stood by his group of tables in the large dining room, ready to take orders. His mind was racing. He had casually asked the doorman what time Issawi was expected.

"I like to see the big grin on your face, Hagar," al-Dyn said. "It makes me happy to see you smile like that."

Hagar had thumped al-Dyn affectionately on the back, and, peering at the large leather diary on the reception desk, told him, "Nine o'clock, my friend. I'll be richer and happier." Then he'd pressed his finger to his mouth, emitting a soft chuckle, as though a thought had flashed through his mind. Al-Dyn wondered if Hagar was already planning what he was going to spend his tips on.

"Will we be seeing much of our rich friend?" Al-Dyn went on, "Because if we do, I can expect you, Hagar, to be permanently rich and permanently happy."

Hagar cocked his head knowingly.

"He's missed us. He's been very busy. The life of a chief advisor is all work and no play. He's asked us to reserve a table for him every second night for the next two weeks. After that, we can expect to be poor again, because my dear rich friend has to leave Cairo on more political business."

"But at least we have him now." Al-Dyn smiled, congratulating himself inwardly on his ability to put Hagar at his ease. It was so easy to fool these gullible, greedy imbeciles.

At nine o'clock to the minute, a sleek chauffeur-driven Daimler drew up. Hagar opened the door and bowed at Issawi, who stepped out accompanied by two security men.

Al-Dyn spotted him from the far side of the dining room—his great bulk, dressed in dinner jacket and black tie, waddling his way towards his table.

His heart pumped wildly. He studied Issawi's face and demeanour, trying to assess his mood. Littoni would want to know everything. The headwaiter showed Issawi to his seat, then unfolded a starched napkin and draped it over his lap. He snapped his fingers in al-Dyn's direction. Perfect, al-Dyn thought. He longed for a close-up of the X's latest project.

He moved forward to take his order.

"Sir?" he said with a servile smile. "A drink?"

Al-Dyn sneered secretly at Issawi's bloodshot eyes, his huge jowls gathering pools of perspiration, his pregnant belly, which wobbled as he wheezed.

"A whisky," Issawi spat huskily without even looking up. "No, make that a double."

"Certainly, sir."

Al-Dyn placed the order and returned with the drink.

Another man had joined him, someone younger, his junior assistant perhaps? His two security guards sat at a table nearby. As he walked towards him to place the whisky on the table, the young man spoke.

"I think you'll approve of the speech, sir," he said. "I am still waiting for the latest figures to come in, but the gist of it leaves no doubt that you were completely blameless in all this. I have written it to absolve you of any involvement, and I am prepared to take responsibility for the mistake myself, sir."

"You certainly will," Issawi snorted, raising his eyes to the ceiling. Then, seeing al-Dyn approaching, he put his hand on the young man's arm to silence him.

"A drink, sir?" al-Dyn asked the younger man.

"Another double whisky," Issawi answered for him. "Leave us alone for ten minutes. You'll be called when we are ready to order our food."

Al-Dyn went to stand by his station and began polishing cutlery, flashing quick looks at the two men from time to time. If he moved closer, he was sure he'd be able to overhear their conversation. Strangely, the dining room wasn't that crowded, although he expected a big crowd later. During the summer months, people dined late at the club. Al-Dyn took a tray of silver goblets, cutlery, and bread plates over to a closer table and replaced one of the settings, keeping his head down as he worked.

"I've ordered four more security men for you, sir," the younger man said.

"You were wise to do that," Issawi said, rimming his glass with fingers. "Your job's on the line as it is."

"We can never be too careful," his assistant went on dully, without flinching.

"No," Issawi said with a laugh, "It's you who can never be too careful. Do you know who I am? Do you have any idea how powerful I am, how I can crush you between my fingers and make your life a living hell. How would you support your family, eh, Salamah, once I spread the word that you are an incompetent nobody incapable of holding his own even in the most menial of government positions?"

Salamah nodded humbly. "I'm sorry, sir," he said. "I'm at your service, sir."

Issawi drank some more whisky.

"The men have been thoroughly checked out," Salamah went on. "There can be no doubt as to their record. They're clean, humble men from poor backgrounds with absolutely no links to any group or organisation."

"Good."

"You leave for Alexandria in two weeks," Salamah said. "Your train will have the fully armed patrol you require and will be thoroughly checked from top to bottom before you leave. I have cancelled most of your engagements for the next week, except for the king's birthday celebrations at the palace. I think it's wise that you changed your mind about your engagements. Hilali and Gamal have told me everything."

"I didn't ask your advice," Issawi snapped. "You want me to fire you? Remember who you are talking to, you useless idiot."

This time, al-Dyn saw the young secretary's face harden in humiliated shame. He decided to move away. It would be dangerous to hover around too much. He risked one last look before he slid through the double doors to the kitchen. Issawi was throwing back the dregs of his whisky. A few moments later, al-Dyn was called back to take their order. He took the younger man's first.

"Very good, sir," he said. And then he leaned subserviently towards Issawi.

"Very good, sir," he said once more.

Littoni could not fault his acting tonight.

The journal of Hezba Iqbal Sultan Hanim al-Shezira,
Cairo, August 23, 1919

I am ready to ride out to the desert. Not for the first time I thank God for my pale complexion, unblemished by sunlight. With my hair tucked under my hat, it is easy to pass as a young officer of the Australian Light Horse Brigade, out on a midnight excursion to visit the family of a new friend—an opportunity to experience true Arab hospitality, perhaps to witness a zikr, something to write home about.

Mustafa is sedately dressed in his servant's garb, a blue turban, and a dark cloak. As we prepare to leave, I order Tindoui to go back to the palace, but he refuses to leave. He stands to one side, looking sullen and anxious.

"I will be back an hour before daybreak, Tindoui," I say. "Make sure you are here to meet me, or send Rachid. Mustafa will stay with me, of course. Don't act as though it is the end of the world. I will be back soon."

I smile at him as I pull on the reins of my stallion, looking up at the glassy sky, blue-black and glittering with worlds I long to know.

"Go back to bed," I say with a laugh at Tindoui, who had crossed his arms angrily across his broad chest.

Mustafa mounts his horse with a look of thunderous anger, and we start off. I have paid him well to accompany me. He has no right to look at me in that way. No one will find out he has helped me. I will make sure of that. We ride off. Disguised as a man—unmade-up, unadorned, and anonymous—I feel ecstatic to be out in the open and to be free.

"Papa did not realise how well my riding lessons would serve me," I say out loud, suddenly unafraid that someone might hear my voice.

As we ride, I don't think about danger. I think about freedom. I am determined, almost fearless. I should have been a boy. I tell myself I am going to Kerdassa to deliver money to the Rebel Corps, Alexandre's underground Nationalist group. But why would they accept money from a girl like me? a little voice inside me says. Another voice says I am fooling myself, trying to make myself believe I am going for a good cause when I am really going because of Alexandre. Another voice mimics Maman's, claiming that England is good for Egypt, that the British have poured money into Egypt. It goes on to say that jewels and silks and gold are more important than the common man and woman. It denies the misery of the wives of the fellahin, the women who bear their farmer husbands ten children and who can see no end to their poverty.

In Mustafa's world, my actions make me unfit to worship, unfit to touch a Qur'an, unfit to speak in the presence of a man, but still he does not say anything. Maybe all men are not the same. Perhaps there are some among them who want women to be free and equal.

Things are changing, slowly, of course, but the seeds have been planted and the radical intelligentsia is questioning the models and beliefs of our religion, separating real faith from choking tradition and fundamentalist dogma. This I know from my studies.

As I ride, I think of my teacher's copy of the book The Liberation of Women *written by the progressive lawyer Qasim Amin. I read a few pages of it some time ago with my heart in my throat. Maman would have sent me away forever if she knew I had read it.*

But Maman was not there when I read it. She was far away, lying on her bed, while her eunuchs fanned her into slumber, with her forever in denial about the change that is happening. She sleeps now while her daughter rides across the desert towards freedom.

CHAPTER FOURTEEN

Nemmat had witnessed Fatima's display at the el-G. She'd seen her choose the sickly looking white-skinned soldier from the crowd, had seen it all from behind the thick curtains separating the backstage alcove from the glare of the stage lights. As usual, it had repulsed her. The soldier's loose red mouth; his watery, drunken eyes; the clownish flush of his cheeks against his wispy pallid features—it had all made her shudder.

She imagined briefly the soldier's hands on her own flesh and shut her eyes in horror. She was not unused to the hands of strange men on her body, but the sight of the ugly soldier had made her feel particularly ill.

Nemmat wasn't convinced that Fatima had chosen well. The soldier did not look like the type who could be easily parted from his wallet. He had a mean face and looked young, but then again, he was a soldier and they were very well paid, the Australians in particular. However, she had no time to think about that now.

She had to focus her attention on the newspaperman and the girl at the club. The girl was cowering in her seat with eyes narrowed. The newspaperman, stony-faced, was watching Fatima with the soldier and then watching the girl, always watching the girl, watching her reaction, leaning over, touching her arm, leaning too close.

From her secret nook, Nemmat could see the desire behind his eyes. If he was at the el-G—even though he was with this girl—he must be expecting Nemmat to perform, expecting a secret nod of affirmation to confirm that the plan was on target. No doubt that was why he was here—and why he stayed, even when it was obvious the girl wanted to leave.

Well, Nemmat wasn't going to perform tonight. Fatima had relieved her of her duties, knowing she had to contact one of the letter boxes. What Fatima didn't know was that Nemmat was expected at a different letter box tonight, that in fact she was expected to take possession of one of Angel's babies and then supposed to take the child to Tashi's house and that the consignment would be sent on once again from there.

She slipped quietly through the dark, musty corridors to her dressing room, cloaked herself in her chador, and left by one of the back doors, pushing through the thinning crowds to the back quarters of Birka.

She didn't have far to go. Nemmat found the narrow doorway and knocked loudly. No answer. She looked around nervously. She did not want to attract attention. She wished Tashi were with her. If he were, it would naturally be assumed that he was her husband and all suspicion would melt away.

She knocked again. At last Angel came to the door. Nemmat bowed her head and hugged the woman's shoulders. A boy stood in the darkness behind her, cradling a bundle of cloth. Nemmat could see the cherubic face of the baby.

"Here she is," Angel said, reaching for the sleeping child. "Be careful with her. She is well padded."

Angel smiled secretly to herself, patting the swathe of cloth enfolding the baby.

"My job is done. Tashi is waiting. My sister is now quite well rested and should be able to change the child. If she is not strong enough to do that, Tashi can help her."

Nemmat gathered the child in her arms and kissed the baby's forehead.

"Don't worry. It won't take me long to get to Tashi's house, and your sister's little darling will be well looked after. I'll make sure the baby is changed and made comfortable before I leave. Do you have any message for your sister or Tashi?"

Angel shook her head, but then her eyes lit up and she said, "Yes, just tell them the baby is fine. Inshallah, God willing, we will claim our victory."

Nemmat smiled and bowed. "Ma'as salaama, peace be with you," she said, and swept away.

She walked briskly through the dark streets, feeling the warmth and the heaviness of the human bundle in her arms. As a chador-covered woman with a child in her arms, she would not arouse any suspicion. She would not be seen for who she really was—a brothel girl who wore an almost-invisible sheath under her chador, whose body moved for the men who paid her, who detested them with passion, who wore her brothel mask for her mother, to whom she owed her life, not for her father, who had deserted her and her brother long ago.

As she held the child in her arms—a young babe only six months old—her heart beat sadly and a lump rose in her throat. For the first time she imagined what it must be like to be a mother. She clasped the sleeping body more tightly to her and checked that she was not being followed.

Angel was a ruthless spy, yet she acted the part to perfection. Her code name suited her brilliantly. Nemmat could not fault the innocence of her face and the demeanour of devoted motherhood she portrayed to the world. She had three sons of her own. This child in

Nemmat's arms was Angel's sister's firstborn. The sister's health had failed when she had delivered the child into the world, and Angel had been looking after the little girl ever since. Now Nemmat was returning the child to Tashi and his wife in a swathe of cloth in which were hidden carefully wrapped slabs of dynamite. All Tashi had to do was unravel the cloth and extricate the dynamite. The baby girl's body was a death trap. Little did she know she was a crucial member of the X. Tashi had considered it unsafe to get the dynamite by the usual methods, knowing that any of the X's letter boxes could be raided at any time. The bomb had to be assembled quickly and moved around frequently to lessen the chance of discovery.

Nemmat found Tashi's door, knocked, and waited with her head bowed. At last he answered and ushered her in, scanning the activity in the street outside as he did so. Nemmat followed him through to the back of the house where Meryiam, his wife, lay on a low couch.

"Give me the child," Tashi said.

Nemmat handed him the human bundle.

"No one followed you?" he enquired.

Nemmat shook her head. Tashi laid the child on the carpet and unravelled the cloth. Meryiam and Nemmat stared at the baby's bare flesh. Tashi looked up at them reassuringly.

"Inshallah, God willing. The baby is fine." He unravelled the bandages that held the soft gelatinous slabs of dynamite to the baby's body, gathered them up in a pile, and passed the child to his wife.

"Here, Wife, take your child."

"Will that be enough for a man like Issawi?" Nemmat asked, watching Tashi roll the slabs in some of the discarded cloth.

Tashi looked up and smiled. "Inshallah, God willing, this will make a right royal mess of the Abdin Palace and your archenemy Issawi," he said. "The perfect revenge, Sayyida, the revenge you've wanted for your mother for so long."

The journal of Hezba Iqbal Sultan Hanim al-Shezira,
Kerdassa, August 23, 1919

We arrive at Kerdassa. Exposed under the cold night sky, I now feel
scared. I am freezing, petrified, and the look of terror on Mustafa's face
as he summons me to a safe place to tie up our horses makes me even
more afraid. We dismount and lead our horses to a nearby stable. The
village is alive with people and noise, and I feel vulnerable. It must be
a local moulid, a festival for the land, for rain, for the fecundity of the
fellahin's crops. I attend to a loose strap on my boots.

My nerves are failing me, but I try to pull myself together. I want
to be eyes only. I want to observe without being seen. I do not want to
fall prey to the preconceived notion that I am inferior because of my sex.
I see two men sitting outside a neighbouring mud-brick house, smoking
a pipe. I feel their eyes hot on me, watching me carefully. To them, I
am a soldier. I know they are wondering what my business is here, in a
desert village at night. Mustafa explains our business to the two men.
His Arabic is servile and hopeful. I do not speak for fear of giving myself
away. He explains he has come to a meeting organised by Hassan, that
he is expected, that Hassan is a friend.

"What is the soldier's business?" one of them asks.

Mustafa explains I am a friend and says no more. After more suspi-
cious glances, we are told, "Come this way." The older of the two men,
quite possibly a sheik of the village, leans on his stick and walks slowly
towards one of the village houses. As he turns, I glimpse by the light of
the moon a flicker of suspicion in his eyes, and my heart thumps even
more violently. This sheik has a thick white beard and a hard face. I feel
my femaleness like a mark on my skin. My walk is too dainty. I am too
cautious, too shapely, too pale, too female, to be anything but a girl. But

the sheik does not take any notice of me. He seems to be too absorbed in his own thoughts to be concerned about two strangers.

He does not talk as he leads us to this mud house. We walk through crowds of people on the main street, women sitting on the ground cradling sleeping children, men arguing and laughing. I hear a loud rhythmic noise and chanting coming from a nearby house—women's voices, hypnotic sounds. A circle of older women in plain, dull clothes—unveiled, wrinkled, and unattractive—is guarding the house. They are holding hands, their eyes are closed, and their heads sway from side to side. We stop, and to my horror the sheik comes up close to me, holding out his hand. From under my soldier's cap, I examine the leathery texture of his skin. My breath stalls for a moment out of fear, but then I notice something that I had not noticed before: He is half-blind.

I realise he takes me to be the soldier I am pretending to be because he grunts at me in a thick voice. "Australian?"

I am mortified. My grasp of the English language is minimal, and I do not have any idea how to reply correctly. Since I speak only Turkish, Arabic, and French, I say nothing, pressing his hand in reply. But then he goes on slyly in Arabic.

"Australians rich. Lots of money."

I shake his hand now, bow, dig deep in my pocket, and put some piastres into his palm. To my relief, Mustafa steps in and draws the sheik's attention away from me. Mustafa raps on the door of the house and it is opened. We go in. Three bearded men in pale blue jalabas are seated at a large table lit by two lanterns. One of them is not wearing a turban, and I can see that his thick dark hair is long and greasy. The group stares at us. Mustafa approaches them with his hand up.

"As salaam alaikum. Peace be with you," Mustafa says. "Sayyid Hassan," he continues, "I am horseman and servant for the sultan pasha, and I am dutifully escorting his daughter, Sayyida Hezba Hanim al-Shezira, to you, at her most esteemed wishes."

CHAPTER FIFTEEN

Farouk wanted to get Aimee away from the club. He did not want to risk being seen by Gad Mahmoud. At the earliest opportunity, they made a discreet exit. He summoned a taxi near the el-G and ushered Aimee inside. He glanced at his watch. It was two in the morning. He slid inside the cab after her, glad of the vehicle's dark cocoon. He was fighting a burning sensation that was crawling up his spine, constricting his heart. He signalled to the driver to wait for a moment while he spoke to the madame.

"Come to my house at Zamalek," he said quietly to Aimee, holding her hand comfortingly.

"But my friend Sophie—?"

"Would you want to worry her? My boy will take care of you. You'll find everything you need there. You can sleep in one of the spare rooms."

"But the police? Surely I should tell them about the raid on my house?"

Farouk shook his head. "Not yet. I have an idea." He paused for a moment, searching her face. "Go to Zamalek to be safe. I'll join you there soon, I promise, but there's something I must do first. Trust me."

He stared at her, at the thick mane of dark hair falling below her shoulders, and felt by the throbbing energy pulsing through him.

He wanted to entwine her fingers in his. He wanted to lean forward and kiss her gently on her mouth, but he knew that would be highly inappropriate, so he pulled back, stopping himself.

Aimee nodded, too tired to disagree. Her body and mind longed for Azi, but her husband was gone. This man was alive. For a moment in the darkness, she felt safe, protected, warm, and glad that she was with him.

But then suddenly he pulled away from her. "I must go," he said.

"Yes," she whispered, not wanting him to.

Farouk told the driver the address and got out of the car. He watched as it drove off down the narrow street towards the Nile.

Aimee leaned back and closed her eyes. Through the open window she inhaled the dark, dusty smell of the earth and the streets, not wanting to look out at the bustling cafés, the still-open shops, the doorways where sleeping bodies lay.

The taxi driver suddenly slammed his fists against the steering wheel. "Wen-Nabi," he shouted in frustration, begging the Prophet Muhammad for deliverance from bad drivers. Aimee opened her eyes again and saw people everywhere. Drunken British soldiers were pushing one another out of clubs, boys were balancing boxed-up pastries and cakes on the handlebars of their bicycles, and men were tugging at carts of vegetables.

She closed her eyes once more, and her mind spun with thoughts of Farouk, her mother, Azi, and the hard-faced prostitute Fatima. Lulled by the motion of the car travelling over the ragged streets, Aimee dreamt of the house where she lived, of the Nile, of her bedroom. In a half sleep, she saw herself telling Sophie about the el-G, Fatima, the break-in, and she saw the look on her face as she told her everything. She imagined Sophie's disbelief and then wondered whether she had actually dreamt it all. The past few weeks had been a kind of living nightmare, and now here she was—on her way to the house of a man about whom she knew nothing. Between jolting wakefulness, she wondered if she had lost her mind.

The car stopped and she opened her eyes. She did not know where she was. Out the window, she saw large majestic houses bathed in moonlight, towering palm trees, and she smelt the scent of burning oud. She leaned forward to clutch the back of the seat in front of her. The driver turned around and smiled at her. He pointed up at a large building on the other side of the street; an old mansion with jutting balconies, mashrabiyya, and spires; a large pale pink house built in the European-Ottoman style of ornate stone.

"This is the address the Sayyid gave, Madame. You are here."

The journal of Hezba Iqbal Sultan Hanim al-Shezira,
Kerdassa, August 23, 1919

I take off my soldier's cap but do not smile or speak. I just study the expressions on the men's faces. Fear, contempt, and disbelief ripple over their features in quick succession. The one with the greasy hair bows, and then a smile edges onto his face. He turns to speak to his partisans.

"I have been told this woman is here to give us money."

"Who has told you?" another asks.

"Anton," he says, and the other men start to laugh. "Anton does not need her money. It is a ruse, a trick."

Despite feeling very scared, I shout, "I am not here to amuse you, Sayyids." Then I tell Mustafa to wait outside for me.

"But, Sayyida, it is forbidden," he says.

"Do it," I shout.

Mustafa reluctantly goes.

For a moment I stand silently. I am cold. The room I find myself in is dirty and uninviting. I am used to more comfortable surroundings. I am anxious to find Alexandre.

He is the reason I am here. Handing money over to the Rebel Corps is the least of my concerns at this moment. The greasy-haired man speaks.

"Are you aware of all the complications you face supporting our group?"

"I am prepared for anything that comes my way."

His companions, a seedy lot, salaciously take in every inch of my body and my ridiculous garb.

The man goes on. "Let me introduce you to my fellow Rebel Corps members, Umar and Aalim."

"But Hassan, a woman?" asks Aalim.

I look this Sayyid Aalim in the eye, squirming inside, hating the filth of his face, the wispy moustache, the way he wrings his hands impatiently, and his eyes screwed up in disbelief at the sight of a woman, dressed in a soldier's uniform.

"Anton's obviously got something in mind. If he wants this woman's money, I know he'll have a use for it," the greasy-haired man says.

"Where is Monsieur Anton?" I ask, impatient to see him, wanting to fold myself in his arms and call him Alexandre. Just then, a woman enters the hut. She is carrying a tray with a coffee pot, cups, and a little pot of sugar. She glances at me and then looks again, affronted by what she sees. I don't think she believes what she sees. It is impossible, I can almost hear her telling herself. Then she approaches me and pinches my arm very hard. I cry out and pull back. The men laugh out loud, and the woman bows in front of them, swearing she has never seen anything so unusual. She moans with outrage and runs out of the hut. All three men have tears streaming down their cheeks as they reach for their coffee cups, loading them with spoonfuls of sugar.

CHAPTER SIXTEEN

Aimee got out of the taxi, timidly climbed the steps of the Zamalek house, and knocked on the door. It was opened by a young boy, barely older than fifteen. She forced a weak smile. The boy bowed his head and asked, "Madame?"

She spoke softly, suddenly embarrassed that she had agreed to stay at Farouk's house.

"I am Madame Abdullah Ibrahim. Your master has invited me to stay here."

The boy bowed again. "I am Gigis, Madame, Sayyid Farouk's housekeeper. I am at your service. The master telephoned. Please come in," he said, watching her silently as he stepped back to let her through the door.

Glancing around the vast entry hall, she ascertained that Farouk had excellent taste. She could see a living room with elegant carved wingback chairs, delicate little tables, lamps lighting the way, and an exquisite painting by Casson, if she wasn't mistaken.

"This is a beautiful house, Gigis. Has your master lived here long?"

"I think so, though I have not been with him that long myself. From what I have gathered, the house belonged to his sister, Madame. When she died, she left it to him. The lady of the house used to live here a long time ago with her husband. There were no children to pass it on to, so she left it to her brother."

Aimee stood for a moment, admiring the ornate ceilings, the elaborately carved archways, and the curls and crests of the plaster-work.

"My master instructed me to put you in one of the rooms upstairs," he said. "I have made up the bed and put out everything you need, but of course, if you should require anything else, please ring for me. There's a bell rope by the bed that connects to my rooms. I'll come at once."

Gigis led the way up the central staircase to the first floor. The house was so quiet that Aimee could hear the soft rustle of the trees in the garden. From the first landing she could see that the French doors were open in the dining room, the curtains swaying in the breeze. A surge of curiosity flooded through her. She inhaled the scent of flowers, felt the cool touch of the marble banister under her fingers as she walked in the low light of the corridors leading to the sleeping quarters. What was she doing here, in a stranger's house, when she could have gone to stay with Sophie at the Continental?

Why was Farouk being so kind? He was an old man and she was unsure of him. She knew so little of men or of life. What should she do? She wondered whether she should leave and go find Sophie. Something was stopping her, though. She'd shut down after Azi's death, but now she was starting to feel a little different—her curiosity about Farouk was drawing her out of herself again.

This was the house of a man who belonged to a more civilised world than the one he and his fellow journalists wrote about in their newspaper. This was clearly a man who enjoyed the good things in life. However, Gigis had not said when the sister had died. The entire house could be a tribute to her and her taste and not reflect Farouk's aesthetics at all. And it was true that there was something feminine about the house, something vulnerable. Gigis opened a door at the far end of the corridor and stood aside, waiting for Aimee.

"In here, Madame."

Aimee slipped past him into the room, uncertain what to expect. She knew that this Monsieur Farouk was being kind by letting her stay here tonight. She feared once again that she had been a little too bold in accepting his invitation. After all, he had held her hand in the cab, and his touch, his warmth, had sent fiery little shivers down her spine, softening every grief-stricken emotion that had occupied her mind and her body since Azi's death. She felt lonely and scared. There was no one to hold her. His gentleness was making her feel alive, when before, in the days after Azi's murder, she had felt dead. She didn't know what she wanted from this Monsieur Farouk, but for the time being, was it wrong to be glad of his kindness? He made her feel she was not alone.

And he had told her he would come to her later. That he had something else to do first. Was he trying to protect her? If so, from what? Aimee walked to the French doors on the far side of the room and stepped out onto the balcony, dappled with moonlight. Gigis followed her.

"I will bring you some tea, Madame. It is late. I am sure you will want to sleep. There are fresh towels on the chair and fresh water in the jug."

Aimee swung around.

"Did Sayyid Farouk say what time he would be returning, Gigis?"

"No, Madame," Gigis replied, backing towards the door. "Now, I'll get you your tea."

Aimee thanked him and heard him shut the door; then she looked out at the garden below, letting her gaze rest on the trees, the little fountain, the terrace. After a few moments she turned and went back inside. She stood still in the softly lit room, hardly daring to breathe, listening to she didn't know what exactly—the ticktock of the bedside clock, the cawing of the night birds, the shout of a youth walking home from a club—but the house itself was silent, deathly silent.

How magnificent the room was. It was beautifully decorated, with a large four-poster bed, a writing desk, a large packing trunk, and a wardrobe. It seemed set in another time, as though twenty years had been wiped away with the flick of a hand.

How much did Farouk really know about Fatima? If she could stay awake until he returned, she would question him further. She went to the writing desk and pulled open the little drawer. She wanted information. Anything. An old ticket stub, a notebook, a matchbox, a pamphlet from somewhere. Anything that might help her piece together who he really was.

All she knew was that he was the editor of the newspaper the *Liberation,* that he lived in this grand old mansion in Zamalek, and that he wanted to help her find out who had murdered her husband.

Could she simply ask him directly why he wanted to help her? Somehow she doubted she would get an honest answer. And the woman at the club? Why did Azi have that photograph in his possession? Every time she went looking for answers, she only came upon more questions. No one could shed any light on why the man she loved had been brutally murdered in the desert near Ismailia. Little clues as to Azi's secret political inclinations could not possibly be linked to his death. Azi Ibrahim was a teacher, a professor who loved his academic life and who had loved his wife. A chill ran down Aimee's spine. Was it possible Azi was not all that he had appeared? She thought back to the early days of their love affair and their marriage, trying to find a clue, something he'd said, some reason for a momentary absence from home, but there was nothing. He'd loved her. She saw his face in her mind, the way his black eyes glittered with happiness when he bent over to kiss her.

Aimee brought herself back to the present. The writing desk was depressingly empty of anything worth noting. It held a sheath of white paper with the address of the Zamalek house emblazoned on the top left-hand corner and some ink pens; that was all.

She flung open the wardrobe and parted the clothes, examining them; a woman's ball gown in pale blue, a suit, a top hat, and a small pale pink vanity case on a shelf above the clothes. Aimee reached for the vanity case, pulled it down, and unsnapped the lock.

Inside it she found some letters, wrapped up with black satin ribbon. She studied the handwriting, the slant of it, but in the gloom she could not make out much. Suddenly she heard the sound of Gigis, padding along the corridor. Startled, she jumped up, snapped the vanity case shut, and slid it into place on the top shelf of the wardrobe.

With her heart thudding, she arranged herself on the edge of the bed and smiled innocently as Gigis knocked on the door, nudged it open with his shoulder, and brought in the tea.

The journal of Hezba Iqbal Sultan Hanim al-Shezira,
Kerdassa, August 23, 1919

At Kerdassa, I find I am losing my patience.

"Where is Monsieur Alexandre Anton?" I demand once more. "I must speak with him."

"He is anxious to see you. He has been waiting for this money you talk about," says Hassan.

I nod and my thoughts turn to Papa. My father, I have heard from Maman's conversation with other women, is much favoured by the British. His good work in the provinces has been observed and celebrated by Hussein Kamel, the former sultan of our beloved al-Qahire, and now here I am in the desert, handing over his money to the Rebel Corps.

I hate myself for betraying Papa. It is a thought that never goes away, and I don't know what I have become. Is it simply a matter of love, a desire for a new life, and a new way of living? Am I really so desperate for a new way of life that I am willing to go behind my own father's back? None of this is about what I want for myself. I want to be part of the change that is sweeping through my country. I want women to be able to serve a purpose, not merely be a decoration for the pleasure of men. I want to educate girls and young boys. I want to help others, those whose lives have been blighted by oppression and poverty, through terrible circumstance, through no fault of their own. Two of the men get up, bow to me, and smile disrespectfully. Then they leave. I feel glad for a very brief moment that my palace does not allow me much contact with men. As they walk out, I think of my dear brother Omar and my father and my childhood; of the pointless war that has just ended; of Turkey, my mother's homeland; of Maman's life as a servant girl in the house of the sultan, her marriage to my father, and her elevation to her position of sultana today. In terms of wealth, I am a privileged woman, so I must do what I can to make things better for others in the future. If my money can help others, then so be it.

Hassan turns to me. "Anton has asked that I take you to his house so you can speak privately. Follow me."

CHAPTER SEVENTEEN

It was half past three in the morning by the time Farouk arrived at Littoni's place. He pushed through the tiny haret at the back of the Café Malta to a door hidden by a jacaranda tree. Anger slithered through him, pent-up but ready to burst out at the slightest provocation.

It was highly likely that Littoni was there, and Farouk wanted to surprise him so that he didn't have time to get on the defensive. He circled the doorknob with his hand, turned it quietly, then slipped into a tiny alcove leading to three doors. He stood still, holding his breath, listening.

Farouk heard the shuffling of papers and saw a light coming from under one of the doors. He moved towards it. There was no time to lose and no nice way of saying what he had to say.

"Farouk?" Littoni gasped, looking up from the desk, where he sat hunched over several maps spread out on the table. "What the hell are you doing here?"

Farouk reached over and grabbed Littoni by the lapels, pulling him violently from his seat.

"What in the name of Allah did you do that for, Littoni? She's going to the police. She's going to report the burglary to the police."

Littoni gulped back breathless splutters, his eyes bulging in their sockets, his hands splaying for something to grasp onto.

Farouk threw him back against the wall. Littoni closed his eyes as his body collided with it.

"Well?" Farouk spat, ramming his face up close to Littoni's. "The girl's house? You weren't very clever, were you?"

Littoni struggled to catch his breath.

"I'm convinced there's a coded document in Ibrahim's house, detailed plans of Issawi's next offensive, the schedule for their next raids. Mustafa is an excellent decoder. It was simply a matter of finding it. The house is not big. It wouldn't have taken long."

Farouk picked Littoni up by his shirt collar once more and pinned him up against the wall, the veins on his forehead pulsing with rage.

"But you didn't find it, did you?" he snarled.

Littoni stared at him through bloodshot eyes. He had never seen Farouk so angry. The man had lost his mind. Littoni had no idea what he was going to do next. Then Farouk withdrew the piece of paper, he suspected was encoded with Issawi's plans, and waved it in Littoni's face.

"Is this what you were looking for?" he said.

Littoni's eyes were the size of dinner plates. He tried to grab the document from Farouk's hand, but Farouk waved it out of his reach.

"Sorry," he said. "Not for amateurs."

"Is that it? Where did you find it? In her house? How did you get it?"

Farouk stepped back, waving the document, then he folded it up and slipped it in the top pocket of his jacket.

"None of that matters, Littoni. I'll just tell you one thing. Judging from what Issawi's networks have up their sleeve, your little plan to go in with a time bomb will never work. You might as well give up right now."

"You evil snake," Littoni shouted. "You're dead, Farouk. You'll see. You'll pay."

In the blink of an eye, Farouk seized his lapels once more and flung him across the room, then kicked him in the stomach as he lay spread-eagled near the door.

Littoni spluttered, spat out bile, then crawled up on all fours, trying to stand.

"Help me up, you imbecile."

Farouk stuck out his hand and helped Littoni to his feet. Littoni pulled a handkerchief from his pocket and wiped his mouth.

Littoni grabbed the wall to steady himself. "Be careful, Farouk," he said, his eyes narrowing with hatred.

"Or what?" Farouk shot back, clenching his fists in front of Littoni's throat, but Littoni batted them away.

"I have my men, and we're watching you. Sectors ten through twenty are on my side. You know the game. I'll be the new president once we've ousted the king and his chief advisor. Do you really want to get on the wrong side of the new president of Egypt, me—Omar bin Mohammod? I can finally ditch my aliases and be proud of who I really am—not like you, Farouk, forced to return to Egypt in shame. Remember, sectors ten to twenty are the chemical warfare sectors—they're the ones I need on my side. We can do without you."

Farouk wasn't going to take any more of Littoni's threats. In one swift motion, he stepped around him, wrapped his arm around Littoni's chest, and twisted him into an arm lock. From this position, he could whisper in his ear and get his message across.

"You'd better tell Hamid, Hossein, and al-Dyn to destroy the dynamite, bury it somewhere in the desert. My journalists are collating the reports on what's happening in Issawi's camp. The night of the twentieth, the night of the celebrations, the whole of Cairo will be on high alert. Now you've risked everything by ransacking the girl's house. I was with her at Achmed's party. I talked to her. She doesn't know anything. She's an innocent. Ibrahim was involved in this, but his wife wasn't. Now she's doubly suspicious, and she'll go to the police at the first opportunity. They'll dust the place, take fingerprints. They probably have every conceivable bit of information on you in their dossiers. It's only a matter of time—hours in fact—before you're picked up, and once they've got you, the whole organisation will start to tumble like a house of cards and Issawi will have slipped through our fingers yet again."

Littoni struggled against Farouk's arm, but the man was strong. It made Littoni regret his declining stamina.

"Al-Dyn has reported back. Issawi was at his club tonight. He overheard him talking to his secretary. There are plans for increased security all-round, so where does that leave us? With the need for a new strategy? A change of time and place? I don't think so. We'll manage one way or another, Farouk. Everything is ready.

"Threaten me all you want with sectors ten through twenty. You think the men in the souks and the hotels, working men will come out in support of you? You, an ousted army general with a big chip on your shoulder. You know nothing of the men in sectors ten to twenty. I know these men, know their families."

He released his arm and pushed Littoni away, then headed for the door.

"Leave the girl alone, Littoni," he said. "Go near her house again and I'll kill you." Farouk pushed his way back out through the haret. Mission accomplished, he was going home to Zamalek.

The journal of Hezba Iqbal Sultan Hanim al-Shezira,
Kerdassa, August 23, 1919

I walk with Hassan down a narrow street to the far end of the village. Men sit outside their shops and smoke. Young boys run around laughing and shouting out little songs. It is now very late, and the earth smells of fire. We come to a squat mud-brick house, similar to the others in the village. Hassan knocks on the door of a house and then opens it. I duck down to enter and remove my cap. Monsieur Alexandre is standing in the far corner of the room, his back to us. He turns around.

"Anton, you have a visitor," Hassan says matter-of-factly.

Alexandre bows and says, "Thank you, Hassan. You can go."

Hassan leaves. We are alone. I stand in silence, watching him. My heart is pounding in my chest. He is dressed in a loose, pale jalaba. Around his head he wears a turban. He comes to me, reaches for my hand, and kisses it. Little flames course through me. I catch his gaze, his scent.

"We haven't much time," I say. "Al-Shezira is very close. He will be at my palace very, very soon. And then I will have to leave for Minya."

He puts his finger to my lips to hush me. I close my eyes. In the darkness of the hut, he wraps his arms around me and holds me against him. In the space of a second, I forget my despicable, torturous marriage and my hateful life at the palace. My body ripples, little shivers pulsating inside me.

Alexandre steers me towards a low couch, his finger still on my mouth. I can hear the thump of his heart. He lays me down, unbuttons my jacket, slips his hand inside, against my warm flesh. He sweeps his hand over my face and hair. Then he disengages himself, removes my boots and trousers, and throws a blanket over us.

"Hush," he says.

He lies down with me. He traces a line with his finger from my forehead to my breasts and then gently gathers me to him, kissing my mouth slowly and tenderly.

When he has removed his clothes and turban, he teases me with little kisses until my breasts and my body are quivering. Then his mouth makes its way to the crest of my womanhood.

Later, in the darkness, I look into his eyes. I feel the hard heat of him as his thighs cover mine. I taste his breath, absorb the fire from him. My body jolts as he joins his own flesh with mine. As we move together, I forget who I am, forget where I have come from. It is only when he wrenches himself from me that I realise that perhaps for the sake of honour I should have stopped him. But I know that I will become his wife and together we can plan for a better Egypt. I want to be by his side, fighting, as he fights. Years ago when I was forced to do my duty as a wife, I cried because I did not want al-Shezira in this way. Now I am different. I want to love Alexandre as a wife loves her husband, physically and with every bit of passion she has. Convention will not stop me. Alexandre caresses my face and after a while he speaks. I have no qualms about being Alexandre's lover. He is my true love—my one and only love—and in my heart, I know that to be with him is my destiny.

Warm flutters ripple through me. I want to hold on to this moment forever. I do not want to go back to al-Qahire. I want to be free among the stars of Africa, a child of the earth.

"I have heard talk of al-Shezira's plans to reclaim all the land within a fifty-mile radius of his palace for himself. This will destroy hundreds of businesses. Your husband has a great deal of political power, but the Rebel Corps cannot allow this to happen. I have many friends among the traders and the farmers, and I know for a fact that many families' lives have been ruined by al-Shezira. He is not a man who pays his debts or keeps his honour. He has enslaved many of the young boys who work the farms for their fathers, and these boys have been carted off as auxiliary soldiers, leaving their families struggling. He has bought up acres of cotton land for nothing and is now reaping extraordinary profits. He plans to do this again in Minya."

I turn away and my tears start to flow.

"Yes," I say, "yes, I know."

He tilts my chin with his finger. "What we are attempting is dangerous, Hezba, but we cannot sit idly by and let this man have his way. The revolution will start with the destruction of al-Shezira's power. By destroying the power he holds, we will change things for good. Al-Shezira and the British are one and the same—you know that, don't you. To get rid of the British, we must start by getting rid of al-Shezira and his political associates. Only then we can restore the power to the people of this country. I know you want that too. With your money and your connections, all this is possible."

I shake my head in despair and humiliation at being al-Shezira's wife and with the knowledge that my father, the sultan, is an associate of his.

"But Hassan and Aalim seem to despise me. They don't appear to want my money or my help."

"Ignore them," he whispers. "They are humble fellah. It will take them longer to get used to the idea of a woman helping us. They are ignorant, uneducated, but deep down they are good men and we are all working for the same thing, for Egypt."

CHAPTER EIGHTEEN

Farouk arrived home just as the eastern sky began to show signs of dawn. Instead of entering the house, however, he went around the side to the garden and sat down on the bench by the fountain. He needed to think. The girl would be upstairs in the blue bedroom, where he'd instructed Gigis to put her.

The sun was rising now, and gold-tinged clouds broke through the black rim of the night sky. Light began to flood the streets of Zamalek. He could not go to bed. He was far too agitated to sleep. He plucked the document the girl had given him out of his pocket and started to read.

At first he didn't understand the code. His mind kept wandering to Littoni and what he had said. The ten sectors on the east side of the city were all personal friends of Farouk's. He counted at least fifty of them, knew their operations, where they worked, what their aliases were, how many code names they operated under, their covers, their fields of speciality, how often they compiled their reports, how their reports were transmitted, how many of the men were decoders, how good they were at their jobs, how many men had access to radio transmitters, who the subagents were—and yet Littoni had tried to fool him into believing he was on his own.

It worried him that Littoni had brainwashed the lot of them into taking part in Littoni's version of the revolution. A thug's revolution was what Littoni wanted—followed by a dictatorship with himself at the helm. But if Littoni were to become Egypt's ruler, it would only result in more poverty for the country, more civilian deaths, and no progress. The country would soon be on its knees and at the mercy of the Germans. He had to get word to Nemmat, fine-tune his plan, and inform her that Ali and Mitali Khaldun were ready to move in on Issawi on the sixteenth, three days from now.

He continued to try to decipher the coded document. He'd once been a skilled code-cracker. He peered closer. The code appeared to address Ibrahim as a member of Security Operations. Yes, he could crack that much. But of Security's specific plans to move in on the X? Well, that was where the code got tricky. Farouk was sure that the document had been double-coded. He would need time to work it out.

He looked up and saw the dark shape he knew to be Gigis standing at the top of the stone steps that led to the terrace. He folded the paper and slipped it back into his jacket, waved to his servant, got up and walked towards him.

"Is the madame asleep?" he asked.

"Yes, sir, I believe so," Gigis replied. "I brought her some tea around half past three and haven't heard a sound since then."

"She needed my help," Farouk said, shaking his head sadly.

"Yes, sir."

"You can take the day off, Gigis," Farouk continued. "But give me the keys to the car. I'll need it."

"Thank you, sir," Gigis said, fumbling in his pocket for the keys.

"Now go." Farouk smiled. "You look half dead from lack of sleep. Have you been waiting for me?"

"Yes, sir."

Farouk patted the boy on the shoulder.

"Well, I'm here now. The madame is safe, and you can go and get some sleep."

Gigis smiled, turned, and left.

Farouk followed him inside, discarded his jacket, and stood for a moment, thinking. Then he climbed the marble staircase to the first floor and padded along the carpeted corridor to the blue room. He just wanted to see her. He could picture her—her pale, striking youth, her unblemished features unmarked by life, her still-forming soul swelling to take its place inside her nearly adult body—yet she had married the evil Ibrahim; it didn't add up. Was there more to her? Was her innocence a useful foil?

He quietly opened the door. In the gloom, he could see her body lying motionless under the sheets. Her dress had been discarded on the chair in the far corner. Her hand clutched the edge of the cotton, like a child seeking comfort. The balcony doors had been flung wide open. Splashes of dawn bathed the room in a soft morning glow. He tiptoed towards the bed and sat down on the edge of it, never taking his eyes off her. Her hair was wild and loose and splayed out like a fan on the white pillow. Her mouth was downturned, her thick black eyebrows highly visible in the shuttered light. He longed to touch her long, straight nose and run his finger gently along the bridge of it towards the pout of her mouth, but he did nothing. He just sat and stared at her. And then he let his eyes wander down to her shoulders and her breasts, partially covered by the cotton sheet.

He raised his hand and let it hover over her skin, not daring to touch her, his breath quickening, becoming laboured, a painful sensation jabbing at him from within his stomach and down around the base of his spine and his groin.

She stirred slowly, moaning slightly in her sleep but did not wake up. He sat back and bit his lip as the haunting refrain of the muezzins signalled the start of a new day.

The journal of Hezba Iqbal Sultan Hanim al-Shezira,
Kerdassa, August 23, 1919

Alexandre gets dressed. I do too. I wish we had more time together. But we don't. I will have to be happy with the feeling of him inside me as I ride back to al-Qahire.

"You know what we have to do, don't you, Hezba?"

"Yes."

"Then it is kismet that you have to go to Minya," he says.

I nod slowly. I know what he is talking about. It is our secret.

"Yes," I say. "I know."

"My sister tells me you want to go to Paris or London where you have friends, that you have begged your family to be released from this marriage."

"Yes."

"Your husband will not divorce you?"

"No, he will not. He wants me to give him children. I am the youngest of his wives, you see, and I have not yet fulfilled my duty."

"And you cannot divorce him?"

"My papa will not allow it. My marriage to al-Shezira is an important political alliance. He has promised to disown me if I divorce my husband."

"Is your father really so cruel, Hezba?"

"My father does not love me. Something happened between us a long time ago. Something even I don't understand. When I went to live in the harem, my papa stopped showing me affection. Our relationship became almost like that of a frustrated teacher and his pupil."

I swallow hard. It was hard talking about Papa like that. I study Alexandre's face as he dresses. Suddenly I feel a pang of fear that I am leaving myself too open, too vulnerable, that I am putting all my hopes in the hands of my lover and I should not be doing this.

I wonder why I have told him these things, things that are so close to my heart. I want to believe he is on my side, but how do I know? By telling him things, I make myself vulnerable to him.

Alexandre wraps his arms around me once more and whispers in my ear. "My men and I cannot forgive a man like al-Shezira for robbing our friends and their families of money and their livelihood. I want to make sure my friends' debts are repaid."

I slip my hand in my pocket and dig out the money I have brought him. He doesn't count it. He puts it in his pocket and kisses me tenderly on the mouth.

"Thank you. I will pass this on," he says. "It will buy us more weapons, more equipment. We are eternally grateful to you, Hezba."

CHAPTER NINETEEN

Aimee was having one of those dreams in which she knew she was dreaming. In her dream she saw a silky, hazy image of a silent court-yard tucked away behind the minarets and the mosques. The sun beat down unforgivingly on the hard pavement and a lone jaca-randa tree. In her dream she saw a pair of large hooded eyes, a hand decorated with henna playing nervously with the voluminous black cloth, in which a figure was draped from head to toe. She recog-nised the face of Fatima, and Azi was standing before her.

She woke up suddenly and cried out. Then she rubbed her hands over her face and calmed herself. She had been dreaming; that was all. She grabbed her dress and underclothes from the chair and went off in search of a bathroom. Two doors down from the bedroom she found one and locked herself in, squatting behind the door on the cold mosaic tiles. Then she turned on the taps and ran a warm bath. She sank into it and washed herself. She examined her thighs and her arms and her stomach and the dark hair between her legs; then she closed her eyes.

After towelling herself dry, she slipped on her underclothes and dress, smoothed her hair into a long plait down her back, and ran her hands over her face. Then she went back to the corridor and stood quietly, not knowing whether she should leave, write a note, or return to her ransacked house on Sharia Suleyman Pasha.

She wanted to thank the monsieur. Then she remembered. He had promised to take her to Ismailia today, to Lake Timsah, to the spot where Azi had been murdered.

She heard the sound of footsteps and saw him. He smiled brightly at her and stretched out his hands to greet her.

"You must be hungry, Madame. I've given my boy the day off, but I'll find something for you in the kitchen. Then we must leave for Ismailia."

Aimee tried to muster a smile.

"Thank you. You are very kind. You've helped me so much already."

He beckoned her to follow him, and together they walked to the kitchen.

"We'll eat outside in the garden," Farouk said.

Aimee quelled her beating heart and went to sit on the little bench near the fountain. A few minutes later, Farouk arrived with a tray of delicacies and two glasses of sweet tea. He handed her a glass and a plate of food.

They ate silently. Aimee stared at her plate and into her glass of tea. She did not want to look at him, but she could feel his eyes burning into her face. Reluctantly, she raised her head and gave him a timid smile.

"Why are you being so kind, Monsieur?" she asked him.

He looked away for a moment, then turned back towards her and met her gaze.

"I liked your husband," Farouk said. "And it stands to reason that I should want to help his young widow with any information that could lead to the arrest of those responsible for his murder."

Aimee hung her head and breathed deeply. He made everything sound so proper, so devoid of emotion. So why was her head swimming? Why did her body feel so weak?

"You are certain you want to go to Ismailia?" he asked. "You realise it's going to be hard for you?"

"I know, I know," she said solemnly, bowing her head. "But it might help me. In fact, I think it will."

"You must change your clothes," Farouk said abruptly, putting down his tea glass. He stood up and pulled her to her feet.

"My sister's bedroom is upstairs near the blue room where you slept. There are lots of clothes in the wardrobes. She was slender too, about your size. I'm sure you'll find something to fit you that will be suitable for the desert. Your dress and shoes are too dainty for this trip." She tried to protest, but he explained. "We must leave the car some distance from where we are going. I know that area. We have to walk through desert scrub to a little village. We will meet someone there, a friend. You would be better off in sensible clothes."

"Must I wear your sister's clothes?" Aimee asked.

Farouk laughed. "Well, nothing of mine will fit you. Now go, upstairs. It's the third room on the right. We'll leave as soon as you're ready."

Aimee found the room. It was musty, with the shutters tightly closed. She pulled some clothes out of the trunk, dressed, and returned to the garden.

"That's better." He smiled, cocking his head at her. "You look remarkably similar, dressed in her clothes." But his voice fell away, and he bit his lip.

"Similar? What do you mean?" she asked.

His eyes flickered sadly. "My sister. In those clothes, you remind me of her. Your eyes are a similar colour and you have the same slight physique. She was a beauty too, much fairer than you with sun-bleached hair but just as striking."

Aimee blushed inwardly. "You have no photograph? No painting?" she asked.

"I don't like to keep things like that. I keep it all in my memory."

He suddenly looked so young, like a little boy. "Finish your tea and we'll go. I have to stop off somewhere first; I hope you don't mind?"

Aimee eyed him curiously. "No, of course not."

"It won't take long," he said. "I have to give a message to my friend Nasser at Nasser's Trinkets in the Muski district. Then we'll be on our way."

"I'm ready," she said.

Farouk led the way to the garage. As he opened the garage door, Aimee asked, "Were you never married, Monsieur Farouk?"

He was silent as he opened the car door for her and she slid into her seat. While he started the engine, she saw that his mouth was pinched, as though he were trying to repress a thought. She realised she had touched a raw nerve.

"I would like to have been," he said as he pulled onto the road. His brow was wrinkled; his long nose twitched. He wound down his window and cursed a group of young boys kicking stones along the road, lingering too long behind donkeys and carts and little trolleys of wares.

"I would have been a most unsuitable husband for any woman."

"Oh, really?"

"I travel a great deal, and I have a restless heart. It's like a sickness. I have given myself to many peoples and places, but I have not yet managed to give my heart to one woman, to settle into family life. And now I am old. I don't see myself changing."

She stared at the road ahead.

"Is it far to Lake Timsah?"

"Not too far. The journey will take about one-and-a-half hours, assuming that we don't encounter any trouble on the road."

"What sort of trouble?"

"There are road blocks, inspection of papers. But you mustn't worry. We should have no problem."

But first they had to go to the Muski district. Farouk parked his car opposite Nasser's Trinkets and went across the street, while Aimee stayed in the car. A man greeted him in front of the shop. He pulled Farouk into his arms and kissed him on both cheeks, shaking his hand at the same time. The man appeared to be talking a hundred miles a minute while Farouk just nodded and shook his head every now and again, staring at the cracked pavement. But as the two of them stood there, Aimee saw the man slip something into Farouk's hand. A few minutes later, Farouk returned to the car, started the engine, and pulled away. They drove in silence, out towards the Moquattam Hills, and then on to the desert road to Ismailia.

The heat of the day was intensifying. Farouk reached behind him, pulled a thermos of cold water from behind the seat, and handed it to Aimee. She took it and drank, but she couldn't stop thinking about the exchange between Farouk and the man at Nasser's Trinkets. For some reason, she had a bad feeling about it. This was not the Egypt of Thomas Cook and Baedeker. She thought about the desert and the long dusty roads to the Sinai, the beach resorts at Alexandria, the houseboats on the Nile and Cairo's palm-fringed mansions, the ragged cafés and clubs, the bars and brothels, the potholed streets, the cracked sun-baked walls of the souks, the mosques and the churches, the throngs of tired citizens starting every day with a new optimism, then going to bed every night with something taken from them, something inextricably vacant.

And she wondered at the soul of Egypt, closing her eyes against the silken link she felt with the soil she walked on every day. She was more French than Egyptian, more European than Ottoman. Sophie belonged. She had an identity, a nationality. She belonged to her parents, to her country, to her uncle, Tony Sedgewick. Aimee wanted to belong—to her father, to her mother, to the traces of desert dust and sky lying flat over a bustling, dry, and irrepressible city—but she felt rootless. Her mother's diary, her aunt, her birth, the story of her early life were hidden from her. She had come back to Cairo full of hope, but she didn't know what was there for her anymore.

"Thanks," he said as he took the flask from her and took a drink himself. He handed her the flask, and she pushed it under her legs.

"If you never married, Monsieur, then you have no children, no family. You are like me."

Farouk smiled and shot her a sideways glance. "Yes, I suppose we are both orphans. I told you my parents died when I was quite young. My mother died first. She was an Egyptian servant girl my father had taken as his own personal plaything. She was just sixteen when she gave birth to me, and she died when I was five or six. I don't remember her. And my father was not a pleasant man. He was extremely rich, but he hated me. He was a drunk, a violent man. And my sister was only my half sister. We didn't share the same mother."

Aimee leaned back and closed her eyes. "Is that why you left home and travelled so much?"

His features hardened. She was asking too many questions.

He continued. "When I was twenty, I fell ill. I had pneumonia. I remained weak for a long time and couldn't do much for myself. One day Papa beat me so hard I crawled away in my own blood.

That was when I made the decision to leave and never, ever go back. And I was true to my word. I was penniless, so I went to live for a while with my sister, who had married by then. Two years later, when I got word that my father had died—an obese drunk lying in a pool of his own excrement—I went out and celebrated. It was the happiest day of my life."

Her eyes widened. She swivelled her body around in her seat and stared at him. He spoke without bitterness. It was a story he obviously knew well, that no longer shocked him. He had lived with it his whole life.

"I've shocked you, Madame Ibrahim," he said, turning his eyes from the road for a moment and smiling at her. He wondered whether he should risk bringing up Azi and Issawi again, but he decided against it for the time being.

"You should take heart in never having known such brutality. You've known love. You married and but for the will of Allah, you would have had a happy marriage, children perhaps, a family. You had a husband who loved you, despite his possible infidelity, and you have a dear friend here in Cairo. You're blessed. There are many people in this world far lonelier than you."

She stared ahead, blinded by the sunlight. Farouk opened the glove box, dug out a pair of black sunglasses, and handed them to her.

"My husband did not love me," she whispered. "His affair with a brothel-keeper is enough to prove that." She felt a stab of jealousy as she spoke.

He didn't reply, instead craning his neck to see what was happening up ahead. She could see an army truck and a group of men waving them down.

"What's happening? Why are we slowing down?"

He bit his lip. "Whatever happens, don't say anything. Let me do all the talking."

He stopped the car. A soldier walked round to the driver's side and spoke in French.

"Where are you going?"

"Ismailia," Farouk said, "to visit friends."

"Papers," the soldier said.

Farouk slid his hand into his inside pocket and pulled out his identity papers.

The soldier peered at them closely, studied Farouk's face, and looked at Aimee. In one fluid movement, he pulled a revolver from inside his jacket and pointed it at them. His face was straining, the veins on his temples standing out against his face.

"Get out of the car, both of you," he shouted. "Quickly. Don't try anything stupid."

Aimee froze in her seat, her heart banging wildly in her throat and chest. And the way Farouk had grabbed and squeezed her hand, jerking his head up towards a sand dune, confirmed everything. This wasn't an ordinary security check.

Five uniformed guardsmen were marching towards them with rifles over their shoulders, shouting at the top of their voices in Arabic.

The journal of Hezba Iqbal Sultan Hanim al-Shezira,
Kerdassa, August 23, 1919

The night grows colder. I hear a sound and I freeze. It is faint at first, but it is an ominous sound, the sound of thunder in the distance, low and dark and growing louder all the time.

I look at Alexandre, who soothes me with a touch of his hand on my arm.

"Come with me," he says. His eyes are strained with worry as we leave the hut. Anton shouts for his men. I hide in the shadow of the doorway, not sure exactly what I should do. I watch in horror as three horsemen ride up, pale, nasty looking men, British officials, no doubt, in government uniform, looking very like the official Turkish zaptieh on parade, their uniforms more elaborate than any I have seen before. They are obviously government officials and not soldiers.

If they discover I am a woman beneath my Australian Light Horse uniform, I will be reported. At first, I hear nothing but the sound of restless horses, pulling against their reins, their hooves pounding the dirt. The horsemen are surveying the village scene suspiciously.

Then one of them speaks. "We are here under authority to investigate an illegal meeting taking place. Do any of you fellows know anything about this?"

One of Anton's group speaks up in strained, heavily accented English. "We are humble farmers, Sayyid. We are celebrating a festival this evening. There is no one in this village acting in an inappropriate way. You would be the first to know if there was."

I catch the arrogance in the man's voice.

"You," shouts one of the horsemen at one of Alexandre's men. "What are you hiding in your robes?"

I hold my breath.

"Give it to me," he orders.

I hear the men muttering in Arabic, interspersed with a few words of French.

One of Alexandre's men speaks. "May I ask you under whose authority you have ridden out to Kerdassa to interrogate us?"

Before they have a chance to reply, he says in a more respectful voice, "We are quiet people here and don't want any trouble."

The horseman dismounts and says, "High Commissioner Wingate has ordered an investigation into illegal meetings. We have orders from headquarters to search rural villages near Cairo for aggressor activity. So do as you are told and hand over what you're hiding."

A scuffle ensues. Aalim draws a dagger. The horsemen draw out their pistols.

"Stand back, keep out of the way," someone shouts. The three horsemen steady their horses with their pistols pointed directly at Aalim. I pray quietly to my God. Aalim is poised with the dagger held high over his head, crying out, "Allah, Allah."

CHAPTER TWENTY

The soldier with the revolver lunged forward, flung open Farouk's door, and stepped back, pointing the gun at him at eye level. Trembling, Aimee got out of her side of the car, arms raised in the air. The soldier pulled Farouk around the car and pushed him next to Aimee. Farouk could see her frightened eyes taking in the five officers marching towards them. He scanned the desert, spread like a yellow carpet all around them; date palm, and acacia trees and a ramshackle service station dotted the road ahead. In the distance he could see a group of old men in long, pale blue jalabas trailing donkeys, accompanied by two large chador-shrouded women, trekking slowly back to Cairo. He saw a huge billboard covered in metallic red and chrome—an advertisement for Coca-Cola; two young men were smoking and laughing underneath it. No one seemed to be taking any notice of them.

The five officers came to a stop a few feet away. Another soldier appeared from behind the car, walked towards Farouk, and gave him a shove. "Move," one of them shouted, "that way."

Farouk felt a sharp jab as the young soldier pushed the revolver into his back. They were marched towards the sand dune from which the five of them had appeared. He saw a mud-brick house and a shack in a little clearing in the distance.

When they reached the hut, Farouk and Aimee were pushed inside. As his eyes adjusted to the gloom, he tried to swallow an angry breath. Damn them all, he thought. He'd been followed, that much was obvious. He was losing his touch. He'd been careful but not careful enough.

The officers followed them in. One of them adjusted a little window so there was some light. Farouk and Aimee were seated at a table and tied agonisingly tightly to their seats with some rope.

The young soldier with the revolver took up his place in front of them, arm outstretched, revolver at the ready. Farouk saw perspiration pouring down Aimee's face. She was licking her lips, her face contorted with fear. He hated himself for getting her tangled up in this.

"What's this all about?" Farouk said, but before he had a chance to say another word, one of the officers struck him across the face with his fist.

"Silence."

Farouk's jaw and cheek tingled. He ran his tongue over his mouth and felt a warm thick trickle of blood slide down his chin onto his white shirt. He could smell its sulphurous scent. He steadied his gaze to regain composure.

One of the men bent down beside him and waved his identity papers at him, sneering as he spoke.

"Do you think you've fooled us, Mustafa Alim?"

Two stony-faced men in suits entered the hut. Farouk felt a deep hatred well up inside him.

"What do you want? Who the hell are you?" Farouk said quietly.

The men laughed. One of them started to circle Farouk's chair, speaking as he went.

"My name is Hilali. This is Gamal. These are three of our officers."

Farouk closed his eyes.

"Our names mean nothing to you, Sayyid? I am the head of Secret Operations for Issawi Pasha, Sayyid."

Farouk flinched, his veins bursting with poisonous hatred, but he remained silent.

"You know Issawi Pasha, Sayyid?"

"Is there a single man or woman in the whole of Egypt who does not know who Issawi is?"

Gamal and Hilali looked at each other and smiled.

"You speak very passionately, Sayyid, which makes us believe you have strong feelings about Issawi Pasha."

Farouk swallowed hard.

"It is easy to have strong feelings about a corrupt despot."

"So you are a Nationalist, Sayyid?"

Farouk sank back into silence.

"What was your business at Nasser's Trinkets in the Muski?"

Farouk blinked. "How—?" he said before Hilali cut him off.

"You were being followed."

"I was visiting my friend there, simply a social call," Farouk said.

Gamal shook his head.

Hilali said, "Men, search him."

The three officers lunged forward and stripped Farouk of his clothes. They fumbled through every pocket until they found what they were looking for.

"A matchbox," Gamal said with satisfaction, sliding open the cardboard.

He withdrew a little packet from the box, unfolded it, then sniffed it.

"Heroin."

"But you're not a drug-taker, Sayyid. If our sources are correct, Mustafa Alim is a family man, a Khalili tailor, and an X sector member. You must have bought the drug from Nasser Sayyid to use for another purpose?"

Farouk remained silent. He simply sat there, nearly naked in his white undergarments, tied to his chair, staring Hilali in the eye, never once averting his glance.

"Is Nasser of Nasser's Trinkets one of the X's letter boxes?" Gamal demanded.

The young soldier advanced on Farouk, pointing his revolver squarely between his eyes.

"I don't know what you are talking about," Farouk said without flinching.

Suddenly men's voices were heard outside. Gamal, Hilali, and their officers sprung to attention. Gamal jerked his head, and he and Hilali went outside.

Farouk strained to hear what was going on. When Hilali and Gamal returned, they were followed by a thickset older man with white hair peeking out from under a general's cap. Hilali and Gamal stood erect, clicked their heels together, and bowed.

"Al-Alfi Pasha," they said in unison.

The man stood back from the others on the far side of the room. He leaned against the wall, then said, "Get them talking, Hilali. I have orders to report back to Issawi on any progress when I meet with him tonight. He does not want to be disappointed."

Farouk scrutinised the man and recognised him as one of Issawi's sidekicks. His body tensed.

"Who is the mastermind behind the X, Sayyid?" Hilali snarled.

Farouk said nothing and shot Aimee a look of warning not to say anything. His eyes darted from face to face, trying to anticipate what was going to happen next.

"Fine, the Sayyid doesn't want to talk. Men, you know what Issawi Pasha has ordered you to do."

They advanced on Farouk. One of them swung behind him, withdrew a knife from his pocket, pulled Farouk's head back by the hair, and positioned the knife over his throat.

The journal of Hezba Iqbal Sultan Hanim al-Shezira,
Kerdassa, August 23, 1919

The officers are violent men. They are looking for any excuse to haul Alexandre and his men away and charge them with being under-ground aggressors. If they are taken back to Cairo, the plans for the revolution will come to nothing. I edge my way backwards against the door and somehow—as though my God is punishing me—I knock over a small bundle of sticks propped up against the house. The horsemen swing round. They dismount and walk over. One of them pulls off my cap. My hair, unravelled because of our lovemaking, cascades down my back.

"Well, well a little Gyppy girl," the older one says, his watery blue eyes shining with contempt.

Then one of the other horsemen speaks, the one with the red hair and freckles, who looks as though he is no older than I am.

"We should take her with us, until this group confesses," he says.

"I am sure these men only want to cooperate with you," I say in French, but this does not seem to please them.

"We don't speak French, Little Missy Gyppy Girl," the older, evil-looking one says. They point their pistols at me now, all three staring at me.

"Please put down your guns, gentlemen," I say in very broken English.

Alexandre shouts. "Leave her alone. She is not involved. Don't touch her."

But the horseman ignores him. "What a beautiful voice you have, Missy," he says.

"Where did you learn to speak the King's English?"

I do not say anything, but I notice Alexandre is moving up behind them with a dagger raised high above his head.

"What? Little Gyppy Missy has lost her tongue? Why don't you give us a kiss then, girlie?"

This is more than I can bear and I explode, a torrent of Arabic expletives bursting from my mouth.

"Get her," one of the Englishmen says, and they lunge at me, forcing their lips onto mine. Their hands are on my breasts, inside my jacket, between my legs, and around my throat. I scream in terror.

Alexandre and his men are on them at once, twisting their arms behind their backs. I run inside the hut, rubbing my mouth with my sleeve in disgust.

"We should kill you right now," Alexandre hisses at them. "How dare you touch one of our women," he screams in Arabic, his voice unrecognisable. "How dare you. Now mount your horses and leave before we shoot you all."

They follow his orders.

"We'll be back for you lot. We know your faces, you bloody Gyppies. We know who you are."

CHAPTER TWENTY-ONE

Aimee blacked out. The glint of the knife, the look of hatred in Farouk's eye as his head was forced back, Hilali's sneering whispers, the stench of human perspiration all washed over her, and the world dissolved about her. When she awoke, she moaned and opened her eyes. For a few seconds she didn't know where she was. Trying to move her neck, she cried out in pain. She was lying sideways on the mud floor, still strapped to her chair. A line of sweat was trickling down her nose.

"Lift her up," Gamal ordered the soldier.

The chair was lifted upright. The soldier bent down and pulled the ropes tighter. She winced and wriggled, her head throbbing. "I need a drink," she croaked. "I need water."

The soldier flashed a look at Gamal who nodded. The soldier poured some water in a dirty tumbler and lifted it to her lips. She could see a dead fly floating in the cup. She pursed her lips and sucked a little water. The fly brushed her lips. Aimee squeezed her eyes shut in disgust.

She tried to move her head to see what had happened to Farouk, but her neck and spine felt bruised. Out of the corner of her eye she managed to get a tiny glimpse, a flash of white. He was still undressed, in his undershorts, but a bandage was now tied tightly over his mouth.

She felt something brush against her cheek. Her head flew round to see Gamal standing an inch away from her. He knelt in front of her and ran his hand salaciously over her face. Aimee froze and closed her eyes.

"It's your turn to talk, lady," Gamal said cloyingly.

Her breath stalled in her mouth, and a shiver of fear coursed through her. He took hold of her chin between his fingers, smiling down at her from where he squatted.

"We know your connection with the X, Sayyida. You are no doubt one of their agents, working in one of their sectors. But which one? We know there are two women who head up sector operations. Where do you live? You'd better tell us, because we'll find out anyway. We'll search your house. We'll find out exactly who you are."

She studied the man's yellowy brown eyes. Seconds passed. Minutes.

"I don't know what—?"

The man Gamal jumped up, leaned forward, and pushed his face up against hers. Aimee recoiled against her chair, her eyes wide with fear.

"I'm losing patience, Sayyida. Your companion, Mustafa Alim, is on our wanted list. I want the names of every person you and Alim have been in contact with in the last forty-eight hours, their addresses too."

Aimee looked at Farouk.

"You've got the wrong man, Monsieur," Aimee whispered. "This man is a friend of my husband. He is taking me to visit some relatives near Timsah. I know nothing of this group you are talking about."

Gamal stood back on his heels, his eyes narrowing in thought. It was obvious to her from the way his eyes were darting from her face to Farouk's that maybe she had convinced him, however briefly, that she really did know nothing. But then, he seemed to change his mind. Suddenly his breath caressed her face again and his mouth was inches from hers.

"I'll give you and Sayyid Alim some time to think about the lies you have just told me," he sneered. "Maybe when you have been left locked in this oven without water for a few hours, you'll come to your senses and provide us with the information we want."

"If not, we'll simply have to follow orders. And in case you don't know what that means—arrested suspects who don't comply will be tortured, in compliance with Issawi Pasha's strict laws governing the treatment of terrorist networks in this country."

The men disappeared. She heard them instruct a lone soldier to stand guard outside the door, heard the key in the door turn, and then twisted her body around to try to get a good look at Farouk.

The journal of Hezba Iqbal Sultan Hanim al-Shezira,
Cairo, August 25, 1919

Two days have passed since Kerdassa. I am back at the Sarai and wish I had never returned. Al-Shezira is here with his party. He will not leave without me this time. Five years ago I falsified a fit of depression and advancing insanity to be free of him. And my plan worked for a while—I was left alone for a long time.

Now there is to be no more reprieve for me. I will be stripped of all my body hair, scrubbed clean, perfumed, dressed, and made ready to escort my husband. I loathe the thought of having to smile in a certain way—a way that is alluring for my husband—when inside my blood boils with rage.

Rachid informs me of al-Shezira's arrival as I lie on the roof garden, smoking cigarettes in the night air.

"Mistress, the pasha has installed himself in the salamlik. His wives and their servants are being conveyed to their harem apartments. The pasha has requested your company tonight. We have orders to prepare you."

I get up and walk to the edge of the roof garden and look out over the city. I can see the Nile shimmering in the moonlight.

"Tell the pasha I am not well enough to receive him tonight. I will see him tomorrow."

Rachid twitches nervously. Something has happened to him. He is changed. He stands there, holding a silver tray on which I can see a small golden box.

"What is that?" I ask him, nodding at the tray.

"Your husband has sent you a little gift, some jewels for you to wear for him."

I go to Rachid and stroke his cheek tenderly. Still he does not move. He does not soften under my touch like he usually does. He does not smile at me.

"Rachid, what's wrong?" I ask him.

"I am your servant, Hezba. I must obey orders." I stare at him in amazement. Then I tell him to go and tell my husband what I have said. But still Rachid does not move.

"Hezba, the al-Shezira pasha is quite firm. He will see you tonight. He has given orders that you be brought to his apartment. It must be done."

A sound wafts up from below, music. Flutes are being played. I can hear clapping. The men are being entertained. No doubt a girl, a young beautiful girl with eyes of fire but a heart of stone, is entertaining them.

"If Allah wills it," I say, "I will receive my husband tomorrow but not tonight. I have heard that Saiza will deliver tonight. I must be ready to be with her if she needs me."

Finally Rachid bows. He does not argue this time as I expect him to. He backs through the archway leading to the stairs and is gone, leaving me feeling desolate.

Of course, it is unthinkable for me to defy the word of my husband. I go to my rooms, and through the mashrabiyya I see the men of al-Shezira's party leaving the palace, dressed in the ceremonial robes and tarboushes of their administration. Al-Shezira is not with them. I fear he has stayed behind and is probably now lying on some cushions, eating and smoking, perhaps with one of his wives, perhaps with the young beautiful dancer the men have just enjoyed watching.

I believe that the men of al-Shezira's party are attending a function at one of the European hotels, and I wonder why my husband does not go with them. Perhaps he is too old now for such frolicking. But then a black feeling comes over me and I know that despite my refusal to go to him, he will have his way.

CHAPTER TWENTY-TWO

Hamid had been sitting in his car outside Issawi's political head-quarters in Cairo for what seemed like ages. He pulled a packet of cigarettes out of his jacket pocket and lit one. This meeting had been going on for hours. He had seen Issawi enter the building. Now he had to see him leave it. Then he would follow him, as discreetly as possible. It was important to get an idea of his movements. If he were driven to an unusual address, Littoni would want to know.

Hamid and al-Dyn were already well aware of his normal routine—the meetings, the dull dinner parties, his frequent travels to the backwaters of Egypt for business purposes, war meetings, the Oxford for a little R & R. Wherever he went, he always rode in his bulletproof vehicle, his entourage on high alert.

At last there was movement. Hamid sat up abruptly, stubbed his cigarette out on the dashboard, and clutched the steering wheel of his car. Several men in formal government attire, neat suits and tarboushes, were leaving the building en masse.

A car drew up. Issawi got in. How easy it would be to shoot at him long range, but Littoni would never forgive him. Hamid followed the car eagerly with his eyes. He let it get a little way ahead, and then he turned the key in the ignition.

The journal of Hezba Iqbal Sultan Hanim al-Shezira,
Cairo, August 25, 1919

*I go and find Nawal. She is in her rooms, combing little Suleman's
hair, scolding him. Her servant is with her. She looks up in fright as I
burst through the door.*

"Hezba, what is it?"

"Nawal, he is here."

*She hands Suleman over to her servant and pulls the bell rope. Two
lower eunuchs arrive.*

*"Come with us to the hammam. Follow us, and bring our things,"
Nawal says to them. Suleman clutches his maman's skirts. Nawal kisses
him, then pushes him away, and we run quickly to the hammam. The
two eunuchs run after us, carrying little silk bags of ointments, perfumes, oils of bergamot, frangipani, rose and neroli, all in tiny bottles.*

*The hammam is located just a short walk through the acacia trees
at the back of our private garden, past the kiosk, the little French fountain, and the marble nymph. It is a large Turkish bath with a grand
main antechamber, tiled in delicate blue-black mosaic where the girls
and women leave their slippers.*

*I understand what Nawal is doing. If it is reported to al-Shezira
that his wife has gone to the hammam, he will believe that she is in
the middle of her womanly blood and she will be left alone—at least
temporarily.*

*We undress in the antechamber. Nawal strokes my cheek, wrapping
me in a loose cotton gown and freeing my hair so that it falls down my
back. She attends to herself. Here, for the time being, we are safe. We
can't be summoned. We have bought precious time. We walk through
a huge archway and through several rooms to the largest bath. It is hot
and steamy, always sending one into a dreamlike trance of relaxation.*

Dour-faced palace eunuchs walk up and down the side of the huge pool with towels, following some of the girls with mesmerised eyes. Usually I love the slow languid pace and the chance to be pampered, but tonight I feel like the living dead.

I wonder how many hours we can waste here, bathing, getting massaged, drinking coffee and eating pastries, smoking and talking. In my heart I want to leave the palace and go to Alexandre. I don't want to be here, in such close proximity to the man I am forced to call my husband.

I discard my robe, wrap a thin piece of cotton around my hips, and slip on my hammam clogs. I feel desperately unhappy, numb inside, and tired. I can't see a future. I long to lie down and let the strong arms of a slave caress my weary body, because Alexandre is not here. I still feel haunted by the awful scene at Kerdassa.

Nawal leads the way through the misty vapours to a row of chaises longues in the far corner of the bathhouse. There we stretch out and are pummelled and massaged by strong, warm hands. Then we wade deep into the hot aromatic bath. Nawal says nothing at first. Then after a while, she looks at me and says, "Are the rumours true, Hezba?"

"What rumours?"

"About Madame Virginie's brother."

'Yes," I say.

She looks at me wide-eyed, her black eyes darting across my face, trying to understand me. I lean back in the bath. I am getting used to the soft, sweet waters, and some feeling is starting to come back to my body.

"Why?" Nawal asks.

"Love," I say.

Nawal looks at me tiredly and says, "I've heard that Sayyid Alexandre Anton is not just a businessman. There are rumours that he is a political man. That's dangerous, Hezba. Because of your papa and our sultan."

I smile. Nawal doesn't understand.

"Alexandre is a loyal supporter of Sa'ad Zaghlul Pasha, our minister for education and leader of the Egyptian Nationalist Party, but that does not mean he is a political man. He is too busy with his work in trade."

I do not tell her about the Rebel Corps.

"That's not what I've heard, darling. I've been told he's a political Sayyid, a Bey."

"So what of it?" I say. Nawal falls silent and lies back in the water, staring at the ceiling. Her full breasts bob on the soft water, and her unblemished ochre-coloured skin glows.

"Don't listen to rumours, Nawal," I say. "Everything will be fine."

She smiles secretly.

"I trust you, Hezba, and you know my secrets too, so I won't say any more about it. I just want you to be careful. There is talk about you. The girls are laughing at you because you cause the sultan so many problems." I smile again, but I don't respond. I know there is talk about me. If I were a man, I would be celebrated, I would be an army general, but instead I am mocked because I speak my mind. I look at Nawal and think about what she said. I know about her love affair with Sigan, her slave.

She stretches out her hands and claps them together, and one of the eunuchs moves towards us. I recognise him to be Ibrahim. He smiles vaguely and bows. We step out of the hot bath into great cotton shrouds. They cling to our bodies, revealing every curve. We walk to a cool pool of freezing water, discard our gowns, and plunge in, crying out at the sensation of ice against our skin. With chattering teeth and clenched fists, Nawal tries to talk once more, but I can't stay in the cold pool for long.

I climb out and am greeted by another eunuch who holds out an elaborate hooded cloak for me, his head bowed. We are then covered from head to toe in coconut oil. Our skin is perfumed and massaged again. We are brought more coffee and sweet pastries and told to relax, but relaxation is impossible for me. My desire to leave the palace is growing stronger by the day.

As the tension in my body finally starts to dissolve, the most terrifying screams explode through the palace mashrabiyya.

CHAPTER TWENTY-THREE

Aimee felt paralysed, unable to move. She'd been sitting rigid in one position for what seemed like a very long time. The heat in the hut was unbearable, and her mouth was as parched as the desert sands outside. She knew she had to try and cut the rope slicing great grooves into her wrists, but what with? No indication had been given of how long it would be before the men returned. When they did, she knew all too well what would happen.

There was no time to waste. She decided to do something. She had to or she'd die. She squirmed on the chair, trying to jerk it across the floor by forcing it off the ground slightly. She managed to move enough to get a full view of Farouk.

She needed direction from him, but how? Could she interpret his eyes correctly? Based on his jerks and nods towards the door, Aimee knew she had to be still and listen for sounds outside. For the moment, there was only the occasional clanking of a tin thermos, the gulping of a thirsty mouth.

She silently communicated her own message to Farouk, with a nod. Then she bent her body to one side and wriggled her wrists around to one side to read the time on her wristwatch: 4:00 P.M. They had been tied up now for more than four hours. The sun was still beating down on the mud hut.

Aimee scanned the room for something she could use to cut herself and Farouk out of their bindings. Then she spotted the small table behind her. If she worked the rope hard against that edge of it, she might fray the rope enough to weaken it. It was worth a try.

She lifted her weight again and moved the chair backwards with deliberate precision so as not to make too much noise. Luckily the mud floor was soft, and any sound was muffled. She positioned her chair as close to the table edge as possible and began to rub the rope against it. After a few minutes, her wrists hurt so much she had to stop. She closed her eyes despairingly for a moment, then looked at Farouk. The dark charcoal gleam of his eyes begged her to continue. She started rubbing again until her arms became numb and she thought she'd lose all feeling in her body.

Eventually, the rope weakened and split in two. She was free. She listened carefully. No sound. She swung around to stare at the door. She risked getting up off her chair, went to Farouk, and tried untying the bandage around his mouth, but he shook his head violently. She knelt down in front of him and put her ear to his mouth, but the bandage was tied too tightly for him to whisper anything coherently. Farouk jerked his head towards his pile of clothes lying on the floor. She did not know what he wanted her to do. She looked back at Farouk, who was shaking his head now. She was to leave his clothes where they were for the time being. What did he want her to do? Then he nodded at his clothes again. Aimee got up and crept towards them. She knew there was nothing in his pockets that hadn't been found, so she picked up his shoes and looked over at Farouk.

He nodded. She examined his shoes and found a tiny raised groove in the inner leather. She pulled at it and removed a section of the inner lining. Inside she found a tiny penknife. She gave Farouk a questioning look.

He was shaking his head again. Then she saw tears rolling down his face. She replaced the knife and sprung up quietly. He was miming, telling her what to do. The tears were part of the act. He hunched over and continued the act, jerking his head towards the door. His eyes lit up in a smile.

She understood. She repositioned her chair where it had been, sat down, wrapped the rope around her wrists, and put them behind her back; then she started wailing, a low-pitched wail at first, growing gradually louder, then more pitiful and desperate.

Her eyes were squeezed shut as she wailed. Eventually she heard the lock shaking and the door was pushed open. The soldier stood there gaping at them. Aimee threw herself into the performance.

"I'm going to die of thirst, Monsieur," she wailed miserably. "I can't bear this heat. Please get me some water? I will die for sure if I don't have something to drink."

The soldier shut the door behind him, eyeing her suspiciously.

"This had better not be some sort of trick. I'm armed."

He was so young. He would not use his revolver on her. He was under the control of his general. He would not dare risk shooting her. His men would return and expect them to talk because they were too mentally and physically exhausted to hide anything from them anymore. The men would expect information. But the boy would do nothing. His was an idle threat.

"Please," Aimee sobbed. "Some water, please."

The soldier examined her suspiciously. Aimee could see his mind ticking over, analysing the scene in front of him. Perhaps he had a sister like her, younger perhaps. The kindness seeped out of him unrepentant. He backed away, pointing his revolver at Aimee and then Farouk. He opened the door and reached for his thermos, poured a small drink for her with one hand, kicked the door shut, and approached her.

This was her chance. As he approached, she held his gaze, slid her wrists out of the rope, and waited. The soldier put the cup to her lips.

Aimee counted down the seconds, sipping as slowly as she possibly could. She stared up at him under gratefully hooded eyelids, and forced an enticing little smile of camaraderie. A faint smile emerged in response on his lips, so faint as to be almost undetectable. Her chance had come.

He turned and began to walk away, satisfied with her subservience to him and convinced that she would not try anything dangerous or stupid.

She stood up and flipped the length of rope in the air. Lassoing him around the neck, she pulled as hard as she could, straining against his strong young body as it struggled to pull away. Then she grabbed the revolver. She pointed the revolver at the boy, who now lay squirming on the floor, and backed away in the direction of Farouk's shoe. Never moving the gun away from the boy's face, she crouched down, retrieved the small penknife, slit the bandages that gagged Farouk's mouth, then cut through the rope that bound his arms to the chair.

Farouk grabbed the revolver, leapt out of his chair, snatched the end of the rope around the boy's neck, and pulled it until the boy's face was pink.

"Don't kill me," he whimpered, wide-eyed.

"I'm just going to tie you up, my friend," Farouk said as he bound him to the chair.

"Quick," she said as Farouk dressed.

Farouk slipped the revolver into his jacket pocket, took Aimee by the hand, opened the door, and peered around.

"Can you run?" he said.

She didn't answer. Shaking, her face and throat coated with dust, her limbs hardly able to bear her own slender body weight, she clasped his hand tightly, and they scrambled over the dunes towards the desert road.

"Who the hell are you?" she stammered hoarsely as they ran squinting in the merciless sun. "And what are you mixed up in?"

The journal of Hezba Iqbal Sultan Hanim al-Shezira,
Cairo, August 25, 1919

"Yallah," I scream. "It's Saiza. Her baby is coming. She needs us, Nawal."

Nawal and I run out of the hammam back to the palace. In a moment, we are by Saiza's side. Saiza is dripping with perspiration, and her eyes are bulging out of her head. Poor child. Her belly is so round. Her eyes are so scared. Her maid fusses over her, draping her with red silk, rubbing perfume into her feet, combing her hair, preparing her for the arrival of the child she longs for. Saiza lies on a long, low chaise, curled up on her side, her robes wet with sweat, her eyes shut so tightly that she has not seen me arrive. I whisper her name gently in her ear. Then I kiss her cheek.

"Her time is very near, mistress," Mohammud, Saiza's eunuch, says.

"We must get her to the birthing chair as soon as she has the strength to move."

I put my arms around her and try and lift her up. Nawal helps. Saiza grits her teeth and pushes.

"Hezba," she says with difficulty, "I hear your husband has come. You must go to him. You shouldn't be here."

I stroke her hair, pushing it off her face.

"No," I whisper, "I will stay with you."

"He will be angry with you if you are found here. You must go."

I do not say anything. I swallow hard and look for reassurance in Nawal's face. She is holding Saiza's hand and kissing her fingertips. The baby makes another push, and Saiza screams again. She squeezes the life out of my arm. I fear her eyes will burst out of their sockets.

"Mohammud, bring the mistress some sherbet to drink."

Mohammud pours a small glass of sherbet, and I put it to Saiza's lips.

"There, this will make you feel better."

Just then four lower eunuchs enter the room and start to perform for Saiza. They do acrobatics, run and jump and fall about, laughing in front of her. They climb on top of one another's shoulders and form a column, balancing their weight carefully. Then they stage a mock fall and land on the Persian kilims with a thud before jumping up and doing more somersaults. Saiza watches them and starts to laugh. It is precisely the distraction she needs. Saiza lies back on her divan and smiles. She stretches out her arm for me.

"I am scared, darling," she says with a little pant.

I know what she is talking about. It is only three years since I went through this.

"I know. I know," I say. It is as though it were yesterday, with the pain of my son Ibrahim's birth. I can feel his bulbous black head forcing its way between my legs. I can feel the pain spreading like fire from my toes to my neck. I can feel my body split in two. I can see his little body slithering out onto soft cotton. I can smell blood. I can hear my own violent screams shuddering through me.

I kiss her cheek again and nuzzle her neck. She is burning up. And I watch her eyes flutter in exhaustion. The birthing maids bathe Saiza's forehead. The eunuchs light candles, casting dreamy shadows on the mashrabiyya and the mosaic tiles of the floor. The clowning eunuchs are brought instruments to play, and soon the mournful sounds of ouds and lutes are heard.

Then I hear the loud echoing voices of the men returning from their evening entertainment. Their laughter wakes Saiza from her sleep. Her body spasms again as her baby pushes forward. She raises herself from her pillows to encourage the baby's pushing.

"Hezba, Nawal, help me," she screams.

"Darling sister, we are here," I say, squeezing her hand.

I massage her belly. I can feel the baby moving under her skin. Then Saiza goes deathly white and lunges forward onto the floor. Suddenly, she is on all fours.

CHAPTER TWENTY-FOUR

Aimee and Farouk walked alongside the desert road in a low trench hidden by the dunes, stopping every now and again to rest. Covered in sweat, with matted hair and dirt-smeared faces, their wrists sore from the rope, they were exhausted and dehydrated. The sun beat down mercilessly on them as it descended slowly in the west.

"I can't go on," Aimee cried out, stumbling towards the shade of an old palm. She stood with her back to it, surveying the vastness of the desert horizon, angry that he hadn't answered her questions.

"Why don't you answer me, Monsieur Farouk or Alim or whoever you are?"

He came and stood next to her, studying her pale complexion and dark features. He didn't trust her. He was sure he'd seen some expression in her eyes, something deceitful, as though she were acting a part, the first time they'd met at the magazine launch, and then again in the garden of his house. He had wondered on those occasions whether she was taking him for a ride, and whether she and her husband had been in it together. He'd been taken in—perhaps—by her youth, but she could be a spy working for Issawi. He scanned the horizon, determined to be careful now, to watch his words. He'd have to feed her a story, something to put her off the scent.

"My identity card was a fake. I have certain papers, in case I am stopped. I do undercover work compiling reports."

"Who for?" she demanded.

"I can't say," he replied. "It's confidential."

"Who were those people?"

"Government thugs," he said.

She ran her hands over her face. She did not understand any of this. She wanted to go to the police. First she would go find Sophie at the Continental, and then together they would go to the police. But she had no information to give them, not really. They would want proof, of which she had none. She felt weak and nauseated. She swallowed hot dusty air.

"Those thugs had something to do with my husband, didn't they," she said.

"I believe so, yes."

"But they talked about letter boxes, Nasser's Trinkets, code names, the X? They must have thought we were somehow involved with a group. I should have told them who I was, that the murdered professor was my husband."

"No," Farouk snapped. "You don't understand. These men are looking for spies and terrorists. I believe they work for the king's chief advisor. The heroin was nothing more than an excuse. I got it for a friend of mine, who did me a favour. He's addicted to the stuff, you see, and Nasser knows how to get the highest quality. I can't explain any more. Those men wanted to frame me, torture us for information. They think I belong to this group, the X, which is ridiculous. I don't belong to any group. They've made a mistake, but that's not so surprising, really. Nothing in Cairo is as it appears. Trust me."

Aimee shook her head miserably, and he went on.

"This Group of the X and Mahmoud are almost certain to have been involved in your husband's murder, and I have heard that Fatima is connected with el-Mudarris, the terrorist group I told you about." He paused and glanced at the horizon again. She was leaning back against the palm, her eyes closed.

"Your husband—did he move in royal circles? Perhaps he was an undercover agent passing information to the British government? Was he possibly trying to blow the cover of a small group of German spies living in Cairo?"

She opened her eyes and studied him incredulously, shaking her head. Then she looked away. Farouk took her face gently in his hands, demanding that she pay attention. "Tell me, Madame Ibrahim, do you know more than you're letting on?" Their eyes met.

"My husband was a professor, Monsieur. He wasn't involved with any group. He was murdered, and you're asking me to believe he was passing information to the British? He hated governments, hated the idea of war, hated it. He just wanted to educate young men. He worked hard. He didn't know any member of the royal family."

Farouk softened, released her, and reached for her hand, holding it gently before lifting it to his mouth to kiss it. "Forgive me," he said. "I shouldn't have said those things. I've got to get you back to Cairo."

He saw the exhaustion on her face change to confusion as she caught sight of his ring, a gold ring worn on the third finger of his left hand, a wedding band. But he said that he had never been married.

He dropped her hand abruptly and turned to scan the horizon once more. Then he saw a vehicle in the distance heading their way.

"There's someone coming," he said, climbing up out of the trench to the road to wave it down.

Shielding her eyes from the sun, Aimee squinted to look. "What if it's them?" she said. "They're probably looking for us. They must have returned by now, found the boy, sent out their search parties. It won't take them long."

"Hide behind this ridge," Farouk said. "I'll check."

He peered ahead. "There's only a driver, no one else," he said. "We'll have to risk it. It's too hot and too far to Cairo to carry on walking."

He jumped up and waved the truck down, flinging out his hand to reach for her when he saw it slowing down for them. He opened the truck door and peered in. The driver was a white man. He looked European. He jerked his head, indicating that Farouk should get in.

"Thank you," he said, helping Aimee to climb in and sliding in beside her.

"You going to Cairo?" the driver asked in French.

"Yes, do you have any water?" The man produced a tin flask, and Aimee drank thirstily.

The driver put the truck in gear and moved off.

Nobody spoke as the truck gathered speed. Every now and again, Farouk squeezed Aimee's hand and smiled weakly, but she could see tiny lines furrowing his brow.

Suddenly the driver slowed to a stop and steered the truck off the road.

Farouk stiffened. "What are you doing?"

The driver didn't answer. He was looking in his rearview mirror and smiling. Farouk turned around and saw three army trucks. Though they were still a long way off, they were coming their way.

"What's going on?" Aimee asked, her voice constricting. The driver reached down beside his seat, picked up a revolver, swung round in his seat, and pointed it squarely at Aimee.

"It seems your friends Hilali and Gamal are a little upset that you left so soon," he said with a laugh. "Well, not to worry, they'll be here in a minute."

In a flash, Farouk grabbed the driver's hand and forced it back hard against the inside of the door. Overpowering him after a brief struggle, Farouk made the driver release the revolver. Then he reached over, opened the driver's seat, and kicked him out onto the gravelly sand.

"Hang on!" Farouk yelled as the truck screeched back onto the tarmac. Even with the truck's accelerator pressed to the floor, the army trucks were gaining on them. He heard gunshots and turned to see the man he recognised as Hilali reaching out of his window with a machine gun. A hail of bullets whizzed through the air. As their truck careened along, Aimee rifled through the glove box and slid her hands under her seat. She didn't even know what she was looking for—some weapons, perhaps, anything to help immobilise their assailants.

She climbed over the seat into the back, throwing herself flat so she was out of sight. She found a box and wrenched it open.

"There's something here," she shouted at Farouk, trying to make herself heard above the sound of the engine. "Grenades!"

"Let me see," Farouk said. "Pass one over."

"I don't know, I don't know," she said. She didn't want to touch them.

"Just do it," Farouk shouted. Sensing the urgency in his voice, she gingerly picked one out and passed it to Farouk who'd reached his arm back over the seat and was waiting for her to put it in his hand.

"Perfect," he said. "How many are there?"

"Six," she said.

"Haul them over to the front."

As Aimee climbed back over, Farouk released the pin of the grenade with his teeth.

"Hold the steering wheel for me," he said. Aimee leaned across him and took the wheel while he threw the grenade out the window into the path of the oncoming army trucks.

They heard an explosion and saw the army trucks swerve off the desert road, collide, and come to a halt.

The journal of Hezba Iqbal Sultan Hanim al-Shezira,
Cairo, August 25, 1919

"Nawal," I say, "help me with Saiza." I pull the bell rope and a moment later, two of Saiza's eunuchs appear, wiping crumbs from their mouths. "Hurry, help your mistress. Her child is coming now."

They support Saiza under her arms and gently position her on the chair, lifting her red silken robes up and fanning her legs wide, while the poor girl leans forward, clutching at their arms and biting back screams. I squat down and crouch at her feet, massaging her horribly swollen calves. The birthing maids arrive with bowls of water and large pieces of muslin cloth. Saiza reaches for my arm. Her eyes are shut. She pants and moans and pushes hard. From between her legs, a tiny head appears, and then the entire body slips out. Another child in the dynasty of the sultan has been born.

"It is here, your baby is here, bismallah, bismallah," I cry. And Saiza smiles, tears welling up in her eyes. The eunuchs holding the baby announce, "A boy, mistress, a boy, as God willed. A boy."

The baby is taken and washed and handed to the wet nurse, and Saiza is carried to her chaise. "Come to me, my sisters," Saiza says, and reaches for Nawal and me with arms outstretched.

We all hug one another, kissing Saiza on each cheek. Just then, the double doors of her rooms are thrown open and two eunuchs appear, calling my name.

"Al-Shezira Hanim," one of them says.

"The master is ready for you. You must come immediately."

CHAPTER TWENTY-FIVE

Aimee decided to return to the el-G that night. She wanted to check out the club again and get more information on the comings and goings of Ibrahim's Fatima and her cronies. She'd spent a few hours at the Continental Hotel with Sophie after Farouk had dropped her off there. Farouk had said little when they'd said their good-byes on the steps of the hotel. He'd reached out to take her hand as she'd climbed the steps, his expression twisted, yearning, but she didn't take it. She'd simply turned away and walked up the steps to the safety of Sophie's suites.

A couple of hours later, Youssef, Sophie's driver, drove her and Sophie back to her house. It was dark when they arrived. Nervous about going in alone, she asked Youssef and Sophie to accompany her.

"Amina's been here." She sighed with relief when she turned on the light. Her housekeeper had put everything more or less back in its place. Apart from the knife gouges in the upholstery, the place looked almost as it had before.

"Look, Aimee, a letter for you and a wire." Sophie picked up an envelope from the sideboard in the hallway and handed it to Aimee. She ripped it open and scanned the contents quickly, reading them out loud.

"Amina has gone away to her eldest daughter's for a while. She's asked me to telephone her at this number. She wants to know I'm all right."

Then she opened the telegram and smiled.

"It's from Saiza, my aunt. She'll be back in Cairo tomorrow afternoon. She'll expect me at her place at around three o'clock. That's wonderful news."

A warm glow flushed through her; then her eyebrows knotted as she wondered whether to tell Saiza about her ordeal in the desert. Saiza would become hysterical, and march her to the police, or, worse, send her away to England to wait out the war, leaving her with a thousand unanswered questions.

She would tell her one day but not quite yet.

At the Sharia Khulud on the edges of the el-Birka district, near the maze of narrow Wassa harets, the crowds were thinning. It was past midnight. Aimee gripped the seat of the car and peered into the gloom.

"Over there, I see it," she said.

Sophie had not seen her friend like this before. Aimee looked different. The heart-shaped charm of her face had melted away. Her mouth had become a thin line, her eyes darted anxiously in all directions, and a feverish glow heightened the colour of her cheekbones.

"Where?" Sophie said.

Youssef slowed down and muttered to himself.

"What's going on?" Sophie leaned forward and pulled herself up between the driver and passenger seats so that she could see the road ahead. Progress was hindered by two men and a donkey. The two men were shouting at each other and throwing punches.

"Oh my God," Sophie said, "it's Sebastian."

Aimee looked at her.

"Who?"

"Monsieur Sebastian, my uncle's friend." A tall blond man in a dark suit grabbed the other man, an Egyptian, by the lapels and was forcing him violently towards the wall of a nearby house. Sophie pushed open the door, jumped out, then exclaimed, "Youssef, stop them!" Youssef got out of the car and walked quickly over to the two men, followed by Sophie. Sebastian looked back, saw Sophie, and then let go of the Egyptian. Sophie pulled at Sebastian's arm and motioned him to the car. The Egyptian, who had been mauled, brushed himself off, adjusted his tie, and walked away.

"Your friend will go with you to the el-G," Youssef said, smiling as Sebastian got into the front passenger seat. "Everyone is friends now."

Sebastian nodded a greeting at Aimee and smiled at Sophie. Sophie introduced them. "Sorry about that," Sebastian said. "That lowlife tried to pick my pocket."

"What are you doing in el-Birka?"

"I was on my way home," he said. "Thought I'd walk off my dinner. What are you doing here?"

Sophie blushed and smirked. "My friend is dragging me along to some horrible club. Come with us?" Sebastian agreed. Youssef found the entrance to the club and turned the car into a small haret, darkened by towering buildings with beautiful mashrabi-yya. Women and girls lingered along the walls waiting for custom-ers. Aimee opened the car door and got out.

"Take Monsieur Sebastian," Aimee said. "I will follow you in afterwards. Pretend you are married and you want to spice up your love life. Don't let the doorman intimidate you. I will see you in there."

"Aimee!" Sophie cried out, but Aimee was gone.

The journal of Hezba Iqbal Sultan Hanim al-Shezira,
Cairo, August 25, 1919

Picture the anger twisting my features at the eunuch's announcement.

"Can't you see that my sister has just given birth? She needs me. Tell my husband I have more important things to attend to here."

Another of the eunuchs walks towards me. I put my hand up to stop him coming nearer. Then I bend down at Saiza's side once more and whisper, "You have a son, Saiza, how wonderful. We will be celebrating for weeks." And then the chanting begins. "God is great, a boy, God is great."

As the servants sing, the wet nurse starts to feed Saiza's babe. I look back at the door. The eunuch approaches me once again, and the other follows. I am escorted away by force. We walk silently through the corridors of the harem, down the marble staircase, the one that leads out to the gardens, and then to one of the dress rooms, where Rachid and Tindoui are waiting for me.

Al-Shezira's eunuchs stand guard outside as Rachid and Tindoui strip me naked. First they check my body for feminine body hair. Seeing that not a hair is visible, they rub oil of frangipani and lime all over my body. I close my eyes and feel the rough rhythmic movement of their hands, massaging the oil deep into my skin, around my knees, my stomach, my thighs, my feet, my fingertips, my neck, and my breasts.

Then Rachid unties my hair and combs it vigorously, with long hard strokes. My head hurts as he pulls. I know he is angry, that rage bursts from every fibre of his being. He hates al-Shezira as much as I do because he sees what I suffer. I want to look at him, but I do not dare for fear of what message I might see on his face.

Tindoui wraps a gold and red bodice around me and ties it up at the back, while Rachid arranges my hair and paints my face. Then Tindoui dresses me in a long purple and gold silk robe that falls to the ground and, cupping my feet in his hands, he gently slips them into narrow harem slippers. Then my arms are decorated with bracelets of rubies, emeralds, and Ethiopian gold, bracelet after bracelet, around and around my arms from wrist to shoulder. My hair is arranged in a simple braid down my back and decorated with gold silk ribbons, then tied up on top of my head. Tindoui adds a simple silver headdress to frame my face. Finally, Rachid dabs gold powder on my cheeks and my eyes and henna on my lips. Tilting my chin towards him, I open my eyes slightly. I can see the tears on Rachid's cheeks and his mouth set bitterly. He is resigned to what is coming, the end of our lifelong friendship.

My life is over, I say to myself, trying not to imagine al-Shezira's gnarled hands on my body and the rough scent of him as the large carcass of his body lies heavy on top of me.

When I am ready, Tindoui and Rachid deliver me to al-Shezira's men, and I am escorted to my husband's apartments. I walk slowly, wanting to delay the inevitable. As I walk, I recall myself as a little girl and feel as though I am looking in on the life of another. The eunuchs do not hurry me. Habrid, walking with al-Shezira's servants, does not say anything.

In my daydream, I sit on Papa's knee. Papa scoops me up in his arms and kisses me repeatedly. I giggle and laugh. I run like the wind alongside my mother in the gardens of the palace.

I look up at the sky, at the birds. I want to be a whisper, a breeze, free like the wind. In the palace of the sultan, I find adventure. My nurse scolds me for being too noisy. I wear boyish pants and little slippers, and my hair is wild, just like my eyes. I play with everyone. I flirt girlishly with Papa. They all love me. They will do anything for me. The harem celebrates that Fire has become a woman. I am eleven years old. I am given my own apartments in the harem of the sultan. I am not allowed to run anymore. I am allowed to see Papa only by appointment. I am to walk slowly, with dignity. I am to speak quietly, not with girlish happiness, but with womanly serenity. I am not allowed to run barefoot in the sand on the beach at Alexandria. I am not allowed to walk about unveiled. And then halfway through my eleventh year, I am married, and my life is signed away by the wakil who legalised my marriage to al-Shezira in my absence.

CHAPTER TWENTY-SIX

After dark, Nemmat made her way to the Café al-Qal'ah near Bab al-Khalq. The night was hot and sultry. The café, in reality a hashish parlour, was off-limits to women. But tonight she was no longer simply a brothel girl, she had become invaluable, indispensable. Behind her chador, she held power in the palm of her hand. She pulled her chador closer and inhaled deeply. The sensation of power was rare, intoxicating, and she savoured it like a sweet elixir.

She was expected to enter around the back. The front entrance was brightly lit, and she was bound to attract attention if she slid between the rough wooden tables where men were playing games of tawlah, which typically served as a front for the pastime of hashish smoking.

She found the alleyway at the side of the café, located the door, and entered. The thick, heavy smell of hashish hit her, and Nemmat felt instantly light-headed. A woman was preparing a large table of shisha stoppers. Littoni, Hamid, Hossein, al-Dyn, and Tashi and his wife were seated on cushions, staring at the woman ritualistically preparing the stones, sprinkling each separate stopper with the black oily hashish resin. Then she turned to prepare the shisha pipe, lighting the charcoal so that the water pipe and the hashish could be inhaled through the long bamboo stem. Tashi's wife, Meryiam, nodded quickly at Nemmat as she entered.

Nemmat squatted down beside Meryiam and pulled off her chador as al-Dyn began to inhale the shisha pipe. Littoni was next, followed by Hamid and Hossein. The pipe was not offered to the women. Nemmat waited for the slow satisfied curl of the men's lips as the effects of the hashish started to flood through their bodies. Littoni cleared his throat and looked around him. His eyes were bright with purpose.

"Men," he said, "this meeting has been called without Farouk's knowledge. We are moving ahead in this way because Sayyid Farouk has expressed a certain dissatisfaction with our plans and we have decided to carry on without him now." His lips pursed around the bamboo, Hossein was inhaling deeply.

"The Muski and Khalili sectors know about this meeting. Sayyid Tashi here will report back to them on the exact itinerary for the night of the twentieth."

Littoni nodded at Tashi, who was anxiously awaiting the pipe.

"The report will be wired in X code to the Muski traders and the Khalili businessmen, and they will be ready."

It was finally Tashi's turn to suck hungrily on the pipe.

Littoni continued. "Tonight, you will receive your instructions. You must memorise them. Nothing is to be written down. You will not talk to anyone about what you have heard tonight, nor relay any of the information you have been given in any form. To do so will guarantee your death."

Nemmat watched Tashi smoking. Littoni's last comment did not cause so much as a raised eyebrow, or a pause to take in the face of the man who had delivered the death sentence. It was a punishment they each knew by heart.

Hamid said, "Farouk is intent on beating you to it. Sayyida Nemmat will report on the latest developments, but coded information sent down the chain has confirmed what we already believed, that Farouk is determined to take matters into his own hands as you say. If he is allowed to succeed, the palace will call off all celebrations. Issawi's death will be a top security priority. There will be no point in sending in a car, as the Abdin Palace will be empty."

Littoni smiled, taking up the pipe again. "And we want Issawi, don't we? But more important than this man is the destruction of the Abdin Palace, which will bring about the revolution. We want the government disbanded and the country in disarray, so we can restore Nationalist order to our beloved al-Qahire."

Hamid said, "How do you know Farouk hasn't rallied his own forces? We might have got the Muski and Khalili sectors on our side, but I know for a fact that the Zamalek, Giza, and Garden City sectors are not so malleable. They might claim to profess loyalty to you, Littoni, but there are many down there who don't like you."

Littoni held up his hand. Nemmat saw his eyes bulging in his head. They were bloodshot and droopy, but she could see he was in a rage.

"Silence," he choked. "Those men won't cause us any problems. We're been planning this for too long. They may be in awe of Farouk's expertise, but they don't respect him as a leader. All the sectors need to be paid and soon. They're all just poor fellahin who are out of work, and so they're easily bought. Tomorrow I'll pay them, and their loyalty to me will be assured. This is the moment they've been waiting for. This will be the biggest coup Egypt has ever seen. The government is weak, preoccupied with the war. There has never been a better time to do this. In twenty-four hours the Group of the X will have swollen to immense proportions. Issawi and his men have no idea how big we have become. They think we're just a small band of thugs, but they're wrong. We've got the people on our side. Forget about Farouk. Once they have some cash in hand and learn that the time has come for them to bring down a government that has oppressed them for so long, any loyalty the sectors claim to feel for Farouk will disappear. You'll see."

Al-Dyn passed the pipe to the shisha woman, who stoked the charcoal in the basket she was using to carry the shisha between the men. Then she started sprinkling more hashish on the terracotta stoppers.

Littoni continued. "We have managed to obtain an invitation to the king's celebrations. All we have to do is get Papadopolous at the print-works to copy it and put the relevant names on it. Sayyid Tashi, dressed in formal black tie, will be masquerading as Suleyman Orhan, the secretary to the Turkish ambassador. The real Suleyman Orhan has been taken care of by the Heliopolis sector. His body won't be discovered for a few days, possibly weeks.

"Fresh identification papers have been prepared by the print-works. Tashi will be driven by Hamid, who will be dressed in an official chauffeur's uniform, to the Abdin Palace. The plan is to plant the bomb inside the palace's grand entry. We have timed it so that the bomb will be detonated when Issawi is standing in front of the king. The destruction will be immense. Our spies have given us detailed maps of the inside of the palace. Tashi, posing as Suleyman Orhan, will be allowed entry to the palace. He will carry the timed device in a trophy. The security men are sector members, so he will have no trouble getting through security. The festivities are planned for the Grand Banquet Hall at the back.

"Tashi will present the trophy to Issawi, then feign illness, and leave quickly. He'll have eight minutes from the handing over of the bomb to Issawi to the point of explosion. His driver will be waiting for him outside, so he should have just enough time to get off the premises.

"From the moment Issawi arrives at the palace, each second counts. Hossein will flash a torchlight signal when Issawi's car is in sight, from the third-floor window of the building opposite the king's palace. This will be radioed through from the networks en route. Tashi and Hamid will time their arrival precisely to the second so that they enter the palace grounds minutes after Issawi has arrived.

"Tashi, as Suleyman Orhan, will follow Issawi up the palace steps. His manner will be that of a statesman. He will not rush. He will carry his gift. The bomb, Hamid informs me, is powerful enough to massacre Issawi, any other politicians and notables in the area, and a sizeable chunk of the palace. During the chaos that ensues, the sectors will storm the building and declare the coup."

Al-Dyn said, "You're sure that the security men at the palace gate who'll be checking the cars are genuine sector members, Littoni? You've checked them out thoroughly?"

Littoni smiled and nodded. "I've known them for a long time. They're with us. The coup will not fail."

The journal of Hezba Iqbal Sultan Hanim al-Shezira,
Cairo, August 25, 1919

Halfway through my eleventh year, my life, as I know it, ends. The husband chosen for me is an extremely wealthy man of fifty, named Khalil al-Shezira. He is one of Papa's closest business colleagues and a powerful pasha. On my wedding day, my husband wears a fine statesman's uniform. I am dressed in a traditional headdress of jewels and my mother's wedding gown. After I have been signed away by the official wakil, I sit with al-Shezira. The palace cheers and everyone celebrates. Jewels are thrown at me, as I am now considered a respected wife. After the celebrations, I am escorted to my husband's rooms. I wait to receive my master. I am scared. My husband arrives and takes my hand. After kissing my neck, he leads me to his bed. Sensing my shyness, he asks his slave to undress me. Then he claps his hands, dismissing his slave, and I am left alone with him. I lie down with him on his bed. The moon shines on us.

He begins to move his hands slowly along my thighs. My breath becomes shallower, and I close my eyes. I feel him climb on top of me. Then he thrusts himself inside me. A searing heat shoots through me, and I begin to cry. I want my maman. I don't understand what is happening. My recollection fades, and I am grown-up Hezba once more.

We have arrived at the salamlik where my husband is staying.

"Wait here, al-Shezira Hanim," Habrid says. Then he enters the apartment.

I stand with my eyes fixed on the marble floor. The night air is heavily scented. I can smell a fire burning somewhere. Someone is smoking nearby. Maybe a group of girls is lying on the roof with a pipe. Habrid returns shortly and nods to the two eunuchs, who escort me into the apartment. His rooms are exquisitely decorated, more beautiful than the harem apartments. The walls are made of gold leaf and the furniture of South African ivory. There are silver pots and marble statues. The room is lit by torches, which throw great shadows on the walls and floors. My husband is seated cross-legged on gold thread cushions in the far corner. One young girl is preparing tea. She holds a samovar and some little cups, while another young girl I do not recognise sits passively beside him. Though I have not seen him in four years, he has not changed. As I approach him, he smiles, but it is not with pleasure—it is with victory. A white robe stretches across his large body, and his tiny black eyes are half closed. The hair crowning his shiny dome is whiter than ever. He holds out his hand to me. I relent and let him guide me to a cushion beside him where I sit down.

"I am pleased to see you, Wife," he says. I say nothing.

He strokes my face and asks the girl with the samovar to pour me some tea. I look at the girls. Their expressions give nothing away, but as I take the little glass of tea from one of them—the prettier one—our eyes meet for a moment. I see a flash of nervousness in the girl's eyes. We drink our tea in silence for a moment. Then al-Shezira claps his hands. The two girls jump up and bow before leaving quietly through a door on the far side of the room. He claps his hands again, and the two dour-faced eunuchs who have been standing guard by the main door bow and leave. We are alone. I do not dare look at him. The last time I saw him was before my son, Ibrahim, was born. He did not come to see me after my baby died, and he left for al-Minya soon after.

"Look at me, Wife," he says, lifting my chin to his face.

"Why are you here, Husband?" I say. "Why have you returned to my palace?"

Al-Shezira drops his hand and laughs. "Your father told me you are ready to return to me. You are my wife, are you not? It is only proper that a wife lives with her husband."

I shake my head. "Papa speaks for himself. He says what he wishes were true."

Al-Shezira shakes his head and strokes my shoulder. I shudder and close my eyes. I do not want him to touch me. I think of Alexandre.

"You will come with me to Minya, Wife. This is expected."

I look at him. I dare to say, "I hear you have taken another wife at your palace, to replace me. Is she not enough for you?"

He pulls me forward abruptly. Suddenly I feel his breath on me, his rough hand clamping down over my mouth.

"You have your place at the Minya palace," he says. "Now don't say another word. I did not come here to listen to you talk. I am not interested in anything you have to say."

I scream, but my screams are muffled by his large, rough hand over my mouth. He slips his other hand inside my tunic and covers my right breast with his fat gnarled fingers. He forces me down on the cushions, but I bring my knee up to his groin. For a moment he withdraws in agony. He is angry now, but I do not act quickly enough. He grabs my throat and holds me down on the cushions.

"You bear me a dead child, and then you further insult me by acting in this way," he says. "People have always talked about you, Hezba. You have betrayed me often enough with your unnatural ways, your defiance. I should have divorced you long ago, but your father begged me not to. He paid me a handsome fee to avoid a scandal."

I can't breathe. I try to turn my face away, but he holds me fast. "Look at me, woman," he says, not releasing me. "I have not finished with you yet."

But I can't look at him. I can't look at his ugly face. He wrenches my clothes from me, fumbles at my skirt, and tears my skin, clawing at the intimate flesh between my thighs. He inserts himself inside me. And when he has finished with me—just when I think it is all over—he delivers a searing blow. I hear the crack of his hand before I feel the pain. He cracks my cheekbone and jaw. I raise my hand to my face and feel the trickle of warm blood.

CHAPTER TWENTY-SEVEN

Nemmat knew her time had come. She knew this from the way Littoni was staring at her. He leaned over and placed his hand possessively on her arm. Every bloodshot male eye turned towards her, and Meryiam flashed her a nervous glance. Even the woman with the shisha stopped what she was doing. "This is where you come in, Sayidda," Littoni said familiarly.

Nemmat nodded coldly. She wanted to get tonight over with. She wanted to return to her mother, but there were many long hours ahead before that could happen. Fatima was waiting for her to get back to work at the el-G, and she doubted she would see her mother and the bed she shared with her before dawn.

"In order for the revolution to begin, we have to dispose of Farouk. He does not suspect your involvement with me?"

Nemmat shook her head.

"I have followed your instructions faithfully," she said quietly.

"And you'll continue to do so if you want your money and your life spared, Sayidda," Littoni continued.

Nemmat nodded. How she hated this man. Hated the way his dead eyes demanded her attention, hated that she had agreed to work with these people, hated her own private master—money. But she did everything because she loved her mother and wanted to protect her from poverty and harm. Her mother had shielded her from the furore of her father and kept her safe when he'd left them with nothing. Now it was her turn to protect her mother. "He trusts me," she said, quivering. "Not tomorrow, but the following night, Sayyid Issawi intends to go to his club. That is when the Sayyid intends to move in on him. Sayyid Farouk suspects nothing of my involvement with this faction of the X. I swear on the Qur'an."

Littoni nodded and continued. "Tell us what has been arranged so far, Sayidda."

"I have got the cyanide. I received it from my cousin Dahshan in Bulaq. Farouk wants me to go to the Oxford as an escort girl. I am the Oxford's gift of thanks to Issawi for his patronage of the club. I am to dine with him and be his playgirl for the evening. Farouk has gotten the heroin for me to put in Issawi's drink. Then Farouk wants me to bring Issawi to the apartment in Abbassiya."

Littoni smirked and nodded. Hamid, al-Dyn, and Hossein continued to take turns sucking on the shisha.

"Do you know what our friend Farouk intends to do with Issawi?" he asked, leaning towards Nemmat.

"He's going to assassinate him there, cut up the body, and have him removed in separate boxes to different locations outside Cairo. I know he's employed two young men to help him."

"What are their names, Sayyida?"

Nemmat shook her head. "I don't know. Everything has been kept top secret so far."

"Still—," Littoni started to say, but he stopped and a smile curled his lips.

Nemmat watched him carefully. He was screwing up his eyes, thinking.

"The night of the coup," he went on, "we want no distractions or problems of any kind—and certainly no traitors."

Nemmat flinched as he said those words. Traitor. The word pounded inside her, making her flesh crawl. It was all she could do to keep her face composed and her body still.

She looked at the other men. Al-Dyn was grinning at her. Hossein had the shisha pipe hose in his hand. Hamid was cradling his knees in his arms. Tashi was stroking his wife's cheek affectionately. The shisha pipe woman had retired, and the lamps had been turned down to a dull glow. The air hung heavy. Littoni stood up shakily, reaching for the table to steady himself.

"The heroin Farouk is expecting you to put in Issawi's drink will dull his senses, is that right, Sayyida?"

Nemmat nodded, her mouth trembling, for fear of what was coming next. Littoni scared her.

"Issawi won't know what's happening to him," she said. "But he wants Issawi conscious enough to know he's about to meet his own end."

"Yes, yes." Littoni grinned. "And you have the cyanide, you say. You're sure it will blend easily enough with his whisky?"

"According to my cousin, it's all in order," Nemmat said. "I only need one capsule. If you don't trust me, I'll give it to you and you can have your laboratory test it."

Littoni's eyes narrowed. "That won't be necessary. Your cousin Dahshan is in one of the Muski sectors, isn't he?"

Nemmat nodded, never for a moment taking her eyes from Littoni.

"I know the man," he continued. "I've had him checked out. He supports us. He's sworn his allegiance to the X."

"Then you are happy, Sayyid, that everything is going according to plan?"

Littoni rubbed his hands together.

"So far, so good. Is everyone clear on their position? We start at the al-Qal'ah end, near the Abdin, on the night of the twentieth. By then, Farouk will no longer be able to bother us. But first things first. We must pray to Allah for deliverance from Farouk. We must pray for our sister Nemmat, pray that she succeeds in her vital mission. If Allah wills it, we will then be free to start the revolution without any interference and to do it properly. Then Omar bin Mohammod alias Fabio Littoni will be president of Egypt. At last."

The journal of Hezba Iqbal Sultan Hanim al-Shezira,
Cairo, August 26, 1919

A letter comes from Alexandre. It is the day after I have been tainted with the stench of al-Shezira's body and endured his violence, but the taint lingers. I cannot wash it away. To calm myself I read Alexandre's letter.

He writes:

Darling Hezba, I will come for you. Wait for me. Rachid has been made aware of this. I have some news for you. My spies have found out that on the night of September 15, your husband is going to hold a conference at the Minya palace, in the Great Hall, for a group of his politician friends. Five pashas will attend the conference. They will arrive at the palace the night before and will be accommodated in the guest apartments. These five pashas are of high interest to the Rebel Corps. This is a fine opportunity, one not to be missed, Hezba. I know you understand my motive in writing to you. These politicians are scheduled to discuss certain topics, including the rights of the Council of Fellahin, the signing of a preliminary Anglo-Egyptian Treaty and what it will mean to our country, and the waiving of certain taxes for the wealthy.

Judgement on these issues will then be presented to government. We have received notification from a branch of our group in Cairo that the execution of our plans on this date will be crucial to the success of our mission. That is all I have to say for now. I eagerly await the moment when I can see you again, hold you to me, and feel your body against mine.

I remain your devoted Alexandre.

CHAPTER TWENTY-EIGHT

Aimee stood shivering on the street corner for a few moments. She was scared. She regretted telling Sophie and Sebastian to go on into the club. But she had to see this woman, Fatima. Azi had been her first love. If this woman had somehow been involved in a plot to murder him, she had to do something.

Two old men in long robes walked past. One of them brushed her thigh with his hand. Peeking around the corner, she saw the el-G doorman, a different one from the night she had come with Farouk. This one was taller, with a hard face, his mouth twisted in a snarl. He wore a billowing black calico robe over filthy trousers. His grey beard was unkempt, and his leering eyes squinted in the low light.

Aimee walked up to him and, steadying her voice, said, "I would like to speak to Sayyida Fatima."

"Oh, yes?" he snapped, his eyes travelling the length of her body. "And who should I say is asking for her?"

Aimee wavered for a moment.

"My name is Amina Khalil. I was told the Sayyida was looking for girls, dancers."

The doorman chewed on his cigarette and then spat it out of his mouth. A faint smile emerged.

"You are just in time then. Fatima is due on stage in just over an hour. Go around the corner to the side door. You'll see an entrance. Knock and wait. Someone will open the door and take you to her dressing room. Tell her Sekmet the doorman sent you."

She turned abruptly and found the door. A dwarf stood guard. He was pulling at his trousers and playing with the zipper. He looked embarrassed for a moment; then he barked.

"Who are you? What do you want?"

"Sekmet has sent me to see Sayyida Fatima," she said. "My name is Amina Khalil, and I am looking for work as a dancer."

He eyed her suspiciously for a moment. It was unusual for girls to appear at this late hour looking for work. They usually came during the day, were auditioned, and told to return later. Still—

"This way," he said, then vanished down the stone steps into the darkness. Aimee followed. Long candlesticks on wrought-iron candelabra lit the way. Finally the dwarf knocked on a door. Aimee heard a woman's voice.

"Fatima," the dwarf said, "I have a dancer for you, a girl called Amina."

Aimee felt faint, and her nerves felt stretched taut. Her heart beat wildly, and little beads of perspiration had broken out at the base of her spine. When the door opened, the dwarf gave Aimee a shove. She stumbled into a surprisingly beautiful room, lit with a hundred candles. Huge mirrors covered every wall. Fatima sat on a silk-draped chair, in front of one of the mirrors. She was dressed in her stage costume, the same jewel-encrusted bodice over loose trousers as the other night. Her hair was tied up on her head, a few black ringlets falling seductively from beneath her tiara.

Aimee steadied her voice.

"Sayyida," she said in Arabic, "I am looking for work as a dancer. My name is Amina. I am very experienced. I have danced in

Paris and in Spain. I have fallen on hard times, and I need to earn a living. The wife of a cousin of mine, Abdullah Ibrahim, told me your club was one of the best in Cairo and—"

Fatima closed her eyes and put up her hand to silence her. Was there any recognition of her husband's name, a flutter of the eyelashes, darting eyes, a jolting of the body, a clue, anything? Fatima stood up and walked over to Aimee. She began circling her like a vulture, examining her from behind and then from the front. Aimee stood still, not daring to move.

At last Aimee said, "Do you know Sayyid Abdullah Ibrahim, Madame?"

Fatima said, "Is he a regular here? Should I know this man?"

"I believe he is rather fond of this club. He told me all about the exotic and graceful Fatima."

Fatima dismissed her with a contemptuous shrug. "Then you will have been told we have high standards. We don't accept riffraff, common girls from destitute homes with no charm or grace to offer. Where are you from? You are not Egyptian."

Aimee grabbed at something to say, tripping over her thoughts. She felt foolish and afraid, out of her league. "I am Turkish. My family came to Egypt a long time ago. I travelled with my mother and danced to earn money. But my mother is dead and I have to earn a living."

"How old are you?"

"Twenty-five," Aimee lied, studying Fatima's full scarlet-painted mouth. She appeared older up close. Tiny wrinkles fanned out from around her eyes. There was a hardness to her face, with lines etched into her forehead.

"Well, you look alluring enough, and much can be done with powder and paint. Did your friend tell you what our customers expect at the el-G?" she said.

Aimee shook her head. Fatima went on.

"The men who come here pay a lot of money to see top-quality girls. They want a show, do you understand, and they don't want to leave the club disappointed. My girls must perform for my men. They dance for them, and then they take them upstairs for any extra services they have paid for."

Aimee swallowed and nodded. What was she doing? She couldn't dance for men. That was ludicrous. But, maybe there was a chance she'd find out more that way. She needed to—somehow—get Fatima to trust her, and this appeared to be the only way to do that. She had seen the way Fatima had whipped the men into a sexual frenzy.

"Do you think you can do that?"

Aimee was tongue-tied. "Do you mean, I must—"

Fatima nodded. "Yes, you must. As you complete the final stages of your erotic dance, you must remove the last of your clothes. Choose a man from the audience, someone who looks as though he has a fat wallet, someone from the front who has paid for sex. Then seduce him while you dance for him on the stage. The other men in the audience must see you do this. It will entice them to buy a girl. After that, you must do whatever the man wants, enticing him with extras, for which he will pay a great deal, do you understand?"

She nodded, her head constricting, a low dull scream hovering somewhere deep inside her.

"Take off your street clothes and choose a dress. Get yourself ready. I will see how you perform tonight."

Aimee wasn't sure she could go through with it, but she had no choice if she wanted to keep a close eye on Fatima. There was simply no other way. Besides, Fatima was already shoving an outfit into her arms—a red semi-transparent stocking dress.

"Here, wear this. And do something with your face and your hair. Change over there and be quick about it. You'll go on in fifteen minutes and remember—I expect a good show or you can forget working here." She thrust Aimee into a room next to hers that was furnished with a long mirror, a dressing table with bottles of cold cream, trays of long ostrich feathers, and rows of spiky-heeled shoes.

She pulled her knotted hair free and combed it, deciding against feathers and tiaras. Azi had to have been crazy to get involved with someone like Fatima. There was nothing alluring about her. She was simply a low-life brothel-keeper. Azi had been worldly and sophisticated. Nothing made sense anymore.

She looked in the mirror, applied some red to her lips, in the manner of Fatima, puckering her lips into a bow. She powdered her skin, which looked deathly in the spotlight of her tiny dressing room. Then she painted her eyes as carefully as time would allow and looked at herself in the mirror. She didn't recognise herself.

The journal of Hezba Iqbal Sultan Hanim al-Shezira,
Cairo, August 29, 1919

My fate is written in the desert sands. From Cairo to Ethiopia, from Wadi Halfa to Rabat, across the length and breadth of North Africa, the vast expanse of land occupied by my ancestors, the signs are there, marking out God's will for me, my destiny. This is the only thought that comforts me now that the inevitable is happening and we are leaving.

The day has been set. Tomorrow at dawn after prayers, a carriage will come to take us to the train station. I will ride with the Minya harem women, seated with the stern but beautiful Iqbal, al-Shezira's favourite, and leave the palace of my birth forever.

Instructions have been given. Al-Shezira's men have given orders to Habrid. Rachid, Anisah, and Tindoui are packing up my things. I have asked to see Virginie. Rachid knocks on my door. He has a message from her.

"Sayyid Alexandre Anton will come tonight," Rachid whispers, and I fold myself in his arms and cry against his shoulder. I cry with sadness because I am leaving my home and with relief because Rachid has been allowed to escort me to Minya. Rachid and I are friends again. He told me he was angry with me for risking my life when I rode out into the desert to meet Alexandre, and he feared that if I continued to act in such a foolish manner, I would die because of it. But now that he has been allowed to escort me, he is happy again. He tells me I am his only friend and my heart aches for him because of this. "I love you, Rachid. You are so good to me," I say. Rachid holds me close.

He releases me and says, "Tindoui and I are to prepare you for your husband. He is expecting you again tonight."

My heart sinks and I shiver. I cannot bear my husband's brutality. The only thing I can do to save myself is to be a wife to him and not talk back to him. But I still want one last night of solitude in the palace of my birth before I leave.

"But Sayyid Anton will still come?" I ask Rachid again to reassure myself.

"Yes, I'll see to it. Now, let me take you to the dressing room. Tindoui is waiting for you there."

Once again, I am escorted to the dressing room. After being washed and made beautiful, I walk as before to al-Shezira's apartment.

"Here she is," al-Shezira says as I am pushed inside the door.

I am alarmed to see a group of about twenty girls—some of whom are harem girls from the palace, others whose faces are unknown to me—sitting crossed-legged on the floor in two rows, their heads covered with sheaves of silk, their hands crossed in their laps.

Seated on the far side of the room, my husband smiles when he sees me. I stand frozen in my silk and my jewels, my hair free and wild around my hips, my feet bare except for the heavy anklets that jangle as I walk.

"Stand in the middle of the room, Wife," al-Shezira says.

I walk to the middle of the room and stop.

"I have something I want to show you, Wife," al-Shezira says.

From each corner, eunuchs appear and lunge at me with rough hands. My clothes are ripped from me, my jewels go flying, my hair is pulled, my skin is clawed, the powder and paint on my face are smudged.

I scream. What is happening?

"Stop," I cry out. "How dare you defile me?"

Al-Shezira laughs and some of the girls snigger. Finally, the eunuchs pull back. I stand naked, my hair in disarray, my mouth bleeding, my clothes strewn around the room.

Then al-Shezira speaks.

"Look at this wife," he says, speaking not to me but to the group of giggling girls seated on the floor. "Be careful that you don't become like her, fat, dull, and ugly, so ugly that no one wants her, not even her husband."

I listen in disbelief. I look at his bulbous face and the slow unintelligent slope of his skull. A rage is surging within me, but I can do nothing. He stands up and walks over to a pretty girl sitting on the floor. I assume she is a Minya girl. He reaches for her and pulls her up. He leads her over to his cushions, sits down, and lays her down across his lap. He strokes her naked belly. Then, pushing the silk off her head, he strokes her face. Finally, he pushes his hand inside her bodice and then down the front of her skirt. She giggles with delight.

I stand naked, shaking with anger. My limbs are giving way, and my head swims. Al-Shezira does not even notice me. He lays his new piece of flesh on a little mattress beside his cushions. He disentangles himself from his robes and lies down on top of her, brazenly entering her while the harem girls hang their heads, stifling nervous giggles.

CHAPTER TWENTY-NINE

Aimee's act was moments away. She hurriedly applied a little gold dust to her cheeks. Then she raised her thin arms above her head and tried to move her hips. There was no way she was going to convince Fatima. The men would laugh at her, and Fatima would get wise to her in seconds.

She had surely lost her mind. She removed her clothes and slipped into the red stocking sheath. It clung to her body like a glove. She pulled the long black gloves off the table and slipped them on. They reached past her elbows, with little ivory buttons holding them in place.

She scanned the room, taking in the cracked ceilings, the rough wooden floors, the antique armoires, the heavy velvet drapes. As she tiptoed barefoot out of the room, a plump old woman sidled up to her and took her hand.

"If you are Amina Khalil, then come with me," the woman said. Her hand felt rough and cold like parchment. Beyond the long corridor, she saw the lights of the stage and the sequinned curtains. Aimee watched a young girl, probably no more than thirteen, swirling, entranced, on the platform. She was wearing a jewelled bodice and loose trousers, and her arms were decorated with silver bracelets.

In the wings on the other side of the stage, Aimee spotted another woman whom she was certain she had seen somewhere before. She peered out at the audience, sizing up the faces of the men through the cigarette haze.

"You're on next," the old woman said, sliding onto a small stool as the music faded out.

Aimee held her breath. The sound of a flute was heard, and then a hush came over the room. She could not think. She thought she would faint. She didn't know what she was doing. The sound of tablas started up, followed by lutes, then pipes.

The old woman gave her a shove onto the stage. She was overwhelmed by that same unpleasant oily smell, which reminded her of the caravansarais and kiosks in the seedier parts of town, places she'd walked past with Azi when they'd explored the city together. She was fairly certain it was opium, an odour so strange her head started to swim.

She moved slowly at first. Then gradually, swaying in time to the music, her movements became more vigorous. She tried to remember the steps of the flamenco dancers who had fascinated her as a young girl. She stamped her bare feet and stretched her arms high over her head, arching her body as she danced. Then a face loomed out of the cigarette haze. It was a good-looking face, the face of a man she knew. Farouk!

She kept dancing. She danced and danced, her body tightening with each breath, the thick, heavy scent sending her reeling. She saw Sophie and Sebastian. Sophie was staring at her in horror, her mouth open. Aimee continued, unable to stop. The face of Sophie's friend dissolved into the blur, and she saw Farouk again. He had left his seat and was pushing chairs and tables out of the way, but Aimee kept dancing to the throbbing music.

She was dancing for Azi, not for Fatima, dancing in her sheath of a dress that clung to her pale flesh, her tiny feet stamping away on the dusty, dirty floorboards, which were spiked with shards of glass from broken bottles. Swirling to the pounding, hypnotic music; she crouched and twirled until she was almost naked, pulling at the thin sheath of fabric that covered her thin body. Still she did not stop. The audience had broken into a frenzy. Farouk pushed them back, leapt onto the stage, and encircled her waist.

"Get off the stage," the men shouted. "She has not yet chosen. You can't just take her. You filthy bastard."

Farouk had wrenched off his jacket, was wrapping it around her, scooping her up in his arms. The dwarf pulled at Farouk, grabbing at him, biting the backs of his legs, but with one swift kick, Farouk sent the dwarf flying off the stage.

The audience roared with laughter. Aimee heard Farouk shouting, but she didn't understand what he was saying. The room was a cacophony of music, laughter, clapping, and yelling. Farouk's eyes were black and wide and hungry. The time had come for her to earn her commission.

The journal of Hezba Iqbal Sultan Hanim al-Shezira,
Cairo, August 30, 1919

Rachid smuggles Alexandre into my apartment just before dawn. My lover comes dressed in a floor-sweeping chador, like a woman. When he arrives, he throws off his robes and gathers me to him hungrily, burying his face in my neck.

After lighting candles on a low table in the corner of the room, Rachid leaves us. He will stand guard outside my rooms, in case Habrid decides to pay me a visit. Anyone who tries to enter will be told I am still suffering with women's business, although this is not true.

Alexandre and I have only two hours together, but it is enough to restore my faith in love.

He says, "Rachid told me that you will arrive at the Minya palace in five days, Hezba. You are stopping for some time at Beni Suef with some close friends of your husband's. This is enough time for me to rally my men. I know the Minya palace and the streets around it. I know people there. I will find you."

"Rachid will bring you to me," I say. "I am certain I will have my own apartment. I have a reputation. They will want to keep me apart from the other women."

"You must be prepared," he continues. "I will draw some of the servants at Minya into my confidence. Behave quietly and do not draw attention to yourself. Do not let al-Shezira get suspicious in any way. Wait for the signal."

Alexandre holds my hands and kisses my fingertips and then takes me over to my cushions. Clasping my hands around my lover's neck, I taste the pleasure of a real man.

I try to take in what Alexandre is saying—that he and his men are going to seek revenge for the injustices inflicted on their people by my husband. He has told me that the Rebel Corps will take control of the Council of Fellahin, allowing the fellahin to run their businesses for profit once more. He has told me that I will be free of al-Shezira before too long. I don't know how it is going to happen, but I am excited. I let myself imagine living in Paris or London and starting a school there. When all the violence is over, I will return to my beloved country.

"I don't know how to thank you," I say, "for loving me, for under-standing."

"You have nothing to thank me for, Hezba. Al-Shezira is an easy target for us. You mustn't be afraid. You must think of your freedom, of our life together, of a free Egypt, of the school you want to start. You

want to be part of a better future for Egypt? You will be, but things have to change, and we're going to make that change happen."

"With you?"

"Yes, we must continue our fight first. The Rebel Corps has work to do. There are too many rich landowners who must pay for their crimes. Then we can free our country."

"I am scared for Egypt," I say, "There is violence everywhere. The men are rioting. Women are protesting on the streets. I am scared, Alexandre."

Alexandre embraces me, and I savour the warmth and urgency of his kiss. I want to tell him of the night I was raped, but I say nothing. We must not make any noise. The women of the harem are sleeping.

We lie together for a little while, flesh against flesh, with a sheaf of silk over us until I see the first glimmer of light and Rachid comes to us to tell us that Alexandre must leave. We have had so little time together, just two hours.

"Habrid has been given orders to wake you, Hezba," he says. "It won't be long before he is knocking on your door, Sayyida."

Alexandre gathers me up in his arms one last time.

"Hezba," he whispers, "don't lose courage. We will soon be together."

After prayers, I am escorted to Maman's rooms to say good-bye to her. She is ill again. I must listen to her as she warns me not to be a bad wife. Then I am fully veiled and escorted to the four arabiehs waiting for us outside the gates of the palace.

I do all this blindly, with the taste of my lover still on my lips. My inner thighs are still burning from his touch, and his mouth on my breasts has left a mark I wear like a badge.

CHAPTER THIRTY

Darkness enveloped Aimee as she came to. The smell of old leather and the familiarly pungent Kyriazi Freres tobacco made her nose twitch with recognition. She thought she heard a voice, low and tender and rich with age, like a seductive whisper, against her ear, but she could not be sure to whom it belonged at first. She opened her eyes and looked around, but had no idea where she was. As she got her bearings, she realised that she was curled up on the front seat of a car, covered by a man's trench coat. The heavy satin lining slid over her naked arms. Her head felt swollen and numb and thick.

She scrambled up, blinking, trying to focus. Farouk was next to her in the driver's seat. The car was parked on the banks of the Nile. She could see feluccas tacking across the river in the moonlight. Up ahead she recognised the Sinan Pasha Mosque, its cool white stone shimmering under the stars.

"God, it's you. How—what? What's going on? Where are we?" Aimee asked huskily, rubbing her head.

"You look ill," he said. "How are you feeling?"

"I feel strange," she said. "What happened? How did I get here?"

"Sssh." Farouk turned and put his finger on her mouth to silence her. He squinted in the darkness and pointed at a group of men huddled near the entry to the mosque. Farouk told her in a low voice that the men had the houseboats along the Nile under close guard. What he didn't tell her was that they were Issawi's men and they were watching the comings and goings along the banks of the river.

Aimee followed his gaze to the men by the mosque.

"Who are they?" she asked.

"Mahmoud's men. They're checking me out. They have their eye on that houseboat over there."

Aimee studied the scene more closely. All she could see was a throng of men lingering around the entry to the mosque.

"Why? Who does that houseboat belong to?"

"I use it," Farouk said.

"What for?"

"As a place to compile my reports," he said.

Aimee sat up straight and pulled the coat over her.

"What am I doing here with you in this car?" she asked him.

Farouk lit a cigarette. "I rescued you. You were dancing at the el-G. A new job?" he added sarcastically. She didn't answer him, instead sinking back against the seat and huddling inside the trench coat. Then she remembered the red dress. Peeling back the coat, she saw that she was wearing the lilac dress she'd borrowed from Sophie. Had he stripped her of her el-G clothes and somehow gotten her dressed?

"How did I get back into this? I was dancing. I had the red dress on—I remember that much."

Farouk wound down the window and flicked ash out. "I collected your things. The old woman took you into a small room and helped you dress. You don't remember that? She told me you were very sick. Fatima was nowhere to be seen. I waited for you. Then I carried you out through the side door. I wrapped you up in my coat and settled you down on the backseat of the car. I had to follow someone."

"Who?"

"Gad Mahmoud. I'm on his hit list."

"Why?"

"He thinks I've done him wrong. He's crazy, a thug."

She chewed her lip, her cheeks burning. She tried to remember the old woman, removing the red sheath, putting on her own clothes, but she couldn't.

"You remember the dwarf and the crowds cheering?"

"Yes, yes. I think so."

"And you remember that intoxicating smell? Opium?"

"Yes, yes."

He reached into his pocket and pulled out a cigarette for her. She took it, and he steadied her hand as he lit it for her. She was shaking.

"I suppose you will tell me in your own time what you were doing dancing at the el-G."

She searched his face. "Why were you there?"

He lit another cigarette for himself and shot her a look. It was the reaction he had expected.

"A friend of mine warned me that Mahmoud was planning on breaking into my houseboat tonight," he said. "I got on Mahmoud and his gang's bad side last year. I didn't know then whether your husband was being targeted by them or not. But recently I've become surer of it. If my sources are correct, Mahmoud is planning something just as final for me."

Something over by the mosque caught Farouk's attention, and he stopped speaking. He straightened up, looking startled for a moment, and then a wide smile spread over his face.

"He's getting into a car. It looks like he's heading in the direction of Shubra with a few of his men. It appears he's given up. None of them have been near my place."

Aimee didn't say anything. Farouk finished his cigarette and threw the butt out of the window. Then he reached for her, slid his hand inside the trench coat, and pulled her to him. He could not hold himself back, and she did not stop him. His mouth, scented and warm, on hers, made her long for him, and all barriers slipped away, dissolving until there was nothing between them. But he pulled back and held her to him in a more restrained fashion, inhaling the scent of her hair.

"You'll tell me why you were at the club, won't you?" he said.

"Fatima," she said.

Farouk disengaged himself from her and pushed her hair tenderly out of her eyes. Then he started the engine and drove the car towards his houseboat. They got out of the car and walked together towards the mooring. The velvet milky darkness of dawn felt cool and soft against their skin. Farouk pulled her face to his, moistening her mouth with a second tender embrace.

"Don't go to the el-G again, Madame Ibrahim," he said. "Mahmoud is a dangerous man. If he finds out you're spying on him or on Fatima, he'll kill you."

Aimee bit her lip. "Did Mahmoud kill my husband, Monsieur Farouk?"

Farouk wanted to tell her. He hated lying to her. At first the lies had come easily, but back then she had meant nothing to him. She had simply been the wife of a man he despised.

He pulled her to him without answering. There was nothing he could say at that moment. He felt her eyes burning holes in him, but he stayed quiet. They reached the steps of his boathouse, and he looked back at her angel face and reed green eyes glittering in the soft dawn light as he helped her navigate the steps. He saw it again, that look of victory, and suddenly he felt afraid. He was losing his mind. He had met women like her before, angels masquerading as spies whose intelligent strategizing outmanoeuvred the cleverest of men. He put his hand in the curve of Aimee's back and ushered her down the tiny steps of his houseboat to the cabin below.

The journal of Hezba Iqbal Sultan Hanim al-Shezira,
Cairo, September 8, 1919

We arrived at the Minya palace earlier today, and it turns out it is just as luxurious as the Cairo palace. My first glimpse of it was from behind my long black traditional burkha. The metal fastening holding the whole contraption together is a constant irritation.

Al-Shezira insisted that I be dressed in full traditional Turkish harem clothes beneath my dull black veil in preparation for my installation in my quarters. Once we had arrived, I was unveiled and paraded in front of the Minya palace harem women in my brightly coloured silk robes. Then I was introduced to everyone.

The White Palace—as it is commonly known because of its ivory stone—is on the banks of the Nile. Pleasantly positioned on the eastside, my private rooms are on the top floor and overlook the water. A small stairwell leads to a roof garden. I have been told that the roof garden is mine alone. Because of my nervous disposition and the concern for my sanity, I am to be given special permission to use it privately for as long as I want. I have fine views of the Corniche and can see families promenading in the evenings. Al-Shezira's home is not so much a palace as a large mansion surrounded by small harets leading in all directions. The nearby streets are lush with palms and wide like the image I have of Parisian boulevards.

My servants Anisah and Rachid have rooms not far from mine. I have a bell rope, as I did in Cairo and can call for them anytime. The decoration of my rooms is fairly pleasing. Instead of my cushions, I have a large, low bed, raised only slightly off the floor. The mashrabiyya is as intricate and as delicate as that of the Cairo palace.

I have Persian carpets, silver bowls, and vases, a little anteroom where I can lie on a couch and read literature especially chosen for me by my husband. I have the services of a lute player—a eunuch boy— who comes to play for me whenever I want. I can eat in my room—I have only to ring for Rachid and he will bring me sweet pastries, little delicacies, fatta, the very best Ethiopian coffee, chocolate, sherbet, very sweet tea, whatever I choose.

The harem is ruled by al-Shezira's aging sister as his mother is dead. She has already visited me and told me the palace routine.

I am allowed one excursion a week, in the company of the other harem women, perhaps to the theatre or to participate in a local moulid, and I am allowed to take a promenade on the Corniche once a day, as long as I am chaperoned.

Prayer time is strictly supervised. I will not be allowed to pray alone in my room, so there will be no room for deceit. Prayers are conducted in the grand hall of the harem to the voice of the mosque's muezzin.

There are to be no lessons of any kind. I am yet to be allocated a night, once a week, to spend with my husband. The night chosen for me will allow me to express my love for my husband. I will be stripped of all body hair, oiled, and perfumed and taken to him. He in turn will have a duty to satisfy me and make me happy, so that I can return to my rooms the following morning, a balanced and serene wife.

Umm Iswis, my husband's sister, has also advised me to have a child as quickly as possible. In fact she has ordered her brother to pay me special attention until I am with child again.

"It will not do for one of the wives of the Minya palace pasha to be without a child. It is not normal. You must have a child right away. Then you must have another, preferably one a year until your husband is furnished with as many as six or seven sons from the belly of the sultan's daughter."

I have everything I could possibly want, but I want none of it.

CHAPTER THIRTY-ONE

Sophie had seen Aimee's disgusting display and watched in horror as her dear friend made a total fool of herself in front of crowds of leering men. Sophie had clung to her seat, shooting hateful glances at Sebastian as he had clapped and laughed. He evidently found Aimee's dancing on stage highly amusing, but it was clear to Sophie that Aimee had lost her mind.

"It's not funny," Sophie yelled. And then that horrible man had climbed on stage and scooped Aimee up in his arms, taking her backstage. Sophie knew that these dancers were expected to seduce a man and earn big money for the brothel madame, the woman who Aimee had said had been her husband's lover. In an effort to find Aimee before it was too late, Sophie had run to the headwaiter and had shaken him by the shoulders.

"Take me backstage. That's my friend who was dancing up there. She's not well. I must rescue her."

The headwaiter chewed his lip and smiled smugly. "It's out of the question. Your friend is a new dancer at the club. No one is allowed backstage except for the girls and the men who have paid for them."

Sebastian tried to calm her. "Sophie, come on. Leave it. Your friend obviously knows what she's doing. Let's go."

Sophie flashed him a look of contempt. "You're joking, aren't you? I'm going to find Youssef. I'm going to get her myself."

Running outside to find Youssef, who was waiting for her in a nearby street, she saw that man hauling an unconscious Aimee into his car. She shouted out, but he was already pulling away.

"Follow him," she ordered Youssef, and jumped in.

Sophie clutched the leather seats anxiously, peering in the darkness at the car in front of them. The man in the car ahead scared her, and she didn't know what she was going to do. When his car slowed down, she ordered Youssef to slow down too and then told him to park unobserved a little way off.

"It's okay, Youssef. Let's just wait and see what happens."

A half hour later, the car remained there, not moving. From a distance Sophie saw Aimee moving inside the car and a man reaching for her gently. They were talking. Aimee didn't look concerned or worried. They seemed to be having an amicable conversation. She wondered if it would be better to wait. Then their car started and they drove off towards the Nile. Sophie ordered Youssef to follow them. They parked away in a shadowy spot, almost out of sight. Sophie was watching them like a hawk. She leaned over the front seat and watched them get out of the car. Sophie reached to open her own car door but stopped. Where was he taking her? They were walking towards the houseboats, and she saw them go down the steps of one. She didn't know if she should follow them now. A few seconds passed, then minutes.

"Wait here, Youssef." said Sophie, slipping out of their car. She sprinted across the pavement, slid down onto the houseboat deck, and peered through the window.

The journal of Hezba Iqbal Sultan Hanim al-Shezira,
Cairo, September 9, 1919

Virginie arrives from Cairo to visit me. I am allowed to walk with her along the Corniche. I am escorted to her by one of the general household servants, a young boy.

Virginie is waiting for me by a row of arabiehs that line the Corniche waiting to take tourists on little excursions. She stands stroking the horses, looking delightful in a fitted sand-coloured jacket over an ankle-length skirt and black boots. She is wearing a smart new hat.

I approach her, and she realises it is me beneath the veil. Her face lights up, and she holds out her arms to embrace me.

"My dear friend, I am so happy to see you," she says.

I am glad I am veiled, because I do not want her to see me cry.

"Dear Virginie," I say softly with a lump in my throat, "I am so glad you have come."

I push my veil away slightly for a moment to study her face properly. I love her shimmering eyes, her soft downy eyebrows, and the curve of her mouth. Then I let my veil fall back into place.

"And your brother? Is he coming too?"

Viriginie takes my arm and leads me away towards the Corniche. The servant assigned to chaperone me stands back and watches us closely, but he does not try to follow us. We watch the feluccas and dahabiehs sailing with the gentle currents of the river. We see tourists aboard. Egyptian children are cleaning their shoes and cooling them with large palm leaves.

"Yes," she says. "But I am scared for you, Hezba. I am scared for your future if you continue this affair with him."

"I can't stop, Virginie. I don't know much, but I know I can't stop this."

"My dear Hezba," she says, "my brother loves you, but your worlds are too different. His mission is a political one. Are you so sure you want to be part of a revolution?"

I lean on her arm, feeling very tired all of a sudden. "Virginie, we are all part of it whether we like it or not. My papa is involved because he is supporting the British. I am involved because I am a part of a world that accepts the old traditions that are crippling Egypt. You are a teacher. You educate people. You are helping things to change, Virginie. Why can't I?"

Virginie pats my arm and then embraces me, telling me to be brave.

"There are terrible times ahead, Hezba," she says. "I am thinking of returning to France, and I am trying to persuade my husband to come too. The Nationalists continue to riot and burn buildings. My brother says he will not leave while the Nationalists are fighting for a better Egypt. He says he has to stay and fight. Forget Alexandre, Hezba. Come to France with me."

I lower my head. I can't leave Alexandre. "Will Alexandre come soon? I will feel better if I can see him."

Virginie rubs my arm to calm me down. "Yes, he's on his way, but your father is in trouble, Hezba. He's being targeted as an aide to the British, as you know. The Nationalists see violence as the only way to force change. They won't be satisfied until Egypt is independent of all British involvement. They are tired of living as servants in their own country. You know that. Things are not safe for your father at the moment. You must write to your father and try to make him see sense. Try to persuade him to leave Egypt for a while with his family. Go to Switzerland, London, France, anywhere but here."

"My father is stubborn," I say. "He's a patriot, but he does not see things clearly. He does not hate the British. He will never leave Egypt, and he will never listen to me."

"Then we must wait and see what happens. It is in the hands of Almighty God," she says, hugging me. "I'll pray for you every night, I promise."

We part and I am escorted back to the palace.

When we arrive, I ask Anisah to make arrangements for me to meet with my father who will arrive in Minya soon on government business.

"I cannot do that, Hezba," Anisah tells me. "He is busy with his government duties."

Anisah does not give me any more information. I feel desperate that I am waiting, waiting for something to happen and no one will talk to me about the things that matter.

"Eat this, Sayyida," Rachid says, passing me a plate of fruits. "You cannot live on pastries alone. You don't look well."

"Come and listen to the musicians tonight in the grand hall, Sayyida," Anisah says.

"You will be measured for new robes, Sayyida," Rachid says.

"Your husband wants you to wear clothes tailored to suit his palace."

I sigh. They talk too much, and they order me around. It is ridiculous to be talking about clothes when Cairo is on fire and our palace is in danger.

"The other women want your company at the baths," Rachid says. "You must go and spend some time with them."

Then Anisah says, "Al-Shezira has sent you this little book to read, a story about a wife's devotion to her family. It is about how the wife longed to have five wonderful little babies and how after the fifth baby boy was born, she planted a little garden for her children and watched the trees and the flowers grow, just as her children grew. It is a lovely story."

I stare at her in disbelief. Rachid and Anisah have had their minds stolen from them. This is all a conspiracy, to make me feel as though I too am losing my mind.

But still I go and listen to the musicians in the Great Hall. Then a fortune-teller comes to the harem to entertain the women. I ask Rachid to arrange a private sitting with her in my rooms.

I am the last to be seen. The fortune-teller sits me down in front of her and takes out a pack of elaborately painted cards. She asks my name, how old I am, and the year of my birth. I tell her I am not sure but think I was born in 1902.

She looks into my eyes and strokes my face gently. I do not like the feel of her fingers. They feel rough and smell of dirt. She tells me I am unhappy, and I nod.

She pulls a card from the pack and sighs. The card has a picture on it of a naked man and woman, entwined like snakes. Behind them, the sky is dark and stormy.

"This card is called the Lovers," she says in a husky voice. "You are in love with someone other than your husband."

She takes another card from the pack. This time the card shows a tower and a bolt of lightning. "Great distress and change," she says.

The next card shows a man on a white horse.

"A stranger is coming," she says, "and he will bring you much luck and happiness."

I don't say anything.

The next card has some gold coins falling to the red earth.

"Luck, wealth, and happiness," she says.

Finally, I say to her, "Tell me who you really are. Have you been sent to me?"

She looks around the room to check that we are alone. "Yes," she says. "I have a message for you." She pauses. "But first," she says, "tell me which night do you spend with your husband?"

"Monday."

"Before the moon rises on this Monday—before you perform your wifely duties—take one last look at your husband's face."

And she presses something cold and hard into my hand. I stare at it in shock. It is a revolver. The fortune-teller looks around nervously.

"Hide it away, Sayyida," she says. "It is ready to use. Your Sayyid wanted me to give it to you."

"Thank you," I whisper.

Then I roll some money into her palm, sit back on my heels, and close my eyes gratefully. When I open them again, she is gone.

CHAPTER THIRTY-TWO

Aimee stood on her balcony thinking about Farouk, Sophie, and the el-G. The look on Sophie's face when she had opened the door to the boathouse haunted her. She had been in Farouk's arms when Sophie had burst through the door, her face ashen at the sight of them together.

Aimee clung to the balcony railing, watching people going about their business. The morning air was soft and silky, but the heat was building. Farouk had held her close, had told her to leave Cairo, had told her she was in grave danger. The reason? Mahmoud and his gang would probably choose to dispose of her as they had disposed of her husband. She had considered his words but knew she would not leave. She was an Egyptian, Cairo was her home, and no war, no dark underworld would make her leave now. She was a woman who would do things her own way, though only a few days ago, she'd felt adrift in this city. Her pride in her heritage was growing. Something was happening to her, and she knew that deep inside her the spirit of her mother was stirring—and with it a determination to stand tall and face whatever the future had in store. Going to the el-G had been a stupid mistake, but she'd read something on Fatima's face when she'd been with her, a hardness. Fatima was a woman without conscience, Aimee was sure of that, from their brief exchange, a woman who was a slave to money who'd do anything—even seduce another woman's husband—if the price was right.

She shuddered at the memory of Farouk's brief and tender kiss on the houseboat. She had allowed him to kiss her, his lips soft against hers, for a matter of seconds, but she had pulled away, standing back to study his face for a clue, for something. She felt torn, drawn to him but very, very wary. As he had reached for her again, cupping her face in his hands, wanting more, Sophie had burst through the door.

She tried to push Sophie out of her mind and focus on what was in front of her. Her neighbourhood entranced her. Booksellers sat on mats alongside kilim sellers, women tended vegetable stalls, and emaciated children ran laughing through narrow harets. Aimee's mind swirled. Though she was still adrift, she couldn't ignore the growing feelings she had for this place of her birth. Neither an outside observer nor a real insider, she was living on the fringes of this hypnotic world, unable to understand any of it. She couldn't help but wonder how her life would have been different if Azi had not been murdered, if her mother were still alive.

Sophie had left the houseboat as abruptly as she had entered it. Aimee had tried to run after her, but Farouk had pulled her back. Then he'd driven her home as dawn was breaking, leaving her there alone at her request. Though the taint of the break-in still lingered, it was her home. She could not stay away forever. He had wanted to stay with her, until Hakim, Aunt Saiza's driver, arrived to take her to Saiza's house, but she had insisted that he leave. She needed some time to herself to think things through, so she had run a bath. Lying in her bathtub, in her little house, she had quivered with the memory of him. She saw Farouk's face, felt his hands stroking her own, the look of longing in his eyes. As she gripped her balcony railing, she knew that something was about to happen—something dark and unspeakable—but she couldn't make any sense of it. The "thing," whatever it was, was a living shadow with no discernible shapes.

In her mind, she pictured Farouk's houseboat, the bookshelves crammed with volumes of literature in French, Arabic, Italian, even Urdu. She could smell the raw oak aroma of the floors and the window frames. She could see the little bedroom with its low bed where they had sat talking. She'd also seen a briefcase with a strange insignia and envelopes on a small desk with unfamiliar names scribbled on them.

Farouk's houseboat seemed so cosy and lived in, with its bookshelves and furniture. It didn't seem like the type of place a man would go to hide out from a pack of assassins. He had his house on Gezira Island. He seemed to live openly. Any group who wanted him dead would be able to find him. None of it added up. Aimee thought about the drama of their desert arrest and their conversation in the trench on their way back to Cairo. Mahmoud, Farouk had suggested to her, *was* the Group of the X. This Group had murdered Azi because Azi was, according to this Group, working with the Germans, trading secrets. Fatima was involved with the X. The name Issawi came to her. She'd heard Farouk mention him, but she didn't know who this Issawi was. If this Mahmoud was after Farouk, why didn't he go to the police? He seemed to be against the idea of any authority getting involved in the tracking down of murderers. So he must have something to hide. Aimee didn't trust him. He seemed so protective of her, and that in itself concerned her. Why would he want to help her? She was nothing to him, not part of his circle in any way. He said he had met Azi, was aware of him, but Aimee got the impression Farouk held some sort of strange grudge against him. He spoke with raw hatred when he mentioned the privileged circles that Azi was supposed to have moved in. And then there was the coded letter that had fallen out of her mother's diary, with the photo of Fatima. She had given him the letter with the strange code, but nothing more had been said about it. She made a mental note to ask him about the letter, but then she realised that they had made no plans to meet again.

She returned to her bedroom to change. She put on a pair of trousers and a blouse, rolled her hair in a tight bun, stroked the soft leather cover of her mother's diary, and thought for a moment.

The telephone rang. The sun was streaming in through half-opened shutters, and the heat hung low in the room. Aimee picked up the phone. It was Sophie. Aimee heard her friend say her name feebly, painfully. Then there was silence. She could hear Sophie breathing into the receiver.

Finally, she spoke. "I don't know what to say. I suppose you know what you're doing."

"Sophie, it's all right. I'm all right. Isn't that all that matters?"

"You know nothing about this man, Aimee. And now you're involved with him?"

"Yes," Aimee said. "Perhaps I shouldn't be, but I am. In some strange way, I am."

"But what will people say? Your aunt?"

"I don't care," she said, swallowing the heavy lump in her throat. "I don't care what people think."

"But he's old, Aimee, at least twice your age. What on earth do you see in him?"

Aimee sighed impatiently. Sophie couldn't possibly understand. The truth was that she hardly knew herself. "I don't know, but I can't let go now. I don't know what's happening to me, but I need you to try to understand."

"But Azi?"

"Azi was involved with a prostitute."

242

Aimee sensed Sophie shiver against the receiver. When her friend spoke again, Aimee could hear the disgust in her voice.

"I don't think you really know what you're doing, but I'm so worried, Aimee. You're my best friend. I don't want anything bad to happen to you. It might be safer if we were to both go to England and wait out this war. What do you think?"

"I can't leave, Sophie. I've got to find out what happened to Azi. I have this feeling that something terrible is about to happen, but I'm not scared. I won't know any peace until I know what happened. He loved me. I loved him. I can't just walk away. It would kill me."

"Aimee—"

"Please, Soph, I think this man Farouk can lead me to Azi's killers. I have to—I don't expect you to understand, but please—don't say any more. I'll telephone you soon, I promise. Please don't worry about me."

Saiza greeted Aimee warmly outside her home in the suburb of Medinet Nasr. Aimee loved Saiza's house, a magnificent villa the colour of butter with a charming garden planted with English trees and shrubs. The garden was where she'd originally told her aunt she was going to marry Azi. She remembered how happy she'd felt that day, how full of hope she'd been for the future. And now?

The Saiza who greeted her with open arms at the front door looked plump and healthy, very different from the person who had disappeared to Alexandria for a rest cure many weeks before.

"I've missed you, Auntie." She wanted to tell her aunt about everything that had happened, but she couldn't. She didn't want to worry her.

"Have you, my dear? You must tell me everything. I have so much more energy now. The doctor in Alexandria gave me a clean bill of health, but he said I mustn't burden myself too much. I must not attend so many of my club meetings. The women's groups will have to do without me for some time, but I can entertain a little, so I shan't be too bored."

"Auntie?" Aimee said nervously. "Professor Langham at the university gave me something that belonged to Azi."

Saiza was quiet for a moment. She peered at her niece curiously. "What, dear?"

"A diary, my mother's diary."

Saiza's face seemed to collapse into itself. She hung her head, chewing her lip as she examined the floor. "Oh, Aimee, I am sorry, so sorry."

"Why did Azi have it, Aunt? Did you give it to him? Why did he lock it away?"

"I'm afraid I didn't give it to him, darling child. He must have taken it. It must have been that day he came to see me, not long before the accident. We were in my sitting room together, talking, and the diary was on my desk. I was going through my things and planned to put it in a very safe place. I remember being distracted by something and left the room for a few minutes. Azi was sitting there drinking tea. When I came back, he said he had to leave. I didn't even notice that he'd taken it, and then my dear—I forgot about it. Oh dear, I am so forgetful these days." She shook her head again and looked away, as though embarrassed. "Oh dear, why would he take it? I shouldn't be angry with the dead, but I am upset. Have you read it, dear Aimee?"

"Some of it," Aimee replied.

"Oh dear, my poor sweet girl. I'm so sorry. I will explain everything, I promise, but first there's someone I want you to meet."

"Who, Aunt?"

"Come with me."

Saiza linked her arm through Aimee's and led her through the house to the small garden at the back. They walked to an old rattan couch in a shady spot beneath the trees. The sun was beating down hard, and Aimee was glad of the palms' shade. Once they'd sat down, Saiza peered back towards the house, evidently waiting for the guest to arrive. She heard a sound, a shuffling, and then the sound of Rose—her auntie's housemaid—talking to a stranger, slowly, soothingly, softly.

A man was being led slowly through the sitting room towards the garden. He was holding on to Rose's arm, and she was guiding him between the furniture. Aimee did not recognise him. He had a plump, smooth face and thin, scruffy greying hair. He was slightly stooped and walked like a very old man, but as the light caught his features, she saw he was probably only in his forties. He was dressed in a loose white jalaba over white trousers. On his feet he wore scuffed scandals. He held on to a white walking cane in one hand. In the other, he carried a little book with a black cover and a silver spine.

"Here he is," Saiza said. She stood up and helped Rose guide him to the couch where she and Aimee sat. Aimee stood up and stared at him. He was obviously blind. His eyes were vague, milky splotches in sunken sockets. He was muttering to himself as he lowered himself, guided by the two women, into his seat. She could understand the words, a strange mixture of Arabic and French.

"Daughter," he said, "Daughter."

Saiza pulled Aimee closer to her and whispered, "Sit down next to him, my dear."

And then she spoke to her housekeeper. "Bring us the tea now, would you, Rose?"

Aimee sat down next to the man. She could not take her eyes off him. The man reached for Aimee's hand, tentatively at first. When he found it, he put it in his lap, and the tears began to flow.

"Aimee dear," Saiza said. "I want you to meet a great friend of your maman. This is Hezba's devoted friend and former servant, Rachid."

The journal of Hezba Iqbal Sultan Hanim al-Shezira,
Cairo, September 10, 1919

Monday, Monday, Monday. I can't get that day out of my mind. I am like a restless child waiting for Monday.

Every day I go through the same interminable routine. I rise from my bed at five. I wash, I pray, I am brought breakfast, I am dressed for the day, I sit on my balcony, I smoke, I eat, I dream, I pray, I walk around my room, I am invited to sit with the other women, I go to the bathhouse, I pray, I am veiled, I walk out for some air, I eat, I wash, I pray, I listen to some of the women sing in the privacy of our apartments, I sit on the balcony and smoke, I wash, I pray, and then I retire to my rooms and lie in the moonlight. Is this all women should expect from life? Really? And what about men? They are off planning military action, learning languages, heading up governments, making money, owning property. Meanwhile I am being attired so I look good for my husband when inside I want to be running a government, building free schools for children, helping women start businesses, and forging a society in which opportunities are there for all, and nobody is scared of a master. I must calm myself.

Turning to sadder news, I hear that Maman has taken a turn for the worse. But she is not interested in hearing news of her Minya daughter, so how can I summon the desire to see her—when I know my presence would probably make her feel worse?

The lack of news from Cairo is horrible. I long to return and march the streets in protest. I would not be afraid. All I can do is lie here and listen to the gentle movement of the Nile as it flows through my land. Tears stream down my cheeks. I find myself missing al-Qahire. I longed to be free of the palace, but that prison has been replaced by another set of walls. In Cairo, I had my friend and my teacher. Now I miss the silly little Bathna, one of my many half sisters. My heart bleeds for simple joys, the companionship of Saiza and Nawal, and I weep for the pleasures I used to enjoy in Cairo, my lessons with Virginie, the hammam, the sight of Papa, despite his usual coolness with me. Last night Rachid looked so different. He has changed. It is not my imagination. He is sadder, no longer my friend and confidant. I think he is tired of his life and is depressed. Everything is changing so fast. The life we knew is fading away. Life now is violence with rioting in the streets of Cairo, the gunning down of ordinary Egyptians by the British. I want progress and change, but I don't want innocent people to die. Rachid is my only friend in the Minya palace. In Cairo, it seemed he would do anything for me. Now in Minya, he seems distracted, as though his mind is on other things. We don't talk like we used to. I hear a knock on the door. It is a girl called Nara.

"Sayyida Hezba," she says, "you are summoned to the rooms of your husband. He has some important news to tell you. Can you come right away?"

At first I am nervous. It is unusual for my husband to call for me like this without my getting perfumed and dressed for him beforehand. Besides, it is not his day to meet with me. I thrust my bare feet into my harem slippers and throw my gold silk wrap over my shoulders and my hair. We walk through the harem until we reach the entry to the main reception hall. From there we are escorted by one of the general servants to the salamlik, the general area of the palace, and then through to the men's quarters, From here we walk to al-Shezira's private suites. I am surprised to see my husband looking very distressed. He tells Nara to stay and does not even invite us into his rooms. We stand at the door.

"You have had a telegram, Hezba wife," he says. "Your mother is very ill. The palace in Cairo insists that you return there for a few days to be with her. You must go immediately. Veil yourself. I have already ordered a horse-and-trap to take you to the station and that your things be packed. You will be accompanied by Anisah and one of my eunuchs. Be sure to return as soon as you can."

But I am too late. By the time I arrive at the Grande Sarai and am escorted to my mother's rooms, my maman, Zehra Sultan Hanim, is dead. I throw myself on her, burying my face in her still-warm flesh. There must still be life in her. My body trembles with sadness. I kiss her sullen face and wiry grey-black hair. She was a beauty, once, so beautiful, Papa could not resist her. My tears spill all over Maman. I hate myself for not being the girl she wanted me to be.

Suddenly I feel strong arms pulling me away from her. I hardly have the strength to look around to see who is wrenching me away, but out of the corner of my eye I see it is Habrid and one of the lower eunuchs.

"Have respect for the dead," Habrid says bitterly. "You are to return immediately to Minya. Your husband wants you with him."

I cry out that I must be allowed to attend my mother's funeral, but Habrid says he is just following his master's orders. I ask to see Papa, but I am told he is too busy. My heart is breaking. Monday, Monday, Monday, please come.

CHAPTER THIRTY-THREE

Rachid squeezed Aimee's hand. It felt hot and large around hers. Tears rolled down his plump face, sliding into the corners of his mouth. Saiza and Rachid and Aimee sat quietly for a moment in the stillness of the afternoon. A timid breeze rustled the leaves. Aimee breathed slowly, staring at him in disbelief. Could it really be him? The Rachid her maman had loved so much?

"Hezba child," Rachid muttered. Aimee let him take her face in his hands. While he patted her face, Aimee studied him closely—his perfect teeth, the sunken sockets that looked out of place on features still relatively unmarked by time, his huge hands and gnarled arms, the same arms that had once comforted her mother.

"This is little Aimee, Rachid. Nur al-Shezira," Saiza said quietly in his ear. "Hezba's baby all grown up."

"Child, child," he sobbed gently, putting his face in his hands to muffle his tears. Rose arrived with tea. She put down the tray and stared at the man solemnly. Saiza shook her head and put her arm around Rachid's shaking shoulders to comfort him.

"Rachid is the last of them," Saiza said almost to herself.

"They will soon all be forgotten," she continued. "No one will remember all those poor scarred eunuchs. Poor Rachid."

"What happened to him, Aunt? Where did you find him?"

Saiza's face clouded, and she squeezed Rachid's shoulder again before lowering her voice to a barely audible whisper. "He came to me quite by accident. It is God's way, I suppose. A friend of mine said she knew of an old eunuch who was being looked after by a family in Helwan. The eunuch was ill and quite useless, having been blind for some time. Though he was usually quite eloquent and lively, he fell into black depressions from time to time during which he would speak to nobody. The family had found him begging on the street, and had taken pity on him as one would a dog.

"I suspect the family originally wanted him to help them, like a houseboy. He appeared to be good with his hands and could mend things, be useful, despite being blind. But then as I said, he would get terribly depressed and start to rant and rave, chanting the name of my dear beloved sister, Hezba. That was when my friend wrote to me. Could it be the same person, she asked? I did not know. While I was in Alexandria, I had Hakim visit him to verify the story. And it was all true. He was once in the employ of the sultan, my father. Though I didn't know him well back then, I recognised him as soon as I saw him. The whole harem knew how close Rachid and Hezba were, but nobody took much notice. Each girl had her own eunuch to attend to her needs."

Aimee listened with her head bowed. Rachid had not released her hand. He held it softly, squeezing it tenderly at regular intervals as though he had been given new life.

"I have brought Rachid here," Saiza went on, "to live with us, though between you and me, I don't think he is well. He cannot tell me what has happened to him since he lost his sight. Perhaps you had better talk to him, dear—you might be able to get something out of him—but first let him show you his little book of snaps. He carries his book with him everywhere. He owns almost nothing else.

He has memorised the pictures, so even with his sight gone, he can tell you who is who.

"Rose and I will leave you two alone so you can have a little talk. Try to get him to open up, dear; I want him to be happy here. He arrived only a few days ago. That was why I was in such a hurry to get home to Cairo. He seems so depressed, so bottled up."

Saiza whispered a few words of comfort to Rachid, kissed his face, and left. Aimee put her hand on his book and tried to take it from him, but he hung on fast, just as she had clung possessively to her maman's diary when she had first discovered it.

"Show me the pictures, Rachid," she said quietly. "I never knew Maman. It would make me so happy if I could just have a little look. You can trust me. You can guide my hand and turn the pages if you like."

She kissed him softly on the cheek, and he smiled and opened it. Aimee swallowed nervously. She had only ever seen one picture of her mother. She had always wanted to be a part of her mother's life and now, the faces in the sepia-toned prints stared up at her. The photos contained unfamiliar faces, dreams never confided, warmth and laughter she would never experience.

Her mother's hatred of al-Shezira, Aimee's own father, had shocked her at first. But in the few days she had been reading the diary, she'd let the hatred flow over her, not allowing it to consume her.

One photograph showed a little girl standing beside a fountain. She had bright eyes, a wide smile, and an air of confidence. Another showed the same girl, older, in a loose calico dress, hair unadorned, holding a smaller child in her arms, a distant cousin, Rachid assured her. In another, the same girl was dressed in a wedding gown, half veiled and smiling, flanked by an elderly man and a woman in ceremonial dress.

"Tell me, Rachid," she said quietly. "Are they all of my mother?"

He spoke slowly at first, timidly as though it took all his energy. "Yes," he said, and then suddenly the words came, like a torrent. "This photograph," he said, jabbing the book bitterly, "this is the day she married her husband. She was miserable that day. You would never guess it, from the look on her face, but she was clever, my Hezba; she could fool people."

"Who are the people on either side of her?"

"They are her parents, Ali Sultan and Hezba's mother, Zehra. The photograph was taken after the signing of the documents. After sitting for the portrait, she was delivered to her husband. She was only eleven years old when the photograph was taken. You can see she is still a child. I thought I would be sent away to work for the men of the palace that day, but I was allowed to continue as her servant because I was docile. I was a good servant. I did not make trouble, and I thank the Almighty I was allowed to stay with her."

"You weren't fond of your master, Rachid. You felt as strongly about him as Maman did, didn't you? Aunt Saiza told me my father, al-Shezira, was a kind man, but that is not what Hezba thought, is it? She hated him, didn't she? It's all in her diary."

Rachid thrust his head to the heavens and sighed, his eyes wet and searching.

"Your aunt has not told you, Hezba child?" he said. "Very likely, she does not know the truth herself, but still—"

He paused for a moment, trying to muster the courage.

"Khalil al-Shezira was one of the most hated men in Cairo. All those years ago, when the poor peasants were trying to eke out a living, when Egypt was trembling like a frightened dog, he was destroying their trade and working their children into the ground and swindling them mercilessly. He was hated even more than the English officials who made the laws and punished any man who dared to question their authority. He was an evil man. I am glad he has gone. You have no al-Shezira in you, thank the Almighty, Hezba child. You were at least spared that."

Aimee lifted her head, gripping Rachid's hand tightly.

"What do you mean, Rachid? What are you talking about?"

Rachid's voice cracked and he turned to her. His heavy eyelids crinkled at the edges, his smokey, dull complexion flushed a little.

"Al-Shezira was not your father, Hezba child," he said, as though he had not heard her question. "Listen to what I am saying. Brace yourself for the truth."

Aimee stared at him in shock. A sickly gasp caught in her throat. Surely he was wrong? Surely he did not know what he was saying?

"That's ridiculous," she said disbelievingly. "Al-Shezira was my father. That is the truth."

Tears sliding down his face, Rachid started to rock backwards and forwards like a madman.

"The Frenchman with the look of an Arab was your father, child. Hezba confided that to me. She told me everything. I believe I was the only person she told about the identity of her baby's father. She might have told Saiza, but she certainly did not want anyone else to know. Imagine the scandal that would have ensued. I'm sure Alexandre himself didn't even know he was the father. It's possible Hezba wouldn't have told him. She was ashamed of bringing yet more scandal upon her family. As much as she wanted to be free, the bonds of tradition were wrapped tightly around her."

"It's not true. It's not true," Aimee murmured to herself almost inaudibly. She tried to fathom what she was hearing, but all she could feel was a pulsing denial in her heart.

"The Frenchman," Rachid continued. "Alexandre Anton was his name. He was Virginie's brother. She introduced them. Her brother, Hezba's lover, your father, had an evil face. He was as dark

as an Arab, a Frenchman with some Egyptian blood in him. He was
a trickster, a rogue who passed himself off as one of our people. Your
father, Hezba child, the Frenchman with the evil face and the look
of an Arab, spoke Hindi and French and Turkish and Arabic as flu-
ently as the natives."

The light grew dull. A cloud travelled across the sun, and the air
was thick and sticky. Aimee stared at the little book of snaps, trying
to understand. Rachid continued to sway back and forth, his eyes
clamped tightly shut, hot tears slipping out nonetheless, chanting a
strange unintelligible gibberish, a soft, sad refrain.

She scrambled up away from Rachid and headed towards the
house. Saiza called for her as she pushed past armchairs and low
tables and flung aside dividing curtains, running for the door.

The journal of Hezba Iqbal Sultan Hanim al-Shezira,
Cairo, September 11, 1919

*There are reports of more bloodshed in Cairo. The people are fed
up, and it seems that things will only get worse. The war and the British
have pushed them to their limits. There is no food for anyone except the
wealthy. In Minya, our people eat well, but I am scared for my real
home, my birthplace.*

*The palace is still in mourning for my maman. What will they do
when the people loot the great houses of the city? Where will my family
hide? Where will they run?*

*I am scared for Virginie. If she has sense, she will leave soon, join
her husband in Malta, then return to France. Here in Minya, we have
been spared the bloodshed, but it will lap against our doors before too
long. It is only a matter of days now. I can feel the mounting tension in
the air. The people have waited long enough, and the government has
done nothing to assuage their suffering. The people hate Papa. They*

blame him for the grip of the British. I hate Papa for basking in the glory of power without lifting a finger to help those less fortunate than himself. He has no right. He was born of the earth. He has a duty to help the fellahin. I despair of all this injustice.

I can hear al-Shezira's men standing guard outside. I am in solitary confinement in a room with only a small window overlooking the Nile, a mattress, some cotton sheets, a low table, a jug of water, and a prayer mat. It is usually one of the resting rooms used by the servants here at Minya, but now it has been cleaned out to be used as a punishment room for wayward wives. I have been here for a few hours. I don't know why I am here. What has al-Shezira got in store for me this time? Where is Alexandre? I have heard nothing, but I have to trust him. Al-Shezira's men bring me food and coffee and then escort me to the walled garden. There I see my husband. He smiles at me and welcomes me to him. I want to ask him why I have been put in solitary confinement, but I stay quiet.

"Are you well rested, Hezba wife?" he says.

"Yes," I say.

I look around the garden, unaccustomed to being here. I see two men I do not recognise, standing by a small flat-roofed kiosk. A fire has been lit, and on a slab next to it are three knives. The men are busy methodically heating the knives over hot coals, unaware of the presence of their master nearby.

What is going on? I feel a scream ready to explode at the base of my throat. I shiver and wait breathlessly for al-Shezira to make a move.

Al-Shezira smiles and claps his hands. In the sunlight I notice once again just how grotesque he is. He has grown fatter, and his belly hangs low. His face is bloated. His hair has all but disappeared, and his moustache appears quite white against the dull mud-brown of his skin.

"Bring the servant," he shouts in the direction of the men in the kiosk.

Rachid is brought forward. His head hangs against his chest. His hands are tied behind his back. Two men stand on either side of him.

Al-Shezira walks towards him and forces his chin up with the end of a stick. Rachid looks at me, and I see his eyes glaze over with resignation and sorrow.

"Take a look at my wife, Rachid," al-Shezira says. When Rachid does not respond, he throws away the stick and pinches Rachid's chin hard, his long ugly nails drawing blood from his poor hairless jaw.

"Take a good look at her," he snarls. "She may not be beautiful, but she is mine."

My poor eunuch does not answer.

"Do you understand, Rachid?"

"Yes, master," he says.

"Ah," al-Shezira says mockingly. "I don't think you do, Rachid. You are devoted to your mistress, are you not?"

"Yes, master."

"Devoted enough to be her aide, to help her defy the orders of the palace."

"Yes, master."

"You poor eunuch. You like to help my wife, don't you, Rachid?"

"Yes, master."

"And you do exactly as Hezba asks, don't you, Rachid?"

"Yes, master."

"She has a lover, does she not? A man in Cairo who pleasures her, who defiles all that is proper. A man who finds his way into the harem of the Cairo palace."

"Yes, master."

"It was not hard to find out about her infidelities. I have my spies, and I know what is going on. I also know you help her, don't you, Rachid. You have helped her become the depraved creature she is."

"Yes, master."

"Take a last look at your heart's desire, Rachid, because you will never see her face again."

I see in Rachid the look of an animal the moment before death. In his wide-eyed stare, I see that he knows his world is coming to an end.

"Men, do as I have ordered," al-Shezira shouts. His servants step forward, raise their white-hot blades, and lunge at my eunuch, gouging his eyes until blood runs thickly down his face.

"No!" I run forward to try and stop them, but another eunuch appears and holds me back. I cannot watch what is happening. My stomach jumps into my mouth, and my eyes sting with rage. My jaw is locked with hatred, and my ears ring with the hysterical, demented screams echoing off the palace walls. I struggle violently as I watch the bloody tears slipping down Rachid's face, his contorted hands and legs, the flash of the knives. Then I hear a different scream, a female sound, haunted, possessed, the most heartfelt sound I have ever heard. I realise it is coming from my own lungs. I never knew I had so much rage inside me. I collapse on the paving stones and splutter for breath before my hysteria rents once more from my throat.

I am thrown back in my rooms. I hear Rachid whimpering with pain in the gardens below, and then I hear nothing. As night comes, I watch the stars twinkle in the sky in a stunned trance. There is something so beautiful about them. Though I try to count each one, it is hard through the veil of tears. At least the counting distracts me from my breaking heart. Rachid, my darling servant, my only friend, is gone, dismissed, blinded by al-Shezira. What will become of him?

Rachid, sweet Rachid, a boy who never hurt a living soul, has been wrenched from my life, and now I will never see him again. My tears splash against my wrists and fall in great salty pools on the stone floor. I don't look at the stars anymore. I curl up, hugging my knees, and sob so violently, I feel my body will break in two. The night stretches out before me like a great expanse of nothingness. How can I help him? I don't know what to do. And with this I sob some more. It's all my fault. I will never forgive myself for the pain inflicted on him. The next day I hear the whisper of gossip on the breeze. I am insane, they say. I will be sent away, locked away in a sanatorium to grow old alone. Rachid is already gone, but I don't know where he has been sent. I cannot find a trace of him. No one will tell me. They are all afraid of al-Shezira. I am desperate, desolate, and pulsing with hatred. Every last pleasure in my life has been ripped from me. When I think of the torture I witnessed, I know there is only one thing left to do: to seek my revenge and wait for no one, not even Alexandre.

CHAPTER THIRTY-FOUR

Aimee had to find Farouk. If one person could help her understand her past, it was he. He was a journalist with access to volumes of newspaper archives. Surely something must have been written about al-Shezira. She wanted to see hard facts, evidence of al-Shezira's cruelty, anything that might shed light on this man.

The air was filmy and the light was fading as she made her way to Bulac, where the offices of the *Liberation* were located. If Farouk was not at his office, she would go find him in Zamalek or on his houseboat. She nudged her way past the street sellers, child beggars, and women with shopping baskets on their heads until she was standing on the street where the *Liberation*'s offices were located. She stopped, wiped the perspiration from her forehead, inhaled deeply, and pushed the door open. She walked down the long dusty corridor. The main door to Farouk's office was not closed. She walked in, feeling vulnerable, impulsive, out of her league. A young man, about her age, told her that no one from the paper was around to help her at the moment, but if she wanted to wait in a small room next to the main office, someone would be returning soon. She heard the young man speaking on the telephone, telling someone on the other end that a young lady was waiting; then she heard him hang up. He came out to tell her he had to run some errands.

"Someone will be here soon, Madame, to help you," he said. Once the young man left, Aimee got up to have a look around. She went through to the larger office and stood there observing how the room was laid out. On a desk were a typewriter and telephone, notepads, maps, boxes of pencils, old theatre ticket stubs, and a large black folder. Musty, yellowing back copies of the *Liberation* were piled high.

She knelt down and flicked through them, slipping back through time, ten, twenty years as she did so. She yanked the bottom copy out from under the pile, saw the date, the year of her birth. She scanned the headlines: riots, demonstrations, arrests, murders, general unrest, strikes, looting, the burning city, history before her.

"Two minds that think alike, Madame."

She felt a heavy lifeless hand on her shoulder. She could smell the whisky and stale cigarettes, the voice was hard, nasty. She held her breath, hardly daring to look up.

"I suppose I should be ashamed of myself, scaring a young girl like you, but I can tell you are up to no good. That lets me off the hook, don't you think."

She turned and recognised the moonface, shiny dome, and whitish hair, the smirk, and the moist red lips. It was Mahmoud, the man Farouk had told her was the leader of the X.

"You know me, Madame?" he asked, smiling demonically, walking over to Farouk's office door. In the few seconds it took him to lock the door, Aimee knew she was going to die.

"Do you speak Arabic?" he said, folding his arms across his fat belly.

"I am French," Aimee said coldly.

"And what would a little lady like you be doing here in the offices of the *Liberation* rifling through newspapers? Tell me that and I might feel generous and let you go."

"I—I."

Mahmoud lurched towards her angrily. "Well?"

She was suddenly rigid with terror. She could see Mahmoud was losing patience. He walked over to her and pushed her slightly so that she fell back into the armchair behind her.

"I was waiting for the editor to return," she said.

A deep, ugly laugh rasped in Mahmoud's throat.

"Really?" he snarled. Aimee could feel his dirty sneer on her, his leering eyes travelling beneath her clothes and up into the most intimate regions of her body. She needed to try to pacify him, put him off guard. She glanced around the room, desperate for some sort of weapon.

"I don't want to cause trouble, Monsieur. Please just let me go," she said in a soft, pleading voice. She even tried to force a weak little smile. Without warning, he lunged at the desk and wiped it clean with his arm, upending chairs and smashing furniture as he did so.

As he turned to her next, he saw her reaching for the walking stick propped up near the chair. Understanding what she planned to do, he launched himself at her like a maniac. Grabbing her chin, he held it so tightly between his fingers that her eyes almost popped out of her head.

"You're coming with me," he said, running his large hand over her face and hair. "And if you give me any trouble, I might just have you for myself; you're pretty enough."

"Where are you taking me?" Aimee cried out tearfully as he pulled her up out of her chair.

"To pay a little visit to someone who really wants to meet you."

The journal of Hezba Iqbal Sultan Hanim al-Shezira,
Minya, September 15, 1919

 Monday has arrived—the Monday al-Shezira is supposed to be holding his conference, the Monday warned me about. I am distraught with the events of the past few days. Al-Shezira calls me to his rooms. I know it is my turn to be punished. His hatred of me is now so obvious. He doesn't even try to hide it in front of others. I am certain he wishes to be released from this marriage, but he has a duty to my papa, having accepted his bribe. Now that he has discovered my infidelity, there is a rumour that he is concocting the most vicious punishment for me. I am terrified but don't know what to do.

 His servants drag me from solitary confinement and prepare me for him. Their faces are cold masks that convey no feeling or warmth. I hold my breath and pray. I can smell death in the air. It lingers in my nostrils like the dug, overturned earth after a funeral. As I walk from my rooms to my husband's quarters, I hear the sounds of music, clapping, tabla playing, laughing, and the stamping of feet. The music gets louder as I walk. Though it is a celebration of a birth in the palace—a new son for al-Shezira—the palace smells of death because life here is so joyless.

 I am not allowed to join in the celebrations. I have not been dressed in my new robes tonight but instead wear a simple gown of red silk gathered at the breasts over my usual bodice and harem trousers. A little pouch is strapped to my waist on the inside of my robes. After al-Shezira's servants dressed me, I feigned forgetfulness and returned to my room to pick up the revolver Alexandre sent to me, loaded with six bullets.

 After collecting some potions and oils—gifts intended to try to pacify my husband—I enter his rooms. Al-Shezira dismisses his servants, and we are left alone. I know then that he has something awful planned for me and wants no witnesses. He smiles at me. I wonder for a moment whether I am mistaken. He walks towards me. As he strokes my cheek, I suck in shallow little breaths and watch him carefully, like a petrified little girl. He slips his hands inside my robes under my bodice and caresses my breasts slowly. I secretly recoil, but I keep my face from showing my repulsion.

"Do you repent, Wife?" he says. "Have you learned your lesson once and for all?"

I say nothing. I simply watch him, trying to anticipate what he has planned for me.

"You tortured my servant," I say coldly. "For that I hate you more than ever."

"So you are in love with a stupid servant too? Is there no end to your deception?"

He laughs and throws back his head, his eyes streaming, his hands thumping his thick thighs. I watch him splutter and quiver.

I feel as though I am being strangled by this anticipation. I cannot take my eyes off him. I watch the saliva in the corner of his mouth, his eyes bursting with scarlet veins. All I can think of is how much I hate this man. I can't stop the nausea from ripping me apart. Suddenly, he lifts his arm and strikes me with his fist. I reel backwards. My hand flies to my mouth.

Then he grabs me by the neck and shakes me so hard, I feel as though my eyes are going to burst out of their sockets.

"Stop, stop!" I scream.

"I'm going to kill you," he says. "Then I'll be free of this marriage, the weight of you around my neck. You're not alone. I've ordered your lover killed too."

Then he pushes me back. I lose my balance and he lunges at me again. He grabs me by the shoulders and throws me on the floor. My head cracks against the stone, and for a moment I think he has killed me. *The pain spirals through my body. He is at my throat again, on top of me.*

"I'll kill you," I splutter, but he rips my dress down the middle and then exposes himself, all hard and ugly. As he forces himself on top of me, I scream out through the fat fingers that cover my mouth.

I try to bite his hand, but he is stronger than me. I try to kick him in the groin, but he has positioned himself so that I can't reach him. He is forcing himself inside me, harder and harder each time, driving into me with a searing heat. I close my eyes. I cannot look at his face. All I can think is that I must get my revolver. But it is impossible while I am being crushed by this monster. Holding one fat hand fast over my mouth, he drives his other balled fist into my cheekbone until I can smell blood.

"You harlot," he screams. "You belong on the streets, not in my palace, and that is where you will end up, dead and forgotten and out of my way forever."

Then his disgusting load builds up to a violent crescendo and is released. When he pulls away, I curl over in a tiny ball, sobbing and clutching my face, hardly able to open my eyes because of the pain.

Panting and puffing, al-Shezira stands up and steps away from me, wiping his mouth and the perspiration from his forehead with the back of his hand. Then he adjusts the swathe of his trousers and pulls his tunic back over his enormous belly.

With all my strength, I too stagger to my feet. I withdraw the revolver from my hidden pouch and point it at his face.

'This is for Rachid," I say, "and Alexandre and my sisters." I am straining against the grip of the revolver.

He looks startled for a moment. There is no time to lose, but suddenly I panic. What if I miss? What if my shaking hand is not able to pull the trigger? My body stiffens and my heart bangs wildly in my chest. I cannot believe I am doing this. The music in the palace has gotten louder and more frantic. I can hear a scuffle in the corridor outside, the sounds of moaning. I turn my head to look at the door. I know I must do this before it is too late. Whatever happens to me afterwards is of no importance. I must avenge my poor Rachid. I stiffen against the revolver and close my eyes. The door to his quarters opens, and I hear boots in the corridor. I hear a tat-tat-tat-tat-tat of bullets firing downstairs and more screaming. I hear French being spoken. I hear Alexandre's voice, deep and loud.

I take one last look at al-Shezira's face, the evil mass of flesh in front of me, and I suddenly feel strong, empowered.

"You won't win," he shouts. "You are a whore."

I am not Hezba anymore. Hezba has died. I close my eyes and shoot. Then I shoot again and once more and watch his body fall to the ground in front of me.

I pump his body with more bullets, anxious to finish the job properly. Then I fall on my knees beside him and reach out to touch one of the gaping wounds. The warm blood on my fingers reassures me that this is real and not some dream.

I feel as though the bullets have been pumped into my own flesh. I cannot believe what I have done. I shiver uncontrollably. Then I hear a loud noise and feel strong arms clamp down on me. I see the flash of a lantern, hear a voice, urgent and pleading, feel the heat of someone's breath against my ear. I notice for the first time that I am covered in blood.

CHAPTER THIRTY-FIVE

Aimee felt a sharp object being rammed hard into her hip. Mahmoud put his arm forcibly around her shoulders and whispered hotly in her ear.

"A piece of me and you'd soon shut up."

She flinched and closed her eyes in horror.

"How would you like that, little Madame? Fancy some of my rough-and-ready?"

He laughed and spat on the ground. Nauseated with fear and disgust, Aimee quivered miserably. What a revolting man. If she'd been a man herself, she would have fought him off, but her fear had immobilised her. If she screamed out, he would use the gun poked violently in her side.

He continued. "When I've finished with you, after I've taken you to meet my friend, I might kill you, just for the fun of it, but not before we've taken a little ride together, out to the desert. It gets very lonely out there at night and very, very cold."

He walked her outside with his arm around her and thrust her in the front seat of his car. "Remember," Mahmoud said, "not a word. I don't want to hear a single sound come out of that pretty mouth of yours."

They drove through dirty streets, on their way, Aimee realised, to Gezira. Mahmoud kept looking over at her. She could feel the hard edge of his gun next to her on the leather seat. Her hands were tied in front of her and a blanket was draped over her, so no one could see. She could feel his watery eyes running over her breasts and her legs. Every time he looked at her, her stomach sank and she could not breathe.

At last the glittering expanse of the Nile appeared, and they crossed the bridge onto the island. They drove towards a magnificent-looking building up ahead, a sandy-coloured mansion surrounded by beautiful gardens. A wrought-iron gate separated a gravel forecourt from the street.

"Remember, not a word or you know what happens," Mahmoud warned her. "You'll be given the order to speak when the time comes."

To her amazement, the sentinel at the gate nodded at Mahmoud, opened the gates, and let them through. He drove around to the back of the mansion, turned off the engine, picked up the gun, and prodded her in the side, laughing.

"You're coming with me," he said, "this way."

He pulled off the blanket and reached over to open the door. Aimee sidled out of her seat. Her mind seemed to have shut down. She tried to think of who she was and why she was where she was, but everything was a blank. All she could comprehend was that the filthy Mahmoud was beside her, walking her inside, up some marble stairs with thick oak banisters, onto a carpeted landing. All she could feel was the prodding of the gun against her hip. Mahmoud's foul breath wafted over her.

"In here," he ordered.

She was pushed into a large and beautiful room furnished with a huge oak dining table and three dining chairs at one end. Mahmoud forced her into one of them. Then he produced a pair of handcuffs from his pocket and cuffed Aimee to the chair. She did not understand. She stared at the handcuffs, stared at Mahmoud. He stood back and studied her with an evil glint in his eyes.

"I still have the gun, Madame. Any funny business—?"

"What is going on? Who are you?" she gasped breathlessly.

Mahmoud perched himself on the oak table, crossed his arms across his chest, and smiled.

"You really want to play the fool with me, Madame? Who I am is not important. It's who you are that matters."

He broke off. Another door opened and two men dressed in smart administrative uniforms entered. They nodded at Mahmoud, and he left the room. As the two men approached Aimee, she realised that she recognised their hateful faces. Fear shot through her again, stabbing at every nerve in her body. She held her breath. The room seemed to go fuzzy, the light suddenly appearing dull and splintered. For a moment, she thought she had passed out, but she knew she was awake. She was, after all, aware of what was going on. She could see the blurred shapes moving about her and discern muffled sounds. She tried to wriggle her toes and her fingers. "We meet again, Madame, and so soon," the fatter one said.

"Let me go. You've got the wrong person," she cried out heatedly. "I have no idea who you want, but I'm not involved in any of this."

Blue-grey shadows slid over the walls. She rammed her ankles against the hard wood of the chair legs, panic-stricken. She knew they would kill her. Aimee yanked hard against her handcuffed fists, to no avail. Defeated, she threw her body back against her chair.

Her mouth trembled, faces appeared before her, first in microscopic detail, then blurring like a brushstroke. Rachid, Maman, Saiza, Rose the housekeeper, Amina, Farouk, Sophie, all of their faces merging and becoming one.

"We want to question you. This time you will not get away," the other said. Aimee tried to focus her gaze. The man's face was expressionless, his lips the colour of pewter, his eyes tight and lifeless, his voice cruel.

"And this time, you'll answer every question put to you on your involvement with the terrorist group, the X."

The journal of Hezba Iqbal Sultan Hanim al-Shezira,
Minya, September 15, 1919

I try to speak, but I am trembling violently. Alexandre gently puts his hand over my mouth and shakes his head. He has an inky-blue turban wound around his head, blue robes, and sandals—desert garb. He looks thin and ill. He is holding a bundle from which he pulls a chador. He wraps me in it, covering my head and my face. My hands are still wet with blood. My head hurts and my face feels bruised and tight. I stare at my hands numbly and cover them with my chador.

I look up and see with him four men whom I don't recognise, dressed in a similar style. They look like Tuareg tribesmen. Alexandre lifts me up and pushes me through the door of al-Shezira's apartment. He shouts to his men, "Stand guard against those double doors, then follow us."

The music has stopped, and all I hear is screaming and whimpering. The slumped bodies of some of the palace's eunuchs are lying on the marble floor.

"The palace—?" I start to ask him.

Alexandre flashes me a look. "Freedom is coming for all," he says, and scoops me up in his arms. He runs with me along the vast network of palace corridors to the back entrance, which leads to the stables.

The night eunuchs aren't where they should be, and I understand what has happened. The price of freedom is the life of others. I have proved that tonight. May my God forgive me.

Alexandre is breathing hard as he marches forward with me in his arms. My face is so close to his that I can see the perspiration on his forehead, the deep frown etched between his eyebrows. I am heavy, but he is strong. When we reach the stables at the back of the palace, he helps me onto a horse and swings himself on. I cling to him and rest my head against his back. He turns to shout to his men. All around me I hear horses pulling against their reins, their hooves thumping on the earth. I hear Arabic and French being spoken. I close my eyes to block everything out. My body pulses with a strange sensation—relief, fear, I am not sure. I wonder what the future holds for me. But for the moment the future does not matter. I am simply calmed by the movement of the horse as we ride. Alexandre looks back at me every now and again and presses his hand against mine. I see in my mind's eye the red of al-Shezira's blood, hear the sound of the revolver exploding against his flesh, watch as his face relaxes in death. Nausea rises from my stomach to my throat.

I squeeze Alexandre tighter. I want to ask him where we are going, but I cannot speak. We seem to have been travelling for a long time. I wish it were all over. I long to be somewhere, anywhere, not riding on this horse. Eventually we stop. We have been following the Nile, which twinkles in the moonlight. I see a village up ahead.

When we reach it, Alexandre sets me down, adjusts my chador, and leads me to a small house. His men follow. Inside, a group of people is sitting on the floor. A man is playing an oud softly. A woman is singing one of the ancient songs of the desert. I recognise it. It was sung to me as a child. I listen to it in a trance. I try to picture my family, but their faces are fading away. It is a terrifying feeling. Alexandre nods at the man with the oud but says nothing as he escorts me to a room away from the group. He pushes the door open, sits me down on a low bed, unveils me, and looks into my face.

"We are safe here for the time being," he says.

"Where are we?"

"A village not far from Beni Suef."

"I killed him," I say, shaking. *My lips tremble and my mouth is parched.*

Alexandre reaches for a jug of water, pours me a drink, and lifts it to my lips.

I drink gratefully.

"Where do we go to from here?" *I say.*

"In an hour, after we have rested and eaten, we will pick up the camel trail to Kerdassa. From there we will plan our journey across the Mediterranean."

I am shivering uncontrollably. "Al-Shezira is dead," *I say. Alexandre puts his arms around me and comforts me.*

"He tortured Rachid and sent him away," *I say.*

He grips my shoulders.

"I know."

"How do you know?"

"I have spies in the palace, servants who are on my side, people who have lived every day waiting for what has happened, to happen."

"Is that why there were no night guardsmen on duty?"

"Yes," *Alexandre says.* "I am proud of you, Hezba. You are the people's hero."

"But I have blood on my hands," *I say, pulling my hands out of my robes and staring at the blood that has dried on them.*

"But there were no witnesses to the killing, Hezba. No one saw or would suspect anything."

"But the gun?" *I say.*

"I have it here. I'm going to bury it deep in the ground. There will be nothing to incriminate you."

"I waited for you," *I say tearfully.* "I was told to wait for a signal . . ."

Alexandre holds me in his arms to calm me.

"It's over now, Hezba," he whispers. "Now we have to look to the future. We have to prepare ourselves for a long and dangerous journey, but first you must rest and change your robes. I must get you to safety in France. Then I will return to Egypt to carry on the fight."

He puts the chador back over my hair, stroking and kissing the swollen flesh on my face, and leads me by the hand to another door, then to a little pathway that leads to the Nile.

"Wash yourself in the river. Take off your clothes and bathe. I will get you more robes and one of our women to bathe your head. Wait here. I won't be long."

CHAPTER THIRTY-SIX

After the evening prayers, Nemmat made her way to her dead brother's apartment in Abbassiya to meet Farouk. Once she and Farouk had gone over the minute-by-minute schedule for the assassination plan one last time, Farouk's men would drive her to the Oxford. Issawi was dining there tonight, and her services as an escort girl for the chief advisor had been arranged. Once Issawi had been drugged, she could bring him back to Abbassiya, where Farouk could get on with his plan. Of course, none of this was going to happen. Nemmat imagined the feeling of power that would come as she ended Farouk's life. She owed it to her mother, for all the wrongs inflicted on her by men. It felt good to be double-crossing Farouk.

Though nervous, she was feeling fine. Her moment had come. Such power. A kind of euphoria had taken hold of her. She wanted to be a rich woman. She had said good-bye to her mother, kissed her soft, downy face, squeezed her frail body, and reassured her that she wouldn't be back too late. She had taken great care with her appearance. She had donned her classiest outfit, a Western-style, ankle-length tightly fitted blue silk sheath that showed off all her curves, covered her arms with her trademark jewelled bracelets, and rimmed her eyes with the usual black kohl. Her hair she'd left loose, brushing it so that it hung down her back, skimming the tops of her thighs.

She pulled on her blue satin gloves, under which she wore wafer-thin mitts to protect her from exposure to the cyanide. Issawi would think the outfit was a tantalising part of the game of seduction. Farouk would know nothing of her protective mitts.

She patted the sash that she'd tied around her waist and smiled. The tiny capsule of cyanide lay hidden in the folds of silk.

Before leaving, she had thrown on her usual black chador, swept any stray tresses behind her back, and covered her head and face with the cloth. Her chador gave her the anonymity she needed. Her heart beat excitedly as she walked out into the street. This job would be much more fun than the Lake Timsah affair. The danger of the operation excited her. Her life excited her. Her mother had wanted her to get married and become a mother herself, but Nemmat could not stop now. How could she ever change when her mother relied on her?

She stood on the corner and waited for the car to arrive. Farouk had ordered one of his men to drive her to Abbassiya. A car pulled up with two men inside. "Jewel?" one of them asked.

Nemmat stepped forward.

"Who asks?"

"Khufu and Amoun."

The code names had been correctly relayed. Nemmat nodded and slid into the rear seat of the car. The traffic was heavy tonight, and the car crawled through the crowded streets. Nemmat glanced nervously at her wristwatch. She was expected at the apartment in ten minutes.

The minutes ticked by. Finally, Mitwali stopped around the corner from the apartment building, as Nemmat had asked him to. She got out, pulled her chador more tightly over her face, and hung her head as she pushed through the crowds, then climbed the stairs to apartment 12. She knocked on the door. She heard a voice and uttered the code word. The door opened. She nodded in greeting as Farouk locked the door behind her. There on a shabby dresser were a bottle of whisky and a few glasses. Farouk motioned for her to sit down on the dirty old sofa.

"I'll stand," she said coolly.

"Let's get down to business," he said.

Nemmat did not remove her chador. She stood as confidently as she could and waited for Farouk to speak.

"The success of this part of the operation comes down to you, Sayyida," he said as he walked to the dresser, unscrewed the whisky bottle, and poured himself a drink. "Do you want one?"

Nemmat nodded. "For courage." She smiled.

"You have nothing to fear," he said. "You have the easy part."

Farouk handed her a tumbler of whisky.

"The heroin I'll give you will dissolve easily into his drink," he said, smiling, as Nemmat took a sip of her whisky.

Farouk took the packet out of his jacket pocket and sniffed it. The heroin he'd bought from Nasser's Trinkets had been hijacked by the desert bandits, but Mitwali had supplied him with some more top-quality stuff. He handed her the packet. Nemmat watched him nervously. Any minute now, she would have to do it. Realising that she had to distract him, she decided to get him talking.

"What will happen when it is all over, Sayyid?"

Farouk gulped down the dregs of his whisky and served himself another.

"You ask too many questions," he said. "Just concentrate on the job you have to do. My men will take care of Issawi's security guards. Once the heroin starts to take effect, he won't be concerned about leaving his bodyguards behind. He'll be looking forward to helping himself to you, Sayyida."

How cold he seemed. It was as though he wasn't the least bit interested in her—as though his heart belonged to another or nobody at all. She didn't understand him. He was an unusual man.

Her heart slammed against her chest as she considered what she was about to do and tried to anticipate his next move.

"This death of Issawi means a lot to you, doesn't it?" Nemmat ventured.

Farouk had just poured himself another double shot of whisky. He put the bottle down on the dresser and turned to face her.

"I have been planning this for a long time."

She felt her face flush under his gaze. There was something suspicious about his eyes. She felt suddenly very afraid—as though the plan was about to go wrong. "And that's all you are going to tell me?"

He jerked his head defiantly at her.

"Why do you need to know more?"

"Because if I know what all this is about, I might be able to do my job better."

Farouk stepped closer to her. Nemmat couldn't wrench her eyes from him. He was studying her face, reading every falsity in her heart and soul. He could see through her; she knew it, and something inside her snapped. A wave of panic washed over her. This was a trap, a setup. Perhaps Farouk had summoned her here because he knew she was in league with Littoni and he was going to kill her.

"Are you ready? You have to go now. My men are waiting. Just get Issawi here. Your money will be here when you return with him."

He was acting strangely. He looked ill tonight, almost feeble and very old. Surely he could not be much older than forty-five?

She took in his features, the long nose, the high cheekbones, the full mouth, the jet-black eyes and olive skin—probably once distinctive, it now appeared slightly withered by approaching old age. She almost felt sorry for him.

"What are you staring at?" he asked.

"I was just wondering—"

His eyes, narrow slits of night-black suspicion, fixed bitterly on her as though he didn't trust her.

"Don't wonder," he snapped. "You know what to do. It's time."

He turned and went to the dresser to get his drink. Perhaps she should do it now?

The journal of Hezba Iqbal Sultan Hanim al-Shezira,
Beni Suef, September 15, 1919

Alexandre leaves. I stand trembling in the night air, in the moonlight, hidden by reeds. There is nobody around. I can smell the dank odour of the river. Crouching behind a dune, I fumble with my clothes and take them off. Then I slip into the Nile and scrub myself with my hands. My hair becomes wet at the ends. I submerge myself briefly, letting the cool water caress my body and my sore head. With my head underwater, I imagine for a moment that I am being purified by the waters and forgiven. Then a surge of fear pulses through me. I am a murderer. I will live with this reality for the rest of my life.

I break through the murky water and focus my eyes in the moonlight. Alexandre is waiting for me on the bank. He stretches out his arm to help me, covers me with a soft woven blanket, and guides me back to the mud-brick house.

A woman comes into the house after us with some ground herbal ointment. She dabs it onto my bruises, cleans the remaining blood from my sores, combs and plaits my hair for me while Alexandre dries me slowly.

When the woman has left, Alexandre takes me in his arms and I fold myself against him, overwhelmed by this all-consuming desire inside me. I am a murderer, running away to start a new life with my lover. Yet, as I stand here in this little village house, all I can think of is Alexandre in front of me, continuing to pat me dry.

I savour the pressure of his hands on my shoulders, the earth-scented taste of his lips on mine. When I am dry, he lets the blanket drop to the ground and lifts me up to lay me on the cushions. He strokes my rounded stomach and my thighs and my feet and my breasts and my face, and then he unravels his robes and his blue turban and lies over me tenderly, moaning my name. I reach out and pull his face to mine, entranced by his full mouth and glittering dark eyes, the slant of his nose and his cheekbones.

He bites my neck and looks lovingly into my eyes, and for a moment I feel as though no harm will ever come to us.

He splays my legs and slips inside me, and I feel the exquisite pressure of his body on top of mine. I'm home, I say to myself. I belong with this man, not to him, but with him as equals.

Alexandre rocks me to a gentle rhythm. I am tired but happy. I forget where I am. All I know is that deep down, I am alive and that death has not overcome me yet. When we are both sated, Alexandre holds me in his arms. He covers me with his robes to keep me warm. I am happy. Thanks to him, I know what happiness and peace are even if it is only for moments. The woman reappears with some clean robes for me to wear.

Alexandre gets up and hands my blood-soiled clothes to her, and she disappears.

"She will wash them," he says.

"But—" I start to say.

"She is one of us," he says firmly.

He returns to me and kneels down in front of me. Holding my hands in his, he kisses my fingers.

"It is written all over your face, Hezba." He smiles. "You don't trust me."

His eyes narrow jokingly, and then he goes on. "No one saw you."

"But the palace? When they discover that I've gone, they will start looking for me."

"Sssh, Hezba," he says. "Cairo in on fire. The Nationalists are rioting. There are looting and killings in the streets. The city is in chaos. It doesn't matter how many troops are sent in to round up the masses— what the masses want is for the rich pashas to pay for lapping up the favours of the British."

I clutch him like a child. He goes on. His voice is no longer playful but mocking and hateful.

"Five men have been murdered at the Minya palace. And then they will find another, the esteemed pasha al-Shezira. The authorities will conclude the same group was responsible for his murder, a group so big and strong that to track down a single culprit will take all their resources and detective work."

"But the sultan's daughter is no longer there," I say. "These authorities will conclude that she escaped because she was guilty of something."

He whispers against my cheek, "There were no witnesses. To arrest the daughter of the sultan of Egypt would be inconceivable. The authorities will do nothing. Trust me."

I want to believe him. I close my eyes. I'm very scared.

"But one of the guardsmen must have seen me go into al-Shezira's apartment?" I tell him.

"Are you sure?" Alexandre asks me.

I tell him I am.

"The guardsmen were called out to the gardens to confront suspected intruders. The man you mentioned was killed in the chaos."

"Intruders?" I say. "Your men had already stormed the palace?"

Alexandre smiles and nods. "We were in hiding."

"So you tricked them, to get them outside," I say.

"Yes."

"And what happened to the night guardsmen when they went to confront these intruders?"

"In the name of our countrymen, they were taken care of," Alexandre says calmly.

I turn away and sigh with sadness. I hate all this death and destruction. "You must get dressed, Hezba," Alexandre says.

"Put on these robes and then follow me. We must go. Our caravan will be waiting. My men will want to set off before dawn breaks."

CHAPTER THIRTY-SEVEN

The uninterrupted drone of a car horn sounded outside—Mitwali's signal that it was time for Nemmat to be driven to the Oxford. Farouk leapt up from the sofa and ran to the window to study the darkening street.

"You must go," he said.

"Your drink? At least have your whisky while you wait for me to bring him back," Nemmat said.

Farouk turned to look at her. He noticed the generous masklike smile spread wide over her face, the too-bright eyes, the anxious rise and fall of her breasts under her chador, the mocha-coloured arm and gloved hand outstretched, holding his tumbler of whisky out to him.

In a flash, he saw the fear in her eyes behind the brightness. And he recognised that fear. It was the fear of a street dweller, the daily fear of being consumed by life itself, of having the precarious balance of power tipped by some outside force from self to other. He took the tumbler but did not hold it to his lips.

The sound of splintering glass shattered the silence. Nemmat screamed as the tumbler shards fell to the floor. He stepped forward and grabbed her by the throat. Her eyes strained with panic, and her flawless, dusky complexion flushed red. "You think I don't know what you were trying to do, Sayyida?"

"What are you talking about, Sayyid?"

Again the car horn sounded, long and forced this time, designed to attract his attention. Suddenly he bent double, a pain rising up through his chest, engulfing him, suffocating him, worse this time, tighter than the spasms of that morning, more excruciating. He started to cough and had to let go of her neck to slam his fist against his chest. And then a more searing pain shuddered through him, as the girl cut through the skin of his arm with her sharp teeth and brought her knee up to his groin. As he doubled over in agony, she made her escape.

He caught a glimpse of her dress vanishing around the front door and managed with difficulty to pull himself up and run after her. Putting one leg in front of the other, his body flaying painfully, he made it down the stairs and saw her disappear into a car that sped off.

But it wasn't Mitwali's car. Mitwali got out and stared after Nemmat confusedly. Ali, his brother, appeared. Shouting, Ali crossed the street, wondering what on earth was going on. Then a round of bullets from a machine gun was pumped into both of them. Mitwali and Ali's blood-splattered bodies fell against the car and slumped to the ground. Farouk knew it had to be the work of Littoni or Security Operations.

He spun around to try to see where the bullets had come from. Women were prostrated on the mud-caked pavement, shielding children, and people were shouting in the streets. He had no time to lose. He jumped into Mitwali's car to trail Nemmat.

She couldn't be far ahead, he assured himself, wiping the perspiration from his forehead with the back of his jacket sleeve as he drove. Damn her! Who was she working for? Littoni? Issawi himself? He'd seen the look of cool betrayal in her eyes. She hadn't been able to conceal it.

He eventually spotted the car ahead and followed them closely through Ezbehieh, al-Qahire, and then on to Giza. When the car pulled around to the forecourt of the Mena House Hotel, he pulled over behind a tree and watched her make her entry like a prima donna. The doorman saluted and fawned over her, then ushered her through the portico to a table in the middle of the dining room. Through the multiple glass doors that led from the entry through the central foyer to the dining area, Farouk watched as Nemmat sat down to join Littoni. His body shuddered with hatred. He reached for his hat and put it on, pulling the brim down low, so that his face was partially hidden. He got out of his car, crossed the street, and went up to the doorman.

He grunted a greeting. "Will you be dining tonight, Sayyid?" the doorman asked.

Farouk shook his head. "No, I need a drink and some privacy to gather my thoughts. Please see to it I am brought a whisky and soda and not disturbed. Tell your boy, I'll be sitting over there, by the palm, reading the newspaper."

The door to the dining room was open. Littoni and the girl's table were not far from the door, and the restaurant was very quiet. He sank down on a leather couch, near the entry to the dining room, picked up a newspaper, and listened carefully.

"You fool of a girl," Littoni said. "A simple task and you failed miserably."

"I had to come straight away, Sayyid. Who knows what Farouk might do now?"

"We'll have to send in our men and get them to finish the job themselves," Littoni said. "He must be got rid of. No mistakes this time."

Farouk held his breath behind his newspaper. He heard the clink of a glass being put down on the low table in front of him.

The conversation stopped abruptly. Farouk panicked for a moment. He would leave but didn't want to do so just yet.

The conversation resumed.

"I need my money, Sayyid," Nemmat said.

"You did not do as the Group instructed," Littoni said. "I should kill you myself for that reason alone. You obviously don't understand the seriousness of what has happened, which is entirely your fault. With Farouk's body holed up in some remote deadbeat apartment, he wouldn't have been found for days, if not weeks. Now, he's out there. Right when the X's moment of glory is so near. Do you think Farouk is going to sit back and wait and watch? Not only will he be more furious than ever, but he's still going to try to take Issawi out on his own—ruining all our plans. The police will be brought in. The king's celebrations will be cancelled. The X will have to regroup and come up with an entirely new plot."

"But if your men kill Farouk first, the X will be able to stage the coup with no hitches," Nemmat suggested.

"You know nothing of how these things work," he said. "Issawi will be waiting at the Oxford for you. But now you're here and we've lost Farouk. We have to find him too before he gets to Issawi. If Issawi is murdered, the king's men will go into crisis mode and a coup will be impossible. The Ibrahim girl seems to have gotten involved too. My men saw her on Gezira, at Issawi's HQ, getting out of a car on Sharia Omar Pasha, evidence that she's in cahoots with Issawi and his cronies, taking over where Ibrahim left off."

Farouk jumped up, raced out of the lobby to his car, and started off for Sharia Suleyman Pasha at top speed. Aimee. Issawi had Aimee. The thought of it burned through him, and he slammed the steering wheel with his fist, like a man possessed, as he drove. It was a trap, a lure. It had to be. He could not believe that Aimee had fooled him into thinking she was an innocent when all along she was in league with Issawi.

As the possibility crossed his mind, his heart exploded with panic. He had wanted to go to her house to check whether she was all right. But now? If what Littoni was saying was true, Farouk didn't know how long he had before the entire network capsized like a doomed ocean liner, before Littoni launched his ill-planned revolution.

The journal of Hezba Iqbal Sultan Hanim al-Shezira,
Beni Suef, September 16, 1919

We set off just before dawn when there is just a smudge of red in the sky. Do I dare believe that I am staring freedom in the face? That I will have a new name, a new country, a new life, free of the torture al-Shezira inflicted upon me? Though I give the impression I have regrets about what I have done—and so I do—I was provoked beyond all reason. And so I should forgive myself. I ride with Alexandre high atop the camel on my little seat, wrapped in the traditional indigo-blue cloth of the Tuaregs. Only my eyes are visible to witness the vast camel train following us.

Our party has grown to include thirty camels, each carrying one, sometimes two men, loaded down with baskets of spices and salt and goods for sale in the desert villages we will pass through. Alexandre has told me that because we are masquerading as the seminomadic Tuaregs, we will arouse no suspicion and we will be far less likely to be stopped by the British patrolling soldiers. I hear him shout instructions to the other men, telling them what will happen when we get to the next village. He tells them to move ahead, and we follow them at some distance to the rear. As I sway with the movement of the huge beast, a wave of nausea washes over me. Desperate for sleep, I close my eyes and surrender to it.

When I awake, the sun is high in the sky, and I'm sure we have been travelling for a long time. The heat beating down through my robes, I stare out at the golden carpet of desert. Behind us, to the south, I gaze upon dunes and mountains and the blinding white light of Africa. My heart throbs painfully at the sight of this landscape that I will soon be leaving behind. A child of the desert, I say over and over to myself. That is what I always was. That is what I will always be, even when I am far, far away.

Up ahead to the north, I see palm trees and the glittering water of an oasis. We arrive at a town and dismount. I am thirsty. I stumble into Alexandre's arms and ask him for water. He hands me a flask and I drink gratefully. Our caravan is coming in through the trees. Alexandre takes me by the hand and leads me to a grass hut. He greets a woman, who is dressed in brightly coloured robes. Her face is beautiful, her smile warm and generous. She bows and departs. Alexandre lays me down on a comfortable mat on the ground and pulls my robes away from my perspiring face. Though I am thankful for the cool darkness of the hut, I look tiredly into his eyes and ask, "Where are we, Alexandre?"

He squeezes my fingers. Since most of his face is covered by his tribesman headdress, I look into his beautiful kohl-black eyes and can read the message within them, that we are together and that despite everything we must be together, that even when I am in exile he will return to bring me home. "We are at Fayoum," he says. "Tonight we will be at Kerdassa. I've instructed my men to rest here while the sun is at its highest. We will set off again at sunset."

I let my body relax as he delicately strokes my enflamed cheeks. "I'll get you some food and tea," he says, and then he is gone.

Another wave of nausea rides over me. I am ill. This is kismet. I have taken the life of a man and now I will pay. I am sure I will die. But the nausea passes. I study the slivers of light penetrating the roof made of reeds. Then I curl into a ball and rock myself into a shallow sleep. Some time later, I wake up with a start.

I sit up and pull my tangled robes away from my face. I can hear Alexandre talking, nearby in French to one of his men.

"I will organise the papers when we get to Kerdassa. We need European clothes and French identity papers. There is no time to waste. I've heard the British Army has sent out hundreds of its men to raid all the villages within a hundred-mile radius of Cairo and Minya. My men in Cairo have assembled as many revolutionaries as they can to demonstrate and ransack the British establishments, the barracks, the clubs. I am hoping the force needed to counteract these attacks will leave the British Army weak and unable to follow through with its village raids. That will buy us some time."

"And the girl? Does she know about her father?"

"No and she must not know. She is vulnerable and weak. If she hears of the Nationalist takeover of the sultan's palace, she will lose the courage to go on. I must get her out of Egypt, before it is too late."

CHAPTER THIRTY-EIGHT

Saiza stood weeping in the upper-floor sitting room of her house. She shouldn't have let Aimee leave like that. She'd run out of the house hours ago and had not returned. What an awful row. And now night was approaching in a cloud of red and bronze. Her dark, misty eyes drooped sadly. She had lost Ali, her son, and Hezba, her half sister. Now she stood to lose Aimee, her precious niece, if she did not sort out this terrible misunderstanding between them.

She huddled in her blue shawl, chewing over the past in her mind. Of course, Aimee had a right to know about her mother and her father, but how much and when?

Saiza had been waiting for a suitably calm moment to have a conversation about her past with her niece, but the time had never been right. As she mulled over what she would have liked to say, one word came to her over and over again: protection. She had wanted to protect Aimee from shame.

Sayyid Alexandre Anton, Aimee's father, had disappeared, but there was somebody who might know where he was and how Aimee could find him if she wanted to.

She came up with a course of action. She would write her niece a letter explaining why she had kept things hidden. Then she would go to Aimee's home and slide it under her door. That way Aimee could absorb the information calmly, in her own time. Saiza started to feel brighter. There was always a solution. She smiled, blowing her nose. She went to her writing desk, pulled out a cream-coloured sheet of paper, found her pen, and dipped it in the ink bottle. Saiza's cousin might be able to help untangle the mystery of Aimee's real father's whereabouts. If she was lucky, her father would be long dead. In heavy black ink, she wrote down the cousin's name and address: *Sayyid Gad Mahmoud, 55 Sharia Mustafa Kamil, Shubra*. After adding a few words of love and support, she slipped the paper in a matching envelope, licked it shut, addressed it, put it into her handbag, and went to find Hakim.

At Sharia Suleyman Pasha, she marched purposefully down the narrow haret leading to Aimee's courtyard garden. She puffed and panted a little up the steep stone stairs, then knocked timidly on the door.

The house was in darkness. Saiza knocked again, then peered through the little window that overlooked the courtyard. She experienced a jolt of panic. Her sixth sense told her something was wrong. She tried the doorknob, but it was locked. She heard running behind her. Was it Aimee? Saiza swung around hopefully, only to see a man at the bottom of the staircase, his hand on the iron railing.

"Sayyid?" Saiza said.

The man ran up the steps two at a time and stopped in front of her. Then he bent over, clutching his chest.

"The lady of the house?" he gasped.

"You must be looking for my niece. It appears she's not at home."

Saiza studied him for a moment. Even with his hat covering half his face, she could tell that he looked ill, distressed.

"Are you all right, Sayyid?" she asked.

He took off his hat and clenched it in his hand.

"I must speak to Madame Ibrahim," he panted. "Do you know where she is?"

There was something about him, Saiza thought. A jolt of recognition that she couldn't quite place gripped her and then faded. "Who are you, Sayyid?"

Their eyes met. Without his hat, Saiza saw that he was about the same age as she was. What could Aimee be doing, associating with a man like him?

"I'm sorry—forgive me. I'm in a hurry. Do you have any idea where Madame Ibrahim is?"

"I—I don't know," she stammered. "I'm looking for her myself."

"Then forgive me for being rude, but I must go."

He nodded and bowed, then turned and flew down the stairs. That face? Where had she seen that face before? A strange premonition came over her, and she knew in her heart that something was terribly wrong. Aimee was in serious trouble.

She steadied herself for a moment on the railing. As she looked down at the shadowy courtyard below, it all came into focus, the face, the voice, the dismissive wave of the hand, the scent of the cigarette he had been smoking.

She started down the steps, reeling dizzily. She tried to grip the railing, but it was too late. The ground gave way under her, and she fell with a mighty thud, her body hitting the slab below.

The journal of Hezba Iqbal Sultan Hanim al-Shezira,
September 13, 1919

I hardly dare speak when Alexandre returns. He bends down and enters the hut carrying a tray with támiyyah, a plate with some sweet kunafah, and a samovar with two gold-coloured glasses. I am sitting up, but I can't bring myself to speak. I can't believe what I have heard.

*Papa? Saiza? Nawal? Are they all right? Desperate for news of my fam-
ily, all I can think about is them.*

Alexandre puts the tray down beside me and pours out some tea.

"Here, eat, Hezba. You must be hungry after our long trip."

*I say nothing. I pick up a small ta'miyyah ball and put it in my
mouth. It tastes delicious, of herbs and chickpeas, very nutty and filling.
I hadn't realised how hungry I was.*

*Then I take some kunafah and find my strength returning with its
delectable orange taste.*

*"What is the news of Cairo, Alexandre? Has the trouble there set-
tled down?"*

*"It has gotten worse," he says. "We have no time to lose. I have
heard that the massacre at the Minya palace has been discovered, and
the army has been called in. The Cairo contingent has sent down its best
men by train to search the surrounding countryside for the culprits. We
have decided to set off again immediately. Drink your tea and finish
eating. The men are preparing the camels. We must reach Kerdassa as
soon as possible."*

*I want to ask him for more information so desperately, but I know
he will not tell me the truth. He will try to protect me from myself. I
realise that I need more information before I can make any plans, and
I can only hope that someone in Kerdassa might know something of the
sultan's palace and what has become of it.*

*When we finish eating and drinking, Alexandre lifts me to my feet.
I feel weak. I thought myself stronger than this. Alexandre undresses me
and covers me in a clean indigo-blue robe. He winds a fresh piece of
cloth around my head and my face, leaving only my eyes visible. I feel
cool in the flowing linen.*

*I pat the little pouch that is always strapped to my waist and thank
the power above that my diary and my bone ivory pen are still with
me. I take such comfort in being able to write down all my feelings and*

everything that happens to me. My diary and I must never be parted, ever.

The camels are still drinking at the oasis, but one of the men starts to rally them together as we walk towards them. I step forward in the sunlight and go to pat our camel. As it is nuzzling my hand, I see beneath its belly, supported by a sheath of fabric tied up with ropes, the protruding end of a machine gun. I suddenly feel very afraid. I turn towards Alexandre, but he is calling over one of his men.

Alexandre helps me to climb up on our camel, and our caravan is off, each camel raising first its back legs and then jolting forward to raise its front legs. The men whip their camels' behinds to get them moving.

The camel's gait sends me into a trance once again. As I pray secretly that Papa is not in trouble and that my dear sister, Saiza, has not suffered, tears of longing well up inside me for the Sarai of my birth. But I know it is too late now, that I am a wanted woman, and there is no going back, even if I wanted to.

Forgive me, I am tired from all these emotions running so hot through me. I am tired of being so close to Alexandre, and yet so cut off from him. I long for the day when we can live together as husband and wife and have a family of our own and start our school. I long for the freedom for which I paid the highest possible price.

The sun slips slowly beneath the horizon in the west. As we make our way north, I make my mind up to find out all I can when we get to Kerdassa, even if it means enduring Alexandre's anger that I have gone behind his back. For Papa is still my papa and my harem sisters are still my family. If anything has happened to them, I want to know. Though I am Alexandre's devoted lover and his future wife, I still love my family and ache for news of them.

CHAPTER THIRTY-NINE

Mahmoud's telephone call to the Oxford relaying the news of the capture of one of the X terrorists—the girl who'd escaped in the desert—forced Issawi to return to Operations HQ in the middle of his dinner. Usually this would have put him in the foulest of moods, but tonight, he felt victorious, ready to threaten her with a menu of torture reserved for die-hard criminals. The escort girl didn't matter. There would be other girls for his pleasure.

He pulled at his shirt collar and mopped his brow with his handkerchief. He had decided to question her in person. Of course it was well beneath him, but he and his men had been playing cat and mouse with this group for years, and Issawi was determined to see the emerging face of the X for himself.

Hilali had confirmed the location of three ringleaders and some ten subsectors. If Operations went in and raided the suspected homes and businesses of the subsectors, word would spread like wildfire and the ringleaders would vanish, regroup at another time, and try again. It would be pointless raiding their homes or acting impulsively. The girl, he reckoned, could be used as a lure, bait to get the rats to scurry out of their holes.

"Hilali, where is the girl?" he asked when he arrived at HQ.

"Follow me, sir."

Issawi braced himself. There would be no concessions for this woman. Hilali opened the door to the dining room and Issawi stepped in. She was seated in the middle of the room, handcuffed to a chair.

His men stood on either side of her. She was younger than he had expected and demurely dressed. She was a beauty, with the palest skin he had seen in a long time—not an Egyptian, that was for sure—but striking all the same with her black hair. She looked tired and ill, her mouth a thin line. She looked up when he came into the room, and he stared at her pale eyes, momentarily unable to believe that his men had the right girl.

But he snapped himself out of it as he walked across the room and stood importantly in front of her.

"Madame, you have been told why you are here?"

"Let me go. You have no right to keep me here. I'll report you."

Issawi laughed. "To whom, Madame? You are talking to the chief advisor to the king. Standing on either side of you are the heads of Security Operations themselves. There is no higher law in this land than the three men in this room. You should consider yourself privileged to be in such company."

Aimee jutted her chin out stubbornly and looked at each man in turn but said nothing.

"You are one of the ringleaders of the X, are you not?"

"I am no such thing."

"What do you know about the X?"

"Nothing. I had not even heard of them until a few days ago."

Issawi's eyes narrowed distrustfully. "But you know about them now."

"They murdered my husband," she said coldly.

Issawi shuffled impatiently. "Your name, Madame?"

"You know my name. Your men know it. I won't sit here and be questioned like this."

Issawi clicked his heels and drew his arms across his chest. "I won't ask you again. Your name?"

"Aimee Ibrahim."

"Where do you live?"

"Thirty Sharia Suleyman Pasha, al-Qahire."

"What do you know of a man code-named the Carpet Seller?"

"Nothing. I don't know anybody who uses a name like that."

"What houses have you visited in the last forty-eight hours?"

"I can't remember. I don't know. I'm tired. I visited my aunt in Medinet Nasr."

"Address?"

"Five Sharia Sheik Mohammod."

"You were picked up on the desert road near Ismailia a few days ago. You were left locked up. We wanted a confession, but you and your companion escaped and then you tried to murder my heads of Security by blowing up their vehicles with grenades. Luckily you did not succeed. Nor will you succeed in anything you try to do. Your companion's name, tell me his name?"

She flinched and raised her head to meet his, her features rigid. "The man I was with is called Alim. Sayyid Mustafa Alim."

"Liar," Issawi shouted at the top of his voice.

She flinched again, closed her eyes briefly, then caught her breath, but she didn't say anything.

"What is his real name?"

Aimee started shivering. She licked her lips. "I don't know. I'm tired. I feel ill. I don't know. Stop asking me these questions. I don't know what you want."

"Yes, you do, Madame. You know that this man uses many aliases. He paid a visit to Nasser's Trinkets on the way to Ismailia.

He stopped the car and went and talked to a man there. You stayed in the car. You know his real name, Madame. You know his friends, his group, the circles he moves in. You simply have to tell us who they are."

Aimee looked up at him again. "I told you I know him only as Mustafa Alim."

"Why were you going to Ismailia?"

"My husband was killed there."

"What was your husband's name?"

"Abdullah Ibrahim," she said. "Do you know him?"

Issawi stepped forward, his eyes travelling the length of her body, the contours of her face. "Should I?" he asked her.

"He was an academic, a professor at the university in al-Azhar."

Issawi shook his head angrily. "Cairo has hundreds of academics. Your husband means nothing to me. . . All I care about is nailing the X ringleaders, locking them up, and throwing away the key."

He walked around the girl. She was a slight little thing; yet for all the lies she told, she had an angelic face and managed to look innocent enough. It was obvious she was a first-class actress, properly trained in deceiving the enemy.

"How long have you known this Mustafa Alim?"

"A few days."

"Has he conscripted you as an agent for the X?"

"No."

He saw her close her eyes. Perspiration glistened on her forehead.

"What do you know about a Fatima Said and the club the el-G?"

Issawi saw her eyes brighten. He pressed her further.

"Well?"

"Sayyid Alim took me there once. I heard a Fatima Said ran this club."

"Why did you go there? It's a man's club, is it not? Barred to ladies."

"I wanted to see what this woman looked like," she said.

"Why?"

"I had been given reason to believe that my husband was having an affair with her, and I wanted to confront her."

Issawi lit a cigarette.

"How did you meet Mustafa Alim?"

"At a party. A gathering of a group of my husband's friends and their wives."

"Address?"

"I can't remember the exact address. The house was in Ezbekieh. It was a literary event for some Cairene poets and the launch of their new magazine."

"Liar," he screamed, advancing on Aimee and raising his hand to swing at her jaw. "I'll see you're tortured for all the lies you have told me. You and your type will be destroyed for what you are trying to do to me."

Aimee closed her eyes and flinched, waiting for the blow, but it didn't come. When she opened her eyes, she saw that Issawi, his arm still raised, was studying every inch of her face. Issawi had had enough of her. He walked over and pulled Hilali to one side and whispered throatily in his ear.

"I've finished questioning her for the time being. Take her to the anteroom at the end of the hall. Lock her in there. I have an idea. I'm going to sleep on it. We'll meet again tomorrow at eight in the morning."

The journal of Hezba Iqbal Sultan Hanim al-Shezira,
Kerdassa, September 16, 1919

We arrive at Kerdassa after nightfall. I smell the wood smoke from the burning fires and watch the innocent faces of the people in the streets. I long to be one of them, I long for a simple life, in a place where I can be myself, accepted, useful. On the far side of the village, we are led to some mud-brick houses clustered in a circle with an arena in the middle. As the men tend to their camels, a woman approaches me. Alexandre nods at her, and she takes me by the hand and leads me to a large house.

The interior is exquisite. Kilims cover the floor. Lanterns light the way. Cushions line the walls. Another woman is pouring coffee from a large iron pot. She comes towards me, and hands me a small glass. I sit tiredly down on the cushions and unwind my turban.

The woman who escorted me into the house kneels down and strokes my cheek. She says, "I have been instructed to cut your hair, Sayyida. You are leaving tomorrow for France."

"Yes," I say, "I must go far away."

She reaches into her dress for some scissors and a comb. Crouching behind me, she combs my hair. Then she starts to cut. Huge chunks of my hair fall to the floor. My hair slopes into my neck and curves around my jaw. After a while, I am given a mirror. I look so different. I look like a European, not an Egyptian. I look fashionable and foreign. I give the woman back her mirror and thank her. She bows and goes to fetch something else. She returns with a tailored suit and some leather shoes with a little heel. She holds them up for me to see. She mutters to herself, saying she thinks it will fit me. The suit is a dull cream colour, low waisted, calf-length. It looks expensive.

"This is what you will wear tomorrow, Sayyida. A carriage will come for you at dawn, to take you along the desert road to the Delta. From there you and Sayyid Anton will take a train to Alexandria."

She hands me a paper packet and I open it. I pull out some identity papers. I study the photograph of the woman. She looks a lot like me. She has the same-shaped face and a similarly shaped mouth, and her hair is cut in a similar style. The name says Madame Alexandrine Chevalier, wife of Monsieur Pierre Chevalier, resident of Collioure, France.

I hand the identification papers back to the woman and tell her to look after them for me until tomorrow.

"You don't have to worry, Sayyida," she says. "Tomorrow you will be transformed and will blend easily with other tourists sojourning in Egypt. Tonight, though, you must rest and prepare yourself for your trip. I will take you to dine with the others."

She leads me to another house across the small central square. It is full of Alexandre's men, who welcome me and ask me to sit on the cushions next to my lover. I know now that I must speak out and ask them what news they have of my palace in Cairo. I must know before I leave tomorrow. I am aching with sadness at the thought of Papa and my sisters, but once I am safely abroad, I will send for them. They will see reason. They will see that it is the only solution.

The meal is laid out before us on the floor. I am invited to pick out what I want, but I have lost my appetite. The nausea I have felt for days has come over me again. Instead I ask for a drink and am given sherbet.

I feel Alexandre's men's eyes on me. Inside I tremble. I should feel at one with these people. This is all I have ever wanted, to be a part of change, to witness it happening around me, but they appear so rough and so unaware of the destruction being levelled all around us. It is the women of this country who will bring about change. I must start my school as soon as I can, and educate my girls so change is possible. Change, progress, equality for all has to come with a feminine blessing and direction. Education and freedom for women, a stamping out of *poverty, men and women working side by side for the sake of progress and real Egyptian independence.*

At last I muster the courage to speak. "Is there any more news of the British Army coming after us?"

Aalim flashes me a look of contempt. Then he says, "The British are too busy at Minya. They will come to Kerdassa, but by the time they arrive there, we will have rejoined our brothers in Cairo."

"Don't you fear being captured there?" I challenge him.

He turns his head and spits on the ground, and I recoil a little. "No one will be picked up," he says. "We were shrouded and unrecognisable when we moved in on al-Shezira's palace at Minya. The Rebel Corps is clever. You doubt us, Sayyida?"

Alexandre reaches over and puts his hand on mine to calm me. He can see the rage starting to boil over in me. If I were a man, I would challenge him, stand up to him. As a woman, I can only speak my mind, and even that is frowned upon.

CHAPTER FORTY

As Aimee was being locked up by Issawi's henchmen, Littoni was in the cellar at the back of the al-Ghawri Mosque near the Sharia al-Azhar. He dislodged a brick in the wall, reached in and pulled out a tube of paper tied up with string. Then he slumped down on the floor near one of the lamps and unfurled the paper tube, smoothing out the sheets on his knees.

The pages were a map of the Abdin Palace. Four of the surrounding mosques were pinpointed on it. Pencilled-in blocks showed the respective sectors. The map also identified the leaders of the sectors and the exact time that these sectors would march into action once Tashi set the ball rolling. Everything lay on Tashi's shoulders. But once the trophy containing the bomb was handed to Issawi, Tashi had left the premises, and the bomb had been detonated, all the sectors would storm the palace and the revolution would begin. Littoni heard a noise. He sprung up, his heart pounding wildly in his throat, and rolled the maps up. The door opened, and Tashi and Hamid appeared. They were wearing long robes tied with a sash at the front and loose hip-length jalabas. Their heads were wound with cloth. They looked like ordinary Muslims on their way to pray at the local mosque.

"You're late," Littoni snarled. "What the hell have you been doing?"

Tashi patted him on the arm and smiled.

"Relax, my friend. Everything's ready."

"You have the bomb?"

Littoni felt as though he were on fire. He imagined that his sectors were on tenterhooks too, watching, waiting.

"The car's ready," Tashi smiled, patting his waist. "The bomb's been assembled. It's small but powerful. It will fit well inside the trophy, our little gift to Issawi. The security men at the palace know what's going on. They're loyal sector men and are anxious for the revolution to start."

"You're sure it will do the job?" Littoni said.

"It's powerful enough to destroy half the palace and anybody in its path," Tashi said.

"You were not followed?" Littoni asked frowning.

This time it was Hamid's turn to answer. "No, we covered our tracks."

Littoni gripped the roll of paper he was holding and furrowed his brow. He spat on the floor and said, "Still no sign of Farouk. I should have gotten rid of him myself and not left it to that prostitute. I radioed to two of our men from the Abbassiya sector to go and check out his apartment, but no one has seen him."

Tashi said, "Forget about Farouk. He's not important right now. We're ready; that's all that matters. The muezzins delivered the signal that the sectors need to get into their places. The evening call to prayer was delivered twice instead of once. Our men are prepared. They were expecting that signal. The time has come, Littoni. What, have you gotten cold feet?"

"Shut up," Littoni snarled. He unfurled the map, held it up, and stabbed it with his finger. "Do our figures tally with the plan?" he demanded.

Tashi and Hamid peered at the map.

"Fifty men from the al-Qal'ah end. A hundred men from the al-Ahzar end. Two hundred and fifty from the Ezbehieh end. The rest from the Opera Square end. Yes," Tashi said, "they're all in place. The men from Khalili, Muski, and Bulac make up the majority. The other sectors from Old Cairo, Bab al-Khalq, and Zamalek will follow later, adding another five hundred men."

"Where is the car? Where are your uniforms?" Littoni demanded.

"The car is on Sharia Abdin near my cousin's camel holding. It is out of sight and ready," Tashi said.

"And your uniforms," Littoni repeated impatiently.

"At my cousin's house. We must go. We have the invitations. Papadopolous did a good job. You must take your place too, Littoni."

"I'm leading in with the Ezbekieh sector," Littoni said.

"What if Farouk shows up?" Hamid asked.

Littoni's eyes narrowed.

"You're all armed. Shoot him—if I don't shoot him first."

The journal of Hezba Iqbal Sultan Hanim al-Shezira,
Kerdassa, September 16, 1919

Aalim stands up and comes over to me. I fear he is going to hit me. Alexandre moves forward to block him.

"You waste your time with such a woman, Anton," he cries out. "She is a troublemaker and has done nothing except hinder our plans. If it were not for her, we could have all gone to Cairo to help our brothers with the revolution. As it is, we are stuck in this half-baked village until dawn, all because you want to see her safely to France."

Alexandre grabs Aalim by the shoulders and slams him against the wall.

"You are as stupid as you are ignorant, Aalim. Hezba is the people's hero. She should be honoured, not ridiculed by you, a common rebel with no future.

"Without her money we would not have been able to buy the weapons we needed. Have you given any money for weapons? No, you haven't. Hezba is risking her life to support our group."

"Is it my fault that I wasn't born into wealth like the little princess?" Aalim says. "No, it isn't. If I had money, I would give it. I don't have money. I have been ruined by the princess's husband. If anything, she owes us. She is repaying her husband's debt to us. We owe her nothing, not one thing. We should kill her, actually. That would be an appropriate fate for her—to preserve the honour of men. Women like her—who think they're equal to men. We're the brains and the power behind this revolution. She's a sidekick, and she's getting in our way. She is nothing to this revolution. A woman—Anton—you just don't see, do you. We're the fighters, the leaders . . ."

"Stop talking or I will kill you," Alexandre shouts, but I move forward and grab his arm.

"Stop it! You are both being ridiculous—I'm on your side. I want what you want. Don't waste your energy fighting over me. Tell me, is my papa alive?"

Aalim spits at me. He is rubbing his throat and gathering up his things to leave.

"He is still alive, Sayyida Sultan," he says mockingly, "but by an inch of his life. Your beloved papa has had his hand in the coffers of the country's wealth for far too long. If I were leader of the Nationalists, I would have shot him long ago."

"No," I shout. "No." Don't you dare speak about my father like that. He has not done you any wrong. His crimes are nothing compared to the crimes of my dead husband. Al-Shezira crushed people like you. My papa has an honest heart."

"*The people will win in the end, Sayyida,*" *Aalim continues.* "*The pashas and the sultan and the heads of state and the corrupt politicians and all the others like them will be forced to realise that justice lies in the earth and soil of this land. The fellahin will rule once more. We will take over the running of this country and turn it around so that it belongs once again to the people.*"

I listen to what he says. He is as passionate as I am, but he is ignoring one simple fact, simply because he thinks I am inferior to him, a mere woman.

"*Al-Shezira was your enemy and mine, and now he is gone and I am the one who made that happen. You dare accuse me of being of the same mind as my father, the sultan. I am his daughter, Sayyid, but I am one of your kind. Yet you dare accuse me because of my sex. You think me lesser than you simply because I am a woman. You did not kill al-Shezira. I did. I am the one who is brave. I am the one who should lead you all. I am the one who people will remember. Al-Qahire should be run by women. You men are not leaders.*"

I gather up my robes and run through the main streets of the village where I find a group of women sitting outside their house, rocking their children to sleep. I am frantic. I beg them for help.

"*A horse, please, give me a horse, please I must have a horse to take me to Cairo.*"

A little boy takes me by the hand, and I run with him to the back of the village. Alexandre is running behind me. I do not stop for him. I must go to Papa. The little boy pulls at his horse's reins, and I climb on. I kick the horse's flank with my heels and gallop away. I will return, but first I need to see my papa. "*Thank you,*" *I shout to the boy, my robes trailing behind me in the wind.* "*Tell the Sayyid I will return. I won't be gone long.*"

Out of the corner of my eye, I see Alexandre skidding to a halt and staring after me in frustration because the boy has the only horse and he cannot follow me.

I feel free as a bird. Under the stars, out in the desert I kick the horse harder so that it gallops as fast as it is able along the desert road. I will keep to my word and return. I have courage now. I feel as though something is born again inside me. I have to see my papa.

I follow the familiar desert road back to Cairo. It is well trodden, and the going is easy. I will be there before long. But soon I begin to shudder hot and cold as I realise the danger I have put myself in and how foolish I have been to act so impulsively.

I am a wanted woman. I am a murderer. I will be caught and made to pay for my crimes. But what if I am clever? What if I manage to avoid the authorities? Alexandre must be right when he says that the armed forces are too busy trying to get control of the streets that are crumbling under the chaos of Nationalist violence.

Within the hour I am in Cairo. I hear gunshots and shouting as I approach my old neighbourhood. Smoke is rising from the buildings. The riots continue. It is too late. I cannot go back now. I need to see my father. I must have courage and continue on.

I abandon my horse as close to my palace as I dare on a surprisingly quiet street. I hear breaking glass nearby. I hide in the alcove of a building and readjust my robes. Then I see a lone soldier coming towards me. He is staggering. I suspect he is drunk. He is mumbling to himself in English—a British soldier. I walk up to him and stand before him. He stops in front of me. I pull my robes over my mouth so that he can see only my eyes. I speak to him slowly and seductively in Arabic. I am sure he doesn't understand what I am saying. Perhaps he has not been in Cairo very long.

I reach for his hand and he smiles lecherously. I know now that he understands what I am offering him. I pull him into the dark alcove and lift up my robes so that he can see the exposed flesh above my breasts. He reaches forward and I step back, pretending to laugh.

How I hate myself for doing this, but I have to get to my papa. I bend down and stroke his legs. As he groans with pleasure, I reach for a rock with one hand. He starts to unzip his trousers, and I swallow a nervous breath. I smile at him as I knock him over the head with the rock. He falls to the ground and lies in a heap at my feet.

With all my strength, I drag him farther into the alcove and undress him. I put on his uniform, cap, and boots, smoothing my short hair behind my ears. I feel momentarily sorry for him. I cover him with my discarded robes to keep him warm and give him a bit of dignity until he wakes up with a massive bump on his head.

Now for Papa. As I set off, I suddenly feel overwhelmed with fear. What will I say to him? How will I ever be able to explain what has happened to me? Will he ever forgive me? I know that he won't, but I go in search of him anyway.

CHAPTER FORTY-ONE

Aimee's head ached when she woke up in the little room. She felt feverish and her body ached. She swung her legs off the bed and sat for a moment with her head in her hands. She had no idea whether it was night or day. She knew only that she had slept and eaten one meal. She curled back up on the bed, realising there was nothing she could do but wait. For what exactly, she did not know. For someone to come, for those pigs to realise it was all a big mistake and she was innocent, not caught up in some terrible terrorist plot. She felt sick, sick with waiting, sick with not knowing what was going to happen to her.

She heard a noise at the door. Then it opened. A man she did not recognise stood in the doorway with a tray on which a bowl, a towel, a samovar, and a tea glass were arranged. A long piece of crimson cloth was draped over his arm.

He put the tray down on the chair near the door and threw the cloth at her.

"Wash yourself and put that on," he said.

Aimee fingered the cloth. It was an evening dress, its low-cut sleeveless bodice sparkling with jewels, the style of dress women had worn ten, twenty years earlier.

"What's going on?" she asked with a lump in her throat.

313

"Don't ask questions. There's a bowl of water, a towel, and a comb," he said, pointing at the tray. "Make yourself presentable. Be ready in ten minutes."

And he was gone.

Aimee stood up and examined the dress. Her mind twisted and turned, trying to understand what these lunatics had planned for her next. The dress was far more glamorous than the one she had worn at the el-G, though a similar colour.

She peeled off her clothes, dipped the towel in the bowl of warm water, and gratefully washed her body and face. Then she dried herself with a second towel, slipped on the dress, zipped the back up as best she could, and combed her hair vigorously.

When she was finally ready, a violent jab of fear spasmed through her. She felt weak and faint. She sat down on the bed and waited. A few moments later, the door was flung open. Issawi stood before her, dressed in black tie, eyeing her lecherously. The other two—she could not remember their names—stood on either side of him. Behind them were three more men in formal attire.

"Stand up," Issawi said.

Aimee stood up mechanically.

"You will accompany me tonight to the Abdin Palace to a ball organised in honour of the king."

"Why?" she cried out.

"It's simple," Issawi went on stonily. "My men and I have reason to believe that your group, the X, are going to try to storm the palace tonight. It appears that my life has been targeted. Despite our intelligence being sure of the plot against myself and the king, the celebrations are going to go ahead anyway. We believe that your friend Alim is one of the key X sector heads. You will be my human shield. With you next to me, your lover will call off the coup."

Aimee listened numbly, trying to take it all in. One of the men grabbed her by the arm and yanked her out the door and along the corridor. Surrounded by the five of them, she was marched downstairs and outside. It was dark outside and the moon was high in the sky. She was held firmly while three of the men did a security check on Issawi's car, shining torches underneath, lifting the bonnet, flashing the light on anything that looked suspicious. Then one of them gave the all clear.

Aimee was nudged into the back. Issawi got in alongside her. His filthy eyes slid over her. As he grabbed her hand, his mouth curled into a salacious smile.

"You realise you are under arrest, Sayyida. You will not escape this time. The X will be watching me. When they see me arrive with you, they will be forced to change their tack. Your Sayyid Alim would not want to put you in danger, would he?" Aimee knew at that point she had to get out of this car.

At last the car drew up to the palace gates. Every chauffeur's papers were scrutinised, every vehicle thoroughly checked before it could enter.

"We're in," Issawi said finally, and the driver turned and smiled at him.

"Come and get me," he said. "I'm ready for you now."

The journal of Hezba Iqbal Sultan Hanim al-Shezira,
Cairo, September 17, 1919—past midnight

With my soldier's cap pulled down, I walk purposefully towards the palace. There is no moon tonight. The atmosphere on the streets is strange. I hear more shouting and see more smoke coming from the old quarter. I walk faster and faster, my heart beating wildly, my mind blurred with the agonising mission ahead of me. Papa, I keep saying

315

over and over, Papa, my papa, the man I have always loved, the one who stood by me when I was a girl, the man who abandoned me when I became a woman. I am split in two, torn between my love of my papa and my desire to change things in this country, for women, for ordinary people. I was born of royalty, but I am not royal. I despise riches and wealth. I am so desperate to see his face again, to curl up in his arms and feel the warmth of his aging body against mine, to feel the old security of his presence beside me. I pray he is all right. I know I am a wretched being who no longer deserves the forgiveness of my God, but I ask simply that my papa be spared.

I see tanks and an army of marching soldiers up ahead. I hide, knowing that if I am picked up and questioned, the game will be up. After the tanks and soldiers have passed, I slip quietly through the narrow backstreets to my palace. I plan to climb the wall to the gardens. I have measured the height of the wall in my own mind many times from the other side, as a frustrated harem girl not allowed beyond it, and now I know why.

If I can find some slabs of stone to pile on top of one another, I will be able to scale the wall and slide down the other side and enter the palace from a secret passageway near the little fountain on the east side.

I hear an explosion and screaming and see people running. Nobody takes any notice of me, and this is good, very good. I find the wall and some rocks and hoist them on top of one another. I don't know where I find the strength to move them, but something inside me is making me strong.

I scale the wall easily thanks to my soldier's uniform. My boots provide a strong grip, and my trousers protect my legs as I drop down on the other side. I have some crazy idea in the back of my mind that I can save my papa and take him with me back to Kerdassa where we can go to France with Alexandre and live as exiles. I find the servants' door and push it open, hurrying inside. The palace corridors echo. All is eerily quiet. I have never heard my palace this quiet before. I am petrified, scared I will pass out with fear. I don't know whether to stay where I am or move into the Great Hall or the salamlik where Papa's quarters are.

Something inside me pulls me to his library. I can't imagine Papa is sitting there writing a letter or reading a newspaper, but I hope he is there all the same. I try to conjure this image in an effort to blot out all the horror I see around me.

Broken marble tiles and mashrabiyya are scattered across the floor, and doors have been violently kicked down. My body pulsates with nausea and fear that mingle together in such a fearsome cocktail that it is almost impossible to go on. The silence is so awful that I fear the worst.

I walk farther into the palace, tentatively, my boots crunching jagged stones and my eyes wide as I examine the bloodstains on the walls.

And then I stand deathly still and listen. I hear the sound of a loudspeaker coming from the front of the palace and the deep, staccato voice of a man talking in English. I try to understand what is being said, but the words fall on uninitiated ears.

The haunting sound of the loudspeaker confirms that something is terribly, terribly wrong. I tiptoe towards Papa's library and see the door ajar. I hear no sound. I move on to the salamlik and find the door to the west wing wide open and the corridors deserted. I do not know what has happened to my people, but Papa, my papa?

I stop dead in front of the door to my papa's quarters. I hear voices that sound low and hard. I hold my breath, straining to see where the voices are coming from. I see his face, my papa's face that comes into focus. I see him up against the wall with his hands in the air. His face is drained of all life. In his eyes I see fear, revulsion, rage. He does not see me. I stand back against the corridor wall again, hardly daring to breathe. I peer back into the room to try to grasp the horrific scene in front of me. Three hard-looking men are pointing machine guns at Papa's belly, thrusting the ends into his waistcoat, making him flinch.

"No?" one of the men says. "You won't tell us?" The men take a step back and raise their machine guns to his chest.

Papa holds his head high and looks away from them. In his eyes I see both anger and resignation that his time has come. His eyes move along the wall and then widen in horror and surprise. Our eyes meet and I choke back a sob. In a flash I see a lifetime of forgiveness on his face, and in that instant I know that one day we will be together again.

Papa, I sob silently, my heart breaking. Writing what happened hurts me like no other pain I have experienced. May my God help me live through this.

Then I hear the bullets pumping through the air into his rounded belly. I see his body spasm and fall back against the wall. My fist in my mouth, I turn and run, biting my knuckles to muffle the searing pain cutting through me. Hot tears burst forth from my eyes. I cannot stop myself from screaming. But the scream that racks my body is a silent scream, the silent agonising scream of too much horror witnessed.

CHAPTER FORTY-TWO

Farouk went home to Zamalek to get his revolver, a 1914 Smith & Wesson Model 3, a sure-shot and a beautiful thing of tapered steel. He had bought it from a friend in 1925, but had never used it, knowing the bullets were reserved for one man only.

He slammed the front door as he entered his house, not caring who heard him now. Gigis stood in the shadows as he passed. Farouk waved him away. He marched into one of the rooms, flung himself on the floor, and yanked out an old packing trunk from under the bed. There it was, gleaming in its leather case. He took it out, jacked open the barrel, counted the bullets, snapped it back shut, and rubbed it with his hands. It felt hard and cold. His heart thumped against his breastbone as he thought of the sound it would make when the bullets entered Issawi's chest.

He went to the garden. It was hot and he needed air. For the first time in his life he didn't know what to do. He lit a cigarette to try and calm himself. As he smoked, he looked up and studied the sky, watching the gold streaks turn a dark shade of indigo.

He thought about the futility of his life. This war, another pointless exercise in territorial domination by a crazed maniac, would be the last war he would witness. In his mind he saw Gladiator fighter planes crossing the Mediterranean, wisps of jet fuel trailing in their wake. Boys, men much younger than he, fighting the Germans in

Europe, waiting for the imminent and inevitable Italian invasion from the coastline of Libya. He was old, had lived his life, but these young boys were fighting desperately for the future. Aimee was their age. He thought of her and the world she would inherit. Littoni was another crazed maniac who was using revolution as an excuse to seize power for himself. And tonight, because Jewel had failed him, the celebrations at the Abdin Palace would go ahead and the revolution would start. He was so absorbed in his own thoughts that he did not hear Gigis approach him. He heard only his voice, sad, urgent.

"The area around the Abdin Palace is on high alert tonight, Sayyid, because of the king's celebrations. You were going to attend a dinner not far from there, weren't you? How will you get there?" Gigis asked.

Farouk swung round, blowing smoke rings into the air.

"I'll telephone my friend and tell him I might be delayed. I'll take a car to al-Qalah and walk from there. You take the night off, Gigis."

"There's news on the wireless," Gigis went on. "If you want to know more."

Farouk went to the drawing room. Gigis adjusted the radio set, and they both stood and listened to the velvety drone relayed in English.

"Security is tight," Gigis said. "Egyptian Intelligence has uncovered a suspected plot to assassinate the king and his chief advisor."

Farouk listened to the report in disbelief. The announcer described the mobilisation of troops and auxiliaries into central Cairo, the talk of massive manpower, truncheons and machine guns and army tanks at the ready in the event of an attack on the king. But the announcer did not mention the sectors or the X. The possible attack was reported in only the most general of terms. It could be political propaganda, a warning, a bluff, a message to the X that they were being watched.

Still, Farouk suspected that Littoni had not anticipated this. He had tried to warn him, but no, the fool had not listened. "Live for the X. Die for the X," had been Littoni's motto and the motto he had drummed into every new recruit.

"I must go, Gigis," Farouk said, and he flew out the door to his car, following the Nile as it snaked its way through the city. He was tired of living, tired of the pain, tired of the rage that wracked his body and poisoned his mind. A voice from beyond the grave compelled him. It was a voice he knew, a voice that told him failure was not an option.

The journal of Hezba Iqbal Sultan Hanim al-Shezira,
Cairo, September 17, 1919

I stumble and fall as I run through the deserted corridors of the palace. I hear glass smashing and then smell the acrid odour of gasoline and fire. Smoke and flames start billowing through the salamlik. The men's voices are loud and violent. I run faster than I have ever run before in my life with my eyes half-closed and my chest heaving with agony. I fly down the huge central staircase two steps at a time.

I see Alexandre in the shadows of one of the alcoves near the red room on the ground floor. He rushes towards me, his eyes expressing both relief and horror. He throws his arms around me, burying his head in my neck.

I fall against him, clutching at him, sobbing violently. I can't go on. "Hezba," he says, "We have to get out of here. Quickly."

"My papa. They shot my papa. Are they Rebel Corps? Are they?"

I am shaking him, shivering with grief. I want to go back and hold Papa in my arms, but I know if I go to him that I will be killed. Alexandre holds my shoulders firm. His face is bitter, mortified.

"No, Hezba, no. My men would not kill the sultan. I don't know who—I don't understand. But right now, we must save ourselves. Quickly, come on."

He yanks me by the arm and pulls me towards the door that leads to the garden. I hear the thud of boots on the paving stones outside and the tat-a-tat-tat of machine guns. I see my dead papa's face in my mind's eye and the look in his eyes when he saw me standing there. He knew in his final moments that I had come back to him, to beg for his forgiveness, to save him. I was the last person he saw, but I couldn't save him. So I have betrayed him twice, by defying him and by being unable to stop them shooting him. Oh God, forgive me, help me. "I can't go on," I sob breathlessly. "You go, leave me here with my papa. I can't go on, do you hear me?" I slump to the floor.

Alexandre scoops me up in his arms and exits the palace into the gardens. I am choking from the smoke. I splutter against his shoulder. Then the crumbling walls of the Sarai begin crashing to the ground. We are in the gardens. It seems like a thousand British soldiers are standing with machine guns raised at us. I hear Alexandre's heart thundering in his chest. I can taste the perspiration trickling down my face into my mouth.

"Freeze," a voice shouts through a loudspeaker.

Alexandre stops dead. He holds me against him, gripping me as though he will never let me go.

"This is the sultan's daughter," he shouts.

"Silence," the general says through the loudspeaker. "Men, upstairs."

A thousand boots clomp past us. Another thousand gather round us, pointing guns in our faces.

"My father," I say, "Those criminals murdered him, and you are arresting us?" The general comes forward. He is a sturdy-looking fellow with a blond moustache and pale blue eyes.

"You're coming with us," he says. We are marched to the front of the palace where I see the full force of the British Army lined up in front, weapons at the ready. Our hands are tied behind our backs, and we are thrown into a police chariot and escorted from the scene.

Alexandre and I sit opposite each other. His eyes are studying the interior of the vehicle, and I know he is planning our escape. My breaking heart cannot take any of this in. I don't know why I am being arrested. For being at the Sarai? For murdering my husband? I know only that my papa is dead and my Sarai is crumbling under fire. My mouth contorts with sorrow. If only I could have saved him. And now I can't even save myself.

Alexandre is looking at me now. He whispers a little poem to me under his breath, something the British soldiers seated on both sides of us cannot understand. He is trying to calm me and give me strength.

> Hezba Sultan
> her name whispered behind closed doors
> in the garden
> in the misty vapours of the hammam
> her name dances with the sounds of harem laughter until it
> disappears forever.

Choking back another grief-stricken sob, I raise my head and look into his eyes. The price of freedom, I think to myself, is this nightmare. When we arrive at the police barracks, Alexandre and I are separated. I am taken to a women's jail. A dour-looking nurse arrives and asks me some questions. I can hardly hear what she is saying, my mind is so consumed with the face of my papa. She raises her voice and tells me to *remove my soldier's uniform. She hands me a bathing gown. Then she accompanies me to another stark, horrible room. On a table is a large iron bowl filled with water, and a towel beside it.*

She begins to wash me. As she does so, she stares at my belly and my swollen breasts and asks if I am with child. I tell her I am. I cannot write about a child because my last child died. I refuse to say any more. I will talk to no one. I will never speak again as long as I live. She wraps me in the towel and takes me back to my cell. There she dresses me in a sack of a dress. She sees my linen pouch lying next to the discarded soldier's uniform and asks me what it is. She starts to take it, telling me she will destroy it as I won't be needing it anymore. She does not know what it contains. Of course, my vow to never speak again is immediately broken.

I snatch it from her and sob violently. "Please don't take this from me," I say. "It is the only thing I have left in the world. If it is taken from me, I will go on a hunger strike."

The nurse stares at me and then takes the pouch gently from me. She peers inside and sees it contains my little notebook and my fine ivory pen. She smiles and hands it back to me, and says she will see it is not taken from me. I close my eyes and nod a thank-you.

She asks me again, "Are you with child?"

I nod. She asks me to lie down on the prison bed and open my legs. She lifts up my dress and pushes her fingers inside me, feeling around deep within. She presses my belly gently and then nods to herself. "I will make a recommendation to the chief of police that you not be kept here," she says. "Because of your condition, the chief might make allowances for you while the courts assess your case. But don't expect any favours. You are being charged with the murder of your husband. Pray to your God, child," she continues. "Inshallah, you are going to need all the heavenly forgiveness your God will allow." And with those words she leaves.

CHAPTER FORTY-THREE

Nemmat crouched down, put her arm around her mother, and whispered in her ear, "Pack your things, Maman. I know a place where we'll be safe." She stroked her mother's lined face and squeezed her hand.

"What on earth are you mixed up in, child?" her mother said. Nemmat didn't answer her. She stood up and listened. It wouldn't be long before Farouk found her and killed her for being in league with Littoni. "Maman, sssh," she said, holding her mother tighter to her.

Nemmat heard men's voices outside the apartment door, and her eyes widened with fear. Her mother clutched at her, and Nemmat put her hand gently over her mouth to signal to her to not say a word. Farouk must have found out where she lived. She flinched. Someone outside was trying to force the door by throwing his body against it. The sound was so loud that she judged there must have been three, four men out there.

Nemmat pulled at her mother's hand, and together they headed out the back door into a small overgrown garden. They scrambled over the broken wall and headed up a haret that led to a wider street.

Nemmat pulled her mother's chador over her head and face and attended to her own. They could not run. It would attract too much attention. The only thing to do was to walk calmly, lose themselves in the crowd, and then find a taxi. Though they had left everything they owned behind in their apartment, Nemmat still had her fortune. She had prepared herself for this eventuality and kept her entire savings in a pouch strapped around her waist. As the women walked through the crowds, Nemmat kept looking back. She was glad of the busy streets. "Tell me, child, tell me, what is going on?"

"I'm afraid, Maman," Nemmat said, bowing her head to the pavement and shooting her mother an apologetic glance. Her mother's eyes demanded the truth. She could not hold out any longer.

"Tell me, child. You are my daughter. Anything that has happened to you affects me. You must tell me what's going on."

"Someone wants to kill me, Maman," she said. "I've been saving money for us to get away. In a few days we can go."

"Go where, child?"

"To Italy. To Seraphina's. She will look after us. You want to see your old friend again, don't you?"

"Seraphina?" she murmured.

"We will be safe with her," Nemmat said. "We can return to Cairo one day, but for the time being we must leave or risk our lives."

"Who wants to kill you, Nemmat?"

"A man called Taha Farouk, Maman."

The journal of Hezba Iqbal Sultan Hanim al-Shezira,
Cairo, late September 1919

The days pass. I lie here waiting. I have counted three sunrises, three sunsets, and countless calls to prayer from the muezzins in the mosque nearby. I don't know exactly where I am, but I think by the spires I can see from my cell window that I am near the Mosque al-Hakim, north of Cairo. I eat little and drink even less. I can feel my baby fluttering inside me, begging me to eat. For her, I will take a mouthful here and there. I try as hard as I can, but I am just not hungry. Then on the fourth day, the nurse arrives. She throws some clothes at me and orders me to get dressed. She tells me to veil myself. "You are to appear in court," she says. "A lawyer has been appointed for you."

My heart starts to beat nervously for the first time since my arrest. I try to read her face, but it gives nothing away.

Once I am dressed in the thick black chador and veiled, I am marched out of my cell. I hear some of the other women laugh as I walk past their cells. They are street workers, deviants, murderers, and I am one of them. Two armed guards meet the nurse at the jail door and accompany us to a carriage that takes us to the courthouse. As we ride through the streets, I see that calm has returned to Cairo, but I still hear occasional gunfire and smell the charred scent of burning buildings. People are sweeping up outside their shops. The cafés are full, the shops bustling, and the hotel terraces crammed with tourists. Camels and donkeys block the way as usual. Men are arguing in the streets, and women are selling fruit in the markets. The odour of mud and spice and donkey droppings is as wonderful to me as the sight of the blistering sky. Every little detail is precious, because it is life.

I watch the scene unfolding outside as though I am a visitor from another world. But this is my world, the world I wanted to leave behind.

How torn I feel, cut in half by my desire to be with Alexandre and my desire to be with my papa and my family. And then I remember that my papa is dead, and my body spasms with sadness. Tears start to roll down my cheeks.

We arrive at the courthouse and are ushered inside. I am made to stand in front of the qadi, the judge. I am completely shrouded. Through my veil I see an ocean of faces around me, all staring at me.

I am made to place my hand on the Qur'an and swear that I will not be deceitful. The qadi asks me a series of questions as though I am an idiot.

"What is your name?"

"Hezba Iqbal Sultan Hanim al-Shezira," I say, trying to steady my voice.

"What is your address?"

"I have none."

"What is your age?"

"I am not sure exactly, seventeen I think."

"Do you know why you are here?"

I stare at him and shake my head slowly.

"You are charged with the murder of your husband, Khalil al-Shezira Pasha."

I blink and don't dare move an inch.

"Do you understand the charge?"

"Yes," I say.

"Is it true you are carrying a child?"

"Yes," I say.

The qadi runs his eyes over me in disgust as though the sight of me in my black robes with my swelling pregnant girth is enough to put him off his lunch. He is an ugly man, with an arrogant bearing and a cruel curl to his mouth.

"It has been recommended that you be moved to more comfortable accommodations for the time being. I will order to have your condition checked by one of our court doctors. If your condition is confirmed, you will be placed under house arrest and will await summons to attend the court again where your lawyer will present your case and your sentence will be delivered."

I stand with my head held high, even though my heart is still breaking and my tears flow easily underneath my veil. The qadi calls one of the lawyers standing nearby and confers with him. After glancing at me, they refer to some pieces of papers in a dossier that the judge shuffles between his fingers. The qadi addresses the room.

"Is the prisoner to be privately represented?"

A man I do not recognise steps forward. "I will be organising the representation of the woman, Qadi. We will be awaiting your instructions with regard to her internment and where she will await her summons for her trial."

The qadi nods and refers to his dossier again. "The Sayyida Virginie al-Fatuh, a close friend of the woman's family, has offered her residence as a suitable place for someone in her condition of disability."

I flinch when he says the word "disability." He looks at me as though my very sex is a disability. I touch my belly softly. My child is my only ally now. And then I realise what the qadi has said. I am going to be allowed to go to Virginie's house. It will give me a moment of reprieve. Surely nothing will happen to me there. I hope and pray I will see Virginie, that she is alive and well. I think of Alexandre and hope for news of him.

"Court adjourned," a man says, and everyone in the room stands up.

I am led out the door by two armed guards. As I walk through a corridor, people stand aside to let me through. Suddenly, a stone hits me on the head, and people begin laughing and calling out my name.

"Murderer," they say. "Shame," they shout.

My hand flies to my head to soothe the pain inflicted by the stone, and I bend closer to the armed guards and hurry with them to the waiting carriage. Stones and pebbles rattle against the roof of the carriage as we drive off. My relief at the prospect of seeing Virginie vanishes. This is the beginning, I say to myself, the beginning of the end.

CHAPTER FORTY-FOUR

Tashi knew that this was the culmination of his life's work. The next few hours would be history in the making. This time tomorrow he would be able to stand with his head held high and take his place as one of the new leaders of the country.

Tashi walked quickly and quietly to an impressive-looking building belonging to one of the richer members. The house, code-named "camel holding," was just off Sharia Abdin. Discreetly hidden in a garage at the back of the property was the bulletproof Daimler, donated by the same Sayyid, an al-Azhar intellectual.

Tashi waved away a group of children who tried to engage him in a game of stick throwing as he passed. It was twenty past seven. Night had blanketed the city in a light-spangled indigo haze, releasing the streets from the suffocating heat of the day. The usual pungent smell of earth and drains, spice and camel dung hit his nostrils. Though he had smelt it a million times before, tonight it was as though for the first time. The energy and the feeling of power coursing through his body made every sense hyperalert.

As he arrived, he looked at his wristwatch for the umpteenth time. There was just enough time to change, check the car, and arm himself with the bomb, the trophy that would hold it, and the detonation device. Masquerading as Suleyman Orhan, the secretary to the Turkish ambassador, Tashi was ready to enter the Abdin Palace just behind Issawi, and hand him the "gift." Last-minute checks had confirmed that the sector men masquerading as security personnel at the palace gates were ready. He put on his evening shirt and black tie, and he ran a comb through his hair. He looked at himself in the mirror, satisfied with the handsome reflection that stared back at him. He looked surprisingly like the Turkish ambassador. The plot was faultless. Hamid and Hossein, with al-Dyn's help, had constructed the bomb cleverly. An almost-imperceptible plate of powerful dynamite was rigged up with detonation wires: minimum packaging, maximum power. The trophy, in which the bomb was to be placed, looked good. It was to be given to Issawi as a thank-you for his latest business venture, a joint venture between the Turkish ambassador, the now-dead Orhan Suleyman, and Issawi. The chief advisor had so many business deals going on, he would be temporarily floored by this little gesture of thanks from Suleyman and would be off guard for a few seconds. He would take the trophy when it was handed to him; of that Tashi was sure.

Hamid arrived in his chauffeur's uniform with his hat under his arm.

"Hurry up," he said.

Tashi adjusted his bow tie and cuff links and patted his breast pocket. In it were his fake papers and the invitation to the palace ball.

"Yallah," he said.

The men walked quickly to the car. Hamid got into the driver's seat. Tashi sat behind him. The brand-new black Daimler looked like embassy material, and its sleek exterior drew envious glances from the crowds as Hamid drove carefully towards the palace. He swallowed nervous breaths. Issawi and the king's hours were numbered.

At last, the outline of the palace was visible ahead. Keep cool, he told himself. Keep cool. His job was simple. He was Suleyman

Orhan Pasha, secretary to the Turkish ambassador. His car would be checked like the others, but the security men were X sector members, so their passage through security with the bomb was assured.

He shot Hamid a look.

"Inshallah," he said. "May Allah protect you."

Hamid nodded and murmured the same. Then Tashi stared nervously, peering into the darkness.

"We must wait, wait for the torch signal."

Hamid said, "There it is," and he pointed up to the third-floor window of the building opposite the palace. Tashi searched the windows. He looked at his watch. Eight P.M. exactly. He saw three faint flashes. Torchlight against the ceiling of a darkened room. Message received. Issawi's car was on its way. The information had been radioed down through the sector networks.

Near the palace, they let a sleek black Daimler like their own overtake them. Tashi and Hamid saw Issawi's face through the window, his white balding dome, his thick neck rolled with fat, the smug grin on his face. He sat in the rear of the car with three men and a woman, dressed in red.

The car slowed to a stop, and the chauffeur got out to speak to the security guards. One of them opened the door and peered in. He smiled as he took their papers; another shone a torch under the chassis, kneeling down to take a good look.

The security guard examining the papers handed them back to man on Issawi's left, nodded, smiled once more, and shut the door. The other security guard examining the undercarriage of the car nodded too, and the car was waved on.

Tashi gulped back a nervous breath and whispered, "The security men, they're not our sector men. What's going on? Oh God!"

But there was no turning back now. Hamid drove the Daimler towards the palace gates. Tashi sat back regally in his seat, breathing hard. The gates to the palace loomed larger. Hamid stopped the car at the security checkpoint and got out.

"Welcome," said one of the guards.

"You have an invitation to tonight's celebrations?"

Hamid handed him the official paperwork with the royal stamp. Papadopolous had done an excellent job. The security guard unfurled the paperwork and studied it for a minute.

Then he opened the door and shone his torchlight on Tashi's face. The trophy, with the bomb inside it, lay on the seat next to him.

"Orhan Sayyid?" he said, checking the photographic identification against Tashi's face.

"Yes?" Tashi said.

"We must check the vehicle before it is given clearance."

Tashi nodded, but inside his body was pulsing with anticipation. "Please," Tashi ventured. "You must take all the necessary precautions."

The security guard nodded to the other guard who knelt down and shone his torch under the car. He then got up and walked around the car a few times. Hamid was holding his breath. Seconds dragged by, then minutes.

The security guard got up and pulled the other aside. What were they doing? What were they talking about? Tashi tried to catch Hamid's eyes, but his face appeared placid, unaffected by the delay. Tashi did not dare get out of the car. That would arouse suspicion. He simply had to wait. The two security guards glanced at him. Then one of them went into the gatehouse booth and picked up the telephone.

The journal of Hezba Iqbal Sultan Hanim al-Shezira, Cairo, late September 1919

When I arrive at Virginie's house, I am shocked to see armed soldiers lined up outside. I long to see Alexandre but know it is impossible. He is in a prison somewhere. I fear we will never see each other again. I am distraught inside.

The door is opened. An austere official-looking Bey, an Egyptian civil servant, wearing a red tarboush, stands at the door and stares at me. The guards who escort me from the carriage pinch my arms as they walk me up the stairs. I am taken without a word to a first-floor sitting room that has been stripped of furniture except for a low bed, a small table, a jug, and a bowl. The floors are bare. No kilims or decorations remain. I am pushed inside, and the door is locked behind me.

I unravel my robe, remove my veil, and go to sit on the bed. I put my face in my hands. My baby is kicking again, and I can tell she is getting stronger. Despite all the adversity, she will not be broken. As I think of her, the fire inside me starts to rage once more.

I have heard nothing of the arrest of the men who murdered my poor papa. It is they who should pay for their crimes, not I.

And what of al-Shezira? The man who ruined so many—including my dear Rachid? Does the truth of his actions not deserve to be revealed? Don't his victims deserve to have their suffering acknowledged? I look around the room, searching for anything that might help me escape. The walls have been stripped of paintings, the window frames of their drapes, the ceiling of its chandelier.

So this is how I am supposed to endure my days until they announce my guilt to the world and pass my sentence? My guilt to them is as certain as the sun in the sky. In the eyes of the qadi and Muslim law, I am a woman who has committed the worst crime imaginable. I am no longer fit to live.

But I will not give up yet. I will not crumble because of the qadi's interpretation of the Sharia. I will seek justice. I remember the words of the Qur'an. There must be a sura, a verse in the Qur'an that will save me. I begin to recite the suras, searching for help from my God, but my recitations come to nothing. I can find no answer.

If only I could see Virginie. When will they let me see her? I go to the window and look out at the garden and the trees. Then I go to the balcony door and try and open it. I am surprised to find it is not locked. That gives me some hope.

I hear something, a woman's voice, inside the house, shouting from down the hall. I swing back towards the door of the sitting room and listen hard. It's Virginie. Her voice is raised in anger. I have never heard her raise her voice like that. It is almost as if she were talking for me, at me, to give me some comfort, to reassure me that she is there.

"What is your charge?" she shouts. "I am well connected here in Cairo, Monsieur. What you are suggesting is outrageous."

I hear murmuring for a while. The Bey is talking, and I cannot hear his voice clearly. Then Virginie speaks again.

"No, I will answer no such questions. I demand to see my lawyer. My dear friend, Hezba al-Shezira is not the person you are after. I know of no such terrorist group. I have never been involved with any plot to murder anyone."

For a moment I hear nothing, and then Virginie screams.

"Get your hands off me. You'll pay for this, Monsieur. The sultan is dead, murdered by your own countrymen, and you have the audacity to accuse me of being an accomplice in the murder of Hezba's husband? I was her tutor, damn you. That was all I ever was, her tutor."

I hear a door open, and Virginie's voice echoes through the corridors of the house.

"My brother has been arrested. I know he has never been involved with any underground rebel group, and I have never heard of the Rebel Corps. I shall consult my lawyer. I shall have you charged with wrongfully arresting us both."

Her voice gets louder. "Let go of me, get your hands off me, don't touch me," she screams.

I hear the front door open and Virginie cursing the guards who are escorting her to the carriage that brought me here. I run to the balcony, but all I see is her hat and the sweep of her skirt as she slips into the carriage. I also see a flash of handcuffs and the slow, evil smile of the guard at her side.

I hear footsteps marching and growing louder. I cover my face with my chador and grip it tightly to me. My door is flung open. The Bey stands there with two armed guards. The Bey crosses his arms across his chest.

"The court doctor will come this afternoon to examine you," he says.

"When will I see my lawyer?"

"Tomorrow," he says. "The day after, you will appear in court before the Qadi."

I walk towards him, but the guards step forward and raise their guns at me. I step back, humiliated and angry.

"Can you tell me news of the man who was arrested with me?"

The Bey juts his chin at me, his eyes lifeless, his mouth rigid.

"I cannot go into details about the man's case. But he is currently in the el-Rizah jail in Shubra. He will appear at the courthouse on the same day as you, although you will both be tried separately."

"Have they arrested the men who murdered my father?"

"Three men have been arrested, yes," the Bey says.

"I want to see them tried and sentenced to death," I say bitterly, tears welling up in my eyes. "I saw them assassinate him with my own eyes. I should be called as a chief witness. I will make a statement."

The Bey shuffles uncomfortably. "That is not possible. The charge against you is very serious. Khalil al-Shezira was a prominent, well-respected businessman and figurehead within the upper echelons of

Cairene society. His death has shocked many. The entire city wants to see the person charged with his murder brought to justice."

Losing my temper, I lunge forward and point my finger at the Bey. Again the guards step forward and raise their guns at me.

"My father was the sultan of Egypt and now he is dead. I am the primary witness to the killing, and you think finding the murderer of a ruthless rapist and corrupt tyrant is more important than seeking vengeance for the life of a great sultan?"

"Enough," the Bey says, his eyes widening with surprise at hearing me speak so freely. "Calm yourself. The doctor will be here soon."

He nods at his guards and leaves the room with them.

I throw myself on my bed and bury my face in the rough blanket that has been left for me. As I pound the mattress with my fists, biting back bitter tears of grief and rage, a thought occurs to me, like a soft dewy rain soothing me. I must do something—for my baby, for my papa, for Virginie, for Alexandre, for Rachid, for these people that I love so dearly.

There is always a way. My God wants me to be strong. He wants me to suffer first and then gain strength from my suffering. He wants me to show my love for my family. At last I realise why I am in hell.

CHAPTER FORTY-FIVE

The air was thick and sultry as Littoni strode purposefully towards Ezbekieh. The streets were filled with the usual throngs of soldiers and brightly painted girls gathered outside nightclubs and cafés.

Littoni didn't dare catch anyone's eye. He was entirely absorbed in his own thoughts, biting back the wave of nervous excitement pumping through his body. He patted his jacket and felt the halter against his shirt that held his revolver. His chest rose and fell painfully from walking quickly.

As he thought about his men moving into place behind their combat lines within their allocated grids, a powerful surge of adrenaline electrified his limbs. Those wealthy Cairene and foreign diplomats gathering to grease their way into the favour of the king and his entourage did not know what was coming.

He screwed up his eyes in the dark. Things were eerily quiet on the military front. There was no sign of any extra deployment of troops nor any visible increase in the number of soldiers scouring the streets. Inshallah, on this moonless night, the X would not be stopped.

He withdrew a cigarette as he arrived at his ground-force meeting in the basement of a sector member's house in Ezbekieh. He slipped inside the building as nonchalantly as he could and made his way to the back. The others would already be there, waiting for him. The tiny basement storeroom, its entrance shielded from view by a rickety old door, was perfect. He stepped in and saw three pairs of eager eyes upon him. A dim lamp lit the room.

"Greetings, fellow rebels," he said. "All armed Sayyids?"

The men laughed as though they were off to a celebration. They were all in high spirits. Dressed in civilian clothes, they could blend easily into any crowd.

"Inshallah, if God wills it, we will succeed," he said. "As the leaders, we will be sending our men in from their assigned streets abutting the palace. Keep well back until the bomb has been detonated. Then we will march in on the palace with all the other sectors. Use your weapons if anyone tries to stop you. Our first destination will be the king's suites and offices. Kamal and Mustafa have been instructed to telephone the radio stations from the palace to let them know the government is no more and the king is dead. They will inform them that the new government will take effect immediately. British martial law will no longer apply. Our men on the ground will make sure of that. The X will disband, and the new alliance government will take over. I will rule as president of the newly independent Egypt."

The men murmured their approval.

Littoni went on. "The sectors have agreed that Tashi, Hamid, and Hossein are to be chief advisors to the new president. The rest of the X will be given jobs within the new government."

Littoni smiled victoriously. In all his years—first as an army officer who was ousted because of his disastrous military manoeuvre abilities, then later during his moderately successful attempts at running various cafés around Cairo—he had always harboured a burning desire to rule. As payback for the humiliation of being evicted from the army, as payback for the bankruptcy he had once faced at the hands of various political hotshots, including Issawi. The only thorn in his side had been Farouk.

"Ready Sayyids?"

The men pushed towards the door.

"Then let's go. Inshallah."

The journal of Hezba Iqbal Sultan Hanim al-Shezira,
Cairo, late September 1919

From the window I see a fat, old, bespectacled man with greying hair arrive. He is wearing a suit and carries a cane. In one hand he is holding a brown leather holdall. He is shown into the house by one of the guards. I stand back and shroud myself. I do not want him to touch me or look me in the eye. The thought that this doctor has been sent by the courts to examine me makes me shiver with repulsion.

I am standing with my back to the wall on the far side of the sitting room when the door is flung open and one of the guards nods the doctor in. My whole body tenses and I feel sick. Then I have an idea. What if he proclaims me insane? My charge might be viewed differently. I decide it is worth a try. It might buy me some time, precious time to get word to Alexandre.

The door is shut, and the doctor stands alone opposite me. For a while he just looks at me. I feel like a poor abandoned animal that someone is trying to rescue. Yet I cannot be tamed.

The doctor smiles at me. "Come here, child," he says, and he beckons me with his finger. "You know why I am here, don't you."

I shake my head but say nothing. I am not going to make this easy for him. I don't want his filthy hands on my flesh. He sets down his holdall and walks towards me. I make a noise, the ugliest noise I can muster. It comes from deep within me. It is horrible, insane.

The doctor stops, his eyes narrowing. Then he goes back to get his holdall, and he places it by the bed. I start to shake and moan. If these sounds make him think I am not of right mind, then all the better. He tiptoes forward and reaches for me. I slide back farther along the wall. He tiptoes closer.

"My dear, I am here simply to examine you, to confirm your state, and to write a report about you for the qadi. Please don't make things worse than they already are."

My thoughts run riot. If I can swallow my revulsion and let him examine me, I might be better able to convince him of my demented state. I try to relax my body. The doctor reaches out for me again, and I let him steer me towards the bed. He is still smiling. I sit down.

"Now then, that's better. I just want you to lie down and lift up your robes. Relax," he says. "Relax."

I lie down and watch him through my veil. He puts on some rubber gloves and feels my belly, pushing down here and there to check the position of the baby. Then he gingerly picks up the corners of my robes and my undergarments and rolls them back so that my legs are exposed. I flinch and freeze. My body is like a rock. I have no feeling left in me. Those large, ugly hands encased in gloves are about to force their way into the core of my body. He moves himself around so that he is standing between my legs, peering down at me through his spectacles. I can't do this. I can't let him touch me.

Suddenly I rear up and push my heel into his groin as hard as I can, sending him flying. He falls back on the floor, groaning in pain. I jump up and grab a syringe from his holdall, the first thing I see, and wave it in the air at him. I am so scared. A million thoughts are running through my mind, galloping like my horse riding into the desert wind. I want this doctor to proclaim me insane. I don't want my life taken away from me.

I don't want to be locked up. I did what I did because of Rachid, because my heart was breaking for him. Am I to be imprisoned for loving so much? At least if I were deemed insane, I would be granted some reprieve from the horrors of prison long enough to plan my escape. The doctor gets up, still groaning, and stares at me in disbelief.

"All right, Sayyida," he says. "Put down the syringe. I have finished with you." He is rubbing his arm and his head where he fell, and then he tentatively reaches for his holdall and heads for the door as fast as he can.

I hear murmuring outside my door. The next thing I know, the guards are inside the room with their guns pointing at me, demanding the syringe. I give it to them. They edge their way out of the room this time, never once turning their faces from me, pointing their weapons all the while. The door shuts and the bolt slides back into place.

CHAPTER FORTY-SIX

That night, at dusk, two hundred members of the Buluk el Nizam—the Egyptian auxiliary police force—gathered at Intelligence HQ, the top-secret military training camp in the el-Gamaliya district. Each of them carried a machine gun over his shoulder. They stood erect, side by side, silently awaiting orders. The atmosphere was heavy. Each man knew of the seriousness of the task that lay ahead of him.

And then they were joined by eight hundred similarly equipped British soldiers. The men waited before a stage. At last five men walked onto it. One man picked up a loudspeaker and started to speak through it. It was Hilali, head of Security Operations.

"Men, you've been briefed on Operation X. Network Intelligence has unravelled this group's intention to strike tonight. And this has been backed up by one of our top secret agents. We have mobilised our largest security operation ever. Now, it is of vital importance that we take the X by surprise. Although it has been widely advertised that security has been increased, the celebrations at the Abdin Palace must appear to go on as normal. The X would expect this. The X sectors will likely plan to surround the palace to wait out the start of the coup. If you are in part of the raid operative, your leader will have informed you to move in on the palace in concentric circles from Garden City, Zaynab, Ezbekieh, the Old

City, and the Sultan Hassan Mosque and to arrive at the palace with enough time to nail the ringleaders who will be watching and waiting close by. We believe the two most senior leaders of the X plan will lead the coup.

"Our top code-cracker has dismantled a radio message that leads us to believe that a meeting will take place tonight. We have the address where the meeting is scheduled to be held. This is a matter for our top security men. What we propose to do is this:

"We are going to deploy a hundred men to secretly fringe the boulevard closest to the main entrance to the palace. The rest of you will be involved in the raid operative. You know who you are and you know what to do.

"The raid operative has been divided into groups of twenty. Each group has been allocated its own area with a list of souks, cafés, mosques, nightclubs, and shops that must be raided. It is important that this happen while the X is mobilising its men into position. They will leave key members behind at certain strategic locations to radio information in. We will leave no stone unturned, and you have been commanded to use as much force as necessary to bring about the desired outcome. We want these men and we want them tonight. There are one hundred men on the wanted list, but we suspect that they are only the tip of the iceberg. We are sending in armoured cars and military trucks, backup forces with cannons and armaments. We will not fail to rid this city of this foul force. The arrested men will be taken to the el-Gamaliya detention centre. While you are working on your assigned mission, our top men will tackle the meeting, which is supposed to take place prior to the coup. Good luck, men. Security Operations's top men will be on the ground with you. My colleague Mustafa Gamal and I will be bringing in the Abdin contingent. Tomorrow, the men and women of Cairo will walk taller and without fear, Inshallah."

The soldiers filed out. The military trucks were waiting. Hilali and Gamal jumped off the stage and walked outside, found their truck, and climbed in. Twenty youths peered gloomily at them from the bed of the truck. They know nothing of war, Gamal thought sadly as he glanced at them. These raids would not sharpen their prowess or harden them to the months of war to come. As he realised that the capture of the X was dependent upon these mere babes' innocence and inexperience, he felt he was staring failure in the face. Hilali's words had had a false ring to them. Tomorrow, the men and women of Cairo would not walk taller and without fear. The X would never die. It would live forever, maybe in a different form, with a new name and new leaders, but it would never be obliterated. They might squash a few of them, might push them underground for a while, but they would be back.

The trucks moved off and began snaking their way through the streets in all directions. Hilali and Gamal's truck was bound for Ezbekieh. It stopped at the fringes of the gardens, and the men leapt out. Hilali and Gamal skirted the houses and shops as invisibly as possible. The rest of the force came in from behind, heading towards a long line of shops, tailors, perfumeries, bakeries, and cafés.

Operation X had begun. If he and Gamal mucked this up, if anything happened to the king or Issawi, both he and Gamal would be finished. A woman in one of the shops they were raiding came towards them and flung her arms at them, pounding their chests. Operations grabbed her and held her against a wall. "Lock her up," Hilali yelled.

The woman burst into tears. From her mouth came an impenetrable tongue-tied mass of expletives. She struggled and bit and kicked as two men held her down to the ground, then held her firm.

"Please," she sobbed. "I am just trying to earn my living. You can't do this."

"Shut up, woman," Hilali shouted.

He motioned to his soldiers to take her to the truck.

"You," he shouted at one of the men who stood near the door of one of the cafés with his arms raised. "Give me your papers."

The man produced them.

Gamal looked at them for a moment and then lunged at him, ramming the angular end of his machine gun into his stomach. The man keeled over and collapsed.

"Take him to the truck," Gamal said.

One of the soldiers dragged the unconscious body along the pavement and hauled him into the back of the truck. Something caught Hilali's eye. A boy of about nineteen, in a café, his face twisted with hatred, was reaching for a lantern. The youth grabbed the lantern off the café bar and threw it across the tiny souk haret to the tailor's shop opposite.

The silk seller leapt up and ran out screaming "Allah, Allah, Allah" as racks of brightly coloured silks exploded into flames. Suffocating smoke billowed out, clouding everyone's visibility. The soldiers ducked, and Hilali and Gamal were thrown back by the force of the flames.

Hilali yelled, "Quickly, the basement!" Gamal led the way. He pushed through an archway to a maze of corridors, through a wooden door, down some steps to a basement. He tiptoed forward, his men right behind him. He saw a light under the door, threw his body against it, and fired a round of machine-gun shots behind him in the air to get their attention.

"Freeze!" he shouted. Before him were four men dressed in civilian clothes, suits, and tarbooshes, their mouths gaping open, their eyes all-knowing, their hatred palpable. One of the men stood up and reached for a gun. Hilali pumped the opposite wall with more rounds from his machine gun.

He shouted, "Which one of you is Omar bin Mohammod, also known as Fabio Littoni?"

Hilali pointed his gun at each of the men in turn, motioning his own soldiers into the room with a jerk of his head.

"Well?" The soldiers rammed their machine guns into the men's stomachs, making each one double up in agony. Littoni slid his hand almost invisibly in his pocket, pulled out his revolver, and edged towards the door. He pumped several bullets into the ceiling, and plaster rained down on the men. He pumped more bullets into the air. The room became hazy with debris, and the soldiers choked and peered through the dust. In the confusion, Littoni slipped through a secret door at the back of the room. He smiled to himself. No bastard was going to stop him now.

The journal of Hezba Iqbal Sultan Hanim al-Shezira,
Cairo, October 1919

I wake up with a start. It is dark outside. I can hear a rustling sound outside my window. I sit up and listen. The sound is rhythmic and persistent, as though someone is trying to attract another person's attention.

I go to the window and look out. I have no idea how late it is, but the moon is high in the sky. I peer into the darkness at the trees near my window. I see nothing at first, but then I look again.

High up in the tree, I see the face of a small child, a girl with huge black eyes in a pool of white, like saucers, staring at me through the branches. She grins, and her white teeth gleam in the moonlight.

She puts her finger to her lips secretively and motions for me to move back from the window by waving her hand. Then she lassoes a piece of rope with a hook on it. The hook catches the ledge of the window. She attaches a small sacking pouch onto the rope and slides it along to the window ledge.

I watch her, my heart beating wildly. Who is this girl? What is she sending me? She can only be about ten years old. Yet she has climbed the palm tree fearlessly and is beaming at me in the moonlight.

When the pouch reaches me, I disengage it from the rope and then dislodge the hook while the girl reels it in and catches it. She turns away, her job done, and starts to climb back down the tree without so much as a backwards glance or a wave. She vanishes like a whisper into the night.

I open the pouch and discover a letter. I unfold it excitedly and read. It is from Alexandre.

Hezba, I have managed with extreme difficulty to get this to you. After reading it, you must destroy it immediately. My men and I will come for you. They are charging me with five counts of murder and for being an accessory to the murder of al-Shezira. My men are behind me. They are out on the streets, plotting to get me out of here. I cannot describe our escape plan in this letter, but rest assured that my men will not put up with seeing their leader in jail. If I can get out of Egypt to France, I will be safe and you will be too. My men have told me that there are only four guards outside of Virginie's house. They change shifts halfway through the evening. You are to appear in court tomorrow. Do not say anything that will incriminate you. I can't tell you what my men plan to do, but I will tell you that you must be prepared. It will be the night after next, if all goes according to plan.

Until I can hold you in my arms again, your devoted Alexandre.

Ecstatic at this news, I tear up the letter into tiny morsels. Then I shove each morsel in my mouth and swallow them one by one. The paper tastes horrible. Then I sit on the bed for a while looking up at the window, watching the moon move across the sky. I know I won't be able to go back to sleep. I try to imagine what Alexandre's men are going to do. Abduct the guards? Steal uniforms and take over one of the shifts, then set me free? Use more violence to avenge my arrest? I know that Alexandre will not stop until he has succeeded in finding a way out of this for both of us.

I also know that he will use whatever violence he thinks necessary to ensure our freedom, because freedom is what he lives for, whether it's freedom from injustice, freedom for the humble farmers and poor traders of Egypt, or freedom from the tyranny of the idle rich.

I eventually lie down and shiver with fear. Alexandre does not like to be wronged in any way. As I start to pray to my God for a better solution, I begin to fall asleep. But I am abruptly woken by the pinkish light of a new day and the call to prayer from the muezzins in the mosques. I jump up and perform my own rakas with a solemn heart.

Later, I am drinking a glass of water when the door opens and a young man walks in, accompanied by the same two guards who point their guns at me.

I quickly cover my head and my face. The man bows and steps forward.

"My name is Mustafa Tora," he says. "I will be representing you in court."

"Where is my family?" I say to him. "Is there no one I can see?"

Mustafa Tora smiles sadly, then says, "Let us talk for a while first, Sayyida."

Once the guards have retreated, I take a good look at him. He is a pleasant-looking man with a kind face. He is carrying a briefcase and he is wearing a waistcoat with his suit jacket. His black hair is wavy and neat. His eyes sparkle confidently, not in a salacious way, but enquiringly, sympathetically.

I feel I can talk to him. I ask him to sit down at the table. I move the water jug and sit on the bed near him. He puts his briefcase on the table and extracts a folder.

He searches for something in the folder, smiling at me occasionally as he shuffles through his papers.

"I want you to tell me exactly what happened," he says.

I flinch when he says this. How can I tell him what happened? I can hardly even bear to think of it myself.

He watches me for a moment, as though he wants to see through my veil to the face behind it, the real me, then he sits back and says kindly, "You had been married a long time?"

"Six years," I tell him.

"You have no children?"

"I had a son, but he died at birth. A little boy I called Ibrahim."

Mustafa Tora nods and writes this down.

"Did your husband ever threaten you?" he asks.

I nod. A cold ache washes over me. It is the ache of misery and regret—regret that I was ever born a girl.

"Did he beat you?"

"Yes, often when we were first married. Then after my son died, he abandoned me for four years. After that time, he demanded that I go back to live with him, but I was allowed to stay in my home because I was considered mentally unwell. Eventually he threatened me with Bait al-Taa."

"And you were sent to live with him recently, is that correct?"

"Yes, I went to live with him at his palace in Minya."

"Did he ever force you to have sexual intercourse with him?"

I feel tears burning my eyes. "Of course, but the courts don't care about that. That is not illegal. It is a man's right to do as he pleases."

Mustafa Tora shakes his head. "I know, but I want to make a case that your husband, al-Shezira, was a violent man and had a history of violence and that he did not treat his other wives in the same way. I am an expert in Qur'anic law, in the Sharias. I believe there are a few suras on which we can draw. You were provoked. Your actions were the consequence of years of emotional and physical abuse."

"I have not admitted to anything."

The lawyer sits back in his chair and strokes his moustache.

"I think you should know that it would be in your best interest to admit to the murder, Sayyida. The qadi has informed me that there is a witness, a young Minya eunuch who saw you that night with a revolver in your hand, standing over al-Shezira. The boy—who will be questioned—saw you pull the trigger and saw the bullets enter your husband's body."

I shake my head in horror. "No, no."

"Where is the revolver?" he asks.

"I don't know."

My head swims, and I begin swaying on the bed. I try to stand up, but my legs buckle underneath me. I can't breathe. I try to walk towards the window, but I fall back against the wall. Mustafa Tora jumps up to help me. He lifts me up and helps me to the bed.

"Are you all right, Sayyida? Can I help you with anything?"

He hands me a drink of water and I press it gratefully to my lips.

"What sort of sentence do you think will be passed?" I ask him feebly.

Mustafa Tora looks at me as he takes the glass from my hand.

"Because of your condition and your status in Egyptian society, your father, and your distressed state of mind, I will try my utmost to get you a shortened sentence at a psychiatric institution."

"You say you will try. What is the worst that could happen to me, Sayyid Tora?"

Mustafa Tora stares at the ground for a moment.

"The Sharia states that a death must be repaid by a death. But there are other factors to take into consideration. And there is always money—a large sum could grant you a reprieve. But—"

"But, Sayyid?"

Mustafa Tora looks at me directly.

"But you are a woman," he says, "and your husband was well-known in public life. I believe that it is possible that Cairo will want to see you made an example of. Al-Shezira's brothers-in-law are demanding the highest penalty in the land."

The room seems to darken. The face of the man in front of me fades away. I do not say anything for a long time. God, then, has answered my prayers. I have nothing left to lose. Alexandre's way is the only way.

CHAPTER FORTY-SEVEN

Tashi felt paralysed with fear. Where were the sector men who were supposed to be masquerading as palace security personnel? Something was wrong. He waited for the new security guard to finish his telephone conversation. The security guard glanced at Tashi, then nodded. He replaced the receiver and walked back to the car. His face gave nothing away. He opened the door of the car and leaned in. The trophy with the bomb inside it lay innocently on the seat next to Tashi.

"Please proceed, Orhan Sayyid," he said solemnly. "Sorry for the delay, but you do understand we must take every precaution. You are free to go in. Have a good evening, sir."

Tashi nodded and discreetly swallowed back a gulp of relief, a flush of heat pulsing through him. Hamid started the engine and drove through the palace gates to the main entry. He saw Issawi's car stopping before a platform at the foot of the stone steps leading into the palace. Men in tuxedos and women in evening gowns were walking up a red carpet towards the huge palace entrance. Guards with rifles slung over their shoulders were parading up and down near the parking area. Another stab of panic jabbed at him. There was no margin of error in this operation. The absence of the sector members at the security gates meant trouble. Issawi's chauffeur was letting him out at the red carpet. He needed to attract Issawi's attention, engage him in conversation, give him the trophy inside the palace's grand entry hall, as planned, and then rejoin Hamid in the car and leave.

"Hamid," Tashi said, "make sure the car is positioned for a quick getaway. Let me out here, and I'll follow Issawi in."

Hamid nodded. "I'll pull the car around and have it facing the exit," he said. "Here's to the revolution, my friend. Long live Egypt!"

Tashi pulled at the lapels of his tuxedo and grabbed the trophy. His heart was hammering in his chest. He thought of his wife and his child. He said a quick prayer and opened the car door. Issawi was walking up the palace steps to the main entry, laughing, with two men and a girl in a red dress. Issawi was holding the girl's arm. He saw that her face was etched with fear. For a split second he bitterly regretted the position of responsibility and glory Littoni had placed on him. He suddenly feared that he would never see his wife, Meryiam, and his baby girl again. What if he wasn't able to leave the palace grounds in time? What if Littoni's plan failed and the bomb was not detonated correctly? But he was prepared to die for his God if he had to. That was the correct voice inside him talking. He would not die a coward. He was not a child. He was a grown man, working to bring about a better future for his country. And he was prepared to pay the price.

He saw Issawi pulling at his bow tie in exasperation, talking to one of his men, one hand possessively on the beautiful, slender, dark-haired girl. Two heavy-looking youths, obviously bodyguards, stood on either side of Issawi and the girl. Tashi slid his hand in his pocket and fingered the tiny handgun hidden there. He looked back and saw that Hamid had positioned their Daimler strategically for a smooth exit. Tashi moved forward up the steps, trophy in hand. The trophy felt heavy. The bomb had been skillfully made by a group of sector members. He had been part of this group and knew everything there was to know about these time bombs. They were small but deadly, and destruction was guaranteed. But, a seed of doubt suddenly played with Tashi's mind, and he wondered whether Issawi would suspect anything from the weight of the trophy. But he squashed his fears. Issawi was a narcissist. This was his big night. He was to be honoured by the king of Egypt for his work, and his thoughts would be entirely focused on the great leader that he considered himself to be.

Tashi examined the scene in front of him. He followed Issawi up the palace steps and then called out to him. "Issawi Pasha."

Issawi turned around. He looked surprised, and Tashi read contempt and irritation on his face.

"Who are you?" Issawi asked angrily.

"Forgive me, sir," Tashi said, approaching him slyly. "My name is Suleyman Orhan. I'm the newly appointed secretary to the Turkish ambassador. I'm a great admirer of yours, sir. We met a few weeks ago at a dinner in Alexandria. I knew I was going to see you tonight, and I wanted to give you this small token of my estimation. I am a partner in the Alexandria trans-Mediterranean packing consortium, the joint venture you have invested in."

Issawi sized him up suspiciously. "Sir, this is neither the time nor the place," he said. "The king is waiting."

Tashi eyed him hatefully. He looked searchingly into his eyes, watching for a sign of recognition. Tashi's heart pounded in his throat, but he felt euphoric.

"Issawi Pasha," Tashi replied. "I have a gift for you. I had my assistant choose it specially for you. It's made of gold, you see, and has both our names on it. It's a gesture of thanks. We are going to be partners and are going to make a lot of money together."

Tashi pushed the trophy against Issawi's torso and the man clutched at it frowning. Tashi saw him look down at the trophy disdainfully, fingering it. He flashed a look at the girl next to him, then at Tashi, and then at the trophy. The sectors, Tashi thought desperately, they must have activated the detonator by now.

Issawi weighed the trophy in his fat hand and laughed. He held it and admired it and continued to laugh. "I do not accept gifts from secretaries of ambassadors," Issawi said, slamming the trophy back against Tashi's chest. He turned to walk away, grabbing the girl by the arm as he went.

Tashi was holding the trophy now. He froze, his eyes wide, knowing the seconds were counting down and the timer must have been activated. The bastard had humiliated him, had dared to walk away, dared to treat him as though he were nothing. He would show him. The Group of the X would destroy him. At that moment Tashi wanted to kill him with a single gunshot to the head, but he held the trophy with both hands and called out to him.

"You want the Group of the X, Issawi Pasha?"

Issawi swung round on his heels. "What did you say?"

"I can give you all the information you need. I've come here to warn you not to enter the palace tonight."

"Just who are you, sir?" he asked. "What do you know?"

Tashi had only minutes. "I came here to give you this gift, Issawi Pasha," he said. "You chose not to accept it. That was not wise."

Tashi saw Issawi swallow nervously. The seconds ticked by.

"What do you know about this Group?" he said.

"I know everything there is to know. I know that you should not go into the palace tonight."

Issawi stood rigid. Tashi could see black fear in his eyes. He felt victorious.

"Tell me what you know, Sayyid," Issawi shouted, "or I'll have you arrested on the spot."

Tashi slipped his hand in his pocket and pulled out his gun.

"That would not be a good idea, Issawi Pasha. You and your bodyguards and this pretty Sayyida are perfect target practice for my men," Tashi said. "Move one inch and my men will fire."

"Who are your men? Damn you!" Issawi shouted, holding back his heavies.

"Sectors five through ten," Tashi said.

"The X." Issawi choked, reaching into his own pocket for his revolver.

Tashi dropped the trophy and backed down the steps, pointing his gun at Issawi's face. He backed up towards the waiting Daimler and got in.

"Open fire," Issawi screamed to the security guards.

A storm of bullets hailed down on Hamid and Tashi's car as Hamid screeched up to the security gate, smashing into the white Ford blocking the way.

The journal of Hezba Iqbal Sultan Hanim al-Shezira,
Cairo, October 1919

Tonight Alexandre and his men will come for me, God willing, but right now I am dressing for court. I smooth my short hair behind my eyes and adjust my beloved journal under my robes. I make sure it is flush against my stomach in its secret little pouch.

I put on my overdress, then my floor-length chador, and I wait to be called. A moment later, the door opens and the guards enter, escorting me down the stairs to the carriage that is waiting outside to take me to the courthouse.

Please God, let me hear news of Virginie. I am sure my lawyer, Mustafa Tora, will be able to tell me something. When I arrive at the courthouse, I am confronted by a sea of faces standing on the steps. Soldiers are pushing people back, forming a corridor for me to walk through. I suddenly feel very afraid, but I decide that I must not let myself be crushed by fear. I must walk tall, for my papa, for Rachid, for Alexandre, for Virginie, for myself and my child.

A hush descends on the crowd as I get out of the carriage. The heat is unbearable, and I am perspiring in my chador. The men gape as I am escorted up the steps to the main entrance.

One by one they start hurling abuse at me until the noise rises to a cacophony, like a swarm of bees ready to sting. *Take no notice,* I repeat to myself, over and over, hardening myself to what is to come.

I walk into the courtroom. There are almost as many men seated there. I go over to a stand and look at the qadi. He introduces himself to me. I do not hear his name because I have started to shake with apprehension. After taking my oath, I am told to sit in the chair provided for me, which is permitted since I have a child in my belly. I sit down on it.

The qadi runs through a seemingly endless list of questions that warrant a simple "yes" answer. Then he says, "You are the only daughter of the marriage of Ali Sultan Pasha to Zehra, his concubine, are you not?"

"Yes," I reply.

"But you have a brother. Tell us his name and where he is at the moment."

"His name is Omar Sultan, and he is studying at Oxford University in England."

"You were married when you were eleven years old," he says, knowing perfectly well that I was.

"Yes."

"How did you feel about your parents' choice of husband?"

"I am a loyal daughter. I had no feeling whatsoever."

"Is it true that you started to hate your husband, from the moment you were married to him?"

I fall silent. There is no way to answer that question, except honestly. "My husband hated me. I was the thorn in his side."

"You did not answer my question," he says. "Did you hate your husband?"

I hesitate, then eventually I say, "Yes, yes I did."

The hush in the courtroom is broken. The crowd murmurs its disgust.

"Enough to murder him?"

The crowd holds its breath. I hesitate, then say, "My husband was an evil man. I was beaten and raped by him."

The qadi smiles mockingly. "So, I repeat, you felt strongly enough about your husband to take his life," he says.

I hesitate, perspiring hot and cold beneath my chador. The courtroom is deathly still.

"It is a simple yes or no answer," the qadi says.

"Yes," I say.

The crowd roars with victory. The qadi silences them. Mustafa Tora gets up and walks towards him. The qadi gives him a stern look. Mustafa Tora plucks a Qur'an from his briefcase and opens it. As he reads the suras, I stare at the qadi, my heart beating so hard I feel I am being trampled to death by wild horses. I have neither the strength nor the courage to face this. The qadi will find me guilty. I have no doubt that Mustafa Tora will not be able to convince him otherwise.

I must preserve my strength for tonight. Alexandre and his men will come for me. I have to believe this, and then I will be free. But I am too choked up to stop myself from passing out, to stop the room from fading away to black.

CHAPTER FORTY-EIGHT

Hidden in a haret off Sharia Abdin, Farouk had seen Issawi's Daimler pull up. Watching in horror, he'd seen Aimee, dressed in her floor-sweeping crimson, being manhandled by Issawi and his cronies as she got out of the car, her face ashen with fear.

He wanted to blow Issawi's brains out, but he was too far away. He would have to get closer. His body trembled so violently that he could hardly hold his binoculars still. The pain in his chest rode him like a demon. He spat out short breaths, trying to regain control of himself. The bomb would be on the shortest possible detonation time, and, with so many VIPs milling in front of the palace and the king on his way from the grand hall to meet them, the scene would, at any moment, become one of mass human destruction. Aimee had so little time left.

Breathlessly studying the scene unfolding in front of him, he knew Tashi's game. Keep Issawi preoccupied while the seconds ticked away. He had to act quickly, get Aimee away from there. He didn't care what happened to him anymore. He was finished—deep down he knew that—but he had to save the girl.

He ran through the crowds, got in his car, and floored it up Sharia Abdin, screeching to a stop just as Tashi and Hamid tried to exit the gates.

He jumped out of the car, clutching his gun in both hands, and pointed it at Hamid and Tashi, then at Issawi and his bodyguards.

"There's a bomb," he yelled at the top of his voice.

The crowds started screaming. Farouk fired some shots in the air.

"Stop!" he yelled. "I know where the bomb is."

The crowds halted and listened. A woman began sobbing nearby, and the men's faces were contorted as the government elite was rendered powerless. Issawi's enormous body spasmed and his face caved in, in horror. The security guards at the gate stood stonily still, waiting for what was going to happen next. The armed guards who'd been patrolling the area raised their rifles, ready to shoot. His eyes strained to take it all in, and perspiration ran down his face, soaking his clothes.

"No!" he screamed at the guards. "Don't shoot. I'm the only one who knows where the bomb is. If you shoot me, you're all lost. It's powerful. It will kill us all."

They lowered their rifles, and he took his chance.

"Release the girl," he shouted at Issawi. "Let her go. She's got nothing to do with all this."

Issawi grabbed Aimee by the wrist and yanked her back into place. Aimee closed her eyes and waited.

"Well, well. The X shows its face," Issawi said. "And we have his favourite plaything." Farouk walked through the gates towards Issawi, his gun pointed at Issawi's face. He held out his other arm to warn the security patrolmen not to try anything.

"Release the girl, Issawi," Farouk snarled. He was close enough now to aim between Issawi's eyes.

"I should blow your brains out, but the bomb will do that anyway if you try and stop me. Let the girl go."

Issawi stared at him, a flash of recognition shuddering through him. "I know you, don't I?"

Farouk didn't answer.

"Let the girl go," he said, stretching his arm out to reach for Aimee. He pulled her fear-rigid body to him and whispered something in her ear, keeping the revolver positioned squarely between Issawi's eyes the entire time.

"Go, Aimee, run as fast as you can, as far as you can."

Aimee gripped his body, eyes wide. Farouk pushed her away. "Forgive me," he pleaded. "Now, run."

She stepped away from him, took off her shoes, and ran for her life, a bolt of crimson gone like a flash in the night. Now Farouk turned to Issawi.

"As for you, Issawi," he sneered, "I'm going to—"

"Farouk," a voice shouted. "Farouk. You will never win."

Littoni was beside him in a flash, pointing his gun at Farouk's temple and smiling.

"The bomb," he said. "It's going to go off. . ." Farouk gritted his teeth and did not move.

"Don't do this, Littoni," he said. "I've got our man. Now I'm going to find the bomb and dismantle it."

"No, you're not," Littoni screamed, his voice echoing off the walls, mingling with the sound of the whimpering women, the ripples of terror emanating from the crowds.

"I'm going to kill you, Farouk. I'm going to—"

A gunshot pierced the air. Farouk stepped back, temporarily startled. A thin trickle of blood ran down the side of Littoni's head. His expression vacant and eyes wide-open, his narrow mouth sagging towards his chin. Another gunshot. This time to Issawi's head. Issawi's body slumped to the ground, dead, not from his gun, but someone else's.

He turned to try to see who had fired, but he could find no one. He swayed in shock. Issawi's bodyguards flinched and raised their handguns, pointing them at him. What looked like a thousand revolvers were suddenly aimed at his face.

And then he heard the crack of the explosion. It rose out of the earth, splitting the sky open and the noise echoed for seconds afterwards as the ground shook. People screamed and the palace walls melted away in a dense fog of dust and debris.

The journal of Hezba Iqbal Sultan Hanim al-Shezira,
Cairo, October 1919

I wake up at Virginie's house. A nurse is sitting next to me. She is peering at me with a concerned expression, her face framed by her starched hair shield. I try to raise myself on my elbows, but she pushes me back gently.

"My baby," I say, "my baby."

She pats me on the shoulder and tells me my baby is fine, that I must rest.

"What happened at the courthouse?" I ask her feebly.

"You are weak and need to lie still. The airlessness of the courtroom made you faint."

"And what are they going to do about my case?"

"The court will reassess your case in a day or so. The qadi has allowed you two days of bed rest. Then you will appear before him once more. In the meantime you will stay here, and I will stay with you for the time being."

I slump back onto my pillow and look at the ceiling. I think of Alexandre and our plan to escape to France. But I ask the nurse, "What about Saiza and Virginie al-Fatuh? Have you heard anything?"

The nurse shakes her head and stands up. "Don't ask so many questions," she orders me. "Now sleep. You are troubled and tired, and it is not good for your baby."

She goes to the door, opens it, and speaks softly to the guard outside.

"Yes, it will probably do her good, but only for a short time," she says. She steps back from the door and Saiza walks in. I sit up and pull Saiza into my arms.

The nurse says, "You're only allowed one visitor before your trial resumes. This Sayyida may only stay for five minutes, and then she must go."

The nurse leaves the room. Saiza puts her finger on my lips to stop the stream of words that threatens to overwhelm me.

"Shush," she says, "keep your voice low."

"Saiza," I whisper, "I am so glad to see you. Where have you been since our Sarai was destroyed? What happened to you?"

Saiza nods and holds me tight. "Our papa, our family, gone." She swallows painfully.

I turn away abruptly. I don't want her to see my tears.

"Did you kill your husband, Hezba?"

I close my eyes and nod slowly. "He gouged out Rachid's eyes in front of me. He found out about my affair with Alexandre. He would have killed me in the end."

"And the baby, is it al-Shezira's or Alexandre's?"

I turn away again. She may be my half sister, but I cannot tell her. I will tell her when the baby is born, but for the moment I must keep the identity of my baby's father a secret. "Don't ask me that, dear Saiza," I say. "Tell me what they are saying at the courthouse."

"They are saying that you will be found guilty, that the qadi is determined to make an example of you."

I shake my head and raise my eyes to Saiza's. She grabs my shoulders and shakes me gently with frustration and emotion. Then she bows her *head and strokes my short hair. She doesn't understand how I can be so resigned about my situation. The truth is I am neither resigned nor calm, but I must preserve my energy for Alexandre, for tonight. I know he will come tonight. I know that we will escape and that my baby will be born in safety. I must keep my spirits up. I say nothing to Saiza. I simply hug her and try to comfort her.*

"Say something, Hezba," she says. "You don't seem to care at all about what I just said."

"I am leaving tonight, Saiza. This is my last chance. I won't be seeing you again for a long time, I am sure, but I want you to know that I love you and I am sorry you lost your baby son, Ali. You see, I have to try and stop this persecution of me, of women. I am not to blame. And if I have even a chance of happiness with Alexandre, then I must fight for it. I do not believe I did anything wrong. Al-Shezira deserved everything he got. I refuse to be sentenced to death for murdering a man everyone wanted dead. I must fight back. I may just be a woman, but this woman is going to fight till the end."

I can see the fear veiling Saiza's face, the way her mouth curls in despair, the tears misting her eyes. I have seen that look before. It is the look that says she knows she cannot stop me, even if she wants to.

"Don't, Hezba, I am begging you. Think about what you are doing. Think about the child in your womb. I am sure there is something we can do. We have money and power in this city. We have connections. I will pay someone to bribe this qadi to let you off. This judge is well-known. He loves money and is easily bought. But please, don't do anything stupid."

"There is no greater power than the power of the Hadith, Islamic law," I say. "I have no choice. Islamic law will condemn me. Islamic law has already found me guilty. I must fight for my baby, Saiza. For a better life for her."

The door opens, and the guards and the nurse walk in.

Saiza hugs me, sobbing, and whispers in my ear. "Have courage, Hezba, but please promise me you won't do anything impetuous, I'm begging you."

I hold her tightly, savouring the sweet scent of her neck. I can promise her no such thing. I wish I could, but it is impossible.

CHAPTER FORTY-NINE

Aimee heard the sound of a gunshot, an ear-piercing explosion, hysterical screams, sirens and more gunfire, then crackling flames. She was running as fast as she could, her dress yanked up around her thighs, her heart burning in her chest from the exertion. As she ran in the vague direction of her aunt's house, she passed screaming people running in the other direction towards the palace.

She tried to breathe, but the smoke and the fumes made her choke. Her bare feet were bleeding. She ran over rough pavements, animal excrement, gushing drains, through mucky and dusty harets. Tears streamed down her face, blinding her. The bomb must have killed Farouk. He had risked his life to save her. She was running free and he was dead. God, he was dead, but she couldn't think about that now. The only safe place for her was with her aunt Saiza. She ran until she could run no more. Finally she saw a cab. Collapsing in a state of exhaustion against the car door, she wrenched it open and ordered the driver to take her to the suburb of Medinet Nasr. She slunk back in the rear seat, dishevelled, out of breath, her cheeks streaked with tears. Her dress was torn and dirty. Her feet were cut to shreds, her arms covered in dirt, her face coated in perspiration. She mustered the last of her energy, leaned forward, and asked the driver, panting, "Do you know what happened?"

The driver nodded.

"The palace, there was a bomb. I wanted to go and help, but I was turned away. It's chaos down there, too many cars, ambulances, and people all trying to get in and out. I wanted to help those poor people, but I could do nothing."

Aimee saw his eyes mist over. He clutched the steering wheel, bit his lip, and shook his head.

"You are helping me, Sayyid," Aimee said. "I was there. I am all right, but I want to go to my aunt's. It is the only safe place for me right now."

The driver nodded miserably.

"We're here, Sayyida," he said, refusing, even when Aimee insisted, to wait for two moments while she got some money from her aunt. She trembled on the pavement as he left, then turned to ring the doorbell of her aunt's house. Rose answered the door. She was wringing a handkerchief anxiously in her hands. Her eyes widened in disbelief at the sight of Aimee.

"Aimee!" she cried out. "The police have been looking for you. Where have you been?"

Rose. It was so good to see a familiar face. She stifled a sob and flung her arms around the housekeeper's neck.

"Rose, where's Auntie? I need to see her."

Rose peeled back Aimee's arms from her neck and looked her straight in the eye. "My dear child. Your aunt had an accident."

Aimee swallowed hard and stared at her.

"What? Where is she? Is she all right?"

Rose stared back at her, her face strained with exhaustion. Aimee noticed the sorrow in her eyes, the downturned mouth, the mask of grief clamped down over her features, the way she hung her head.

"Aimee, you must prepare yourself for a terrible shock. Your aunt Saiza had a fall. She was taken to the hospital, but she did not survive."

Aimee stared at Rose blankly, incredulously. Her arms went limp; then her legs buckled under her. She sank to the floor and covered her face with her hands. She felt Rose crouch down beside her, put her arms around her shoulders, then get up and walk away for a moment. Then she felt a glass being nudged slowly into her hand and Rose's fingers encircling hers.

Aimee stood up, and Rose put her arm around her to steady her.

"When did this happen?" she asked in a choked whisper.

"Yesterday," Rose said, stroking a stray strand of hair from her cheek.

"Where did it happen?"

"She went to your house. She slipped down the steps that lead from your front door to the courtyard below. She hit the ground hard. The hospital tried to save her, but she hadn't been in the best of health. The fall from such a height brought on a heart attack. She died a few hours later."

Aimee opened her mouth, but no scream came. Instead she hung her head and closed her eyes. Her head was swimming. She couldn't breathe. Her thoughts turned to that terrible scene the other day when Rachid had revealed the real identity of her father and she had stormed out of the house. She had almost accused Saiza of lying to her. That was the last time she had seen her aunt.

"Come and sit down, Aimee," Rose said soothingly. "You've had a terrible shock." Rose walked her slowly towards a small sitting room off the entry hall. Aimee reached for an armchair and slid into it, unable to grasp where she was or what had happened.

She looked up blearily at Rose.

"There was a bomb at the palace," she whispered.

"A bomb? I heard something, far away, I wasn't sure."

"I had to get away. I ran and ran as fast as I could to get away. It's terrible. The people, that terrible noise, the smoke, the Abdin Palace has been destroyed."

Rose's hand flew to her mouth.

"My God. I must telephone my friend at the radio station and find out what's going on."

Aimee's head fell back against the armchair. She closed her eyes. She suddenly felt cold, bitterly cold, and began shivering. The shivering grew more violent. Rose found two blankets and gave her some more brandy.

"You're in shock, my dear. I'll call for the doctor, straight away. I'll stay with you until he gets here. I can telephone my friend later."

Aimee opened her eyes slightly and peered at Rose through tired slits, pulling the blankets closer to her.

"No, please, Rose, don't telephone the doctor. I'm all right," she lied. How could she tell Rose what she had been through? She could hardly believe it herself. Compared to the fact that her beloved aunt was dead, none of what had happened meant anything anymore. Her ribs ached and her wrists were still sore from being tied up. She shivered and closed her eyes as she remembered Farouk's face, the gun he held pointed at Issawi, the rage in his voice.

"Is Rachid still here, Rose?"

"Yes, he's been in his room all afternoon and refuses to come out. I tried to bring him some tea, but I heard him chatting to himself. I thought I would leave him for the time being, poor thing. He had become fond of Saiza since he arrived." Saiza. The mention of her aunt's name dragged her back to earth. She was dead, she told herself again and again. But she couldn't accept it. It couldn't be true. Her teeth chattered violently, and she tucked herself more deeply under the blankets to get warm. At last the brandy started working its magic and she drifted off to sleep.

When she woke, Rose was there beside her. Rose smiled sadly at her.

"I'll get you some tea," she said. "You've slept for a couple of hours. Have some tea, and then I'll make up one of the spare bedrooms for you."

"What time is it, Rose?"

"Nearly midnight."

Aimee sat up and rubbed her eyes. "The bomb at the palace? Have you heard anything?"

Rose shook her head.

"I didn't want to put the wireless set on in case it woke you," she said. "I'll listen in while I'm making the tea. We must pray that not too many people were hurt."

Aimee bit her lip.

"Don't fret, Aimee. Let me get you that tea and then I'll put you to bed. Tomorrow I'll get the doctor to examine you. I'm sure we're safe here."

Aimee slumped back again. She wished Rose were right, but somehow she didn't believe it. The feeling that everything was so very wrong gripped her throat and made her stomach churn with anxiety. Rose had left the room, and finding herself alone, she was petrified. As she looked around the room, her eyes fell on Saiza's handbag on the floor near her chair.

Aimee groaned as the reality of her aunt's death flooded through her again. She reached for Saiza's handbag and stroked the leather sadly. Then she opened the catch and looked inside. She pulled Saiza's appointment diary out, opened it, then put it back. She saw her face compact, her comb, her keys, her little photograph album of snapshots. It was difficult to touch any of her things. Saiza had touched all of these things. She had run the comb through her hair, dabbed her face with the powder in the compact, and flicked through the appointment diary to check the day's schedule, her women's club meetings, her volunteer work for the war. She had opened the leather address book to retrieve the address of a friend. She had unscrewed the ink pen and written a note to someone. Then Aimee spotted an envelope inside the bag. She pulled it out and saw her own name scrawled across it. She opened the envelope, unfolded the notepaper inside it, and began to read. She had difficulty deciphering the words through her tear-blinded eyes, but something was written in heavy black ink at the top of the page.

It was a name and an address. *Sayyid Gad Hassan Mahmoud, Sharia Mustafa Kamil, Shubra.* Though she recognised the name, the address was not familiar. Surely it couldn't be the same disgusting lunatic who had threatened to rape and kill her in the desert? One of Issawi's cronies, the thug that Farouk had pointed out at the el-G?

Farouk had told her that Gad Mahmoud belonged to the X, but Aimee now knew differently. He was part of this man Issawi's group. The nightmare she had just endured at the hands of the lunatic Issawi had taken place with Mahmoud looking on. Mahmoud had kidnapped her and taken her to Issawi's headquarters. Mahmoud had locked her up in that room, on Issawi's instructions. Mahmoud wanted this Group of the X found and imprisoned. And now his name was linked to her beautiful dead aunt. She felt imaginary hands grabbing at her throat, panic overwhelming her again. To see that name written down on the page horrified her. The rest of the letter was even more shocking. This Gad Mahmoud was someone Saiza wanted her to meet, someone who could help her solve the mystery of the whereabouts of her real father.

The journal of Hezba Iqbal Sultan Hanim al-Shezira,
Cairo, October 1919

The moon casts a brilliant light over the gardens. Everything is quiet. I have been sitting perfectly still in the corner of my room for hours, waiting with a pounding heart for the rebel attack to begin. I go through every little detail in my head of Alexandre's rescue of me, the time, what I have to do, where we will go, asking myself a hundred more questions, which I know Alexandre will answer when the time is right. His men are powerful. They have at their disposal enough weaponry to blow Alexandre's way out of prison. Then, in the ensuing chaos, they will come to Virginie's house and get me out.

I hear the night guards assume their position outside the house— two outside my door and two outside the front door—relieving the day guards of their duties. I will wait with bated breath for Alexandre's rebel forces to arrive. I start counting the minutes, slowly, purposefully, watching the splash of moonlight on the shuttered slats of the balcony doors.

Aside from the two night guards outside the door of my room, Virginie's house is empty. I fear she is still being held in a detention centre on the other side of Cairo. I have to assume that her husband has not yet returned to claim her. There is no doubt he will have been wired about the terrible news concerning the death of his dear friend, Ali Sultan, and the questioning of his beloved wife, Virginie, and will be on his way back to Cairo.

My own breathing sounds loud and laboured. I try to quieten myself by muffling my breathing with my hands.

Then I hear it, a faraway rumbling. I hold my breath. The sound grows louder. I hear the night guards talking among themselves in alarm. I hear them moving across the pavement. I go to the balcony to watch. Five men dressed in British military uniforms ride up, pulling *back on their reins. One of them has a holdall over his shoulder. Their caps are pulled down over their eyes, so I cannot see any of their faces. The guards ask them who they are. They answer that they have been sent from the army barracks near the British headquarters to check on things. My heart sinks. Alexandre's Rebel Corps has been found out. It's all over. I clench my teeth miserably.*

The guards reply that everything is all right and look up hopefully, as though waiting for the soldiers to turn their horses around and leave. Then, in one swift motion, the five soldiers withdraw their revolvers and point them at the guards. There is hardly time for them to answer before the horsemen have fired dozens of bullets into their bodies.

I hear the guards stationed outside my room run down the stairs at the sound of the gunfire. They fling open the door and open fire with their own guns, but the horsemen have vanished.

I watch the guards tread carefully down the steps onto the pavement. They spin around, taking stock of the situation, then separate and sidle around the house, guns raised.

Footsteps sound on the staircase within the house and the door is flung open. Alexandre stands there. He drops the holdall on the ground and wrenches from it a British officer's uniform, complete with cap and boots.

"Hezba, put this on. Quickly."

I rip off my hated robes and climb into the scratchy uniform, do up the buttons, pull on the boots, pull my hair behind my ears, and put on the cap. Alexandre grabs me by the arm and we fly down the stairs. Suddenly he pushes me back against the wall of the hallway. I hear bullets firing and a trilling sound of victory.

Alexandre leads us to the horses and helps me to mount one of them. As the others mount theirs, I notice that the fifth soldier, whose horse I have taken, waves us off and marches off into the darkness. I do not dare ask questions about where he is going. Suddenly we're off. I do not dare look back. I pray as I gallop that my baby is all right, hoping it is God's will that my baby will not suffer any harm. I do not know where we are heading. All I know is that we are leaving Cairo. Now is not the time to ask questions. I have to trust Alexandre.

Some clouds race across the moon. I smell the scent of oud, of damp earth. We head out of Cairo like bolts of lightning. Then we come upon the lush and verdant soil of the Delta, and ride through cotton plantations, date palm forests, and mud-hut villages, at one with the flooded plains around the Nile. At last, just as the moon is setting on the horizon, we reach Alexandria.

We have stopped only twice, to drink and eat a little midnight supper, but we were back on the desert road once more without delay. Once in Alexandria, we make our way to the district of el-Gomruk.

When we arrive, Alexandre dismounts and goes to knock on the door of a whitewashed house. A woman answers. She nods and he summons us in. The woman takes me by the hand and leads me into a small room lit with lamps and furnished with plain wooden furniture. On the floor is a mattress. She bids me to lie down.

But I can't stop the thundering of my heart. I can't stop the terrible feeling that nothing will truly be all right until Alexandre and I are as far from Cairo as we can possibly get.

The woman tells me she will get me some refreshment and leaves the room. I hear the men talking. Alexandre is bidding them good-bye. He is thanking them with all his heart. He is swearing continued allegiance to their cause. He is making them promise to keep safe. He tells them he will send them money and that one day he will return.

I hear them laugh as though what they have done is all in a day's work to them. I shudder regretfully. We are all wanted murderers. What have I become?

CHAPTER FIFTY

The foul-smelling odour at the Kubri el-Kubba detention centre was nothing new to Hilali. He was familiar with el-Kubba, one of Cairo's most inhumane holding centres for the lowest of criminals. Tonight, the smell—a mix of human excrement, sweat, and open drains—was particularly pungent. A fitting place for the X, he mused.

His mouth and hair were still coated with dust from the explosion, and his body was still quivering, but he had to pull himself together. As he walked, he pulled a comb out of his pocket and ran it through his hair, tugging at bits of plaster lodged there. He was safe; he could thank Allah for that. His men had arrested most of the terrorists from the basement meeting in Ezbekieh, and the ones who had gotten away had been shot dead. He'd arrived at the palace with his men just in time to witness it.

Shortly afterwards, the dynamite had rent the concrete underfoot, and the world in front of him had been engulfed in a wall of flames, consuming men in tuxedos, women in ball gowns, and his own security forces alike. The power of the blast had been so great that bodies had literally flown through the air.

He shuddered at the horror of it. The X was finished. He would see to it personally. Some of his best men had been lost in the explosion. Though he tried to compose himself, his rage was all consuming. He looked around at the slime-coated walls of the building he was walking through, stifling a retch that was threatening to overwhelm him. In the name of Allah, the smell was awful. His nose twitched in disgust.

Gamal and Major General Nesbit of British Intelligence walked by his side along the long dank corridor to the main interrogation room. On the left-hand side were the cells. He heard groans permeating the darkness of one, saw the whites of an inmate's eyes as he peered through the bars.

"Where have they been put?" Hilali asked Nesbit.

"Fifty of them are in cell A. The remainder are in cell F," Nesbit replied.

"Call them one by one to the interrogation room, Major," Gamal said. "We'll interrogate each one individually."

Nesbit patted Hilali on the arm.

"You'll be rewarded for your diligence, Hilali," he said.

"The king, once he has recovered from tonight, will hear of the success of Operation X."

"And Issawi's murderer?" Gamal asked.

Nesbit's eyes flashed triumphantly.

"A girl was spotted by one of our men. She was arrested immediately and brought in. She is the one you will be interrogating. She's a live wire, but I have no doubt she'll break if we apply the pressure."

"Okay, men, let's get on with it," Hilali said. "We'll see the girl first. Get your men to bring her through, will you, Major?"

Nesbit clicked his heels and walked away.

Hilali opened the door to the interrogation room. Gamal followed. Four military officers holding batons with rifles slung over their shoulders stood by a large square wooden table. The room was brightly lit, windowless, and soundproof.

"Men," Hilali said, "Operation X is still missing one of the masterminds. We'll be interrogating every one of the men and the woman we've caught for information. Any sign of trouble and I'll give the order, okay?"

The door opened. In walked the girl, held firmly by two of Nesbit's men. They sat her down on the wooden chair next to the table and tied her arms behind her back.

Gamal walked over to her.

"Name?" he shouted.

"Fatima Said."

"Age?"

"Twenty-nine."

"Address?"

"Forty-eight Sharia Ibn Tulun, Ezbekieh."

"Occupation?"

"Businesswoman."

"And what is your business, Sayyida?" Gamal went on.

"I run a nightclub in Wassa."

"What type of nightclub?"

"A gentleman's club."

"Name of the club?"

"The el-G."

"Do you sell women's services?"

"Yes."

"Have you ever heard of a man, code name Centurion?"

"No."

"I'll ask you again. Have you ever heard of a man, code name Centurion?"

Fatima shook her head. Hilali studied her. She was a pretty thing, a little cocky though.

"Do you know why you are here?"

Hilali watched her black eyes narrow with hatred as she stared at him.

"No."

"You murdered the chief advisor to the king, Haran Issawi, one of Cairo's most prolific politicians."

"I did not. I am not a murderer."

"You're a liar, Sayyida. Not only were you seen aiming and firing at Issawi, but as soon as you fired, you made the mistake of dropping your gun and running. I should congratulate you, Sayyida, for being such a good shot, but I'll save my breath. However, I will warn you, do not make the mistake of lying to us. Your sentence is predetermined. Egypt does not view murderers with any favour whatsoever, especially not if they are female, and especially not if the victim was at the pinnacle of public life. You are being interrogated now because we believe you know the real identity of the Centurion, the mastermind behind the X, and we want you to reveal his identity immediately."

Hilali nodded at one of the military officers, who marched up to Fatima.

"I'll ask you one last time, who is the Centurion?"

Fatima bit her lip and looked around. She saw the man questioning her nod at the soldier standing next to her.

"Tell us the truth, Sayyida," Hilali shouted.

The officer grabbed Fatima around the neck and slammed her head against the table with such force the table's legs cracked and slid forward on the damp stone floor.

"I'll die before I tell you anything," Fatima said, her voice cracking. The soldier had not released the grip on her neck. Gamal stared at her face squashed against the table, her eyes bulging, blood trickling from her lip.

"We have ninety members of the X incarcerated. Every single one of them will remain in prison for the rest of their lives. There will be no trial. Military Intelligence has this power, and the X will not get away with their reign of terror. We know two of the ring-leaders died in the bomb blast. You saved us the trouble and murdered another one. Why? Were you working as a counter-operative to the man you murdered? If so, on whose instructions did you murder him? We want a name, Sayyida, all aliases, and addresses. Is he the Centurion?"

Fatima did not move. Her head was on the table. Her eyes were closed. She opened them briefly, then shut them again. She did not answer.

Hilali nodded at the soldier.

He lifted Fatima's head again and smashed it violently against the table. Tears of rage slipped from her eyes, and she tried to open her mouth to speak.

"Centurion is also Smith, Carpet Seller. It depends on his business enterprises of the week," Fatima stammered.

Hilali smiled.

"You have decided to talk, Sayyida. You are wise. The owner of the newspaper the *Liberation* is an Italian called Lorenzo," Hilali went on. "Does the Carpet Seller ever use the offices of the *Liberation* as his headquarters?"

The soldier raised Fatima's head. She winced and closed her eyes.

"Well?" Gamal said.

"No—I don't know—no."

"What do you know of Abdullah Ibrahim, the young professor murdered in the desert recently?"

Fatima shook her head, wincing.

Hilali nodded at the soldier who slammed Fatima's face against the table again. Bloody welts began to appear on her cheekbones. The table was covered with blood and saliva.

"Nothing, Sayyida?" Hilali said. "Are you sure about that? You use your nightclub to network and sign up men for your cause, don't you? You were paid to befriend Ibrahim, weren't you? By whom?"

"No one," Fatima groaned. "I don't know who you're talking about. I don't know anything about this man Ibrahim."

"Throw her back in her cell, men," Hilali said. "A pitch-black bout of solitary confinement in the company of the flies, the overflowing excrement bucket, and the rats might make her change her mind."

The soldier dragged her up and marched her out the door. Hilali heard her jail door crank shut and the key turn. This was going to be a long night, he thought to himself.

"Now bring in each of the arrested men," Gamal ordered his other officers.

"Use maximum violence this time," Hilali ordered. "Each and every one must be broken. This Carpet Seller, the Centurion, this man Smith, is the one we need. We need to know exactly where we can find him if he is still alive. If we start smashing their knuckles and cutting off their hands, one of them will talk."

The journal of Hezba Iqbal Sultan Hanim al-Shezira,
Alexandria, October 1919

In the house in el-Gomruk, Alexandre comes to me. I sit up to greet him. He kneels down on the floor beside me, takes my face in his hands, and kisses me passionately, lovingly. In this moment, it is just the two of us, encircled by the haunting light of the lanterns, safe in this private world we have created, free of repression and domination. In this moment, I believe I am truly his equal. The fact that I have ridden with him through the desert to freedom is proof.

"Hezba," he whispers, "look to the future. Think of our life together."

He smiles and nuzzles my neck, and then I ask him. "How did you escape, Alexandre?"

"My men blew up the wing of the prison where I was incarcerated. I was in solitary confinement on the north side. No one was hurt. My men are clever. But we haven't time to talk about that now. I am here. You are here. There are other things we need to discuss."

I grip the lapels of his soldier's uniform and pull him to me.

"But were we followed? Is there any chance at all that we were followed?"

"The jail will have alerted the police. The Mamur Zapt, the head of Secret Police, will be rounding up his entire force at this minute. That is why we haven't a moment to lose."

"I need identity papers, the ones given to me at Kerdassa. I don't have them anymore. They were lost. What am I going to do?"

"It's all right," Alexandre says. "I have another set for you."

I nod. Alexandre continues. "The woman whose house we are in now has some Western clothes and shoes you can wear as disguise. We are going to board the early-morning boat, La Princesse, *which is bound for Marseille. Once we are in France, we will be safer, though we will have to disappear for a while. I have arranged for us to live out the next few months in a hideout in the mountains near Perpignan."*

"Thank you my love, thank you, for everything," I say.

Alexandre nods. "I love you, Hezba," he says. "I will always love you. You are my hero and my love, and I want us to be together forever. I want to look after you. I will do whatever I can. What we have been through together has made me sure of this. And I want to protect you from harm so that you never have to experience violence or abuse ever again."

I close my eyes and sigh.

"I heard you say to your men you will return. Do you mean it, Alexandre?"

He looks at me sadly. "I am going to return, Hezba, yes. I can't leave my men. We have to see this revolution through to its conclusion, but after that, I will return to you in France. I will always come back to you. And one day, we will return together to Egypt, to a better Egypt. But we must not talk about that now. We have to get changed. The boat leaves in one hour from the port. We must be quick."

"I was privileged, Alexandre," I remind him. "I could have done more for our people."

"Don't say that. Don't talk anymore. He kisses me and leaves. The woman enters the room carrying my disguise. She helps me dress, powders my face, combs my hair, adjusts my hat and the buckle on my shoes, gives me a suitcase to carry and a little handbag for my papers.

Alexandre comes in next. He is dressed in a cream suit with a waistcoat beneath the jacket. He is wearing spats, the type Virginie's husband wears, and a hat, and he is cleanly shaven. He no longer looks like the desert nomad he wants to be. He is the French aristocrat of his heritage, the man he really is but would never admit to being.

Alexandre nods for the woman to leave and we are alone again. He smiles at me and takes me in his arms.

"You are my French wife, Hezba," he says, getting into the role that we are about to play, a husband and wife returning to France after a short holiday. He kisses me on the mouth. I feel strange and light-headed. The low-waisted jacket fits me snugly and I think again about the child growing inside me, Alexandre's child, for I know it is his child, of this I am as certain as the dawn of a new day. I so want to tell him about our child but I know, right now, I cannot. The time is not proper and correct yet. My journal is snug against my skin. My identity papers are in my handbag. My heart is firmly in the future. I

am no longer Hezba al-Shezira, wife of the murdered statesman. I am Madame Alexandrine Chevalier, wife of Pierre Chevalier, returning to Marseille and then continuing on to Perpignan.

"Are you ready?" he asks me.

I nod. I have never been more ready than I am now. My whole life before this moment seems to have vanished in a dreamy haze. I am a woman on the threshold of my own future. I think of the school I am going to open. I am going to be like Virginie, teaching girls so that they can become the next leaders of Egypt. In twenty years these young women will be running businesses, heading up political parties, building their own wealth so they are protected from the oppression of poverty. I think of my marriage to Alexandre and the birth of my baby. I think of a world that is better than this, of a place where women can live free of the shackles men and religion place around their necks. I want my daughter to be raised without a religion, to grow up free, allowed to live the life she desires without fear. I see this. This is what I want more than anything. We say good-bye to the woman. Alexandre takes her hand in his and bows with gratitude. She smiles at him kindly. There is a carriage waiting outside to take us to the port. The driver nods at us as we mount. Dawn streaks the sky. The streets are deserted. How different Alexandria is from Cairo. I can smell the scent of the Mediterranean on the soft breeze that blows in from the sea.

I pull my cloche hat down over my eyes and huddle into myself, not wanting to be seen. Alexandre holds my hand and says nothing. He is scanning the streets as we set off. I know his heart is beating wildly, just as mine is.

The driver tries to make conversation with us, but Alexandre pretends he does not understand Arabic. The driver then changes to French, and Alexandre knows he has to answer him.

"To the port?" he says, and Alexandre nods. A jolt thunders through me. What a strange question, I think to myself. Surely the driver must *have known where he was supposed to be taking us. Alexandre flashes me a look, a warning that he too suspects something.*

"Are you sure, Sayyid? Which boat are you catching?"

Alexandre tells him that we are scheduled to leave on La Princesse *bound for Marseille. He glances at me again and pats his jacket. I know what he has in there—a revolver. The driver picks up the pace and we feel the swift movement of the carriage under us.*

Alexandre leans forward and says to the driver, "This is not the way to the port, my man. What do you think you are playing at?"

The driver pretends not to hear, and this makes Alexandre angry. He leans forward farther and grabs the driver by the neck. The horses pull against the reins. I can see the perspiration on Alexandre's cheeks, the straining of his temples as he wrestles the driver of our arabieh. He sideswipes the driver and kicks him out of the moving carriage. Then he grabs the reins and begins driving himself.

"Now to the port," he says, and I hold on to the seats for grim life. When we arrive, we see that the ship is in the port. Among the crowds milling around the embarkation area we see police and throngs of soldiers.

"What are we going to do?" I whisper, clutching at his arm. "We can't do this. An entire army is waiting for us."

CHAPTER FIFTY-ONE

Aimee waited until Rose had gone to bed that night. She stood behind the door of her bedroom, listening to the sounds of Rachid's moaning fading away. She heard Rose visit the bathroom and then finally retire for the night. What she had to do couldn't wait. She didn't want to worry Rose any further by telling her what she was going to do or where she was going.

She went and sat on the bed for a while in the moonlight and looked at the dressing gown she had put on after her bath. Then she got up and, as quietly as she could, she opened the door to the wardrobe in her bedroom and found some clothes to wear. There was a pair of Saiza's black trousers. She put them on. They were far too big for her, so she grabbed a belt. She threw on a thin beige sweater, slipped on some boots, and cloaked herself in a dark shawl. She folded the piece of paper with Gad Mahmoud's address on it and put it in her pocket along with some money she'd found in Saiza's purse.

Ready, she thought, bracing herself for what she had to do. She opened the bedroom door quietly and crept across the dark landing to Saiza's bedroom, opened the door, and slipped inside.

She didn't dare turn on the light for fear of being caught. She knew Saiza kept her gun in a secret velvet-lined compartment of her jewellery and makeup box. She saw the box on the dressing table. "Forgive me, dear auntie," she murmured to herself.

With the gun in her pocket, Aimee crept downstairs, out the front door, through the gates, and onto the street. She pulled her black shawl over her head, wound it around her neck, and started to walk.

In the distance she could see a hazy cloud of smoke billowing out from the direction of the Abdin Palace. But she wasn't going to the palace. She was going to pay Gad Mahmoud a visit in Shubra.

She found a cab and instructed the driver to take her to the address in the letter. She was soon standing in front of Mahmoud's house. It was a strange place that looked like a Swiss chalet, near the Church of St. Anthony that she knew well, bordered by a small garden filled with wild shrubs and plants. She stood for a moment, clutching the letter, drops of nervous perspiration from her hands smudging the ink.

Aimee recalled Saiza's words to her in the letter.

I could never find it in my heart, my darling Aimee, to tell you who your real father was. You were brought up as an al-Shezira to avoid any possible repercussions or gossip. I have tried to keep so many things from you, my dear, because I wanted to protect you. Your maman was a wilful child. There seemed no point in revealing the scandal of her life. As for the journal, it was something I had wanted to destroy, but after a lot of soul-searching, I decided to let you have it when you got much, much older, after you had married. This you know. What more can I tell you?

She'd read on.

The details of my innocent brand of deception are something that must be discussed in person, Aimee. It is for this reason that I am writing you this letter, first. I want to tell you how sorry I am. The pain and suffering must be truly unbearable. Not only are you having to cope with the death of your dear Azi, but you now know the scandal surrounding your birth and the truly horrible events that followed. Go and see Gad Mahmoud. He is a kind man. He might—and I say, might—know where your real father is. I can only hope that perhaps your father, Monsieur Anton, is dead, because I don't suppose he can be any use to you now.

She had to be brave. If the Mahmoud mentioned in Saiza's letter was Issawi's Mahmoud, she had her gun. She was no longer afraid.

She adjusted her scarf, pulling it down farther over her forehead and covering her mouth, so that only her eyes could be seen, and knocked on the door. It was a long time before a manservant opened the door. He had a surprised look on his face.

"I have come to see Sayyid Mahmoud," she said.

The manservant was wearing a dressing gown and slippers. He looked at his wristwatch.

"It is two in the morning, Sayyida," he said. "I am not sure the Sayyid is awake."

"Please, it's urgent."

The manservant showed her into a small sitting room, lined wall to wall with books. He put on a lamp in the corner and asked Aimee to sit down. Photographs stood in frames on a small oak desk. While she waited, Aimee studied them closely. She saw a pretty woman with a small child and then in another, three young men with broad smiles on their faces.

Suddenly Aimee felt panic-stricken. She had been crazy to come. What if this Mahmoud was the same Mahmoud who had tried to kill her? She fingered her gun and waited, her heart beating wildly in her chest. A man entered, adjusting the cord of his dressing gown, squinting in the low light of the little sitting room. He was portly with age, his face intelligent and open. His complexion was as black as ink.

"Sayyida?" the man said. "I am Gad Mahmoud. Is something the matter? How can I help you?"

Aimee sighed and blinked with gratitude. Gad Mahmoud! It was a fairly common Egyptian name! And yet she had been so certain of the possibility of it being Farouk's Mahmoud that she had practically convinced herself of the fact, but it wasn't. Thank God, it wasn't! She wanted to cry with relief. Instead she stepped forward, removed her headscarf, and smiled weakly.

"Sayyid Mahmoud?" she said. "My aunt Saiza, a very distant cousin of yours, sent me to see you."

A frown clouded his face, and he went to sit opposite her in a low armchair.

"I see. Well, it's a pleasure to meet you, I'm sure, even at such a late hour. I've just been listening to the news on the radio. There was a bomb. Half of the palace is destroyed. It's terrible. They're saying a hundred people are dead, but they are still counting the bodies."

Aimee bit her lip. "I know. I saw the smoke on my way here tonight."

Mahmoud clasped his hands together and said, "It's also been reported that the Abdin Quarter is on fire. The Military Police are in charge now. The king is safe. Apparently he had been called away for a moment just before the bomb went off. There's been a massive roundup of the suspects. Quite a few perished in the bomb blast. And one was murdered in cold blood, a man called

Omar bin Mohammod, alias Fabio Littoni, along with two of his sidekicks. One of the ringleaders is still missing, but he too is presumed dead."

Aimee put her face in her hands and breathed deeply, fighting back tears. Mahmoud moved forward and asked, "Are you all right, Sayyida? Sorry. I don't think I caught your name? Can I get you something to drink? Water? Tea? Coffee? Whisky?"

She wiped her eyes and tilted her head so that she faced him with a composed expression.

"Please call me Aimee, Sayyid," she said, her heart in her throat. "I'm sorry—I—my aunt passed away yesterday. I'm sorry for disturbing you like this. That is why I am here."

The man's mouth dropped. He bowed his head and closed his eyes.

"I'm so terribly sorry. I had no idea."

"I have only just heard the news myself. I'm deeply shocked. I can hardly believe it."

Aimee went on. "She had a fall and did not recover. She wrote me a letter before she died, advising me to come and visit you. She said you might be able to help me."

Mahmoud, evidently confused, shook his head, his features twisting sadly.

"I only just returned from the Sudan, Sayyida," he said. "I really am so terribly sorry. How did it happen?"

"She tripped and fell down some stairs, and, well, she was not young. She had a weak heart. The fall was bad. Her heart gave way, and there was massive damage to the brain."

"I see." A shadow passed over Mahmoud's face. Aimee shivered.

"Sayyid Mahmoud, my aunt told me you might know where to find a Frenchman called Alexandre Anton. I believe he is in Cairo. I wanted to come straight away to find out if you have his address."

His eyes flickered.

"Anton? Why yes, I used to know of his whereabouts, but as I said, I have been in the Sudan and have only just gotten home."

Aimee clutched her scarf, closed her eyes, and bowed her head.

"What do you know of him, Sayyid Mahmoud?"

"As you say, he's a French gentleman," Mahmoud went on tentatively.

"He was a very old acquaintance, someone I knew quite well, long ago. He came to Egypt about twenty-five years ago because his sister was living here. She was married to an Egyptian and lived in one of those magnificent old houses built by the Europeans at the turn of the century."

Mahmoud's eyes rested kindly on Aimee's face. Aimee stared at him. Her breath quickened.

"And now?"

"I believe the sister died many years ago and Anton left Cairo. He had a troubled past. I last saw him about ten years ago. We ran into each other in Alexandria. I hardly recognised him. His hair had faded almost to grey. His face was thin, and his cheekbones had become razor-sharp. He looked tired, ill. As I said, I had trouble recognising him because he had always been such a dashing young man with olive skin, a fine nose, and flashing black eyes. But when I saw him, he looked broken. I took him to a little café in Alexandria, and we chatted about the old days. He told me he was importing perfumes and household goods."

"And you have not seen him since?"

"No, I have not seen him. We lost contact, you see. However, I heard he left Egypt again and worked for a while in Turkey. Apparently, he returned to Cairo recently."

"Have you any idea where I can find him? It's very urgent."

Mahmoud studied her face inquisitively before he answered.

"I can make some enquiries for you, telephone a friend of mine who might know. Although it is very late, lucky for you, my friend is also an academic, a night owl who will probably still·be awake."

"Thank you."

Mahmoud got up to leave the room. He tilted his head, his hand on the doorknob.

"Anton, I think I heard, had reconnected with some of his old friends from the Wafd days. You are young, obviously. Maybe you are not aware of who the Wafd were? They were the original Nationalists, the political party that stood behind Sa'ad Zaghlul when he demanded Egyptian independence twenty years ago."

Aimee chewed her lip and nodded. "He did not marry then? He did not have a family?"

"I don't believe so. There was a woman I believe, a long time ago, but I have never heard of a wife."

"Could I ask if you would be able to make those enquiries, Sayyid Mahmoud? It is important that I find this man. Any information you have or can get would be most helpful."

"I will ask my man to bring you tea while I telephone this friend. If you wouldn't mind taking tea here, I will use the study to make my call. I won't be long."

He opened the door and shouted for his servant. He was about to leave when he leaned back around the sitting room door.

"Would it be impolite of me, Madame, to ask why you want to find this man?" he said.

Aimee stiffened, swallowed hard, and raised her eyes to his.

"He is my father, Sayyid. I'm sure you will now be able to appreciate why I have to find him."

The journal of Hezba Iqbal Sultan Hanim al-Shezira,
Alexandria, October 1919

A determined look flashes over Alexandre's face.

"We have no choice," he says. "If we try and catch the next boat, we will have to wait another day, and that would be disastrous. The longer we wait, the tighter security will be. We have no choice, Hezba." His voice is dark now, angry. I can feel by the grip of his hand on my arm that his decision is final. We must go on. We must carry out our charade. I pray quietly for deliverance, but my legs feel weak, unable to support me.

Alexandre and I start to walk towards the embarkation station. The fear of being discovered slices through me.

I whisper, "I will say nothing. My French is fluent, but my accent might give me away. You do all the talking."

Alexandre nods but does not look at me. His eyes are fixed on the soldiers checking identity papers, examining faces and luggage, and ushering people up the ramp to La Princesse.

I feel as though I am walking the plank, like prisoners in those pirate books I have read. I count the seconds as we march slowly towards the destiny God has willed for us.

"Halt," a soldier says, stopping us with his rifle.

Alexandre stops and puts his arm around my shoulders.

"Papers," the soldier orders.

Alexandre asks me sweetly in French to get my papers out of my handbag as he fishes his out of his pocket.

The soldier studies the papers, examines the photographs, compares our faces to those staring up at him from the cardboard.

"How long have you been in Egypt?" he asks.

"One month."

"And where were you staying?"

"With a friend at Giza."

"What has been the purpose of your visit?"

"A holiday, my friend," Alexandre says cloyingly, and the soldier flinches, his eyes narrowing.

I can hardly breathe. I have eaten so little and rested even less. Whatever source of strength has kept my child and me alive this long is leaving me now.

"Do you plan to keep us long?" Alexandre asks the soldier. *"My wife is not well. It is not good for her to be standing around."*

The soldier examines our papers again. There is a suspicious look in his eyes. Fear pulses through me like a vicious heat.

"Stand aside," he says, waving his rifle away to the left.

I lean against Alexandre and try to remain calm. I try to think of other things to distract myself. I can almost hear Alexandre's heart pounding in his chest. The sun is climbing slowly in the sky now. Though the air is fresh and pleasant, I look solemnly upon the city and the Mediterranean, our gateway to freedom.

The soldier calls over a more senior officer and points at us. The senior officer marches to a shabbily constructed hut and goes inside. A few minutes later, he comes out again, this time accompanied by three other officers, all armed, all stern-faced.

Alexandre holds his head high as they approach. Then he demands angrily in French, "What's going on? My wife needs to rest. We have our tickets for La Princesse. *Our papers are in order. Why are we being kept waiting?"*

"You are under arrest, sir," the army officer says.

Alexandre smiles mockingly and reaches in his pocket for his revolver.

I lunge forward to stop him, screaming, "No!"

Soldiers storm in on all sides. Alexandre is thrown to the ground and handcuffed. His head is pushed against the ground, and he is kicked in the stomach. His head is bleeding. I am screaming. I hear my screams, husky, dust-coated, violent, desperate. Two soldiers grab me by the arms and lift me off the ground. They take me to a waiting carriage, and I am driven through the city, then marched into a women's prison and pushed inside a cell. The steel door clangs loudly as it is slammed shut and locked. I listen to the echo of the warden's hobnailed shoes on the flagstones. And I hear the screams that continue to rent unabated from my throat.

CHAPTER FIFTY-TWO

Nemmat danced for her lover that night, but her body was prostrate with anxiety. Though the Abdin Quarter was burning, the head of Secret Police, Mehmed Abbass, was adept at commanding operations while attending to the more pressing need for personal gratification. His radio operator delivered news on the progression of events from the adjoining room channelled in from Intelligence HQ at regular intervals. Whenever Abbass decided he wanted a break, he summoned Nemmat for further entertainment.

But Nemmat was not her usual self. According to Operations, a man fitting Farouk's description, seen holding a gun to Issawi's face, was now missing. His body had not been found, which meant only one thing. If Farouk was still alive, he would soon come looking for her to exact his revenge. She swallowed painfully, forcing a thin smile for her lover. Littoni's assassination gave her little reason to rest easy.

Intelligence and Military Operations had managed to round up ninety of the suspected terrorists and now had them in custody at the el-Kubba detention centre. The night was still young, but the round-the-clock news reports were talking of torture and life imprisonment for anyone associated, even vaguely, with the terrorist group, the X.

Nemmat had made her to way to Abbass in Shubra and decided to hide out there for the next twenty-four hours. At least in Shubra, she felt safe—for the time being. She had one last card to play, but for the moment, pleasuring Abbass would secure her a few more nights' protection for her and her mother, who was asleep in the room next door.

She twisted and turned in the moonlight, carving the air with her body. Mehmet Abbas sat round-bellied on a velveteen sofa, moist about the lips, entranced by her mocha-coloured skin. She removed her clothes and stood over him. Abbass reached for her, cupping her breasts, pulling her towards him with one hand while he fumbled with his own clothes with the other. He adored her exotically scented dancer's body as though it were a heavenly thing. And with her thighs clamped tight around his portly waist, he became hers and she became his. But it was hard for her to purr like a Siamese cat, stretching her naked body before his when all she wanted was to know that Farouk had been captured.

"Ninety, Jewel," Abbass said exultantly. "We've got ninety and counting. The rats have being forced out of their holes."

"You are the master of this operation, Sayyid," she cooed, "despite what Intelligence might say. You'll be promoted for sure."

Abbass laughed. "And you'll be paid well, Sayyida for your involvement in their capture."

"How much?" Nemmat asked. "What we agreed?"

"You'll have enough money to keep yourself and your mother going for a few years."

"I need complete anonymity, police protection, and an escorted passage to Sicily to stay with a friend of my mother's for a while."

Abbass raised his eyebrows. Nemmat went on.

"I have more information for you," she said. "But you must promise to give me more money for it." Nemmat rubbed herself against him and bit his neck sensuously.

Abbass squirmed with pleasure.

"What's it worth to me?" he asked.

"You want the Centurion, the Carpet Seller, don't you? With the other ringleaders dead, he might very well be the last remaining X mastermind."

"He's missing, presumed dead. That's good enough for me," Abbass said.

"Are you sure? Think of the prestige, the glory of seeing the most prolific terrorist Egypt has ever seen behind bars for the rest of his life."

"Yes." Abbass smiled. "Yes—"

"The Carpet Seller is missing, but I'm convinced he will have crawled home somehow. If you're quick, you'll find him there. If he survived the bomb, he'll try and leave Egypt. I did a little extra undercover work. Though this man has many addresses, I've discovered this rat's favourite sewer—the place he'll go before he disappears forever. But you'll have to be quick."

The journal of Hezba Iqbal Sultan Hanim al-Shezira,
Cairo, October 1919

I have been transported back to a Cairo jail. I am waiting to be seen by the Mamur Zapt, the head of Secret Police. I have been told what to expect. The Mamur Zapt will want to know about my involvement with Alexandre's Rebel Corps and will want a signed confession that I murdered Khalil al-Shezira.

I know that Mustafa Tora, my lawyer, can do nothing for me now. I should have listened to Saiza, but it's too late. The jail I am in is far worse than the one I was put in before. It is crawling with rats, the walls are filthy, and there are fleas in my mattress. I am allowed to bathe daily to avoid infection. That is my only luxury. A thin English nurse comes to escort me to the prison office of the Mamur Zapt. I am allowed to sit down. The questions begin.

"Who are you working with?"

"No one."

"Your escape was organised by the Rebel Corps, was it not?"

I look up at his ugly, evil face and wonder whether he ever loved anyone, whether a woman could ever have loved him. "What is going to happen to me?"

"You are going to answer my questions and then you will see," he snarls.

"I know nothing of the group who rescued me from Zamalek," I say.

"Liar," the Mamur Zapt shouts. I flinch when he raises his voice to such a pitch.

"But you are Alexandre Anton's lover. You murdered al-Shezira Pasha while Anton and his men murdered the other politicians on the same night at Minya. Tell me where I can find the men involved with the group and you will be spared."

I look up at him in surprise.

"I can't help you. I don't know where these men live or what their names are."

"You are a stubborn, disrespectful woman," he says. "I'll see you're tortured, make no mistake."

"But—"

"Tomorrow you will appear before the qadi and your sentence will be heard."

He turns to one of his men and says, "Take the woman away."

I am delivered to the English nurse who takes me back to my cell. The door slams shut. I look out through the bars up at the sky, holding my belly. The sky is streaked with the remains of the day. I close my eyes for a moment. Then I go to the little jug of water in the corner and wash my arms, my face, and my feet. I kneel on the hard floor to pray. When I have finished, I lie on my mattress and fall asleep, dreaming of Papa and the heaven he has gone to, hoping, praying that I will go there soon.

In the morning, I am summoned early. I am washed by the nurse and given a clean robe. The robe is a lemon-yellow colour, bright and cheerful. I think the nurse feels sorry for me. Then she gives me a new black chador. She combs my hair before I veil myself. She squeezes my arm supportively as she asks me to follow her to the waiting carriage that will take me to the courtroom.

The streets around the courthouse are lined with people. It seems that I am a spectacle once more, and they have come to gape at me. Ushered into the courtroom, I am seated before the altar that will accommodate the qadi.

The room lulls to a deathly silence as we wait for his entrance.

At last the qadi comes in and walks slowly to take his place. He is carrying a Qur'an. He does not look at me. He looks at the floor as he walks, deep in contemplation. A boy, one of his assistants, announces his presence as though he were a god.

He says, "Qadi in this case."

The qadi reads out my name and my crime. He opens the Qur'an and reads a sura. Then he closes it and announces to the room, without even looking at me, "Death to the woman who murdered al-Shezira Pasha."

The room cheers. The boy assistant steps forward to me and asks if I want to say anything.

I stand up, remove my chador, and unveil myself. The crowd stares in disbelief and then begins to mutter obscenities.

The qadi still does not look at me. I say this: "I am the daughter of the sultan, a royal princess who dared to love and choose her own destiny. I was raped and tortured by my husband. Yet I am still considered a criminal. The law gives men permission to treat me this way because I am a woman. Yet I am the mother of all the men in this room. If you sentence me to death, you are sentencing the whole of womankind to death and depriving the entire world of its only nurturer. My father was murdered, but still you find it necessary to condemn me before you condemn the murderers of my father. I damn you all to hell with no God, no Allah to spare your souls."

Screams of hatred erupt from the crowd. Still the qadi does not look at me. This qadi could not be more of a coward. I am escorted out of the courtroom and into the crowds.

I am still unveiled. I have resisted all attempts to cover me with that foul headdress. I have nothing to lose now, nothing to be afraid of. Rocks pierce my face, and I feel blood trickling down, warm and salty into my mouth.

I close my eyes in the arabieh, the carriage that will take me back to my cell, as I am gripped on both sides by two armed soldiers. But I am taken to Virginie's house and locked once more in the sitting room. Another doctor comes and informs me what will happen to me. This time I allow the physician to examine me.

"Your baby is healthy, Sayyida, thank God for that," he says kindly. He looks me in the eye because I will no longer wear the veil that has shrouded and oppressed me for so long. In his eyes I see sympathy. I see humanity. I see a warmheartedness in his features. I smile at him weakly. I do not know what has happened to force such violence into the hearts of men. The qadi and the prison wardens, the soldiers and the men in the courtroom are Egyptians like me, with wives and daughters and mothers and grandmothers. Yet they want me dead—because I

dared to live my life the way I wanted, because I dared to try to put an end to my suffering.

"I am so glad," I say without emotion.

"I have ordered that you be allowed to stay under house arrest in Zamalek for the duration of your pregnancy. Nothing will happen to you until you have given birth. I estimate that your baby will be born in around five months. You must rest as much as possible and avoid fits of depression or anxiety. Then, I am afraid, I have no choice but to follow the orders of the court and to release you back to them."

I hang my head.

"You have a visitor," he says.

"I do?"

The doctor goes to open the door to the sitting room. Ushered in by a new set of armed guards, is Saiza.

CHAPTER FIFTY-THREE

Aimee waited patiently for the Sayyid Mahmoud to return, but her heart thundered unabated in her chest. She felt as though she were waiting for the delivery of a death sentence. Finally, after what seemed like an age, he returned. She stood up eagerly to greet him as he entered and watched him as he inhaled deeply. He steadied himself against the door as he shut it quietly.

His complexion had turned a murky shade of grey, and his mouth had become a thin slit. He hung his head, shaking it. His teeth were clenched, and his arm was trembling. When he looked up at her, he stammered as he spoke.

"I don't know how you will take this news, Sayyida. I managed to reach my friend. It appears I was correct. The man you say is your father, Alexandre Anton, is still in Cairo."

Aimee clutched her headscarf, wide-eyed and dry-mouthed. "I see. Do you have an address?"

Mahmoud swung his head away. He sighed, then ran his hands over his face. He walked over to the sitting room sideboard to pour himself a whisky from the decanter, and gulped the drink down.

"Yes," he said, "yes, I do."

"Well, Sayyid, may I have it?"

Mahmoud threw back another swig and put his glass down again on the sideboard.

"I don't think—"

"I am his daughter, Sayyid," Aimee insisted, trembling. "Please don't keep me waiting any longer."

"I am so sorry," Mahmoud said. "I am so very sorry."

He stared at her long and hard, little beads of perspiration erupting on his forehead.

"I have an address, but I don't think it will be any good to you."

"What do you mean? What are you talking about?"

"Your father is missing, presumed dead."

"How? What—?"

"He was last sighted at the Abdin Palace tonight."

"My father? At the palace, tonight?" Aimee gasped. She was suddenly chilled to the bone.

"Please," she begged. "Let me go to him. At least give me his address."

"Are you fully prepared for what I have to tell you?" Mahmoud said.

Aimee nodded.

"Your father is wanted by Intelligence and by the Military Police."

Aimee stared at the floor. She did not understand. Her father? A wanted man? Surely he had gotten it wrong?

"Why was he at the palace tonight? Had he been invited to meet the king?" Aimee asked.

"No, Sayyida. You did not hear what I said. Your father will be arrested when he is caught, but he might be dead already because of the bomb." She slumped down in her chair and said nothing.

"Your father belongs to the Group," Mahmoud went on.

Aimee shook her head and gritted her teeth. She knew what he was going to say now. There was only one thing he could possibly say.

"You know about the X? It's been on the radio. They are believed responsible for the bombing at the palace tonight."

"The X," Aimee whispered.

"Your father—my source has told me," Mahmoud started to say. Then, gauging her reaction, he paused for a couple of seconds before continuing. "He has many aliases. The last name my friend heard he was using was Taha Farouk."

Her body felt numb. When she looked up, she saw Mahmoud mouthing some words, but she didn't remember much after that.

She remembered vaguely her aunt's cousin calling her a cab, getting into it and telling the driver where she wanted to go. She remembered feeling absolutely nothing, as though her body were an empty shell incapable of any human emotion.

As the car rumbled along, the words of a poem came to her, Maman's song, the song Saiza had sung to her as a little girl. It was the song she'd written down in her exercise books at boarding school, the Arabic swirls and loops the only legacy passed down from her dead mother.

Hezba Sultan
her name whispered behind closed doors
in the garden
in the misty vapours of the hammam
her name dances with the sounds of harem laughter until it
disappears forever.

And as she mouthed the words with stony resolve, she rammed the handgun, discreetly hidden in her trouser pocket, hard against her left thigh, leaving bruises on her skin. She was going to find Farouk, going to Zamalek.

The journal of Hezba Iqbal Sultan Hanim al-Shezira,
Cairo, October 1919

"You are allowed fifteen minutes together," the guard says, and the doctor presses my arm gently before he leaves the room, shaking his head in anger at the guard's callousness.

"Saiza," I cry out, enfolding her in my arms and sobbing violently against her neck.

"Hezba, shush," she says, holding me close, rubbing my neck and my back soothingly.

"Saiza, I am so tired," I say, and she takes me by the hand and tells me to lie down on the mattress, while she bathes my face.

"They've sentenced me to death," I tell her. Saiza bends over me and kisses my face. Her tears splash over my cheeks and her body spasms with sobs.

"We will get you free, darling," she says.

"Have you news of Virginie?" I ask her.

"She is not well, Hezba," Saiza says. "She has been removed to a hospital in Old Cairo. Her husband has been exiled. Virginie faces a prison sentence for harbouring two criminals."

My heart is breaking, for all the wrongs that are my responsibility, for Virginie, for Rachid, for Saiza who is sobbing. These are the people I love, and I am the cause of their suffering. "And Alexandre?" I ask her.

"He has been sentenced to ten years in prison."

Turning away from Saiza and without looking at her, I say, "Saiza, you must take my diary, hide it away, please give it to my child when she is old enough to understand."

Saiza leans over me and turns my tear-streaked face to hers. "I'll do anything you say, darling sister," she says.

"The court could never have seen it, you know that, don't you?" Saiza hangs her head but carries on stroking my hair.

"I know."

"When my daughter has grown up, and she has married, give it to her then. Only then might she understand. And tell her I love her. I love her already, and I'll carry on loving her, even after I have gone."

Saiza stifles another sob and says, "Don't talk like that. Don't say those things. We will get you free, Hezba."

I nod quietly, but I am too tired to hope for this outcome. I think about my diary and how it has been my only friend. I feel desolate. I kiss Saiza and feel the wetness of her tears against my mouth.

"I trust you," I say, "but tell me you will allow no one to read my journal, Saiza, not even you. It is for my daughter, the daughter I will never know."

"What if your child is a boy?" she asks.

"Then destroy it," I say. "It is not a journal to be read by a boy. But I know you won't have to do that, Saiza. I know my child will be a girl."

"You can trust me," Saiza says.

"I am getting tired now," I say, "too tired to carry on writing in this thing. I have struggled to continue with it these last few weeks. I have written it because I want it as a witness to my life, the only true account there is."

"Of course, darling," she says, and I turn away from her again and look out through the window at the evening-streaked sky.

I watch night spread its fingers across the earth. I feel my strength leaving me, ebbing away. For the time being, I am content to lie here and drift in and out of sleep with Saiza holding my hand.

I can hear Rachid's voice as I doze, hear in my memory the lilting laughter of the harem children as they play in the gardens of the palace. I fall into a shallow sleep at last. I dream of Nawal, of Maman and Papa, of the peddler woman and riding across the desert at night with the wind in my face and fire in my veins. I dream of Alexandre, my Alexandre, our love, our past, our future. I dream of the house at Kerdassa, of the sweet coffee, thick as mud, of the scent of oud and the palm trees bending in the wind, of a hammock gently rocking, of a baby, my baby, a little girl, who will grow into a woman, a little girl who lives in a better world than this one. A little girl I will call Aimee.

CHAPTER FIFTY-FOUR

Just before dawn, Farouk stood smoking in his garden. Watching the heavenly shafts of orange and gold light emerging on the horizon to the east, he shivered. The shock of the coup, the bomb blast, the destruction, Aimee's haunted face as he pressed her to him and then released her to the streets of Cairo—it all sickened him.

The whisky decanter stood on the stone table, half empty. The whisky made him feel a little better. It had blocked out some of the pain. Bruised and blood-soaked from the night, he contemplated his own death for the hundredth time. He should have died tonight. He'd seen Issawi's expression of wide-eyed shock as the bullet had entered his brain. He'd felt Littoni's massacred body fall against him.

How he wished the bomb had killed him. Instead the force of the blast had simply sent him flying. He had landed hard against one of the palace outer walls. He had suffered no real injuries, except cuts and bruises bruising and a slight ache in his left ankle. In the ensuing chaos, he had crawled through the smoke to a side street and found a car. The driver had wanted to take him to the nearest hospital—such wonderful Egyptian warmth and caring, Farouk had thought at the time—but he'd insisted the driver take him home to Zamalek.

At Zamalek, he thought about Aimee, and guilt slivered through him. He had lied to her because he had wanted her to lead him to Issawi. He had been convinced that she and her husband had been in league with Issawi. Where was she now, her angelic innocence destroyed? She had vanished, and now he would never have the chance to explain.

He pulled himself together and drank some more whisky. His thoughts turned to Gigis, his houseboy. Gigis had been like a son to him and would have the house. Gigis would marry and could bring his bride to live here. Gigis would preserve the Zamalek house as a living shrine to Farouk's sister. None of the antiques, the paintings, the ornate chairs, the massive bookshelves filled with important volumes or the letters he'd written to her in his early years could be sold or disposed of.

Poor Gigis would find him, of course. He had it all planned. Gigis would remove the blood-soaked will from the grip of his hand and organise the dismantling of his estate.

What better way to die than by his own Smith & Wesson Model 3 revolver, his favourite weapon. A bullet through the head would leave no room for mistakes. He had nothing to live for now that the tumour had taken hold of his lungs, nothing to live for now that Issawi was dead. His work was done. He stubbed out his cigarette and went inside.

It was Gigis's night off, and he was visiting friends at Giza. A whisper of a breeze fluttered through the rooms. He sat down and put his head in his hands. Then he looked up and swallowed back a lump in his throat. The sweet scent from the flowers in the garden drifted in on the wind.

For a moment he ached to carry on living, but it was too late. He was wanted, wanted by Security Operations, by the Secret Police, by Intelligence. His sentence would not be light. He heard his sister's voice in his head, comforting him, telling him that everything would be all right. She had been so caring, his sister. She had cared about everyone. He pictured the soft gold of her hair, her pale eyes, and her skin, the colour of peaches and milk.

He slammed a fist against his chest and coughed up blood into a large white handkerchief. He had so little time. He wanted to see Aimee before it was too late. It was his last wish. He wanted atonement for the way he had treated her, for deluding her into thinking that Mahmoud and Issawi had killed her husband, for trying to lure her into a trap for his own selfish reasons. He walked inside and went upstairs to his study, where he normally slept on a low makeshift bed. He poured himself a fifth whisky, opened the double doors to the little balcony, and sat down in an old rattan chair. He was a Perpignan baby, born at the grand old mansion of Le Comte Cavaille d'Anton. He could not even remember his maman's face, the poor Egyptian slave his father had impregnated. How he had hated his father for his treatment of his maman. His father had been a hardened criminal, a toothless mass of odious flesh with his hands in the corsets of all the women of Roussillon. Farouk knew he would see both his sister and his beloved soon enough, the two women who had never really left him through all these years. He sat rocking himself backwards and forwards, hugging his chest, like the boy he had once been—a hungry, sad Alexandre, beaten and prodded by his papa, while Maman was raped and cast aside.

All grown-up, Alexandre the man was tall and magnificent, with a head of shocking black hair and flashing black eyes that he'd been told he'd inherited from Bouchra, his dear Egyptian maman. He wished he could remember her face. He couldn't. But he remembered her tenderness and the way she had loved him as a child. And when she had died, he had been heartbroken.

His entire adult life he had vowed to revenge the wrongs his own father had perpetuated.

That was a long time ago.

The journal of Hezba Iqbal Sultan Hanim al-Shezira,
Cairo, June 12, 1920

Written by Saiza Ali Sultan

I can hardly see the words I am writing because my eyes are misty, my body is trembling, and my hand is shaking so much that it is almost impossible to move the pen across the page.

Thank God my little niece is safe. She will live with me until she is old enough to be removed from this foul, atrocious city full of murderous criminals.

Then I will send her to live in France to be brought up under the loving guidance of Catholic nuns at the wonderful Institut de Neuilly, near Paris. It is run by my friends, and I trust them to take good care of her. The scandal surrounding baby Aimee's birth and life must be kept hidden. In France she will live as Aimee Nur al-Shezira, the legitimate daughter of Hezba and her husband, Khalil al-Shezira. If she were to stay in Egypt, people would talk. One day perhaps things will change. One day, I hope, little Aimee will be part of a different world. Until that time, I hope and pray that the God of us all, be we Muslim or Christian or Jew, protect us from evil and the insanity of men.

Hezba is gone. She was assassinated, butchered by three of al-Shezira's male family members. Al-Shezira's younger half brother, Haran Issawi, was the instigator.

He walks free, while my sister is dead.

The qadi has not ordered any investigation into it, because it is deemed an honour killing and considered just punishment for her actions.

The qadi, I am sure, is glad to wipe his hands of the affair.

My darling sister did not have enough strength in the last months of her life to continue writing in her diary. The doctor looking after her insisted that I be allowed to visit her every day, and she drew great courage from that. He also ordered that she be made as comfortable as possible in her temporary jail at Zamalek.

He arranged for her to have a few pieces of furniture put in her sitting room, reading material given for her, and instructed that her food and drink to prepared with the health of her baby in mind.

The qadi who sentenced her to be executed had connections with al-Shezira. This was reported in the newspapers, and a British high official was appointed to look into the case and identify any evidence of the perversion of justice. This news of a trial steeped in corruption was a great shock to my half sister. Her anger made her uncomfortable. She would not rest and insisted on pacing around her room most of the day. She demanded that I find out as much as I could about the British high official looking into the case.

She asked that I go and see him, and I did.

This kind man, Errol Simmons, had reviewed all the paperwork and was about to make official his decision to overturn the sentence and for the case to be brought before a Western court, with a new set of lawyers, full admissions by witnesses, written statements, and another court hearing.

A new court case was to take place after Hezba had had her baby. When I told Hezba this news, she was ecstatic. She talked about Cairo changing for the better and a chink of light appearing in the darkness that surrounded all women, from the humble wives and daughters of the fellahin to the richer women enclosed in harems.

I told her that her defiance in taking off her veil had received as much admiration as it had hatred and that gradually the women of Cairo were starting to take off their veils too.

Many lawyers had come out in her support, men who believed that the inequality Egyptian women face was the foremost reason for our lack of economic progress and dependency on the British for aid. Hezba was confident up until the end that justice would prevail.

And she was right when she suspected she was going to give birth to a girl. Her tiny girl-child came into this world at dusk on March 1, 1920, as Hezba lay on her favourite rattan couch behind the mashrabiyya in the first-floor sitting room of Virginie's house.

I tried to move her with the help of one of the servants to a more comfortable place, but she didn't want to be moved.

She delivered the baby without too much trouble. Despite the changing world around us, we paid tribute to our family's tradition by dressing Hezba in golden robes for the birth and by singing and lulling her through the pain just as we had done in the harem.

She was allowed a wet nurse and was up and in good spirits shortly after the birth. Though still under house arrest, she embraced her new role as a mother to Aimee and began preparing for her new trial.

I had just appointed a new lawyer for her when word came that she had been murdered during the night. Her baby, just two months old, asleep in her cot in the next room, was spared. It has been reported that Haran Issawi bribed the guards to let him and al-Shezira's brothers-in-law into the Zamalek house.

Not only does Haran Issawi walk free, but rumour has it that he was recently promoted to a higher position within royal circles.

I insisted that Hezba's body be cremated. I took her ashes out to the desert where I threw the powdery dust to the wind and watched her remains swirl through the air, so that she could be as free as she had always wanted to be.

I have not read her journal. I have respected her wishes that her daughter will be the only person allowed to read it, but only once she has become a woman. I will finish this sentence, then package up this diary with string and put it away safely until the time is right to give it to Aimee. God forgive all this evil in the world.

CHAPTER FIFTY-FIVE

Aimee stood looking up at the outline of Farouk's Zamalek mansion in the softening dawn light. She held her pistol tightly inside her pocket. A soft breeze caressed her face, and she inhaled the pungent scent of earth.

The front door opened. She held her breath. Out of the shadows came Farouk. He was smoking. His shirt was bloodied and torn. He looked old and ill. He saw her and he froze.

"You came," he said. "Thank God you came. I thought I'd never see you again."

Aimee did not answer. She walked towards him, up the steps, and stood in front of him. Her heart thundered in her chest. She searched his face, the grey-black of his hair, the rough razored flesh of his time-worn cheeks, the twisted line of his mouth, the coal black of his eyes. She looked for herself in his features. She was his child.

"Come out to the garden and have a drink with me. You look ill," he said.

She didn't say anything. Words were lodged painfully in her throat. He ushered her through the doorway, and she followed him to the back of the house and into the garden.

"Where is Gigis? Are we alone?"

"He's not here. He had the night off. He went to a party in Giza. Thankfully, he was a long way from the Abdin Palace when the bomb exploded. He will be home soon."

She listened to him speak but could not take in what he was saying. She felt her body swaying and her legs about to give way.

"Aimee, sit down. You're so pale, you look like you're going to faint."

"I don't want to sit down. I came to find you."

He held out his hand to support her, and he noticed her flinch when he touched her.

He pulled back and examined her face sadly. He reached for the whisky decanter that stood on a stone table and poured her a drink.

He put the glass into her hand and circled her hand with his as she held it. Again he felt her flinch.

"Aimee, tell me you're all right. I was so worried. I was praying that you had made it to safety."

"I thought you'd been killed," she said coldly, and then she took a sip of the whisky. "The bomb killed a lot of people, didn't it? Half the Abdin Palace has been destroyed. You can still see the smoke from here."

He hung his head guiltily. "Yes, yes."

"I thought you might have been one of them. I thought your boy might have news of you."

He flinched a little at the tone of her voice. She appeared changed. There was something cruel in her expression. He studied her vivid green eyes, which were sparkling intensely. Her skin looked deathly white, her charcoal-coloured hair contrasting with her pallor. She held herself rigidly as though made of stone. She sipped the whisky calmly, looking more human, less rigid. He saw her chest rising and falling shallowly.

"Aimee—? Come here, let me hold you. We had a very lucky escape. Tell me what happened to you after the explosion."

"I went to Madinat Nasr to see my aunt," she said, stepping back from him as he approached her. He wondered why she had done that and looked at her quizzically.

"But when I got there, my aunt's housekeeper, Rose, told me that my aunt had had a fall, and that she had died."

Farouk tugged at his shirt pocket and retrieved a cigarette, his eyes never leaving hers. His eyebrows knotted over a frown, and then he said, "I'm sorry, I'm so sorry."

He offered her a cigarette. She refused. He lit his own.

"She wrote me a letter before she died," Aimee continued. "I found it in her handbag."

He cocked his head, screwing up his eyes in confusion, but he didn't say anything.

"A couple of days ago, before Gad Mahmoud kidnapped me from your offices"—she held her hand up to stop him from inter-rupting her when she saw his features stiffen—"I'd been to see her. My aunt wanted me to meet someone, a man."

She stopped for a moment, waiting for him to say something. His breath had quickened, and he held her firmly in his gaze. "The man was a eunuch who'd been found roaming the streets of Aswan. He'd been brought to live with my aunt."

What was she talking about? A eunuch? Aswan? What did this have to do with him?

She continued. "My aunt said this eunuch was someone I would want to meet. He had known my mother, you see, had been her slave a long time ago."

"Why are you telling me this?" She did not answer him.

"His name was Rachid. He was my mother's servant, as I said. He loved her. His master blinded him with red-hot pokers because he had helped my mother betray him. My mother had a lover, you see, and Rachid helped orchestrate their meetings."

She watched him as she spoke. The black of his eyes had intensified, and his mouth had opened slightly. She continued.

"When I met him at my aunt's house, Maman's eunuch gave me a little photo album of pictures to look at. He showed me photographs of my mother, photographs of her house, scenes from her life in Cairo during the Great War."

He was shaking his head as a hardened cough tugged at his throat. He stood back, rammed his handkerchief to his mouth, spluttered into it, and wiped away blood from his lips.

Aimee reached forward to steady him. "You're ill," she said. "There's blood."

Farouk wiped his fingers and folded the handkerchief. "I'm all right, don't worry. What's all this about a eunuch?"

She knew what she had to say, confront him, come face-to-face with the hateful reality of what she had found out. She started to shiver, not able to frame her words. She wanted to tell him that she knew who he was, but the reality of it seemed too incomprehensible, however she looked at it. There were words she could say, though, words that came easily.

"You murdered my husband, didn't you, Monsieur Farouk."

Farouk shook his head, his face screwed up in agony. He gripped his bloody handkerchief, stepped back from her, found the stone bench, and sat down with his face in his hands. "You don't understand, Aimee. You don't know."

She closed her eyes and reached for her revolver, wanting to withdraw it from her trouser pocket but knowing she had to wait for exactly the right moment. The broken man in front of her had once been so handsome. She saw him now as her maman had seen him, his black hair sweeping a smooth forehead, his black eyes flashing with passion, his bearing upright, almost soldierly, his mouth full, his love for her maman, for his country, driving him on. He had wanted to destroy every evil he had witnessed throughout his young life, and this determination to right the wrongs of his ancestors had pushed him forward, possessing him entirely. Maman had written about Alexandre Anton's hatred of his French father and his love of his Egyptian mother. He had become a revolutionary fighter for Egypt. He had loved the women in his life—Hezba, his half sister, and his own mother—for their inner fire and their determination not to let centuries of tradition repress them.

For that Aimee should have loved him, but as she stood before him watching him curled up in agony, she felt no love at all. He was a murderer. He had killed her husband, and for that she had a bullet reserved for him.

"Why did you do it?" Silence followed. "Why did you murder my husband?"

He looked up at her, to where she was standing over him. He was unable to wrench his eyes away from hers, unable to answer her. His breath became laboured.

"Come with me," he said, uncurling his body and grabbing her hand. He pulled her into the house towards the central staircase, squeezing her hand so tightly that she was afraid.

"You're hurting me," she said, but he didn't seem to hear her. Farouk pulled her along, her body jolting against his.

"I want you to understand. I want to show you something." They reached the little sitting room on the first floor. Farouk pushed open the door and pulled Aimee in. There was a mashrabiyya on the far side of the room that cast dappled light onto a chaise longue. Farouk held Aimee's hand firmly. He would not let her go.

CHAPTER FIFTY-SIX

The sitting room had been closed up, and the atmosphere felt stuffy. In the low light, Aimee studied the layout of the room. Maman, she sobbed inwardly. This had been her mother's room, the place Aimee had been born, a royal daughter with a scandalous heritage. Maman had described the room so vividly in her journal that she knew it straight away. Aimee's identity had been hidden from her. The sins of our ancestors, Aimee thought bitterly.

She managed to wrench herself from Farouk's grasp and pulled the revolver from her pocket. She slammed it hard against his temple. It was fully loaded. She would kill him. He was her father, but she hated him. She hated him for murdering the only man she'd ever loved. He had brought her to the place she had been born. He had brought about the death of her mother and deprived her of a normal life. Her maman had loved him above all else. Hezba had given her life for this man. Hezba had died for him, yet he had lived. He had walked free from prison and gone on to murder the man she had loved too.

With the gun against his temple, Farouk relaxed. He focused on the feeling of the hard metal against his skin. He heard doves cooing in the soft morning air. He did not look at Aimee, but he could feel the stiffness of her arm as she held the gun against his face. Inwardly he was smiling. It was time to die, time to see his loved one again. The scent of jasmine from the garden filled his nostrils, and he heard a voice, Hezba's voice, singing a little song.

Hezba Sultan
her name whispered behind closed doors
in the garden
in the misty vapours of the hammam
her name dances with the sounds of harem laughter until it
disappears forever.

Farouk brought his hand up slowly and covered her fingers with his hand. He felt her soften and yield. He gently peeled her hand away from his face, but she clung to the pistol like a child to its favourite soft toy. He wanted to die—he was practically a dead man—but he had to explain himself to her, tell her everything.

"Your husband was passing information about me to various departments in the ministries," he said. "My men found out that your husband was going to the village near Ismailia to pass on detailed maps of all of the sector addresses and hideouts. My men and I went there. They held him down and I slit his throat." He didn't dare look at her.

"I am so sorry, Aimee. Please—please understand. There was a woman, you see, whose murder I needed to avenge, a woman I loved, who was assassinated by this man Issawi."

He swallowed bitterly as he watched her. "Your husband was moonlighting as a spy, a double agent for the British and Germans, but he was also working for the king and his chief advisor, Haran Issawi. I knew I would be arrested soon enough. It was only a matter of time before the Group of the X was caught. I knew I didn't have long. If I was arrested, if the Group of the X was rounded up,

I would die never having been able to see Haran Issawi murdered. I knew I had to finish him off before the tumour grew too big."

Aimee felt weak. She held the revolver in her hand with difficulty. Her body was about to give way. She pumped her hand to hold the revolver tight.

He continued. "Issawi's Intelligence forces were subpar, swept along by baksheesh and corruption, but then they signed up a young university professor, Azi Ibrahim, and everything changed. We found out that your husband had several special skills. He was an expert code-cracker. He worked invisibly, using his job as professor as a front. He had contacts everywhere. Nobody knew how to say no to Azi Ibrahim. All of a sudden, after years of being impenetrable, the X was being undermined. Your husband had to be eliminated."

Farouk felt the force of the revolver slam harder against his temple. He wanted to tell her he'd even planned to give himself up after he'd assassinated Issawi, to tell Security Operations what Littoni was planning, the exact location of the proposed bomb detonation site, and the entire plot, but it had all gone wrong. He'd been double-crossed by Jewel. In the end, all he could do in the hour before the bomb exploded was to send a wire anonymously to Security Operations HQ with the address of Littoni's basement lair, where Farouk knew he often held meetings with some of the sectors.

"And Fatima?" she said.

"Fatima works for me. She's an X agent."

"She seduced my husband."

"Yes."

"Why?"

"I paid her to. If she could seduce Abdullah Ibrahim, she would get to know all his secrets, who he was passing information to and when. She was my spy on the ground."

"Is that why you befriended me? For information? So you could get Azi's information?"

"Yes, but then I fell in love with you. I initially thought you were working with your husband, and I wanted to find out more. I thought you'd denounce me to the authorities if it all came out. I thought you were lying to me about being so innocent, but very soon, none of that mattered. I loved you, Aimee. I still love you."

She closed her eyes.

"And Zaky Achmed, the professor who held the literary evening, does he work for the X?"

Farouk nodded. "I love you, Aimee," he said again with more force this time. "From the moment I first met you, I loved you."

Aimee drew herself up and slammed her revolver back against his face.

"You want to kill me, don't you?" he said. "Understand, Aimee, Ibrahim, your husband, was stopping me from getting to Issawi. I had to eliminate him because of her, because of Hezba."

"Hezba," she said. "My mother."

He jolted, and his sad eyes widened in disbelief.

"Hezba?"

She bit back a sob and stiffened against the revolver. "Do you know a baby was born in this house twenty years ago?"

His body spasmed and his eyes flashed. "What are you talking about?" he said.

"Your sister had a friend, didn't she? A great friend, one of her students, in fact."

"Yes."

"And that girl, that friend was your lover, wasn't she?"

He squeezed his eyes shut.

"The girl had a baby in this house, in the bedroom upstairs."

His eyes grew wider. His voice was strangled in his throat.

"Yes, there was a child. How do you know all this?"

Farouk's face had turned to stone.

Aimee went on. "A very distant cousin of my aunt's, Gad Mahmoud, knew Alexandre Anton, apparently. I have just come from this man's house. Mahmoud told me he had been a friend of Anton's. He rang a colleague to check where Anton might be because he hadn't seen him for quite a few years."

Aimee was shaking, but she continued. "He told me Anton was working with a terrorist group called the Group of the X. He told me your alias, told me Anton had become Taha Farouk."

Aimee stiffened against the revolver. "Where did you go when Hezba Nur al-Shezira died?"

Farouk's eyes snapped shut. Hezba. Her name. Aimee was saying her name.

He closed his eyes and, shaking violently, fell to his knees in front of her. He wrapped his arms around her shins. He was sunken and beaten at her feet. In his agony, he mumbled and sobbed.

"It's not true. It can't be true."

She felt stronger, harder. She would finish him. She had the pistol. All she had to do was pull the trigger.

"My aunt Saiza was Hezba's half sister. My birth name is Nur al-Shezira. I was given my father's name, or at least the name of the man I always believed to be my father."

She pulled him up by the hair so she could look at him one last time. "I grew up believing my father was the kind, respected Khalil al-Shezira. Then, when Azi was murdered, I was given a journal, Hezba's journal. You murdered my husband, and my mother died because of you. I'm going to kill you," she said bitterly. "I'm going to kill you."

"Aimee, you are my daughter?" He looked up at her, trying to see Hezba in her face.

"Yes."

"Hezba's baby girl?"

She heard a strange sound from outside, like army trucks lining up along the street, then the sound of men's voices, shouting military orders. She heard Farouk's name being called and the sound of gunfire.

Farouk raised his head in alarm.

"They're here," he said.

EPILOGUE

Madame Aimee Rigaud
75 Rue Victoire
Versailles
France
February 5, 1946

Madame,

It is with great pleasure but also with sadness that I write this letter to you.

I hope with all my heart this communication reaches you at the above address and finds you well.

Recently I was fortunate enough to meet a gentleman at the Oxford club in Cairo, a Mr. Tony Sedgewick. In our conversations we discovered that we had a mutual association. His former ward, Mrs. Sophie Brennan, née Mersault, gave me your address when I wrote to her in London on the advice of Mr. Sedgewick. She very kindly gave me your address so that I can relay some information that will, hopefully, be of interest to you.

You might not remember me, but I hope you do. We met once when you came to my house in Shubra, that awful night in August 1940, the night of that devastating bomb at the Abdin Palace.

On that terrible night, you were very distressed and wanted to know the whereabouts of your father. I wanted so much to help you then.

Please believe me when I say that it is with great sadness that I write to tell you of the passing of your father, a month ago, at a prison sanatorium near the Sinai. After our meeting, I spent many months wondering whether you ever managed to get in contact with your father. Not long after our meeting, the news came out that Monsieur Alexandre Anton had been arrested by the head of the Secret Police, Mehmed Abbas, at Zamalek, and placed in a detention centre on the outskirts of Cairo to await trial.

The people of Cairo wanted to see him get life imprisonment. It was only then that they would feel vindicated. The newspapers reported that he was dying. Eventually your father was tried and convicted of terrorist activity and was incarcerated for life.

I am not sure if you are aware of the court case that brought the Group of the X to justice. A young woman, a brothel owner, called Fatima Said, was tried and convicted of the murder of Haran Issawi. She will never be released. It was reported that she was in fact an agent working for your father, the key mastermind, Farouk-Anton-Lorenzo-Carpet Seller, all aliases or sector names, as they called them.

Three hundred other members of the Group of the X—some of whom were surprisingly well-known members of the Cairene intelligentsia—were arrested over the course of the next two years.

I believe the authorities decided long ago to make an example of your father. I'm sure Mehmed Abbas had some influence in seeing that he received the harshest sentence. Your father was sent to live out his years in a high-security jail at el-Tor in the Sinai, a horrible, inhumane place. I'm sure your father hoped for a quick ending to his suffering, but as is sometimes the case, the cancer lingered on, for years.

Your father passed away on the fourth of January, this year, in his sleep. He was in solitary confinement after bouts of psychotic behaviour. It is with deep regret that I write to you with this news.

You are wise, Madame Rigaud, to have left Cairo for France. The situation here grows worse every day. Under King Farouk, our beloved country remains in the stranglehold of corruption and suffering. There are no jobs for the young. Taxes have risen. The landowners are struggling under chronic poverty, and rents are rising. It is only a matter of time now before the armed forces will bring matters to a head and force the government to take action. It reminds me so horribly of the days after the First World War when the Nationalists took to the streets in protest and anger, seeing like-for-like violence against British rule as the only option. I fear Egypt has not progressed much. The Muslim Brotherhood now actively seeks to bring its vision of independence to the fore. The newspapers report daily on the violence between the fundamentalist factions and the last of the British soldiers stationed here. I am convinced no man or woman ever really sees violence as a solution. Mrs. Brennan informed me of your marriage four years ago to Dr. Rigaud of Paris and of the birth of your two children, Alexandre and Virginie. You remain forever in my thoughts, and I wish you and your family good health and happiness both now and for many years to come.

Yours most humbly,
Gad Mahmoud

ABOUT THE AUTHOR

 Jo Chumas is a British writer living in Barcelona, Spain. She grew up in Belgium and England, and spent her childhood holidays exploring Europe and North Africa with her parents. She worked for many years as a journalist in Australia, the United Arab Emirates, and the UK while also writing fiction. A profound fascination with early twentieth-century Egyptian political and cultural history led her to write *The Hidden*.

ACKNOWLEDGMENTS

A massive thanks to Christina Henry de Tessan, editor extraordinaire.